"Well, well," he murmured, "with every look and every word, the little lamb with the big brown eyes proves she's not as defenseless as she first appears."

Clara felt a spark of frustration at his description. She might be plain and possess a shy, quiet disposition, but she was not some helpless, dependent creature.

"Is that what I am?" she asked as they turned in a circle, moving in the steps of the dance. "A little lamb?" She opened her eyes deliberately wide. "And I'm lost in the woods, I suppose, and you'll come save me?"

"Save you? I doubt it." His gaze lowered, pausing at her lips. "Ravish you would be a sight more likely."

Clara's heart gave a panicked thud, slamming into her ribs with such force that it broke her concentration. She trod on his foot, lost her balance, and would have stumbled, but he caught her, letting go of her hand to wrap his arm around her back. "Careful," he murmured. "Dance with me much longer and you'll be in danger."

"You warn me, Lord Galbraith, but I cannot help wondering why."

"You're in my arms." He pulled her a fraction closer. "Make no mistake, my lamb. You are in very great danger."

By Laura Lee Guhrke

LAURA LEE GUHRKE

The Trouble with True Love

AVONBOOKS

An Imprint of HarperCollinsPublishers

THE TROUBLE WITH TRUE LOVE. Copyright © 2018 by Laura Lee Borio. All rights reserved. Printed in the United States of America. No part of this book may be used or reproduced in any manner whatsoever without written permission except in the case of brief quotations embodied in critical articles and reviews. For information, address HarperCollins Publishers, 195 Broadway, New York, NY 10007.

First Avon Books mass market printing: February 2018

Print Edition ISBN: 978-0-06-246987-8
Digital Edition ISBN: 978-0-06-246988-5

Cover illustration by Jon Paul Ferrara

Avon, Avon & logo, and Avon Books & logo are registered trademarks of HarperCollins Publishers in the United States of America and other countries.

HarperCollins is a registered trademark of HarperCollins Publishers in the United States of America and other countries.

FIRST EDITION

18 19 20 21 22 QGM   10 9 8 7 6 5 4 3 2 1

To Sophie Jordan, Gayle Callen, Margo Maguire, and Jennifer Ryan. Not only are all of you great writers, you rock at brainstorming, too! Many thanks.

The Trouble with True Love

Chapter 1

Clara Deverill was twenty-two years old before she discovered in herself a flaw she hadn't even known she possessed.

It wasn't her shyness, for she was already quite familiar with that aspect of her character. It was something she battled on a daily basis.

Nor was it her unremarkable looks, for she'd long ago accepted the fact that brown hair, a round face, and a freckle-dusted button nose were not characteristics that set the average man's pulse racing, particularly when combined with a figure that was more reminiscent of a young girl than a fully-grown woman.

And it certainly wasn't her traditional views and values, for though her bold, very modern sister, Irene, often teased her about her hopelessly old-fashioned outlook, most people, including Clara herself, regarded the desire to find a good man, get married, and become a mother as a perfectly reasonable goal in life.

No, Clara admitted as she cast a gloomy eye over the pile of letters on her desk, procrastination was her greatest flaw, and a facet of her character she had only begun to appreciate a mere ten days ago.

She plunked an elbow on the desk and her chin in her hand, staring at the telegram that rested atop the pile of envelopes before her. There was no need to read it, for she'd done that so many times already that the words were engraved in her memory.

```
Glad papa is well Having wonderful
time Want to extend trip eight weeks
see greece and egypt You can manage
lady truelove cant you darling Dont
worry You will be splendid Respond via
cooks venice by 07 may Irene
```

Clara was glad her sister was enjoying her honeymoon, but she couldn't summon any enthusiasm about Irene's plan to lengthen the trip, for things here at home were not going quite as smoothly as her letters to her sister might have implied.

Their father had always had a fondness for brandy, a fondness that had only increased since his eldest daughter's departure for the Continent. As for Jonathan, their brother had agreed to come home from America and take over management of the family newspaper business, but nearly two months after his promised arrival, he had still not appeared, and Clara's letters to him inquiring on the subject had been answered only with vague promises. Her cable a few days ago demanding a specific date had not yet garnered a response.

Still, Clara had no intention of worrying Irene with any of that when she was on her honeymoon, and she had cabled her sister a positive reply at once. There was nothing else to be done. Irene had always taken care of her and provided for her, never once asking for anything in return until now, and Clara would rather have cut off her arm than object to her sister's once-in-a-lifetime trip.

Still, as she stared down at Irene's cable and the pile of correspondence beneath it, she appreciated that sisterly loyalty did have its drawbacks. Irene had composed only enough iterations of the Lady True-love column to last until her intended return. Now that she'd extended her trip, Clara would be offering advice to London's lovelorn until Jonathan arrived or her sister came home.

Don't worry, darling.

Clara wasn't the least bit encouraged by those words. All very well, she thought darkly, for Irene to say such a thing.

Her sister never worried about anything, and why should she? Irene was beautiful, accomplished, and filled to the brim with self-confidence. After their mother's death ten years ago, she had taken over the household and managed it on nearly nothing a year. She'd reinvigorated the family's deteriorating newspaper business by producing a profitable society paper, and in doing so, she had also created Lady Truelove, London's most popular advice columnist. She'd then capped those triumphs by marrying the handsome and very eligible Duke of Torquil, and upon her return to England, she intended to use her influence as a duchess to help achieve the vote for women. Clara had no doubt her sister would succeed there, too. Irene succeeded at everything she touched.

You will be splendid.

Would she? Clara couldn't share her sister's faith in her abilities. A woman who was shy and plain, who stammered when she was nervous and had never caught a man's eye in her life, could hardly be splendid at advising people about love and romance.

That was the gist of the problem, of course, and the entire reason she'd spent over a week with the letters stacked, untouched, on one corner of her desk. But now, she was running out of time, and she did not have the luxury of procrastinating any longer.

Reminding herself of all that Irene had done for her, Clara took a deep breath, shoved aside her sister's telegram, and reached for the first letter on top of the pile.

A knock on her door gave her pause, and Clara felt an irrational wave of relief. The emotion was short-lived, however, evaporating the moment the door opened and Mr. Beale entered her office.

Augustus Beale was the editor of the *Weekly Gazette*. Before her marriage, Irene had been both the newspaper's editor and publisher, but before leaving on her honeymoon, she'd hired Mr. Beale to take over the editorial portion of her duties. It had proved a surprising and rather uncharacteristic error in judgement. Despite substantial experience and laudatory letters of character, Augustus Beale was, at least in Clara's opinion, an odious man. At this moment, she noted, he was also a very angry one.

"Miss Deverill." He ground out her name as if its utterance took great effort. "Is there any word of your brother's arrival?"

A question the man asked every day, and one to which she always gave the same answer. She tried to give it with cheer. "I'm afraid not. But," she added, crossing her fingers under the desk, "I'm sure he'll be arriving any day. In the meantime, can I be of help?"

He frowned, his thick dark brows coming together over his nose in a shape rather reminiscent of an overgrown yew hedge. "I doubt it."

"I see. Well, then . . ." She paused, casting a hopeful glance at the door. Sadly, Mr. Beale did not depart.

"I still do not have Lady Truelove's column."

"It hasn't arrived?" She worked to put an expression of innocent surprise on her face, for the famous columnist's real identity was a closely-guarded secret, one even the *Gazette*'s editor wasn't allowed to know. "Oh, dear. I can't imagine what is causing such a delay. Lady Truelove is usually most reliable."

He strode to Clara's desk and dropped the layout of Monday's edition on top of the letters on her desk. It was opened to a page bearing the typed headline, *Dear Lady Truelove*.

"Do you see this?" he demanded, stabbing a finger at the vast expanse of white space below the headline. "It's blank," he added, as if she couldn't see that for herself. "The blasted woman is two days late now. You and I seem to have very different definitions of reliability, Miss Deverill."

Clara grimaced, guilt pricking her conscience. She might not like Mr. Beale, but he had every right to be frustrated. "I shall pay a call upon Lady Truelove immediately and see what—"

"Do," he said, snapping out the order as if she were a hired member of the newspaper staff. "Tell her she has until four o'clock. If her silly advice column isn't here by then, I'll choose something to take its place and your Lady Truelove will be out of a job."

Have Irene come back to find the *Gazette*'s most popular feature had vanished from its pages? Appalled by the prospect, Clara jerked to her feet. "I'm sure that won't be necessary, Mr. Beale. We don't go to press until tomorrow night. There's still plenty of time for me to fetch her column myself, and for you to edit it. The word count might differ slightly from what you've allotted here, but I'm sure you can—"

"My working week comes to an end at five o'clock on Fridays, Miss Deverill, and that's three hours from now. My wife puts dinner on my table an hour after that, and I'll not be kept from it because of silly women who would rather have careers than be at home making dinner for their own hardworking husbands."

Clara had never longed for a career, nor had she ever been the sort to march in the streets for women's rights as her sister had been known to do, but nonetheless, Mr. Beale's words stirred within her some of her sister's suffragist sympathies. Any other time, she might have taken issue with his disparaging ideas of what constituted a woman's place, but at this moment, she was in no position to defend Lady Truelove's tardiness. "I'll edit it myself, and ensure it fits the space you've allotted before Mr. Sanders begins the type-setting."

"See that you do," he barked, and without another word, he turned and walked out, slamming the door behind him.

Though glad he was gone, Clara found her mood decidedly worsened by her encounter with him, and instead of getting on with her task, she scowled at the door, feeling a sudden wave of resentment that included not only him, but also Jonathan, Fate, and even her beloved sister.

This wasn't how things ought to have gone. They had all agreed that Jonathan would become the publisher after Irene's marriage. Jonathan was supposed to be the one sitting behind this desk, managing Mr. Beale and worrying about Lady Truelove, while Clara was supposed to be with the duke's family, working to overcome her shyness and learning to move in good society. The season was officially set to begin next week. With Jonathan's defection and Irene's delayed return, how would she ever make a successful debut?

Panic rose up inside her, mingling with her resentment, but she forced both emotions down, along with any inclination to feel sorry for herself. She had work to do. Clara reached for her letter opener, but before she could resume her task, she was again interrupted by a knock on the door, and Annie, the family parlor maid, came into her office.

"Begging your pardon, Miss Clara, but your father wants to know if you'll be joining him for tea upstairs this afternoon."

Since it was after two o'clock, her father was probably well on his way to being drunk by now, and she had no desire to watch him get any drunker. "No, Annie, give him my regrets and apologies, but I'm far too busy to break for tea. I shall come up to bid him farewell, though, before I return to the duke's house this evening."

"Yes, miss." With that, Annie departed, but the door had barely closed before there was yet another knock.

"Oh, for heaven's sake," Clara muttered under her breath, tossing down her letter opener and rubbing a hand over her forehead. "What is it now?"

The knock came again, and Clara lifted her head. "Come in," she called.

The door swung wide, and the *Gazette*'s secretary, Miss Evelyn Huish, entered the room. "I've sorted the afternoon post," the auburn-haired secretary said as she approached Clara's desk. "Lady Truelove's column still hasn't arrived."

Clara wrinkled up her nose. "Yes, so Mr. Beale has taken great pains to tell me."

Evie might have noticed the acrid tone of her voice, but since the other woman's secretarial duties were divided between Clara and Mr. Beale, she wisely made no comment. Instead, she shifted the bundle of correspondence she carried onto one forearm and plucked an unopened letter off the top. "Nothing from Lady Truelove," she said as she held out the envelope, "but there is a letter from your brother."

"Jonathan?" she cried, relief welling up inside her as she jumped to her feet and took the letter from Evie's outstretched fingertips. "At last!"

But when she glanced at the return scrawled across

the back of the envelope, her relief faltered. He was still in Idaho, a remote part of the American wilderness nearly five thousand miles away. No closer to London, in other words, than he'd been when he'd last written a month ago.

Fearing the worst and cursing his name, Clara tore open the envelope and scanned the words written in her brother's careless, nearly illegible script.

"Not bad news, I hope?"

Evie's voice had Clara looking up. "Awful," she replied in dismay. "The worst news possible. He's found silver."

"Silver?" Evie laughed in surprise. "He's a miner?"

"My brother," she muttered in disgust, "transforms himself into whatever will enable him to avoid his responsibilities at home. Silver?" She rustled the letter in indignation. "Now, after seven years of roaming around America chasing every wildcat scheme possible, now, when I need him, he finds a mine with silver in it? That scoundrel!"

Evie laughed, much to Clara's chagrin. "But if he's found silver, that means he's rich," she pointed out.

"Damn it, Evie, you're missing the point. He's not home, and now, he has no intention of ever coming home. That is the point." She groaned. "And Irene's surely halfway to Greece by now. What am I going to do?"

But even as she asked that question, she already knew the answer. She was stuck, stuck not only with Lady Truelove, but also with the paper, Mr. Beale, and all the headaches that came with them until Irene came home.

"Miss Huish?" called the irate voice of Mr. Beale
from the outer office. "When you've stopped rattling
on with Miss Deverill, I need you out here."

"Go," Clara said as Evie hesitated. "Just put the
rest of my correspondence on the corner of my desk."
Turning, she reached for her leather portfolio from the
shelf behind her. "I'll deal with it tomorrow."

"You'll be coming in on a Saturday?"

"I have to, I'm afraid. With that wastrel brother of
mine ducking out on his promises, I've no choice. Right
now, however," she went on, reminding herself of her
most immediate priority as she stuffed letters into the
portfolio, "I must go and deal with Lady Truelove. If I
don't return with her column in hand, Mr. Beale will
probably have apoplexy. Hmm . . ." She paused. "Upon
reflection, I'm not sure that's a bad thing."

Evie gave a chuckle of laughter and set Clara's correspondence on her desk. "Is there anything else you
need, Miss Deverill?"

"No, Evie, you go on. But I would ask you not to tell
Mr. Beale the news about my brother. If it becomes
necessary to inform him, I will decide when and how
to do so."

"Yes, ma'am."

The secretary departed, and Clara finished putting
Lady Truelove's correspondence into her portfolio.
She then added Irene's telegram, a stack of notepaper,
and a fountain pen, and left her office, ignoring the
editor's malevolent glare as she departed. On the sidewalk, she turned left and started up Belford Row as if
she knew just where she was going, though in truth,
she really had no idea.

It had to be somewhere quiet, she decided as she

walked, a place with no distractions or interruptions or cranky editors, where she could compose the advice column in peace.

She paused at the corner, and as she glanced to her right to check for traffic, she spied a sign for Mrs. Mott's Tea Emporium halfway down the block.

Mrs. Mott's, she decided, would suit her purpose admirably, for at this hour it was bound to be empty and quiet. She turned her steps in that direction, and when she entered the tiny shop a few minutes later, she found that it lived up to her expectations. The place was empty but for a pair of gentlemen who didn't even look up from their tea as she came in.

The waitress led her to a table beside that of the two men, but with a thick cluster of potted palms between them and herself, their presence wasn't likely to prove a distraction. She sat down, ordered a cream tea, and pulled out the letters and stationery supplies from her portfolio. Bracing herself to finally conquer the task she'd been putting off all week, she chose an envelope from the pile in front of her and pulled out the letter.

Dear Lady Truelove,

I am a girl of noble family and strong social position, and I wish to marry, but though my parents provided a sizable dowry and launched me into society last season, I was unable to find a husband. I am painfully shy, you see, and because of that, I proved a social failure.

At every ball or party, I stood against the wall, agonized because I was being overlooked and yet terrified that some young man would notice me. And whenever I was presented to any

*member of the opposite sex, particularly one I
found attractive, my shyness overwhelmed me.
I stammered, I blushed, I could think of nothing
to say, and I ended up making an utter fool of
myself at every turn. This, I hardly need add,
did not make a favorable impression on any of
the young men introduced to me.*

*Another London season is about to begin, and
I am terrified that I will fail again. What if I meet
no one? What if I die a lonely spinster? I am
writing to you, Lady Truelove, in the desperate
hope that you can suggest ways I might become
more attractive to gentlemen and overcome my
shyness with them. Can you help me? Signed, A
Devastated Debutante.*

Clara was more sympathetic to this girl's plight than
the girl herself could ever have dreamed. With only
a few changes, this letter might well have been written by her own hand, and she would have dearly liked
to assist this girl, but what assistance could she give?
If she knew any method for overcoming shyness and
transforming from wallflower to shining social success, she'd have employed it on herself, found a husband of her own, and been off on her own honeymoon
long before now. With reluctance, she set aside the
letter from the Devastated Debutante and picked up
another from the pile.

Dear Lady Truelove,
　　*Having reached my twenty-fifth year, I have
decided it is time for me to choose a wife, and
since I have very specific requirements, my*

*search for a bride will require your assistance.
My circumstances are straitened, so she must
possess a substantial dowry. In addition, she
must be very pretty, for it would be unthinkable
that I should have to wed a plain girl—*

Clara stopped reading with a sound of disdain. Having been deemed a plain girl herself by most of the men who met her, and having had no dowry at all to offer until very recently, she was not the least bit sympathetic to this shallow young man's predicament. She ripped his letter in half, set it to one side, and tried again.

*Dear Lady Truelove,
    I am in such desperate straits that I don't
know if you can even help me. I am in love with
a young lady, but she takes no notice of me, for I
am not, sadly, the most eloquent or handsome of
men. I am writing to solicit your advice on how
I might gain her attention, initiate conversation,
and begin my courtship. I would be grateful for
any suggestions you can offer. Yours, Speechless
in South Kensington.*

Clara stared down at the inked lines before her, lines that once again demonstrated why putting her in charge of Lady Truelove was laughable. What advice could she offer any of these people?

She looked up, staring across the empty tables of the tea shop, thinking of the countless times she'd stood to the side of a ballroom with the other wallflowers, of the parties where she'd lingered unnoticed in a corner of the room. What did she know of gaining the attentions of the opposite sex? Of initiating conversation? Of courtship?

She shoved aside the pile of letters and leaned forward, plunking her elbow on the table and resting her forehead on the heels of her hands, swamped by inadequacy. She couldn't do this, at least not alone.

"Dear God," she whispered, desperate for a bit of divine guidance. "I'm in over my head, and I could really use some help."

"Indeed?" a male voice murmured, a voice that was deep, low, and quite obviously amused. "How might I be of assistance?"

Chapter 2

Clara bolted upright in her chair, but when the voice came again, she realized it was not the Almighty who had uttered such prescient words, but one of the two gentlemen seated at the table on the other side of the potted palms. Though he was facing her direction, he was not looking at her, and she realized that he had not been speaking to her at all, but to his companion. He was also, quite obviously, a mortal man.

Mortal, perhaps, she thought as she angled her head for a better view of him between the palm fronds, but certainly good-looking enough to be a god.

His hair, short but unruly, was of dark, burnished gold and seemed to catch and hold every glimmer of light through the windows of the tea shop. His eyes, the clear, azure blue of a Grecian sea, were focused completely on his companion, granting Clara the undeniable treat of studying him unobserved. His face, of perfect symmetry, lean planes, and chiseled contours, seemed as unyielding as a marble statue, but then he smiled, and at the sheer, dazzling brilliance of it, Clara's heart turned over in her chest.

"I'm happy to help," he said, "but I hope it's not money you need. I'm absolutely flat at present."

His companion said something in reply, but Clara didn't catch it, for her attention was fully occupied by the man opposite. And who could blame her? It wasn't every day that a golden, windblown Adonis came down from Mount Olympus to grace an obscure little tea shop in Holborn.

His body—what she could see of it above the table—was sheathed in the fine white linen and dark gray morning coat of a proper English gentleman, and yet, his wide shoulders and tapering torso made his physique seem far more suited to some ancient Olympiad or Roman coliseum than the civilized London of 1893.

This god, this delectable feast for feminine eyes, stirred in his chair, his splendid shoulders lifting in a shrug, and the move caused Clara to tear her gaze away. She did not want him to catch her staring. But as he spoke again, she couldn't resist leaning closer, curious to hear more.

"What does every man spend his money on, Lionel?" he said, his voice light and careless. "Wine, women, and song. And cards, of course."

"But especially the women, eh?"

The two men laughed together at that bit of raillery, but Clara couldn't help feeling let down. Adonis seemed rather a rake. Not, she feared, a noble god at all. And rakes, as she well knew from her father's example, never truly reformed.

She had no chance to speculate further on Adonis's character, however, for the voice of the man called Lionel returned her attention to the conversation at hand. "No, what I need from you isn't money, old chap. I need advice about love."

Those words reminded Clara that she was expected to dispense some of that particular commodity herself this afternoon, which meant she ought to stop eavesdropping on other people's conversations and return to her own task. But before she could reach for another letter, Adonis spoke again, giving her pause.

"Good God, Lionel, why would anyone want advice about love from me?"

Clara, who had been asking that very question of herself, wondered what Lionel's answer might be.

"It's Dina, of course," he said. "She's dropping hints about matrimony, and I've got to find a way to slip the hook. That's where I'm hoping you might be able to advise me. You're so good at that sort of thing."

Clara was a bit shocked. Adonis, however, merely seemed amused.

"And which is my talent?" he asked with a laugh. "Staying free of marriage, or advising others how to do so?"

"Both."

This was not the sort of problem Lady Truelove would choose to tackle in her column, but nonetheless, Clara was intrigued. She'd asked for help, after all, and help did often come from the most unlikely places. Keeping her head down so that the man opposite wouldn't detect her eavesdropping, she leaned even closer.

"Are you sure you want to slip the hook? Your inamorata is rather a catch herself, you know. She's not only a rich widow, she's also young, exceedingly pretty, and most agreeable company—quite a prize for a lowly MP like you. There's many who'd deem you a very lucky chap."

"True," his friend agreed, sounding as if he considered himself anything but fortunate. "You wouldn't, though. Everyone knows *your* opinion of marriage."

"Not everyone, sadly. Despite my aversion to that outmoded and wholly unnecessary institution, certain members of my family are determined to see me chained to it, and in pursuit of this goal, they insist upon hurling desperate debutantes at me every season. But not many men share my cynical view. I certainly never thought you did."

"I don't, really. It's just that . . ." Lionel paused and gave a heavy sigh. "I'm not sure I want to marry right now."

"Ah." There was a wealth of understanding in the word. "What you mean is that you're not sure you want to marry *her*."

"I suppose that's it," Lionel mumbled, and Clara felt immediate compassion for the young lady in question. "She's not really my sort, you know. I'm such an ordinary chap, and she's part of the *ton*."

"Poor girl."

"That's just it. Dina's not a girl. She's five years older than I am. And being a widow, she knows her way about all right. When she made her attraction to me so plain, I thought all she wanted was an affair. I thought, 'Why not?' I was flattered. What bloke wouldn't be?" He sighed again. "It all seemed so simple. So straightforward."

"You're talking about a woman, Lionel. Nothing is ever simple or straightforward."

"Don't I know it? The point is, I never thought she'd want *marriage*."

"Ladies usually do, once we've slept with them," Adonis murmured, and at those blunt words, heat flooded Clara's cheeks. She knew just what "slept with" was a euphemism for, thanks to the explanations of her forthright sister, and she felt a growing indignation on this Dina's behalf. Whoever she was, the woman was obviously being quite ill-used.

"Deuced inconvenient of them, I know," Adonis went on, "but there it is. That's why I steer clear of respectable young ladies as often as I can. Invariably, they expect marriage."

And why shouldn't they? Clara wondered, feeling prickly and a bit defensive. *What's wrong with wanting to be married?*

"Dancers and actresses," he continued, adding to her ire, "are much less bother."

Bother? Clara bristled at the word. Women who wanted honorable marriage were a bother?

"That's all well and good, but hardly helpful."

"My dear Lionel, what is it you expect me to say?"

"I want you to help me stay out of the trap! Though how I ever got snared in the first place escapes me."

"Haven't we already established that? You fell into the trap when you fell into her bed."

The blush in Clara's cheeks deepened, spreading heat through her entire body. Heavens, who'd ever have thought such nefarious conversation could take place in the respectable confines of a tea shop?

"And everything was going splendidly, too," Lionel murmured in a gloomy tone while Clara pressed her hands to her hot cheeks. "But barely a month later, she's making wedding plans."

"Women," his friend replied, "can be so unreasonable."

Clara had to clamp one of her hands over her mouth to stifle an exclamation of outrage before it could escape her lips and give her away.

"Rather," Lionel agreed and gave a laugh, though he sounded anything but amused. "My family has never met her. Hell, they don't even know about her. And her family certainly doesn't know about me. We've managed to be very discreet until now. If her people found out, the fat would be in the fire, for it would be a comedown for her, and they'd never approve of it. And yet she doesn't seem to care. She's prepared to tell them all to go to blazes—for my sake, she says. My sake? Damn it, man, what am I supposed to do?"

Adonis was silent a moment, considering the problem. "Could you go abroad?" he asked at last. "Take a jaunt to Paris or Rome for a few months? The season's just beginning, and Dina will surely be caught up in the social whirl. I daresay by the time you come back, she'll have forgotten all about you."

"Or she'll follow me. Dina isn't a meek and mild little flower, you know. Being so rich, and a widow, she doesn't have to worry about neither costs nor chaperones."

"Perhaps, but why should she bother? Other chaps will be lining up soon enough, I daresay, and paying her so much attention that she probably won't miss you a jot."

"I suppose you're right."

Clara couldn't help noting that Lionel didn't sound relieved by the prospect. *Isn't that just like a man?* she thought, feeling a stirring of her sister's suffragist sympathies. *Wanting to have the cake and eat it, too.*

"And besides," Lionel went on, "going abroad isn't possible for me. I'm a hardworking MP. I am," he insisted as his friend made a sound of derision, "and Parliament is in session. I can't go trotting off to the Continent."

"Then your course is clear. You have to break with her."

"Must I?" Lionel paused and sighed again. "Why can't we just go on as we are for a bit, see where it leads us?"

"You can't, I take it?"

"I made the suggestion, but she said she didn't see the point. Since we love each other, she said, marriage is the only possible way forward."

"Love?" Adonis's voice was suddenly so hard and so sharp that Clara was startled. Forgetting caution, she lifted her head and watched as he leaned forward, his perfect countenance suddenly grim. "You told her you love her?"

The palms beside Clara's shoulder rustled, agitated by Lionel's restless elbow as he wriggled like a guilty schoolboy. "May have done," he muttered. "In the . . . umm . . . heat of the moment, as it were."

His friend groaned and fell back again in his seat, impelling Clara to once again duck her head. "Of all the idiotic things to do," he muttered. "During the twenty years we've known each other, has nothing I've told you about women penetrated your thick skull? Really, Lionel," he added, sounding thoroughly exasperated, "you're a hopeless business."

"She said she loved me, and I just . . . I got caught up . . . oh, what does it matter? It's too late for recriminations now. It's not as if I can take the words back. So, what am I to do?"

"If you don't want to break with her, and you don't want to marry her, then your only course is to persuade her that what you have now is preferable to the other two alternatives," he said, a reply that seemed to prove beyond doubt Clara's earlier conclusion about men and their cake. "You'll have to do it in a way that doesn't make her feel you're being dishonorable."

But he is being dishonorable, Clara wanted to shout. *And so are you for advising him to continue being so!*

If Clara was tempted to give voice to her outrage, however, Lionel spoke before she had the chance.

"Just how am I supposed to accomplish that? It's impossible."

"Not impossible. It can be done. But to be honest, Lionel, I'm not sure you're the sort who can carry it off." He paused, and though she was not looking at him, Clara could just imagine those blue eyes giving his friend a dubious glance across the table. "It's a tricky business."

"Tell me anyway."

"You'll have to suggest breaking with her."

"I've told you, I don't want to do that."

"I said you have to suggest it. You don't have to actually do it. Knowing Dina, if you're the one to suggest breaking it off, it won't seem nearly as appealing to her."

"Or she'll think it sounds like a fine idea and drop me flat."

"That's why it's important to go about it the right way. You need to take her hand, look deeply into her eyes, paste an expression of utter devastation on your face, and explain that marriage between the two of you is just not possible."

"And what reason could I give?"

"The facts are reason enough. You haven't means to support her."

"That's true. I've very little money of my own, and she knows it."

"Remind her of that and suggest—gently—that perhaps the two of you should go your separate ways? You don't want to do it, of course, because you're wild about her, and you can't sleep or eat for wanting her, and your nights with her are the most amazing thing that's ever happened to you, but for her sake, you feel you must tear yourself away."

At this self-serving diatribe camouflaged by noble self-sacrifice, Clara nearly bounded out of her chair, but she managed to refrain by curling her hands into tight fists on the table. Staring down at them, she wished suddenly that she were a man so she could call these scoundrels out and put her clenched fists to good use. Of all the outrageous speeches.

"I can't say that," Lionel protested as Clara worked to keep her temper in check. "It's ridiculous."

"Is it ridiculous? You want her, don't you?"

"Yes, but—"

"You don't want to let her go, do you?"

"No, of course I don't. I've already told you so."

"Then, unless you want to find yourself standing in the nearest parish church a few weeks from now, pledging your entire future and what little you have in the way of worldly goods to a woman you barely know, you'd better find the words to persuade her to an alternative that doesn't mean farewell."

"But even if I could manage to say all the things you suggest, how can I make it seem convincing?"

"I advise you to spend a night or two beforehand going without food and sleep. That will give you the appropriately ravaged appearance."

"God," Lionel choked, laughing a little. "You're such a clever fellow."

Unlike Lionel, Clara felt no inclination to laugh. By heaven, her blood was up. To think of that poor young woman being deceived so thoroughly and persuaded by such nefarious means to continue an illicit liaison—why, it was unbearable. To stand by as another woman clung to the hope of marriage when the man she loved had no intention or desire to offer it, was unconscionable. If people found out about her illicit affair, she would be disgraced and shamed. And if she became with child, she'd be beyond the pale, ruined forever, and the child would suffer the stigma of illegitimacy and shame.

Until now, Clara hadn't had any idea of the devious depths to which some men could sink, but this conversation was providing her with a quick and brutal education. In her opinion, the young lady in question would be gaining a lucky escape if she walked away from this Lionel fellow now, before it was too late. As for his friend . . .

Clara took another peek at the man she'd likened to Adonis, and when she did, she found that the spell was broken. Though he was still every bit as good-looking now as he'd been a short while ago, she could no longer see him as some sort of golden, windblown god. All she saw was a deceitful cad who toyed with women and encouraged others to do the same.

Lionel spoke again, and Clara found that her indignation on this Dina's behalf was not stronger than her curiosity. She leaned closer to the palm trees as he said, "Even if I can convince her I'm shattered by the idea of ending things, I don't see what good it will do. What's to stop her from simply agreeing with me and saying good-bye?"

"She probably will, but I'm willing to bet any farewell on her part will be halfhearted. Parting from you isn't what she really wants, you see. She wants a sweeping, romantic gesture on your part to reassure her that you care, even if you're not prepared to marry her."

Clara bit down hard on her lip, fearing this man knew far too much about women.

"What sort of gesture?" Lionel asked, sounding bewildered.

"If you want her, you'll have to throw your pride to the winds and plead with her not to leave you. Even if it's only another night, another week—whatever crumbs she offers you, you're willing to take. That's what she wants to hear."

"I suppose, but it sounds like utter rubbish to me."

"It won't if you do it properly. I'll show you."

Too curious for caution, Clara slid another side-ways glance at him, watching as he lifted his hand to beckon to the waitress who was passing their table with a laden tray that looked to be Clara's tea and scones.

The waitress stopped at once, so quickly in fact, that the contents of the tray almost slid to the floor. "Oh," she gasped as Adonis stood up and faced her. Clara, meanwhile, readjusted her position, ducking her chin even as she slanted her gaze up so that she could con-tinue to watch out of the corner of her eye.

"May I help you, sir?" the girl asked, her voice be-traying an eagerness to please that went a bit beyond the polite civility usually provided by the employees of a tea shop.

"Indeed, you may, Miss . . . ?"

"Clark, sir. Elsie Clark."

"Miss Clark." He smiled, and though Clara was now immune to the potency of that smile, the waitress was not. When he pulled the tray from her hands, poor Elsie Clark scarcely seemed to notice.

"I do need your help," he went on, turning to set the tray on the table beside him. "You see, my friend here has been most injudicious with his feminine compan-ion."

That seemed too much for the poor girl to take in, for she frowned in bafflement. "Sir?"

"Honor demands he break with a girl," he explained. "She's far too good for him, and he knows it. He also knows the right thing to do is abandon his courtship, for he's a considerate, gentlemanly chap."

Clara gave a snort, but fortunately, the other three didn't seem to notice.

"But he can't bear to let her go," Adonis went on. "He's quite shattered about the whole thing, really, and he has asked my advice on the subject. I should like to demonstrate for him how he can postpone the inevitable end as long as possible, and that is where you shall be of invaluable assistance to me, Miss Clark."

To Clara's way of thinking, a man who bedded a woman, declared love, refused to offer honorable marriage, and saw nothing wrong with continuing to bed her with no intention of ever doing right by her was not in any way a gentlemanly chap. She glanced between the palms at the man seated beside her, and though his appearance seemed that of a benignant and amiable fellow, Clara knew he was nothing of the sort. He was a contemptible deceiver, and so was his friend.

Her gaze slid up, and she watched as Adonis lifted the waitress's hand in his own. "So, Miss Clark, are you willing to assist?"

If Miss Clark's beatific expression was anything to go by, she'd have been willing to do anything this man asked of her. When she nodded, he pulled her hand, bringing her closer.

"My darling girl," he began, "you talk of marriage, but how can that be possible between us? I am no one. I have nothing. You are a lady of breeding and quality, so lovely, so fine." He paused, cradling her hand in both of his, then he said, "You deserve so much more than I could ever offer you. You may think right now that the vast difference in our station doesn't matter, but it does, and I know that one day, you will realize it. And when you do, it will come between us and cast an unresolvable pall over our happiness."

Damn, Clara thought, a hint of reluctant admiration breaking through her anger, *this man might be a rake, but he's a talented one*.

She dared another peek at him and found that he was still gazing at the waitress, his attention fully fixed on her. As for Elsie, her upturned profile and enraptured expression only served to confirm Clara's opinion of this man's rakish character and talent for duplicity.

"Marriage," he went on, "brings harsh realities that, little by little, turn love to dust. I couldn't bear for what we have, the mad passion we feel, to be eroded and destroyed by the mundane tedium that marriage inevitably brings. What would become of us then?"

Elsie didn't answer. She probably couldn't, poor girl.

"No, my dear. Marriage isn't possible for the likes of us. You deserve it, of course, but we must be honest about our circumstances. I don't have the blunt to support you, and I certainly don't have the breeding to be worthy of you. And what of your family? They would surely turn against you if you married a lowborn chap like me. How could I ever cause such a breach between you and your relations? Do you really think me such a cad?"

"I think you're lovely," Elsie whispered, a declaration that further outraged Clara's feminine sensibilities, partly because of the worshipful tone in which the words had been uttered, and partly because she'd had the very same mistaken opinion of him not a quarter of an hour ago.

"It tears me apart, for I'm wild about you, but I cannot bear the torment that would come with knowing

I've ruined your life with matrimony. If a husband is truly what you want, I shall have to step aside, for I am not worthy of the role. Thus, I fear we must part forever."

He moved to pull his hand free, but the girl clutched it tight, obviously unwilling to end what was perhaps the most romantic moment of masculine attention she'd ever had. "Is there no place for us?" she asked, sounding nauseatingly desperate as she clung to his hand.

There was a pause. "I can think of only one, and that is where we are now. One day, you will end things between us, I know, and it will break my heart. But I beg of you," he added, pressing a fervent kiss to her hand, "do not let that day be today."

Elsie sighed again, the fact that he had just reversed his entire position on ending things seeming to go right over her head. She stared up at him in dazed and silent wonder, but she was given little time to savor the romance of the moment. With a dexterity Clara couldn't help but admire, he slipped free of Elsie's grasp, leaving the girl's hand still hovering in midair.

"You see, Lionel?" he said in a conversational tone as he resumed his seat and forced Clara to again look away. "It can be done."

"I suppose so, if one does it the way you just did," his friend agreed, laughing.

"What do you think, Elsie?" Adonis asked the waitress, obviously so confident of his powers of attraction that he felt free to call her by her Christian name, the cheeky devil. "If you were the lady, would you go? Or would you stay?"

"I believe . . ." Elsie paused and gave a little cough

as if working to recover her poise. "I believe I'd stay," she managed at last. "Not forever, mind you," she added, as if to emphasize that she still possessed a scrap of pride. "A girl's got to look out for her future, you know."

"Quite right." Teacups rattled, and Clara's gaze slid sideways to watch as he lifted the tray and held it up to her. "Thank you for all your help."

However amiable his voice, his words were clearly a dismissal, and the girl realized it. "You're very welcome, sir," she mumbled. Taking the offered tray, she dipped a curtsy and departed.

"Well?" Adonis asked, returning his attention to his friend as Clara turned hers to the waitress coming around the palms with her order. "What do you think?"

"I think you should be on the stage," Lionel said as Elsie set Clara's tray on her table and began placing tea things before her. "And I believe you have resolved my dilemma."

"Doing this buys you time, Lionel. That's all. Put that time to good use."

The two men stood up. Clara's pot of jam hit her table with a thud, and then Elsie was off like a shot, bustling toward the front to assist the gentlemen with their departure.

As the two men came around the palms and followed the waitress toward the front of the tea shop, Clara snatched up one of the letters she'd previously opened and ducked her head, pretending to take no notice of them whatsoever. Adonis turned toward the door, Lionel came around her table to follow him, and Clara lifted her gaze to watch their backs as they settled their bill, and all she could think about was the nefarious trick about to be employed on an unknowing woman.

Someone ought to warn her what was afoot, Clara thought, her gaze narrowing on the architect of this scheme as he followed his friend out of the tea shop. Someone ought to tell her just how despicably her affections were about to be abused. But how, Clara wondered, could such a feat be accomplished?

She frowned, pondering the question.

This Dina was, she knew, part of the *ton*, a fact which did present certain opportunities. Clara was, after all, the granddaughter of a viscount and was now also the sister-in-law of a duke, so she possessed the proper entrée into this woman's circle, but did that matter? She hadn't really begun moving in society, hadn't yet met many ladies outside the duke's family, and among the few she had met she'd encountered no young widow named Dina.

Clara sighed and sat back. The girl's surname would have been much more useful to know than her Christian name. Still, she could at least inquire of the duke's sisters. They might know who the woman was.

But even if Clara could identify her, what then? She could hardly walk up to a young lady she didn't know and blurt out that the woman's secret lover was a deceiving scoundrel. Her good deed would probably earn her a slap across the face.

And besides, she thought, casting a gloomy glance over the pile of correspondence before her, she had her own troubles.

Suddenly, an idea flashed into Clara's mind, a crazy, incredible idea that could not only solve her most pressing problem, but also save a fellow woman from future heartbreak and ruin.

Clara straightened in her chair, pulled a sheet of notepaper closer, and took up her fountain pen. She considered a moment, then she began to write. Only a few minutes later, she set down her fountain pen and placed her composition on top of the letters before her, feeling a sense of grim satisfaction.

Her first Lady Truelove column was now complete. She could only hope Dina Whoever-She-Was read the *Weekly Gazette*.

Chapter 3

Rex wasn't the sort for high society parties. Given his rather wicked sense of humor, he found low society far more entertaining. Nonetheless, he was Viscount Galbraith, the only son of the Earl of Leyland, and with that position came certain social obligations, most of which involved his great-aunt Petunia. Auntie held not only Rex's sole source of income at present, but also his deepest affections, and when she decided to open the season by holding a ball, he knew his presence was *de rigeur.*

Which was why Rex allowed his valet to put him into a white tie and tails, capped his head with one of those ridiculous top hats, and trundled off from his own modest town house in Half Moon Street to his great-aunt Petunia's lavish and fashionable home in Park Lane, and braced himself for at least two hours of having his toes smashed and his ear talked off by nervous debutantes.

His aunt's ballroom was only somewhat crowded, for his familial obligation demanded a punctual, rather than fashionably late arrival. But he wasn't, he soon discovered, punctual enough to suit Auntie.

"Well past eleven before you finally decide to make your appearance, I see," she said as he paused where she stood just outside the ballroom doors. "I feared I'd die of old age waiting for you to arrive."

Anyone else might have thought such a greeting denoted a coldness of feeling, but Rex wasn't fooled, and he leaned close to buss her wrinkled cheek with an affectionate kiss. "Past eleven, is it? A most uncivilized hour for you to still be awake, Auntie Pet." Pulling back, he pasted on a look of concern. "Perhaps you ought to have a dose of cod liver oil and go to bed? At your age, you can't be too careful, you know."

"Impudent cub." With a toss of her head, she gestured to the opened doors of the ballroom behind them, where people were milling about in anticipation of the dancing soon to begin. "Your reward for your saucy tongue shall be to open the ball."

He groaned. "Must I? Can't Uncle Bertie do it? Where is the old boy, by the way?" he added, glancing around for his uncle.

"My nephew caught a bit of a chill this afternoon and he's gone to bed. He'll be all right in a day or two. My dear Lady Seaforth," she added, looking past Rex to the next arrival and giving him a pointed nudge with her foot.

Appreciating what would be required of him in Uncle Bertie's absence, Rex moved to stand beside his great-aunt and offer his share of the required greetings to Lady Seaforth and her daughters, both of whom—thankfully—had husbands, and were, therefore, unavailable as fodder for Petunia's favorite hobby.

Auntie, being unmarried with no children of her own, had a very romantic nature and had made it her main ambition in life to arrange matches for all six of her as-yet-unwed grand-nephews and -nieces before she departed this earth. Because he was heir to the earldom, Rex was of particular interest to her in that regard, and she proceeded to underscore that fact the moment the Seaforth contingent had passed into the ballroom.

"You needn't worry about finding a partner for the opening dance," she said. "I've chosen one for you."

That bit of news was no great surprise, but he decided to pretend obtuseness. "Is it Hetty?" he asked, turning to glance over the crowd as if searching for his favorite cousin. "How marvelous. I shan't mind opening the ball if it's with Hetty."

"It is not Henrietta," Auntie informed him in a dampening tone. "You are free to seek a partner for life amidst a much wider circle than your own cousins."

He'd already made it clear many times that he wouldn't be seeking a partner for life anywhere, ever, but such assurances never seemed to put the slightest dent in Petunia's resolve.

"Really, Auntie, I don't see why you should be so against Hetty marrying me," he said instead, keeping his expression earnest and sincere even though his tongue was firmly in his cheek. "You'd get two of our lot married off at once. And marrying one's cousin was good enough for the Queen, wasn't it?"

Her answering look was wry, showing she knew quite well he was teasing. "Victoria, being royalty, was forced to matrimonial considerations that do not bind the rest of us."

"That's one way of calling a goose a swan," he said with a grin. "But you needn't worry about Hetty ever making a match with me. She'd scream with laughter at the very idea."

"And yet, I fear you are the one who refuses to take matrimony seriously."

"On the contrary," he replied at once, "I take it very seriously—the avoidance of it in particular."

"Really, Galbraith, you make me so annoyed. You'll be thirty-two this autumn. How much longer do you intend to circumvent the most important responsibility of your position?"

"Until I'm in the ground. Even longer, if possible."

"With no consideration of what happens to the title and the estates. Your father expects you to wed, and rightly so. You've no brothers, and your uncle Albert, being my late sister's son, can't inherit. If you don't marry and have sons of your own, everything goes to your father's third cousin once removed."

As if he didn't already know all this. Rex repressed a sigh as Auntie went on, "Thomas Galbraith is a man neither of us has ever met in the whole of our lives. He's older than you and yet he has no heir. In fact, he's not even married, so—"

"Then perhaps you should have invited him to your ball, eh?"

She ignored that bit of raillery. "He owns a boot-making establishment in Petticoat Lane. Boot-making,

I ask you—is that any sort of preparation to be the next earl?"

"A boot maker as the Earl of Leyland?" He pretended horror. "Heavens, what an idea."

"I'm not referring to his profession. It's his lack of knowledge and preparation that are of concern. Thomas Galbraith knows nothing of running a great estate like Braebourne."

"What's to know? Dane's a capable steward. And since Papa's moved to London and leased the house—"

"Only until you marry."

This time, his sigh would not be suppressed, but when he spoke, he worked to keep his voice as gentle as possible. "That isn't going to happen, Auntie Pet, as I've already said many times. And if we intend to quarrel about it again," he added before she could reply, "I shall need a drink."

With a glance down the main corridor to verify that the next guests were still removing their wraps in the foyer, he excused himself and walked into the ballroom. He made for the nearest footman with a tray of silver mugs, keeping his eye on the door as he pretended vast indecision over whether to choose a claret cup or rum punch.

He loved Petunia dearly, and he knew she was equally fond of him, but there was a steely glint in her eyes tonight that told him the evening ahead—and the entire season, for that matter—might be especially trying for both of them.

Any other time, he could have avoided any possibility of a row by going off to mingle, but with his uncle unable to act as host, duty required him to stand by and help his great-aunt greet arriving guests until the dancing began. So, when the newest arrivals started down the corridor toward the ballroom, he plucked a mug of rum punch from the tray and returned to Petunia's side. Once those guests had moved on, however, his aunt returned to their previous discussion, seeming not to care if a row resulted.

"Both your parents are quite disappointed, I daresay, by the utter disregard for duty that you display."

He gave a bark of laughter at that declaration and took a hefty swallow of his drink. "Mentioning my parents is hardly likely to spur me to the altar, Auntie Pet."

"Your parents' marriage has always been . . . difficult, I grant you, but at least they fulfilled their primary duty. And," she added before he could reply, "their situation does not provide you with any excuse to ignore yours. Nor, I might add, is their unhappiness a reasonable basis on which to condemn the entire married state."

"I'm not sure our general acquaintance would agree with you there." He turned, gesturing with his glass to the crowd in the ballroom behind them. "Thanks to Mama and Papa's deep mutual loathing and complete lack of discretion, the gutter press was able to keep all of society *au courant* regarding the miserable state of their marriage, from Mama's first affair, through every scandal and every retaliation, all the way to the final legal separation. Given the misery they managed to inflict upon each other during their fourteen years of cohabitation, I think our friends fully appreciate my contempt for matrimony."

"That all ended a decade ago when they separated. Everyone's quite forgotten about it."

He turned his head, meeting his great-aunt's exasperated gaze with a hard one of his own. "I haven't."

Her expression softened at once. "Oh, my dear," she said with a compassion in her voice that impelled him to look away and divert the conversation from himself.

"It's not as if Mama and Papa have forgotten, either," he said. "They have not, I assure you."

The moment those words were out of his mouth, he regretted them, for Petunia pounced at once. "And how would you know that?" she asked.

Now embroiled in a volatile discussion he always took great pains to avoid, Rex knew he had to tread with care. "I called upon Papa when he arrived in town, whereupon he immediately began to expound on his favorite topic: my mother's faithless character. My call, therefore, was brief."

"I'm surprised you bothered to call upon him at all. He's none too fond of you these days, you know, and in no mind to reinstate your income from the estate until you marry."

"And yet I remain a dutiful son," Rex countered lightly.

The irony of that wasn't lost on Petunia. "Only in some ways," she said, her voice dry. "Your father desires you to marry as much as I do."

"Ah, but there's a difference. Your greatest care is my happiness. Papa's is the succession."

"Either way, I wasn't curious about your father's opinion," Auntie replied, wisely not bothering to assure him of his father's questionable affections. "It's your mother I'm thinking of. How do you know her present feelings on the subject?"

So much for treading with care. He grimaced and took another swallow of punch.

"Don't tell me you've been in correspondence with her again?" Petunia made a sound of exasperation before he could decide how to reply. "His discovery of your communications with your mother—and the fact that you were giving her money—are the entire reason he cut off your income in the first place. It is fortunate for you that I have been able to replace it."

"Very fortunate," he agreed. "You're a brick, Auntie Pet."

"Why? For spiking your father's guns, or for providing you a source of funds to spend on a bachelor's shallow pursuits?"

He grinned at her. "That's a no-win question if ever I heard one. I think I'll refrain from answering."

"Unlike your father, I recognize that attempting to force your hand only makes you more determined. Still, if he finds out you have been writing to your mother again, I can't think what he'll do. Disinherit you completely, I expect."

"He's bitter enough for such a course, I grant you, but I did not write to Mama. And if she chooses to write to me, what would you suggest I do about it?"

"Inform Mr. Bainbridge. Give him her letters."

"Tattle on my own mother to the family solicitor?"

"By communicating with you, she is in direct violation of the terms of the separation decree."

"Bainbridge would tell Papa, who would then take away what little income Mama receives from the estate. I am her son, Auntie Pet. Her only son. It was very wrong of Papa to forbid her to see me or write to me."

"She's fortunate Leyland granted her an income at all!" Petunia's voice held some heat, reminding him there was no reasoning with her on the subject of Mama. "She shamed him and the entire family with her wanton behavior. And," Petunia added before Rex could remind her there had been grievous wrongs on both sides, "nothing's changed since, from what I hear. Her affair with the Marquis of Auvignon is over, and since he's not supporting her, money must be what she's after, though why she'd apply to you escapes me. It's not as if you can afford to give her any, for you spend every cent I'm giving you as it is—Gaiety Girls, drink, cards, and heaven-only-knows what."

"Quite so," he agreed, managing to utter the lie without a blush, even though he hadn't had a woman or a round of cards in over a year. His reputation as a wild-living bachelor had been well-earned, but nowadays, it was nothing more than a convenient way to explain his perpetual lack of funds. If Auntie Pet found out where the money she gave him was truly going, the fat would be in the fire. "And yet, my irresponsible spending habits don't seem to be as great a sin as Mama's."

"If you married," she went on, ignoring his point completely, "all this frivolous living would stop, of course—"

"And no frivolity at all would be better?" The question was incisive, his voice razor-sharp as his restraint began to crack. "I look at Papa, and I am inclined to doubt it."

She sighed, studying him with a sadness that cut him to the heart. "You are made of stronger stuff than your parents."

To his mind, that wasn't much of a testament to his character, but he hated quarreling with Auntie, so he decided to change the subject.

"You've chosen my first dance partner this evening, have you?" He paused, drawing a breath and bracing himself for whichever young lovely was about to be thrust upon him. "Am I entitled to know who she is?"

"I wish you to open the ball with Miss Clara Deverill."

The name was unfamiliar, and he gave his aunt a teasing grin. "Ah, trying new tactics this season, I see."

"I don't know what you mean."

"I've never met this Clara Deverill in my life, and I can only conclude that, having exhausted all possibilities amongst the young ladies of our own set, you are now attempting to cast your nets a little wider."

"Miss Deverill is part of 'our own set', I'll have you know. She is the granddaughter of Viscount Ellesmere. And she has other connections as well, for her sister married the Duke of Torquil earlier this year."

Rex was not the least bit fooled by this mention of the girl's connection to Torquil. "Ellesmere? Isn't he the chap you almost married back in '28, or whenever it was?"

"Heavens, dear, I'm not that old. It was 1835. More to the point, this is the girl's first season, always a nerve-wracking time for a young lady. So, you see? This isn't about you at all."

He grinned. "Then it's clearly about you doing Ellesmere a favor. Still carrying a torch for your childhood love, are you?"

"Don't be absurd," she remonstrated with a sniff. "Viscountess Ellesmere is alive and well, as you already know, and she asked my help in bringing her granddaughter out."

"Why should a girl with such valuable connections need help—oh, God," he added at once, dismayed as another possibility occurred to him. "She's ghastly, isn't she?"

"Miss Deverill is a nice, sweet girl."

That description only reinforced his suspicions. "I knew I should have stayed away," he muttered. "I knew it."

"Miss Deverill," Auntie went on, ignoring his self-recriminations, "has not had much opportunity for society. Her father's family is in trade—newspapers, I believe. Naturally, Ellesmere was opposed to his daughter marrying the fellow—"

"Naturally," he echoed, thinking of the mud the gutter press had slung at his parents years ago. "A newspaper hawker in the family? What an awful prospect."

"But she was determined to have him," Petunia went on, "and because of that, she became estranged from her parents and turned her back on good society. She's gone now, poor dear, but Ellesmere wishes to mend the fences with his granddaughters."

"Well, there is a duke in the family now."

This rather cynical contention did not sit well with his great-aunt, who gave him a look of reproof. "That's hardly in the girl's favor at present. Torquil's widowed mother married that notorious Italian painter last summer. It caused quite a stir, let me tell you. Harriet's a fool. The fellow's nearly twenty years her junior."

"A younger man," he murmured. "Oh, the horror."

"My point is that Miss Deverill hasn't been out for

very long, and between her unfortunate background, the scandal in the duke's family, and the fact that her father's ill and she's required to manage that newspaper business while her sister's away on honeymoon and her brother's in America—well, she's in a most awkward social position through no fault of her own. So, I am determined that she have a successful launch into the season tonight and enjoy herself. As for you, do not think one dance with Miss Deverill fulfills your obligations this evening. Not only do I expect you to be amiable and entertaining company for Miss Deverill, but I also expect you to dance with at least six other unpartnered ladies as well. No dashing off when my back is turned to play cards at your club or to meet some Gaiety Girl."

Resigned to his fate, he downed the rest of his punch, then set down the mug, straightened his cuffs, and nodded toward the ballroom. "So where is this Miss Deverill? Can I at least see what I'm in for?"

"Her physical appearance is hardly relevant."

"On the contrary," he answered with cheer, "I think it's quite relevant, since she is about to be hurled into my arms. And the more you prevaricate about pointing her out to me," he added as she gave a huff, "the more I imagine an Amazon of twenty stone with bad breath and warts on her nose."

"Don't be absurd. The odds of pairing you up with someone are bad enough as it is. I wouldn't dream of making them worse." Auntie moved through the doorway, and as he followed her inside, she took a glance around the ballroom. "To the right of the refreshment table, by that big vase of lilacs," she informed him as he paused beside her again. "Brown hair, white gown."

Rex's gaze traveled to the appropriate spot, where a tall, willowy figure in filmy layers of white illusion stood against the wall. In that first cursory glance, he knew just why her grandmother had deemed her in need of some social help. The girl was, quite obviously, shy.

Her back was pressed flat against the wall, as if she wished the room behind her would open up and swallow her. She had fine eyes, large and dark, but they stared out at the crowd with the combination of dismay and anxiety shy people so often displayed at social gatherings.

Her hair, fashioned in an austere braided crown atop her head, was that indeterminate brown shade halfway between blond and brunette. Her figure was slender, but her face was round as a currant bun, with a pale-pink mouth that was too wide, dark brows that were too straight, and a nose so small it was barely there at all.

Many, he knew, would have deemed her plain. Rex wasn't prepared to go that far, but in this room of glittering, bejeweled beauties, she did seem easy to overlook, rather like a bit of shortbread on a tray of French pastries.

As he studied her face, it struck him suddenly that she seemed familiar somehow, and yet, he was positive they'd never been introduced. He'd probably encountered her over the punch bowl at some previous affair, or sat next to her at a concert, but he found it a bit odd he should recall even that much about her, given that she was the sort who tried hard not to be noticed.

That thought had barely crossed his mind before

someone in the crowd caught her attention, and it must have been someone she knew and liked, for she gave a little wave, and then she smiled.

In that instant, alchemy happened. Rex sucked in a surprised breath, for with one simple curve of her lips, the girl's entire face was transformed. Her tension vanished, her face lit up like a candle, and those who might have dismissed her as plain would surely have had to eat their words. Whoever she was smiling at must have been a woman, for had she directed that smile at any man in the room, he'd have responded like a puppet pulled by a string. Even Rex, usually immune to the charms of young ladies, felt a bit dazzled by it.

"There, now," Petunia said beside him. "Are you satisfied that I have not saddled you with a wart-faced Amazon?"

He didn't reply, for he knew if he expressed an opinion of the girl that was even the slightest bit favorable, Auntie would be finagling invitations for her to every possible occasion, and his entire season would become a game of duck-and-hide.

"Oh, very well," he said instead, and heaved an exaggerated sigh. "Let's have this over with."

Those words were scarce out of his mouth before Auntie was tucking her hand into the crook of his elbow and pulling him toward the girl.

Miss Deverill looked up as they approached, and the moment she laid eyes on him, any trace of a smile vanished from her face and all her previous tension returned. Somehow, her appalled reaction to the sight of him made her seem even more familiar than before, and it was a good thing he'd already realized she was shy, for if he hadn't perceived that, he'd be racking his brains now, trying to figure out where and how and under what unfavorable circumstances they had met before and what he'd done wrong.

"Miss Deverill," Auntie said as they halted in front of her, "I should like to present my great-nephew, Viscount Galbraith, to you. Galbraith, this is Miss Clara Deverill."

"Miss Deverill." He bowed. "A pleasure to meet you."

She clearly didn't share this sentiment, for her face was as pale as milk. She didn't smile a greeting or move to curtsy, but remained utterly still, so still, in fact, that he wondered in some alarm if she might have stopped breathing. She looked as if she might faint, and though there were men who would find that a most gratifying feminine response to an introduction, Rex did not. If she fainted, it would be terribly embarrassing and make him the butt of the most tiresome jokes amongst his friends. Worse, it would subject him and this poor girl to the wildest speculations, and that sort of talk was something they could both well do without. He was obliged to prompt her. "Miss Deverill?"

At the sound of his voice, she inhaled sharply and color flamed in those pale cheeks like spots of rouge. "L . . . likewise, I'm sh . . . sh . . . sure."

Her eyes were now round as saucers, reminding him of nothing so much as a lamb about to be dispatched, and any momentary flicker of interest her previous smile might have evoked was snuffed out at once. He was, perhaps, something of a wolf, but defenseless little lambs had never held much appeal for him.

In desperation, he turned to Aunt Petunia, but he discovered at once that he would be receiving no assistance from that quarter.

Instead of jumping into the breach, Auntie murmured something about the orchestra, excused herself and walked away, leaving Rex on his own.

Cursing Auntie's devilish matchmaking, he returned his attention to the girl, and the sight of her staring at him in mute agony was all the reminder Rex needed of just why he avoided high society parties.

Chapter 4

It was him. The god of the tea shop, the good-looking rake who charmed women as easily as he dispensed advice on how to deceive them, was standing right in front of her. And he now had a name other than the one she'd given him in her mind. Not Adonis, but Lord Galbraith.

In itself, the discovery of his true identity wasn't particularly shocking. One didn't have to be in the newspaper trade to know that Rex Pierpont, Viscount Galbraith, only son of the Earl of Leyland, was one of the *ton*'s most notorious bachelors, well-known not only for his wild ways but also for his disdainful view of marriage. The fact that he would do all he could to assist another man in evading wedlock was not a surprise to Clara at all.

Nonetheless, it had never occurred to her that she might see the Adonis of the tea shop again. Only now, in hindsight, did she appreciate that his fine clothes and conversation should have warned her that an encounter such as this was possible. She could only guess that her own desperation and anger the other day had blinded her to other considerations.

Now, with their introduction hanging in the air, she felt transfixed, as if she'd been turned to a pillar of salt, or transformed into a tree stump, or debilitated by some other equally horrifying impediment. But though her body seemed frozen into immobility, her mind was racing.

Did he know who she was? Did he recognize her as the girl peeking at him between the palm fronds at Mrs. Mott's Tea Emporium a few short days ago? She had been sure at the time that he hadn't noticed her—because, after all, men almost never did—but what if she'd been mistaken?

She scanned his face, looking for any sign of recognition in his countenance. There was none, but that didn't do much to alleviate her alarm, for she'd seen firsthand this man's talent for duplicity. If he did recognize her, the fact would only matter if he also read Lady Truelove and if he'd read this afternoon's edition. In that case, he would surely put two and two together. And that would be disastrous.

The fact that Lady Truelove's identity was unknown provided a mystique that was a great part of her appeal. People were forever speculating about just which matron of high society was the real Lady Truelove. If Galbraith realized the truth and determined what she'd done, spite could motivate him to reveal her as the famous columnist. If that happened, the *Weekly Gazette*'s most successful feature would be compromised, perhaps ruined, and it would be her fault. Irene would be devastated by the loss of her most successful creation. She might even be disappointed in Clara for allowing it to happen.

That notion was unbearable, like a knife going into Clara's chest.

"My aunt tells me your father is a man of business, Miss Deverill," Galbraith said, forcing her out of these frantic contemplations and forcing her to gather her scattered wits. "Newspapers, I believe?"

Was he toying with her? "Yes," she answered, a squeak of a word that made her grimace.

He didn't seem to find such brevity satisfactory. He waited, watching her, his brows lifted as if he expected further elucidation.

"One newspaper," she went on, striving not to sound like a panicked mouse this time. "The *Weekly Gazette*. Do you . . ." She paused, and gave a cough. "Do you . . . umm . . . ever read it?"

His expression became apologetic. "I'm afraid not. I don't read the papers much."

"Oh," she breathed, relief washing over her, easing her apprehensions a little. "That's good."

He frowned in puzzlement at this seemingly nonsensical reply, and she rushed on, "I mean, so many men seem to just lounge about in their clubs all day, reading the papers, don't they? It can't be healthy."

Even as she spoke, she appreciated how inane she sounded, and his polite, perfunctory smile confirmed her conclusion even before he replied.

"Quite," he said.

Silence fell between them. He shifted his weight and glanced around, looking trapped and a bit uncomfortable, a reaction from men with which she was, sadly, quite familiar. But given what she knew of this man, and what she wanted to keep secret from him about herself, she felt none of the awkwardness she usually experienced in such encounters. Now that she could be reasonably sure he had not recognized her, all she wanted was to make some excuse to depart and return to her friends. He spoke, however, before she had the chance.

"My aunt has asked me to open the ball, Miss Deverill."

Horns sounded from the orchestra as if to herald this pronouncement, and he held out his hand to her. "Will you honor me?"

Clara stared at him, dumbfounded. He was asking her to dance?

Once upon a time, she'd dreamed of charming princes with tawny-gold hair and brilliant blue eyes, men so good-looking it took one's breath away. As a young girl, she'd waltzed with imaginary partners like him in the privacy of her room, but those girlish imaginings had never materialized into reality, and on the rare occasions when she'd had the opportunity to dance, her partners had usually been young boys, old men, or the husbands of her friends. Now, with her first serious foray into good society, her silly girlhood dreams seemed to be coming true at last, but with an unexpected and ironic twist: her Prince Charming wasn't a prince at all. He was a cad.

It was so ridiculous that a laugh came bubbling up out of her before she could stop it.

His smile stayed in place, though it may have faltered a bit around his eyes. "Did I say something amusing?"

"No," she choked, smothering her laughter at once. "I mean, yes, y . . . you did, obviously . . . but no . . . that is, I wasn't laughing at you. I m . . . mean . . . I just . . . it was only . . ." Her voice trailed off, and she gave it up. There was no way to explain. And it wasn't as if he would suffer much from her amusement at his expense, except perhaps a sting to his conceit, which to her mind, was no more than he deserved.

"Was that a yes, or a no?"

His question reminded her she hadn't yet responded to his invitation, and he seemed of no mind to withdraw it. Hand still outstretched toward her, he continued to wait for her to reply.

She couldn't think of any man she had less desire to dance with, and she grasped desperately for an excuse. "Oh, I had not . . . that is, I don't really—"

"I beg you not to refuse me," he cut in smoothly, "for if you do, I shall feel no end a fool." His smile seemed to stiffen even as it widened. "Everyone's watching us, you see."

Oh, God. Her cheeks flamed with heat, for she hated being conspicuous, and she had to suppress the urge to glance around. He was probably exaggerating, but even a single pair of eyes seemed a pair too many.

Unfortunately, he had just conveyed upon her what anyone watching would regard as a great honor, and since she had not been engaged for this dance by another partner, there was no excuse possible.

"Thank you, yes," she murmured and took his hand. As he led her onto the ballroom floor, she appreciated with a sinking feeling that even if no one had been watching them a moment ago, every pair of eyes in the room was certainly fixed on them now.

She paused with him at one end of the ballroom, waiting as other couples desiring to dance lined up along the edges of the dance floor, preparing to follow them in the Grand March. A few moments later, he glanced at her, gave a nod, and started forward.

Clara moved with him, acutely uncomfortable as they paraded across the ballroom floor under the scrutiny of over a hundred people. How ironic that she'd spent her entire youth wishing she could make a successful debut into society, and yet, once Fate had at last decided to grant her the chance to fulfill that seemingly impossible wish, all she wanted was to make a mad dash for the nearest door.

At the top of the room, they turned to face each other. He looked at her, and she looked at his white tie as he lifted their clasped hands. The other couples who had followed them ducked beneath the arch formed by their raised arms, then circled back around to line up along the edges of the dance floor, men on his side, women on hers.

When all the couples had gone through, Galbraith turned and so did she, and they started back across the room, other couples in their wake.

"Surely we must have a bit of conversation, Miss Deverill," he said, breaking the silence between them.

"Must we?" The moment she said those words, she regretted them, for it wasn't in her nature to be impolite. "I'm sorry," she mumbled, casting a sideways glance at him. "That s . . . sounded rude. It's just that I'm not . . . I don't . . . that is, c . . . conversation isn't . . . my greatest talent."

"I see." In his extraordinary eyes was a hint of what might have been sympathy. Or pity.

She stiffened and looked away, wishing she hadn't been so frank. "It's only with strangers."

They paused where they had started, turning to face each other, and as they waited for the other dancers to move into the proper formation, she felt impelled to underscore a lack of familiarity. "I don't know you, you see."

"A fact which is wholly my loss."

Given what she knew of him, Clara was inclined to agree, but of course, she couldn't say so. "Rather the opposite, I should think," she said instead, forcing a laugh, trying to make light of this awkward situation. "Your invitation to dance was at your aunt's behest, I'm sure."

A kindlier man might have rushed to deny it. Galbraith did not. Instead, he studied her face for a moment, then his lashes lowered, the gold tips catching the light as he glanced down.

Heat rushed into Clara's cheeks at once, for she knew what he was looking at, and she was quite aware that there wasn't much to see. Resisting the urge to squirm, she lifted her chin a notch and endured it, reminding herself that she didn't care two straws what a man like this thought of her or of her figure. But when his gaze returned to her face, something in his grave expression made her catch her breath just the same.

"You hide your lights under a bushel, Miss Deverill."

"Do I?" she muttered, feeling a bit frantic as he leaned forward and took up her hand. "No wonder I can never find them."

He laughed, though Clara couldn't understand why. "You have wit, I see," he said as he began turning them in a circle, the first movement of the quadrille. "What a delightful discovery."

"An odd one," she replied as they switched hands and began turning in the opposite direction. "Since I have no idea what I just said that was funny."

Still smiling a little, he lifted their clasped hands above their heads, entwining his arm with hers as his free hand held her free hand tightly between their bodies. "No," he agreed, looking at her through the opening formed by their upraised arms, his smile fading away, his gaze roaming over her face as they turned in a circle. "I suspect you don't."

Entangled with him this way, his open stare on her face, his absurd compliment hanging in the air, she felt trapped and terribly vulnerable. Even through the layers of her clothing, she could feel his knuckles brushing against her belly, sending a jolt of panic through her entire body and impelling her to speak. "Do you flirt with every woman you meet, Lord Galbraith?"

He seemed surprised, though whether that was due to her question or the tartness of her voice as she'd asked it, Clara couldn't be sure. "Not usually, no," he answered. "Not with young ladies anyway. It's a rule of mine."

"I shouldn't think a man like you had any rules," she muttered, and immediately wished she could take the words back, for a little frown knit his brows, and his gaze narrowed speculatively.

The steps of the dance caused them to separate before he could reply, however, and as they moved through the next figure with other partners, Clara reminded herself that her best means of keeping her secret was to keep quiet, something she'd never had any trouble doing in her life before.

Galbraith, unfortunately, did not seem inclined to let her take refuge in silence. "A man like me." He echoed her words in a musing voice the moment the dance brought them together again. "What sort of man is that, exactly?" he asked, grasping her hand in his and moving them in a circle. "Your choice of words makes me curious."

Oh, Lord, his curiosity was the last thing she needed.

"Come now, Miss Deverill," he said when she remained silent. "Despite your declaration of reticence, you seem to have little trouble conveying what you think of me." He gave a rueful smile as they changed hands and reversed direction. "Seems a bit unsporting to form a judgement so quickly. After all, we've only just been introduced. Unless I'm mistaken?" He paused, and though he was still smiling, Clara saw the sudden watchfulness in his gaze. "Have we met before?"

"Of course not," she denied at once, and cursed herself for how unconvincing she sounded. Taking a deep breath, she tried again. "At least, I don't believe so. I don't move in society much, so if we'd met, I'd remember it."

"Then what have I done to earn your low opinion?"

The best thing was to deny any such view of his character, but something in Clara resisted giving him a lie that would spare his feelings, even if it was the safest thing to do. "You have quite a scandalous reputation."

"Yes, so my aunt often reminds me. And people do seem quite inclined to gossip."

"Gossip?" She raised an eyebrow at his attempt to brush off his wild manner of living. "The newspapers talk about you all the time, Lord Galbraith. And I should know, since my family is in that trade."

"So, it is your family's livelihood that has inspired your low opinion of me? Well, I have a low opinion of newspapers, so we're rather even there."

That flicked her on the raw, due to his aspersion of her family's means of earning a living, or his disregard for his own notorious reputation, she couldn't have said. "Many seem to share my view."

"I refuse to worry about what other people think of me."

"You don't even try to earn their good opinion?"

He grinned, demonstrating the truth of her accusation. "Why try to be good, when being bad has so many rewards? Besides," he added with a shrug, "most women love a rake."

That was more true than she liked to imagine. "Clearly, then, I'm not like most women," she muttered.

"No," he agreed, and unexpectedly, he pulled her close—closer than decorum allowed—as he lifted their joined hands overhead. "I'm beginning to believe you're not."

The implications in that soft reply sent her stomach plummeting, but Clara forced herself to hold his gaze. "You don't deny what is said of you, then?"

"I am hardly in a position to deny it. I enjoy life, Miss Deverill, and I fail to see why I should be condemned for that."

"In other words, you want people to think well of you whilst you do whatever you please?"

She rather hoped her words would sting, but he only

laughed, shaking back his unruly hair and causing the tawny strands to glint in the light of the chandeliers overhead. "I suppose I do, yes."

She thought of him in the tea shop, conspiring to help his friend do that very thing at an unknowing woman's expense, and she couldn't suppress a sound of derision. "Men and their cake," she muttered.

The steps again separated them, and Clara decided that since he seemed determined to have conversation for the entire dance, the best thing was to turn to innocuous topics, but when they came together again, he gave her no opportunity.

"I take it," he said, picking up her hand and the thread of their earlier conversation, "you believe all men just want to have our cake and eat it, too?"

"Not *all* men."

He laughed softly as he lifted their joined hands overhead. "Well, well," he murmured, "with every look and every word, the little lamb with the big brown eyes proves she's not as defenseless as she first appears."

Clara felt a spark of frustration. She might be plain, with a shy and quiet disposition, but she was not some sort of helpless, dependent creature.

"Is that what I am?" she asked as they turned in a circle, moving in the steps of the dance. "A little lamb?" She opened her eyes deliberately wide. "And I'm lost in the woods, I suppose, and you'll come save me?"

"Save you? I doubt it." His gaze lowered, pausing at her lips. "Ravish you would be a sight more likely."

Clara's heart gave a panicked thud, slamming into her ribs with such force that it broke her concentration. She trod on his foot, lost her balance, and would have stumbled, but he caught her, letting go of her hand to wrap his arm around her back. Above their heads, his fingers tightened over hers to keep them both in the pose as she found her feet again.

"Careful," he cautioned. "Dance with me much longer and I fear you'll be in danger." With that, his arm slid away, his hand freed hers, and he was gone.

The change to other partners was a welcome respite, but as she moved through the steps, the imprint of his arm was like a steel band against her back, and his words were echoing in her ears more loudly than the music.

Ravish you would be a sight more likely.

Heavens, no man had ever expressed the desire to *ravish* her before. What a pity, she thought, aggrieved, that the first one who did was a man she didn't even like.

But was it such a pity? He was so good-looking that it almost hurt to look at him, and had she liked him, had she cared about earning his good opinion, she'd probably have been too tongue-tied to ever hold a word of conversation with him. With this man, however, it was different. Despite his looks, his true character was clear, and since she didn't care a jot what he thought of her, she had a certain degree of power over the situation that she otherwise wouldn't have possessed. No wonder she was being so uncharacteristically forthright this evening. Why shouldn't she be? With him, she could say anything, and what did it matter?

"You warn me, Lord Galbraith," she said as they came together again and clasped hands. "But I cannot help wondering why. Is it the steps of the dance I should fear?" she asked, emboldened in a way she'd never been before. "Or you?"

He raised a brow, and no wonder. From a *little lamb* like her, such words were bound to be unexpected.

"Oh, me, definitely," he answered. "I'm far more dangerous to you than a mere quadrille. If this were a mazurka, now, that might be different."

She laughed, disarmed by that bit of wit in spite of herself. "I doubt I'm in any danger from you."

"You're in my arms." He pulled her a fraction closer. "Make no mistake, my lamb. You are in very great danger."

Clara's throat went dry, and as they turned slowly on the ballroom floor, staring at each other through the circle of their upraised arms, she felt her newfound sense of power slipping.

He seemed to perceive the change. His smile faded away, his gaze roamed over her face, and her heart began thudding hard in her chest. She feared the sensations he evoked in her were due not to her fear of recognition, but to something else entirely, something she'd never experienced in her life before. Worse, she knew what it was.

This was what Elsie Clark had felt that afternoon in the tea shop. This was how it felt to be caught in the sights of a devastatingly handsome man. He was looking at her as if she was the only thing in the world that existed, as if nothing that had come before or would ever come after was more important than she was. A rake's version of the siren song.

It wasn't real, and yet, even as she reminded herself of that, heat curled in her belly.

Thankfully, the steps of the dance again forced them apart, and by the time they came together for the last figure of the quadrille, Clara had regained her composure. "I thought you said you don't flirt with young ladies. You make it a rule, you said."

"So I did. But rules . . ." He paused, a faint smile on his lips. "Rules, they say, are made to be broken."

"You have certainly broken a few."

He laughed as he lifted their hands overhead. "I have indeed," he said, studying her through the circle of their arms. "But you haven't, I suspect."

She thought of what she'd done with Lady Truelove. "You'd be surprised," she muttered.

"Would I? You intrigue me, Miss Deverill." He pulled her closer, his fingers tightening around hers, his knuckles brushing against her belly. "Perhaps we should break some rules together?"

"Which ones did you have in mind?"

That provocative question came tumbling out of her mouth without any thought, but thankfully, the music stopped before he could reply, and Clara was profoundly relieved. She pulled back, expected he would let her hands go and offer his arm to escort her back to her place, but to her astonishment, he didn't free her. He didn't even move.

"Several ideas are going through my head, I confess," he murmured, answering her question. His vivid blue gaze lowered to her mouth. "A kiss during a dance would break quite a few rules, wouldn't it?"

Clara imagined it, his arms around her and his mouth claiming hers, but though it was just a flash through her mind, her knees suddenly felt like jelly, even as her feminine pride railed against the notion that she could be conquered so easily.

"Many rules, I should think," she agreed, pulling her

hands free and heaving a sigh of feigned disappointment. "But kissing me during the dance is impossible."

"Is it?" He stirred, moving closer. His head bent down a fraction. "Why?"

She began to laugh. "Because the dance is over."

He blinked as if that were the last thing he'd expected. "What?"

Noting his blank expression, she realized he'd been so caught up in her that he hadn't even noticed the end of the dance. She laughed, exhilaration rising inside her like a sudden burst of fireworks, overriding everything else this man had made her feel. She had her own siren song, it seemed. Who'd ever have thought that?

He glanced about as if working to come to his senses, and she took that opportunity to turn away and start for the nearest door. It was a breach of good manners, for it deprived him of the opportunity to return her to her place, but Clara didn't care. For the first time in her life, she'd said the perfect thing at the perfect moment, and she didn't want to spoil such an unexpected triumph by talking with him any further.

But when she glanced over her shoulder, she found that her escape was not to be so easy. He was in pursuit. Why he should be, she couldn't imagine, but there was an unmistakable half smile on his lips and a determined cast to his countenance that made Clara quicken her steps.

She had the advantage on him, for his momentary daze had enabled her to put a good twenty feet of distance and half a dozen couples between them. But once she left the ballroom, those advantages would evaporate. Her vague, half-formed intent had been to duck into the ladies' withdrawing room, but only now did she realize she'd never ascertained where it was and she had no time to go looking, for he was on her very heels. And even if she could spare a moment to find out that information, there was no one to whom she could put the question because when she stepped into the corridor, she found it was empty.

Cursing her sudden and most uncharacteristic impulse to be a flirt, Clara glanced around. Ahead of her was the main corridor that led to the foyer, a vast expanse with no side doors and no hiding places. To her left and right, the ballroom wall was flanked by large marble statues, and she saw only one possible means to evade him.

She turned to the right, running for all she was worth down the corridor, but she'd barely managed a dozen steps before she heard the door to the ballroom open, and she veered sideways, catching the glint of his tawny hair out of the corner of her eye just before she slid between two statues. She drew in her breath and stiffened her spine, hoping her body was slender enough and her skirt narrow enough to sufficiently conceal her from view.

Voices and music floated to her down the corridor, and then the door closed again, muffling the sounds of the ball going on in the room behind her. She didn't know if he'd gone back inside or not, but there was no way to find out, for she didn't dare move. She waited, listening, hardly daring to breathe.

"What the devil?" she heard him mutter. "How does a girl just vanish into thin air?"

Clara bit her lip, smiling to herself. How, indeed.

The grandfather clock by the stairs began to sound the hour and as the twelfth chime died away, a sudden chuckle of laughter echoed to her along the corridor.

"Midnight, eh?" He laughed again. "Well, then, Cinderella, it seems I must bid you good-night."

Her smile widened into a grin. She didn't like him, nor did she have the desire for his company, but none-theless, it was exciting to be caught up in a real-life fairy tale—to be, for the first time, the lovely ingénue who captured the interest of the handsomest man at the ball. Even if he was a cad.

The door to the ballroom opened and closed again, but Clara continued to wait, counting a full thirty sec-onds before she dared to emerge from between the statues.

Thankfully, the corridor was empty.

Chapter 5

Rex could not imagine how the girl could have vanished in the blink of an eye, but he knew she couldn't have gone far, and any other time, he'd have willingly lingered for a more thorough search. Unfortunately, he had other obligations to fulfill, and wandering the corridors of the house in search of one cheeky girl wasn't among them, a fact brought home to him with force the moment he reentered the ballroom.

Auntie Pet's stern gaze honed in on him at once, reminding him that he had at least half a dozen dances to go before he could return his attentions to the provoking Miss Deverill.

He glanced around for a suitable partner, and when he spied Lady Frances Chinden a few feet away, he approached her for the waltz. From his point of view, Lady Frances was a perfect choice. Her father had massive gambling debts, so Petunia would never approve of her as a possible future Countess of Galbraith. She was also distractingly pretty to look at and quite enjoyable company, but even Lady Frances's considerable charms did not enable him to dismiss Clara Deverill from his thoughts. The girl's face, lit with laughter at his expense, remained crystal clear in his mind even as he danced with another woman, the orange-blossom scent of her hair still lingered in his nostrils, and her words echoed in his ears more loudly than the strains of Strauss's "Blue Danube."

Kissing me during the dance is impossible, Lord Galbraith . . . because the dance is over.

He pictured himself as he'd been a few minutes ago, dazed, stunned, even aroused—on a dance floor, he appreciated with chagrin, in full view of society. He'd been so occupied with delicious notions of kissing her that he hadn't even realized the music had stopped and they were no longer dancing. No wonder she'd laughed at him.

Still, he did have an excuse. She might not be the sort a man noticed in a first cursory glance, true enough, but when she laughed, the transformation was a bit shattering. When Clara Deverill laughed, when she smiled, it lit up her face—hell, it lit up the room—and sent any notions that she was plain straight out the window.

She didn't realize it herself, he suspected, or have any idea that she had a unique charm all her own. He'd have been happy to show her, but she'd never given him the chance. She'd been off like a shot the moment the dance was over, leaving him standing there like a chump and feeling like a prize idiot.

Where she'd gone still baffled him. She must have slipped into the ladies' withdrawing room, though he couldn't see how she'd managed to reach it in time. She must have run hell-for-leather.

But why? Without being unduly conceited, he knew he wasn't the sort ladies usually ran from. So why such a desire to escape? Had she merely been flirting with him? Running away, expecting him to pursue as the next move in the game?

That didn't quite square. She had not wanted to dance with him, that had been clear enough, and despite a few flirtatious words here and there, her manner toward him had been for the most part coolly indifferent, even disapproving.

Who was she to approve or disapprove of him? he wondered, a bit nettled. They'd only just met.

With that thought, he felt again the curious sense that he knew her somehow.

She had flatly denied it, but the more Rex tried to dismiss a nagging feeling of familiarity, the stronger it became. They must have met, and she was denying it for some reason. But why? To pay him out for some slight, perhaps? Had he offended her in some way?

Before he could explore that rather unsettling prospect, Lady Frances's voice intruded on his thoughts.

"You seem preoccupied, Lord Galbraith."

With an effort, Rex set aside his contemplations of his former dance partner and returned his attention to the one in his arms, hastily conjuring an excuse for his inattention. "My apologies, Lady Frances. I am preoccupied, I do confess. On my uncle's behalf, I'm playing host this evening, and I'm not accustomed to the role. It's giving me cause for anxiety."

"There's no need for that. You're doing splendidly. The role of host suits you well."

Like most men, Rex found praise an agreeable thing, but only if he deserved it, and in this case, he didn't, since he'd been playing host for less than an hour. No, he thought, looking into Lady Frances's pretty face, this was the meaningless sort of flattery debutantes seemed to feel was expected of them. Most debutantes, anyway.

You do have quite a scandalous reputation.

Rex muttered an oath.

"I beg your pardon?"

Lady Frances was staring at him, and for the second time, Rex forced his thoughts back to his present dance partner. But despite his best intentions, he occasionally found his gaze scanning the room for a glimpse of a willowy figure in white illusion and a crown of light brown hair. To no avail.

It wasn't until he had returned Lady Frances to her parents and started toward the refreshment table that his efforts seemed rewarded, and when he spied a tall, slender figure in white slipping onto the terrace, he wasted no time in going after her. When he reached the terrace, however, he discovered that the woman he'd been following was not Clara Deverill, but the slightly scandalous Lady Hunterby, who gave him a wicked smile just before she dashed down the steps and out into the gardens.

He moved to the balustrade, watching with a hint of envy as Lady Hunterby crossed the lawn toward the folly in one corner of the garden. A tryst, he couldn't help but feel, was far more entertaining than dancing with women he had no interest in, or searching in vain for an aggravating girl who clearly had no interest in him.

"I took your advice."

Rex turned at those words, glad of a distraction, and found Lionel Strange coming toward him across the terrace. "Lionel? What an agreeable surprise to see you. I had no idea you'd be at Auntie's ball."

The other man shrugged, but there was a curious tenseness in his demeanor that belied the nonchalant gesture. "I'm sometimes invited to these things. I suppose even your aunt Petunia finds it hard to scrounge up enough single men for a large ball."

Rex noted the slight slur in Lionel's words and his unsteady gait as he came across the terrace, and he felt a glimmer of surprise. Lionel was seldom drunk. "I'm sure that's not why she asked you," he said as the other man halted in front of him. "It's probably because she knows we're friends and I think quite highly of you."

"We're friends?" Lionel echoed, laughing a bit too loudly. "Are we, indeed?"

"Of course we are."

"Then you have some damnable notions of friendship."

Rex frowned, his surprise deepening into concern. Even on the rare occasions Lionel had indulged in alcoholic excess, Rex couldn't recall him becoming belligerent or boorish. "I haven't the least idea what you mean, but either way, I'm sure you weren't invited just to balance the numbers. My aunt would never invite anyone of whom she didn't have a good opinion. And you're an MP, a man of position in your own right. It's not as if you're an insignificant nobody."

"Perhaps, but we both know I'm not top drawer." There was an unmistakable bitterness in the words. "Geraldine knows it, too, apparently."

Rex's frown deepened at the mention of Dina, and so did his concern. "What do you mean?"

"As I said, I took your advice. This very evening, as a matter of fact. Do you want to know the result?"

Rex wasn't sure he did, given his friend's obviously inebriated state, grim countenance, and bellicose manner, but a man couldn't shirk when a friend was in difficulties. "I do want to know. Tell me what happened."

Lionel shook his head, laughing a little, but there was no humor in it. "Exactly what I predicted. She agreed wholeheartedly with my suggestion that perhaps we should part, declared that I was right—that she in fact *was* too good for me. And then she left me flat."

"What?" Rex blinked, a bit taken aback by this piece of news. Dina was, first and last, a flirt. It didn't seem like her to walk away without leaving Lionel some means to pursue. "Did you go after her? Give her the speech I suggested?"

"Oh, yes." Lionel's expression got a bit grimmer. "But I barely got halfway through it before she stopped me, declaring that she knew I'd try something like this."

"Something like what?"

"Lady Truelove had warned her to expect it, she said."

Rex blinked, still utterly at sea. "Lady Who?"

"Lady Truelove. It's an advice column. *Dear Lady Truelove.* God, Rex, surely you've heard of it. Don't you ever read the papers?"

"You know I don't."

"People write to Lady Truelove with their romantic problems, and she advises them on what to do."

Rex studied his friend's angry face and began to wish the other man had sought advice from this Lady Truelove instead of him, but of course, it would never do to say so. Instead, he tried to make sense of the situation at hand. "Geraldine wrote to an advice columnist in the paper?"

Even as he said it, he knew how absurd that notion was. Dina might be a flirt, but she was also discreet. She'd never do such a thing.

"She says not. But it hardly matters either way. The letter described a situation so much like her own that she decided to take the advice Lady Truelove had offered the correspondent. It was Providence, Dina said."

"You're not serious?"

"Oh, but I am. The letter, from some woman calling herself 'Bewildered in Belgravia', claimed that the man she loved had led her to expect marriage, but that he was now expressing reluctance to actually marry her."

"Well, that is rather a common tale, I daresay—"

"Just like us, Dina said. She said it was as if Lady Truelove was talking straight to her. After reading the column for myself, I could see why she came to that conclusion."

"Nonetheless, it is just a coincidence."

"The correspondent comes from a much higher station than the man she loves. She is a widow of the aristocracy, while he is merely middle class. They have each declared their love for the other. They meet in secret and their families know nothing of their amour. They've been together a month. That's quite a string of coincidences, wouldn't you say?"

"But what other explanation could there be?"

"That is what I've been asking myself. Lady True-love advised her correspondent that the man in question was a rotter, a scoundrel who was clearly out to take advantage of her in the most reprehensible way possible."

"Don't tell me you're taking this personally? Really, Lionel, it's not as if this woman is referring to *you*."

"You think not?"

"How could she be? She doesn't know you."

"Perhaps she does, even if I don't know her. She told the girl," he went on before Rex could respond to that rather enigmatic remark, "that the man would try to get 'round her somehow, that he would work his wiles on her and attempt to persuade her to continue this liaison."

"Well, of course any man who found himself in such an agreeable situation would want it to continue for as long as possible. You certainly do. Dina's far too discreet to air her private concerns to a newspaper columnist."

"She is discreet," Lionel agreed, and his expression hardened even more. "Which brings me to you."

Rex stiffened, suddenly wary, not liking the resentful way his friend was glaring at him. "Just what are you implying, Lionel?"

Instead of answering, his friend reached into the breast pocket of his evening jacket, pulled out a cutting from a newspaper, and unfolded it. "Allow me to share with you Lady Truelove's assessment of the situation and the advice she offered."

Looking down at the page in his gloved fingers, he began to read. "'I doubt that simple procrastination is the explanation for this man's lack of action. My dear young lady, it is clear, I am sorry to say, that honorable marriage is not in his plans at all. To be blunt, he is using you in the most dishonorable way a man can do. Should you question his motives, I daresay he will attempt to make his reluctance to wed you sound honorable, even noble. He may declare that he cannot marry you because you are too far above his station, and that he hasn't the means to support you in the way you've been accustomed.'"

"Any man would feel the need to underscore a vast difference in station between himself and his lady love," Rex pointed out. "To marry with such differences between them would be precipitate and unwise."

"'He will say that you deserve more than he can provide,'" Lionel went on, ignoring Rex's point altogether, "'and that you are too good for the likes of him. He might make a token effort to break things off. He might say that he does not want to do this because he's wild about you, that he can't eat or sleep for wanting you, that your time together has been the most amazing thing that's ever happened to him.'"

At this exact repetition of his own words from the other day, Rex gave a laugh borne of pure astonishment. "But how would—"

"'Do not be fooled,'" Lionel interrupted. "'Such a speech as this is not intended for the honorable purpose of ending what can only be regarded as an unsavory connection. Quite the opposite. Every word he speaks shall be designed to work on you, my dear, to play on your affections and bind you to him even more tightly than before. Following this attempt to break things off, I have no doubt that he will plead with you to continue as you are a bit longer. He might even throw himself on your mercy, expressing his willingness to settle for the merest crumbs of your affection—'"

"What the hell?" Rex snatched the newspaper cutting from his friend's fingertips and scanned the entire column from top to bottom, and as he read the words of his own speech, a picture formed in his mind's eye—a picture of that little tea shop in Holborn, a spray of palm fronds, and a pair of dark brown eyes looking at him with disapproval, and he suddenly knew just why Clara Deverill seemed so familiar.

"Because of this column, Dina has broken with me completely," Lionel said, his voice rising. "She's told me to leave her alone and never contact her again. This is all your fault."

Despite his friend's raised voice, Rex paid little heed, for in his mind, his aunt Petunia's information was echoing far more loudly than Lionel's angry words.

Her father's family is in trade—newspapers, I believe.

His gaze moved to the masthead at the top of the sheet in his hand.

The Weekly Gazette.

"What cheek," he cried, his temper rising as he realized what must have occurred. "What damnable cheek."

"God, Rex, I thought you were a discreet chap, I really did. I thought I could trust you to keep my confidence."

The implications of that caught his attention, and he looked up. "What? Lionel, surely you don't think—"

"But seeing you dancing with the Deverill girl," Lionel cut in furiously, "made me realize that my trust has been misplaced."

Rex could not reply, for anger was rising within him. *That minx*, he thought, his hand tightening around the sheet of newsprint, crumpling Lady Truelove's column in his fist. *That clever, eavesdropping, opportunistic little minx.*

Taking a deep breath, he tried to explain what must have happened. "Lionel, I didn't tell this girl anything. It's clear that she—"

"Don't," his friend snapped, cutting off explanations. "Don't even try to justify yourself." He jabbed at the paper balled in Rex's fist. "Her father is the publisher, you realize that?"

Rex set his jaw, beginning to share his friend's grim mood. "I have appreciated that point, yes."

"I've always thought you knew so much about women." Lionel gave another laugh. "But this one's made quite a fool of you, hasn't she? How long has she been pumping you for information on her columnist's behalf? How many of our other friends have seen their private affairs used as newspaper fodder, I wonder?"

"For God's sake, I just met the girl less than an hour ago, and besides, I would never—"

"And when next week's column features another supposedly fictitious offering that depicts the exact situation of another of our friends, that will be coincidence, too?" He shook his head and laughed again. "I'd never have thought you could lose your head over any girl, but I've been proved wrong now, it seems."

"I have never lost my head over a girl in my life," Rex assured him. "And your fear for our friends is misplaced. I intend to see to it that this is the only time such a thing will happen—"

"It's a bit late for that now, don't you think? Because of you and your lack of discretion," he added, his voice rising to a shout, "I've lost Dina for good!"

A movement past his friend's shoulder caught Rex's attention, and he spied Lord and Lady Flinders strolling out onto the terrace. "If discretion is what you're after, old boy," he murmured, "I suggest you keep your voice down. We're no longer alone out here."

Lionel cast an impatient glance over his shoulder, then looked at Rex again. "Damn it, man," he said, making no effort to follow Rex's advice or keep his temper in check, "is that all you can say after what you've done? After you've betrayed my confidence this way?"

"Lionel, listen to me," he said quietly, trying to employ reason in the face of his friend's anger and inebriation. "As I told you, I just met the Deverill girl this evening. And I would never tell anyone—"

"You lying bastard."

Quick as lightning, Lionel's fist came up, slamming into the side of Rex's face before he had the chance to duck. Pain shimmered through the entire left side of his face and knocked him back a step, but when he saw Lionel's other fist coming for an uppercut to his jaw, he blocked the move, knocking the other man's arm sideways. He didn't want to fight, especially not at Auntie's ball, but it wasn't as if he had a choice.

He hit back hard, landing two quick blows before his friend could strike again. And since he had no desire to be attacked a second time, he pressed his advantage, tackling Lionel and sending both of them stumbling across the terrace, a move that sent Lord and Lady Flinders scrambling to stay out of the fray, along with several other guests who'd come out to see what the commotion was about. Among those guests, unfortunately, was Auntie Pet, who stopped just outside the doorway to the ballroom, looking so aghast and appalled that the sight of her face stopped him in his tracks.

The blow came out of nowhere, striking with such force that stars shot across his vision like flashing sparks. He felt himself falling backward, pain exploded inside his skull, and his only thought before everything went dark was that he really needed to stop giving people advice.

THE BLACK EYE wasn't so bad—a barely noticeable blotch, his valet assured him. The concussion, however, was another matter. The morning after the ball, Rex discovered that the world had the inclination to spin violently every time he sat up, and his body had developed a most inconvenient tendency to heave the contents of his stomach.

It took another forty-eight hours before he was on his feet again, and by that time, the barely noticeable blotch beneath his eye had quadrupled in size and turned a lurid shade of purple.

"God, Cartwright," he muttered to his valet as he stared into the mirror. "I look like an apache. Any woman sees me coming, she'll clutch her handbag and cross the street."

"I think you exaggerate, sir." The valet set aside the razor and reached for a towel. "Mrs. Snell has prepared breakfast, if you're feeling up to it?"

He was famished, he realized in some surprise, but before he could offer his valet an affirmative reply to the question of breakfast, there was a tap on the door, and his butler, Whistler, entered the bedroom.

"Begging your pardon, my lord, but Lady Petunia is downstairs."

"Again?" Rex lowered the mirror in his hand. "That's three times since the ball."

"Four, my lord. She seems quite anxious to speak with you."

"Dear Auntie Pet," he murmured, smiling. "She's obviously concerned about me."

The butler gave a discreet cough. "I wouldn't quite say that, my lord."

Rex stiffened. His memories of the other night were still a bit vague, but one image was suddenly clear as glass in his mind: Auntie Pet, standing by the doorway to the ballroom, staring at him in horror. Any inclination to smile vanished at once, and he turned in his chair, facing Whistler directly. "What did she say? Tell me her exact words."

"When I explained that you were still in no condition to receive callers due to your injuries, she said . . ." Whistler paused, giving Rex a pained, apologetic look. "She said that in her opinion, any injuries you sustained were no more than you deserved. Given that you had taken to offending young ladies on the dance floor and—"

"The girl dashed off," Rex interjected, stung. "Then she vanished into thin air. What was I supposed to do? Hunt her down all about the house?"

"She also mentioned something about neglecting your duties as host."

"Well, I was knocked unconscious," he pointed out, even though it was hardly necessary to defend himself to his own butler.

"Yes, she mentioned that as well, my lord."

"Oh, did she?"

"Her description, I believe, was that you had taken to brawling at her balls like a Limehouse longshoreman."

Rex grimaced, his foggy memories of the other night becoming clearer with every word his butler spoke.

"She has expressed the wish to discuss with you the matter of your recent conduct." Whistler's voice interrupted his thoughts. "Do you wish to receive her?"

He ought to, he supposed. Let her call him on the carpet and have it over. After all, the fight was probably his worst offense, and it wasn't as if that had been *his* fault. Lionel had struck first, and Auntie would surely agree that any chap had the right to defend himself. Once he explained—

He broke off that train of thought to reconsider. On the other hand, it wasn't as if he really could explain, for he couldn't betray Lionel's confidences. As for the grievance Auntie had against him regarding Miss Deverill, he certainly couldn't tell Petunia it was his naughty suggestion about kissing the girl that had spurred her to depart the dance floor. And, he thought, lifting the mirror in his hand for another look, his battered face would hardly help him to regain his aunt's goodwill.

He handed the mirror to Cartwright and returned his attention to his butler. "You did explain to Lady Petunia just how serious my injuries are?"

"I said you had concussion, my lord, and would probably be unwell for several more days."

With that, Rex decided the best thing to do was to let things lie and allow Auntie's temper to cool. In the meantime, he could perhaps fashion a palatable way to explain the fight without having to reveal anything about Lionel's secret affair with Lady Geraldine Throckmorton. As for the rest . . .

His gaze moved to the crumpled sheet of newsprint on his dressing table as more memories of the other night came back to him. "Tell my aunt that my head injury—my *massive* head injury—still prevents me from receiving visitors," he said, turning to the butler. "I will call on her when I'm fighting fit. When I'm feeling better," he amended as Whistler raised an eyebrow.

"Very good, sir."

The butler departed, and Rex reached for the wadded-up newspaper cutting He'd pay Auntie a visit in a day or two and find a way to make amends, and in the meantime, he'd see Lionel, try to patch things up there. As for Miss Clara Deverill . . .

Rex set his jaw grimly as he smoothed out the scrap of paper in his fingers. Where she was concerned, he had no intention of making amends or patching things up. Quite the contrary. When it came to her, he was itching for a fight.

Chapter 6

Newspapers had been the mainstay of the Deverill family for many years, once encompassing a vast journalistic empire that in its heyday had included seventeen newspapers and twelve magazines. Clara's father, however, had never been much of a businessman, and under his tutelage, the business built by the two previous generations had rapidly deteriorated, dwindling at last to only one paper, the *Weekly Gazette*, with its offices in what had once been the family's own library.

It was Irene who had salvaged this last vestige of the Deverill newspaper chain, a fact which had often led Clara to laughingly accuse her sister of having ink, rather than blood, running through her veins. For her own part, though Clara enjoyed reading the papers, she'd never really shared Irene's passion for the business of running one.

Clara's primary ambition in life had always been a simple one: to marry and have children, but hampered by her acute shyness, she'd found this goal an elusive one to achieve. Making matters worse, her father's estrangement from her mother's family had left her few opportunities to move in society and meet young men. She did have one marriage proposal to her credit, but the unappealing circumstances under which it had been offered had impelled her to refuse it, and since then, no other chances for matrimony had presented themselves.

Clara knew that if she was ever to achieve her most cherished dream, she had to find a way to overcome her reticence with strangers and take an active rather than passive role in her future, so when Irene married Torquil, Clara had accepted the invitation of the duke's family to stay with them for the coming season, and despite the extension of Irene's trip and Jonathan's now-permanent defection, Clara had no intention of abandoning her own plans.

She soon discovered, however, that Fate was not going to make this easy. For one thing, Mr. Beale was becoming more truculent with each day her brother did not appear. She knew she ought to tell him the truth, that Jonathan wasn't coming after all, but afraid he'd quit, she kept putting it off. She tried her best to ignore his sour demeanor and work with him as amicably as possible, for at present, she had a much more serious problem than one cranky editor.

Clara stared down at the two letters in front of her, the same two letters to Lady Truelove that she'd been perusing in the tea shop the other day. Many more letters had come for the columnist since then, of course, but these two had engendered within her a powerful sense of empathy. She badly wanted to find solutions for them, perhaps because she knew that in doing so, she might also find a solution for herself.

But as she sat at her desk studying their letters, she was forced to acknowledge that no advice for either of these correspondents had magically invaded her brain since that afternoon at Mrs. Mott's. And Lord Galbraith was not located within earshot to provide her with any inspiration.

In a way, that was rather a pity. For though the man's advice to his friend had been morally appalling, it had been based on a solid, if cynical, awareness of human nature. He'd make, she realized in chagrin, a better advice columnist than she was proving to be. He knew a lot about people, particularly women. And he certainly knew how to charm them. Hell, she knew him for a rake, she didn't like him a jot, and hadn't a shred of respect for him, and yet, as a woman, she'd felt his pull like the force of a magnet.

Ravish you would be a sight more likely.

Remembering those words, Clara felt rather aggrieved. The only time in her life a man had ever expressed the desire to ravish her, and it had to be a man she had no use for. Just her luck.

A kiss during a dance would break quite a few rules, wouldn't it?

"Enough rules to ruin a girl's reputation," she muttered, and with that, she reminded herself that she had work to do and returned her attention to the task at hand.

After several moments of consideration, she decided to focus her efforts on the Devastated Debutante. After all, the girl was someone with whom she had so much in common. If she could determine how to advise her, maybe she could apply that same advice to herself.

A knock on the door interrupted her contemplations, and Clara hastily pulled a handful of other correspondence over the letters she was studying. "Come in," she called, and when the door swung wide, Evie came through the doorway.

"The evening papers, Miss Deverill," the secretary said, bringing them to Clara's desk.

"Are our competitors penning anything of interest?" she asked, even as she appreciated that she could not allow herself to be distracted by any of the competition's juicy tidbits.

"Nothing much." The secretary set the stack on one corner of Clara's desk. "The *London Inquirer* has an advice column now. They are calling it 'Mrs. Lonely Hearts.'"

Clara gave a snort of derision. "Mrs. Lonely Hearts? Mrs. Copycat is more like it."

Evie laughed. "I put that paper on top, in case you wanted to have a look at it."

Clara wasn't sure she did. If their fiercest rival was trying to steal the *Gazette*'s readers with their own version of Lady Truelove, that made it even more crucial for Clara to do her job well. "Thank you, Evie. You may go."

The secretary departed with a nod, closing the door behind her, and Clara opened the *Inquirer* to take a peek at the latest threat to Lady Truelove's reign as queen of the advice columns, but after turning only a few pages, she stopped, her attention caught by a particular headline.

"Oh, dear," she murmured, a little smile curving her lips.

It wasn't right, she supposed, to take a measure of delight in someone else's difficulties, even if that someone was Lord Galbraith. On the other hand, the man's notorious reputation had been well-earned and something he seemed proud of.

I enjoy life, Miss Deverill, and I fail to see why I should be condemned for it.

Clara glanced at the headline again, and her smile widened. The viscount, it seemed, was about to pay a price for all his enjoyment of life.

Feeling a rather wicked sense of anticipation, Clara decided she could spare five minutes from her task to find out just how he'd blotted his copybook, and she settled back in her chair to read the article she'd stumbled upon. She'd barely finished the first paragraph, however, before her attention was again diverted by a tap on her door.

She straightened at once, wiping any trace of a smile off her face as she folded the paper and placed it back on the stack Evie had brought her. "Come in," she called, reaching for her pen, striving to appear hard at work as the secretary once again appeared in the doorway.

"There's a gentleman here to see you, Miss Deverill," she said as she approached Clara's desk, a certain amount of awe in her voice and a card in her hand. "Viscount Galbraith."

"What?" That the subject of her reading material and the primary object of her thoughts today was right outside her door brought Clara to her feet. Dismayed, she snatched the card from the other woman's outstretched hand. "What on earth does he want?"

Even as she asked the question, she began to fear she already knew, and a knot of apprehension formed in her stomach.

"Does it matter?" Evie countered, grinning as Clara looked up. "He's such a treat to look at, who cares what he came for?"

Clara offered a reproving frown in reply, and the other woman's smile vanished at once. She gave a cough and resumed her usual air of brisk efficiency. "He didn't state the purpose of his call. He merely asked me to inquire if you will receive him."

"No, I—" Clara broke off, reconsidering even as her apprehension deepened. She could refuse to see him, of course, but would that do her any good? He could pay a call at the duke's house any time, or ask her to dance at the next ball, or corner her at some party during the season. If he had found her out somehow, it might be better to face the music here in her private office than in front of anyone else's prying eyes. And if he hadn't told anyone Lady Truelove's identity, she could reason with him, perhaps persuade him somehow to keep mum.

"Show him in," she said, tossing his card onto her desk.

The secretary departed, and Clara worked to dampen her growing apprehension as she gathered up the letters on her desk. She might be wrong. Galbraith might be here for some other purpose, something wholly unconnected with Lady Truelove.

Ravish you would be a sight more likely.

Clara sucked in a deep breath, that unthinkable notion doing nothing to calm her jangled nerves. She shoved the letters to Lady Truelove into a drawer and strove to find some of the same bravado she'd managed to display the other night, but the attempt faltered the moment Galbraith entered the room.

Unmistakable anger glittered in those gorgeous eyes, and there was a hard, uncompromising cast to his countenance that confirmed Clara's worst fear and told her reason or persuasion would probably prove useless. Every line of his body as he halted in front of her desk made it clear he'd come to do battle, an impression underscored by the dark purple bruise under his eye and the gash at his temple.

Clara swallowed hard, looking past him. "Thank you, Evie," she said, donning a pretense of unflappable calm she was far from feeling. "You may go. And close the door behind you."

The secretary's auburn brows lifted at this rather scandalous instruction, but she complied, smiling a little, a smile that widened into a meaningful grin and a girl-to-girl wink just before she closed the door.

"Lord Galbraith," Clara greeted him, dipping her knees in a quick curtsy.

"Miss Deverill." He bowed in return. "Or," he added, straightening, "perhaps within the walls of your own offices, it would be more correct to refer to you by your nom de plume?"

Her worst fear now confirmed beyond any doubt, Clara nonetheless worked to keep any hint of emotion off her face. "I don't know what you mean."

He tilted his head, studying her for a moment. Then, unexpectedly, he gave a laugh, though Clara feared there was no humor in it. "Appearances can be so deceiving," he murmured. "You look the sweetest, most dulcet little thing, with those big brown eyes of yours, and yet, you are also one of the coolest liars I have ever encountered. I doubt butter would melt in your mouth."

Clara stirred at his accusation of deceit, not only because she was in no position to refute it, but also because to her mind, it was a case of the pot and the kettle if ever she'd heard one. "Do you have a point?"

He raised an eyebrow, but he didn't answer her question directly. "When we first met, I thought you looked familiar," he said instead, "that I'd seen you somewhere before, but I couldn't place you. You, however, insisted otherwise, and I was inclined to think I'd been mistaken. But later that evening," he added as he reached into the breast pocket of his morning coat and pulled out a newspaper cutting, "when my friend Lionel confronted me with Lady Truelove's most recent column, I realized I had made no mistake."

Clara's heart sank as she watched him unfold the wrinkled, ragged-edged sheet of newsprint. Not only he, but also his friend, knew her secret. Even if she could somehow convince Galbraith to exercise discretion, she could never ensure that his friend would do so. Lady Truelove's identity would soon be known to the world, the mystique would be utterly spoiled, the column condemned, and Deverill Publishing's competitors overjoyed. And it would all be her fault. What would she tell Irene? How could she face her sister with the news that Lady Truelove was ruined because of her?

"In offering advice to her correspondent, your columnist made some very specific predictions as to the behavior and motives of the gentleman in question," he went on, looking down at the cutting in his hands. "So specific, in fact, as to be uncanny. Both Lionel and I appreciated how familiar her words seemed. Lionel actually suspected me of being Lady Truelove, but when he saw me dancing with you, he formed an alternative theory."

"Oh?" Clara swallowed hard, stalling for time as her mind raced to find a way out of this mess. "What theory is that?"

"That I had been played for a fool." He looked up, his eyes glittering like aquamarines. "He concluded that you and I were acquainted—so well acquainted, in fact, that I had betrayed his confidences to you. And that you, in your role as the publisher of Lady Truelove, had passed on these confidences to your columnist, who then used them as inspiration."

Clara seized on that contention at once, feeling a faint hint of relief. If he could be persuaded that his friend was right, that she had merely overheard and passed on the information, perhaps it could all end here and Lady Truelove's identity could remain a secret.

"Lionel," he went on before she could speak, "did not take kindly to what he perceived as my betrayal of his confidence." His free hand lifted, gesturing to his own face. "As you can see from the state of my appearance."

Despite the awful situation, Clara's lips twitched a little. "Your friend is the one who hit you in the face?"

"He did." Galbraith shoved the cutting back into his breast pocket. "I'm gratified you find that fact amusing."

She pressed any hint of a smile from her lips at once. Laughing at his expense would hardly help her cause. "Lord Galbraith," she began, but he cut her off.

"I knew Lionel was a bit out in his assumptions, of course, for I hadn't told you anything, and that's when I realized why your face was familiar. You were in the tea shop that day in Holborn. You were the girl at the next table. You eavesdropped on our conversation, our *private* conversation, and used it as newspaper fodder. Do you deny it?" he asked when she did not reply.

"Would there be any point?" she asked, spreading her hands in a gesture of capitulation. "I doubt you would be convinced of any denial I might make."

"I don't often read the papers, it's true. God knows, I've no use for them, but in making inquiries of friends today, I have learned that Lady Truelove's identity is a closely guarded secret. It is also, from what I gather, a matter of intense speculation, and one of the main reasons the column is so popular. What would happen, do you suppose, if people discovered who Lady Truelove really is?"

Clara's heart sank, but she tried to rally. "You don't know who Lady Truelove is. You don't know to whom I may have passed on the information I overheard."

"On the contrary, I know exactly. It wasn't necessary for you to pass on the information to Lady Truelove, because you *are* Lady Truelove."

She forced a laugh. "And what is the basis for this absurd conclusion?"

He smiled grimly. "Your eyes, Miss Deverill. Your big, expressive brown eyes."

Clara didn't know what she'd been expecting him to say, but that wasn't it. She stared, unable to fathom what he was talking about. "What do my eyes have to do with anything?"

"You noted the other night that I have a notorious reputation. How do you suppose I acquired it?" He leaned over the desk, coming close enough that she could see the gilded tips of his lashes and the dark blue ring around each of his irises, close enough that she caught the scent of sandalwood shaving lotion. "I acquired it because I know a great deal about women."

"Obviously," she snapped, her tension fraying. "But I don't see—"

"When we danced, I discovered that my reputation had preceded me, and in a most unfavorable way, for you made it quite clear I cut no ice with you. It was not only in your words, it was in your eyes, narrowed on me so disapprovingly when I shrugged off the things that have been said about me. I didn't take your disapproval of me seriously—in fact, I found it rather refreshing. Most women are quite happy to overlook my peccadilloes and forgive me for them."

"What a nauseating fact about my sex," she ground out. "But I'm gratified you found me such a novelty."

He ignored the biting sarcasm of her latter remark. "When I was with Lionel, and he was expounding his theory about how my exact words had managed to appear in your paper, a picture formed in my mind. I saw the same narrowed eyes, the same disapproving look, of the girl I'd just been dancing with, only the setting was different. In my mind, I saw an image of those eyes peeking at me from the other side of some potted palm trees, and I realized just why you seemed so familiar."

"I still don't see how you can possibly conclude—"

"You were feeling more on that day than disapproval, weren't you, Miss Deverill? You were angry. The conversation you overheard had outraged your maidenly sensibilities."

"All right, yes, I was angry. Upon discovering how cavalierly your friend—and you—treat women, anyone would be angry. For a gentleman, you seem to have a quite a flexible moral code."

For some reason, that description made him smile, though the smile didn't quite reach his eyes. "You might be surprised if you knew the vast number of people who find morality a flexible concept."

She didn't want to think about how true that might be. "Well, I don't."

"Quite so. And your moral outrage spurred you to write what you did?"

"I already told you—"

"You did it purely out of spite," he interrupted. "You wanted to pay us out. You wanted to get revenge for what you perceived as a slight upon your sex—"

"I didn't write it for spite or revenge!" she shot back, exasperated beyond bearing, beyond caution. "I wrote it to warn an innocent woman that she was being taken advantage of in the worst possible way by a deceiving scoundrel!"

The admission made her want to bite her tongue off, especially when she saw the gleam of satisfaction in his eyes. "Oh," she breathed, her frustration deepening into outrage, at him for trapping her, and even more at herself for falling into that trap. "You are a devil."

"Yes, morally outraged ladies often deem me so." He paused, donning an expression of penitent earnestness as he pressed a hand to his chest. "But only until

I am able to convince them of the true goodness of my soul."

"There is no goodness in you. You are a cad. And so is your friend for attempting to play on a young woman's affections with such cavalier disregard. It's disgraceful. It's appalling."

"So, you decided to interfere in something that was none of your business?"

"When I perceive that another person is in harm's way, I think it a good idea to warn that person. I'm strange that way."

He made a scoffing sound. "And just which party did you think was in jeopardy?"

She stared at him. "Her, of course!"

"Or perhaps," he countered, "it's my friend who is truly in danger? Have you considered that?"

"Nonsense."

"Dina's starting to feel guilty about what they're engaged in, that's what this is about. The morality she's been stuffed with all her life is starting to prey on her conscience. That's why she's bringing marriage into it now. It's expected of her to want it. Is guilt a good reason to jump into matrimony?"

"People don't want marriage merely to soothe their consciences!"

"Many do. Society's prudish, downright ridiculous dictates about where love should lead play merry hell with people's minds, filling them with guilt about physical desires—desires that are natural and just, and almost always transient."

Clara stirred, hot embarrassment flooding through her at the mention of physical desires. "This is hardly an appropriate topic for conversation."

"As a result of their guilt," he went on as if she hadn't spoken, "people often feel compelled to chain themselves to each other for life when they barely even know each other and haven't the least understanding of whether or not a life together could make them happy."

"Barely know each other?" she echoed. "The two people we are talking about are intimately acquainted."

The moment the words were out of her mouth, she wanted to take them back, for she knew what he would make of them.

"Very intimately," he agreed, his voice grave, the corners of his mouth curved in a faint smile. "But only in a biblical sense."

Clara gave a laugh, one borne of astonishment and embarrassment, not amusement. She pressed her hands to her burning cheeks, hardly able to believe that she was discussing this sort of thing with a man, though from what she knew of this particular man, she supposed she shouldn't be surprised. "You speak as if such intimacy is a trivial thing!"

"Not trivial, no, but it's a poor reason to wed. Lionel and Dina have known each other a month. One month," he added, as if to underscore the point. "Do you really think they are in any position to commit to each other for the rest of their lives?"

"They are sleeping together!"

He gave a shout of laughter. "God, I hope that's not all they're doing. I should hate to think their trysts are for a purpose as dull as mere sleeping."

She folded her arms, glaring at him. "This is not something to laugh about. Although the fact that you would describe this sort of situation as a harmless entertainment is quite in keeping with what I know of your character. As is your attempt to take the credit of it."

"Well, I think I'm entitled to take a little credit. I did introduce them."

"And yet, you don't feel any responsibility for the fact that you encouraged him in a despicable courtship?"

"We're not talking about an innocent young girl here. Dina knew just what she was getting into when she launched this affair with Lionel—and yes, she was the one who launched it. To put it bluntly, she wanted to bed him and she did."

"More fool her, then, for ever wanting more?"

"That's not what I'm saying. I'm saying both parties are culpable here, so describing his actions as despicable is a rather harsh judgement, don't you think? In any case," he added before she could reply, "they are not involved in a courtship. Courtship implies a view to matrimony, and as I said, neither of them is ready to take that step. They may never be ready."

"She seems quite ready, from what I overheard. She's in love with your friend, though why that is so, I'm sure I can't fathom. And he has told her he's in love with her—"

"Yes, yes, they're in love. At least, they're madly infatuated with each other and both are willing to call it love. Why should they ruin such a blissful state of affairs by getting married?"

Clara shook her head, wondering if this man's capacity for depravity would ever cease to shock her. "Ruin it?"

"Yes, ruin it. Again, they have been acquainted for a month. Do you think that's a sound amount of time for two people to decide they want to spend their lives together?"

"It doesn't matter what I think, since it's not my decision to make. It's theirs."

He laughed. "Says the woman who blatantly interfered in their love affair and brought about its end, thereby causing a great deal of unnecessary pain and heartbreak to both parties."

Clara shifted her weight, hating to think he might have a point and that her judgement may have been a bit clouded by anger.

"If they are indeed heartbroken," she said after a moment, "then I am sorry for it. But though a month isn't much time, I grant you, not everyone finds it insufficient. My sister and the Duke of Torquil had known each other three weeks when they became engaged, and they are quite happily married."

"It's called a honeymoon for a reason," he countered dryly. "When the duke and your sister have been married a dozen years or so, if they're still blissfully happy, I might deem them an exception. Either way, right now we're talking about Dina and Lionel, two people I know quite well, and I can honestly say they are not ready to get married, despite any guilt over their affair Dina may be feeling at the moment."

"Perhaps your low opinion of marriage is affecting your judgement."

"Miss Deverill, I'm not so against marriage that I don't think anyone should ever do it. If my friends decide, after serious consideration, to wed, then I shall don my best morning coat, put a carnation in my buttonhole, and give a congratulatory groomsman speech at their nuptials, expressing my absolute belief in their true love and their bright, happy future. I daresay I shall even manage to make it sound convincing. But it is my fervent hope that they take a bit more time to enjoy each other and confirm they are ready to spend their lives together before committing to it irrevocably."

"And in the meantime, free love is an acceptable option?"

He shrugged. "As long as marriage remains a situation from which it is virtually impossible to extricate oneself, then yes. And why not? There's no harm in it."

"It's harmful in so many ways, I can't begin to list them all!"

"Try. I'm curious what you would define as harmful."

She could have done. She could have pointed out the burden borne by the bastard children of free-love unions. She could have talked of the inevitable degradation of a society that did not have the bedrock of marriage to support it. She could have mentioned the comfort and emotional sustenance that a lifetime together could bring to a couple. But she didn't have time for all that. She had an important problem, one that would not be resolved by arguing with him or antagonizing him.

Having inadvertently confirmed that she was Lady Truelove, she now had to find a way to persuade him to keep silent. It wasn't as if she could appeal to his chivalry, but what other card did she have to play?

"Lord Galbraith, it's clear you and I do not see eye to eye on this subject, so perhaps we should set it aside and discuss why you are here. You have stumbled upon my secret. What do you intend to do about it?"

"Hmm . . ." He paused as if considering. "That is the question, isn't it?"

She worked to muster her dignity. "If you do indeed have such goodness in your soul as you claim, then I hope you are willing to demonstrate it by keeping Lady Truelove's identity to yourself."

"One could argue that, in this case, goodness is best demonstrated by warning people. You're fond of that particular activity, after all."

"Warning people? Of what, in heaven's name?"

"That the woman dispensing all this knowledgeable advice about love and romance is really the daughter of the publisher, perhaps? That she is unscrupulous enough to eavesdrop on private conversations, and meddlesome enough to interfere—"

"It's my scruples that impelled me to interfere!"

"To interfere," he went on as if she hadn't spoken, "in affairs that do not concern her, and to offer her advice even to those who have not asked for it."

"You have no proof that I am Lady Truelove."

"I may not move much in respectable society, Miss Deverill, but I have many influential friends who do, and with the exception of Lionel two days ago, not one of my friends has ever had cause to question my word. If I were to tell them you are Lady Truelove, they will believe me. If I were to warn them about you and how you use private conversations as fodder for your newspaper, they will warn others."

"And if your friends ask how you have come by this information, you will have to reveal your part in what happened, as well as Lionel's illicit relationship. He is a Member of Parliament, and such news would hardly impress his constituents favorably. He is your friend. Would you really be such a cad as to expose him?"

"I don't have to reveal the source of my information. I merely have to assure my friends that my source is reliable. You may be the sister-in-law of a duke, but Torquil and his family are not being viewed with favor this season, so that connection will do you little good. And you may be the granddaughter of a viscount on your mother's side, but on your father's, you come from a line of newspaper hawkers. In addition, you are presently in charge of your paper's operations. All these things will come back to hurt you if what you did is exposed. I am the son of an earl, and my friends know me to be a discreet and loyal friend. If I warn them about you, they will accept my word without questioning the source of my information. And once that happens, your debut in society will come to an abrupt and ignoble end."

She glared at him, hating that he was right. "With that, I think we can put paid to any notions of goodness in your soul."

That shot seemed to hit the mark, for a trace of his earlier anger flashed in his blue eyes and tightened the corners of his mouth. "My friends are brokenhearted wrecks because of you. I can think of no reason not to tell my entire circle of acquaintance about you."

Clara began to feel desperate. The notion of being conciliatory with this man flicked her decidedly on the raw, but what else could she do? "Lady Truelove is the *Weekly Gazette*'s most popular feature, and the main reason for our advertising revenue and our income. Shall you enjoy taking away a family's livelihood?"

He made a scoffing sound. "Do not make me out to be the villain here. I think I would be quite justified in warning others about your so-called advice column. And since your brother-in-law is a duke, I hardly think you and your father will be turned out into the street if your identity is exposed."

"That's not the point—"

"One of my best friends, a man who has known me since we were boys at school, has questioned my discretion, accused me of betraying his trust, and struck me in the face. The latter action not only gave me a black eye, knocked me unconscious, and gave me a concussion, it also seems to have appalled my great-aunt, who has been chomping at the bit the past two days for the chance to give me a sound lecture on the subject."

"The desire to lecture you is one your aunt no doubt experiences with tiresome regularity."

"Either way, Miss Deverill, I'm finding it hard to care about how your decision to meddle affects you."

"You meddled as well."

"I was asked by my friend for my advice. I gave it. You can claim no such high ground. As Lady True-love, I'm sure you adore offering your advice to all and sundry, but in this case, your advice was catastrophic for all concerned."

She grimaced, fearing this episode might very well be a metaphor for her future as the famous advice columnist. Unless—

"Lord Galbraith," she said abruptly, "do your friends often ask you for advice?"

He blinked, startled by the abrupt question. "Yes," he said after a moment, "I suppose they do."

"Why?"

He laughed a little, as if bemused. "I suppose because I'm a good listener? Or perhaps it's because I have a knack for finding solutions to problems? I don't know, really."

He might not know, but she did, and suddenly, she also knew how she could persuade him to keep Lady Truelove's identity a secret. The idea in her head was wild, downright mad, in fact. On the other hand, she seemed to be developing quite a talent of late for wild, mad ideas.

Her gaze slid to the stack of newspapers on her desk. And it wasn't as if she didn't have leverage—

"Miss Deverill?"

The prompt brought her attention back to him, and she lifted her hands in a gesture of seeming capitulation. "You've uncovered my secret, but I'm still not quite sure what you want from me."

"What makes you think I want anything?" But even as he asked the question, she knew she was about to be offered a bargain. That boded well for her own crazy plan.

"Because you wouldn't have come here otherwise," she answered. "If your intent was to reveal Lady Truelove's identity to the world, you'd simply have begun doing so. Warning me of what you are at present only thinking to do seems to serve no purpose. I can only conclude that you want something from me, in exchange for which you will keep my secret."

"I applaud your perspicacity, Miss Deverill."

She gestured to the chair opposite her own. "Perhaps we should sit down and discuss it, then?"

He frowned, looking understandably skeptical of this sudden show of amiability on her part, but when she sat down behind her desk, he took the offered chair opposite her. "There is very little to discuss. There is only what I require you to do."

"And what is that?"

"Lionel is no longer speaking to me because of you. When I paid a call on him today, he refused to see me. I want you to go to him and tell him the truth. You will explain who you really are, what you did, and why you did it, and you will assure him that I did not betray his confidence in any way."

It was bad enough that circumstances required her to trust Galbraith with her secret, but Clara knew she could not afford to trust the discretion of his friend. Nonetheless, she pretended to consider his demand. "If I tell your friend the truth," she said, straightening the stack of newspapers on her desk as her mind raced to consider the ramifications of the idea rattling around in her head, "he'll never be convinced."

"He might, if you underscore the fact that you are sharing a piece of information that would damage your column's success if it came out publicly. Lionel, you see, is rather susceptible to women in distress, especially those with big brown eyes, and he might soften enough that he'll let me talk to him."

"If I tell him the truth, I have no guarantee he will keep my secret."

"True, but if you don't tell him the truth, I definitely won't keep your secret. What he does with the information," Galbraith went on before she could reply, "I cannot predict. Nor do I care. Your choice is simple:

you have a slim chance of keeping your columnist's identity unknown, or you have no chance. You must decide which possibility you prefer."

She left off fiddling with the newspapers, her mind made up. "I cannot do what you ask, Lord Galbraith. I do not know your friend, and I cannot afford to trust his discretion. But . . ."

She paused, taking a deep breath and shoving down any misgivings over what she was about to do. "But I would like to offer you an alternative proposition."

Chapter 7

Rex couldn't quite believe what he was hearing. He had her backed into a corner, and she wanted to negotiate? She had gumption, he'd give her that. "An alternative proposition? Is that a joke?"

"Not at all. You know my secret." She paused, her gaze narrowing on him, a look he was coming to know well. "Though that is only because you goaded me into revealing it."

He donned an air of false modesty, brushing at an imaginary speck of dust on his waistcoat, smiling a little. "Yes, that was rather a neat trick, if I do say it myself."

If his words aggravated her, she didn't show it. "Either way," she said, leaning back in her chair, "telling that secret to yet another person presents a risk I am not willing to take."

"That's a pity." His smile vanished, and he gave her

a hard, level stare across the desk. "Since it's not as if you have a choice."

"My only choice," she went on, ignoring his point completely, "is to convince you not to carry out your threat to expose me."

He had no intention of carrying out his threat, but he wasn't about to let her know that. "I doubt there's anything you can say to convince me."

"I think perhaps there is. You see, I'm prepared to offer you something that would make keeping mum worthwhile."

She hadn't meant her words to be suggestive, but Rex couldn't resist speculating on some provocative possibilities. He glanced over her, his gaze skimming the long, delicate column of her throat, moving past the prim collar of her shirtwaist, over the gentle swell of her bosom, pausing at her absurdly tiny waist. Though the desk blocked any further study of her body, that didn't matter, for he already knew her shape. He'd had plenty of opportunity to form that picture the other night during their dance, and as he envisioned the slender hips and long legs that were presently hidden from his view, as he remembered the brief, tantalizing brush of his arm against the small of her back, the baser side of his masculine nature began imagining some of the naughtier means of persuasion she could employ, and his body began to burn.

But when he looked up again into her face, the delicate flush of pink in her cheeks told him she'd perceived the direction of his thoughts—at least to the extent an innocent lamb like her could do—and reminded him that the delicious picture forming in his mind had no chance whatsoever of becoming reality. And despite her opinion of his character, he was—sadly—a gentleman, which meant even if she were of a mind to offer such things, he could not accept. Innocent young ladies were not his line of country. Shoving down reprobate images of what Clara Deverill looked like without her clothes, he spoke. "What exactly are you offering?"

"A job, Lord Galbraith. I'm offering you a job."

That was so unexpected, so absurd, and so damnably different from what he'd been imagining that Rex couldn't help a laugh. "Doing what, in heaven's name?"

She gave a shrug of nonchalance, but he could see the tension in her slim shoulders, and he knew she wasn't as nonchalant as she wished to appear. "I want to hire you to write the Lady Truelove column for me."

This was sliding from absurdity into farce. He laughed again, confounded. "Now I know you're joking."

His amusement seemed to vex her, for a tiny frown knit her brows. "I'm quite serious. I don't see why you think I'm not."

He took one more glance over her body with a sigh of profound regret. "Let's just say my mind was traveling in a wholly different direction."

The blush in her cheeks deepened to absolute scarlet. "I am making you a bona fide offer of employment. It would only be temporary, until my sister returns from her honeymoon. She is expected home in about two months' time."

"She married in March, if memory serves. Four months is quite a long honeymoon."

"You have no idea," she agreed with a sigh. "Once she returns, she will find someone to take charge of

the column on a permanent basis. In the interim, I'd
like to hire you to do it."

She really was serious. He leaned back, rubbing a
hand over his face, thinking a moment. "Setting aside
the fact that I have no need to earn my living—thank
God—why would you want someone else to do it for
you? And even more baffling, why choose me, of all
people?"

She made a rueful face, her wide mouth twisting a
bit and her button nose wrinkling up. "You find that
odd, I take it?"

"Odd? Hell, no. I find it incomprehensible. Aside
from the fact that I loathe newspapers and can't imagine working for one, you think I'm a cad, a disreputable
rakehell. Why," he added, driven by curiosity, "would
you want me to take on the task of penning advice to
the lovelorn?"

"Because I'm no good at it."

He laughed at that nonsensical admission, but before
he could remind her of her well-established success,
she rushed on, "You, however, have a certain insight,
shall we say, into matters of romance. I am prepared
to employ you for that insight. In a literary sense," she
added as he raised an eyebrow.

"And you think I would find such an offer of interest? I am a gentleman, Miss Deverill—"

He was interrupted by a derisive snort that told him
what she thought of that contention.

"*Gentlemen*," he went on, emphasizing the word,
"don't have jobs."

"You'd be surprised, Lord Galbraith, if you knew
the number of gentlemen who work for newspapers.
I know of at least five who secretly write articles for

our competitors under assumed names. And at least a dozen have given their endorsement to various products advertised in our newspaper, recommending everything from shaving soap to patent medicines in exchange for a fee."

"Then perhaps you should hire one of those good gentlemen?"

"Why should I do so, when I have you?"

"You don't 'have' me, as you put it." Even as he made that point, he saw her straight brows arch as if disputing that contention, and when he looked into those dark eyes of hers, he felt a sudden, vague uneasiness. "I'm the one with the leverage here, Miss Deverill," he said, feeling the need to remind her of that point.

"Are you?" She straightened in her chair, and with that abrupt move, something changed between them, something that only deepened his uneasiness.

"My leverage," he went on, ignoring her question, "would vanish if I were to accept this offer. If I took on the job of being Lady Truelove, I could hardly start revealing to our acquaintance that you are she."

"Yes," she agreed, sounding quite pleased by the prospect. "Exactly."

"So that is your true intent in offering me this position? Buying my silence? What makes you think I would agree?"

"Because it's a winning arrangement for both of us. I am prepared to pay you a generous salary, and your perpetual lack of money is well-known. You will be obliged to keep my secret, as you have already appreciated, and I can stop writing an advice column I am obviously ill-equipped to compose—"

"Why obviously?" he cut in, diverted for the moment. This was the second time she'd disparaged her abilities as the famous columnist, and he couldn't help wondering why. "You're quite good at the job, from what I hear. The column is wildly popular."

She squirmed a little in her chair, making him even more curious. "Why would you disparage yourself in this way?" he asked. "Surely your success speaks for it—"

"I'm far too busy nowadays to write it properly," she said, cutting him off. "Now that the season has begun, I wish to move more in society, and with all the other duties of the newspaper that require my attention while my sister is away, I wish to hand off the task of writing Lady Truelove to someone else."

"Perhaps that's true," he conceded, "but that's not what you first said. You said, 'I'm no good at it.'"

"You were right," she muttered, rubbing four fingers over her forehead. "You are a good listener."

He didn't reply. He simply waited, and since he knew or had guessed most of the facts already, she capitulated with a sigh. "My sister used to write it. She prepared enough columns to cover the time she originally anticipated she'd be away, but then, she and Torquil decided to extend their honeymoon, and she cabled me, asking that I take it over until she returns."

"In addition to managing the paper? That's a lot to ask."

"Since my mother died, my sister has always protected and cared for me. In return, I am happy to do whatever I can for her at any opportunity. But when it comes to Lady Truelove—" She broke off, lifting her hands in a hopeless gesture, then letting them fall to her desk. "I am utterly lost. Offering advice to the lovelorn," she added with a little laugh, "is hardly my forte."

He studied her face for a moment, noting its lack of conventional prettiness. No rosebud mouth here, no Grecian nose, no delicately-arched eyebrows. But it was an agreeable face for all that, with its own unique charm, though he doubted the young chaps gadding about town ever halted their gazes on her long enough to see it. She wasn't, as he knew from his first cursory glance at her, the sort to draw masculine attention. "I see," he said gently. "And how does your father feel about having someone else assume Lady Truelove's mantle?"

"My father?" She stiffened, frowning, looking suddenly prickly. "What does he have to do with it?"

"He is the publisher, is he not? He is the owner?"

"Actually, no. He was, but his health has put paid to any involvement in the running of the *Weekly Gazette*. My sister now owns the paper, along with my brother, Jonathan. He was supposed to come back from America and take over, but circumstances forbade, and as a result, I have been obliged to assume the position of publisher until my sister returns. So, you see, it is within my purview to offer you this position. And with all my social obligations, I would be quite relieved to delegate Lady Truelove to someone else. This would also work to your advantage, since as I said, I'm prepared to pay generously. Say . . . one hundred pounds per column?"

The amount rather surprised him. A hundred pounds a week totaled more than his quarterly allowance from the estate—when his father was of a mind to pay it—and it was nearly double what Petunia was so generously providing him while he and his father were on the outs. He didn't know anything about how writers of newspaper piffle were compensated, of course, but it seemed a rather high sum. It was also an indication of how desperate she was to keep her secret safe.

Rex, however, had no desire to be an advice columnist, nor did circumstances require him to do so. "That is quite generous," he agreed, "but whatever the salary, it's hardly an incentive for me, since despite my irresponsible spending habits, I don't need the money. My aunt has been kind enough to provide me an income."

"Yes, well, about that . . ." She paused, giving a cough, and the uneasiness inside Rex stirred again. "It's clear that what you said the other night was true," she went on, reaching for the newspaper on top of the stack at one corner of her desk. "You really don't read the papers, do you?"

Rex frowned at this seeming change of subject. "What does my lack of interest in newspapers have to do with anything?"

Instead of replying, she opened the paper in her hand and began flipping through the pages to locate one page in particular. When she found it, she folded the sheet back, turned the paper around, and held it out to him. "You might want to reconsider your aversion to the daily news."

Taking the paper from her outstretched hand, he looked down, his gaze honing at once on the prominent headline at the top of the page.

LORD GALBRAITH CUT OFF BY SECOND EXASPERATED RELATIVE!

He read it three times, and yet, the words were slow to sink in. And the words after it, as he skimmed through them, seemed little more than a jumble of journalistic insinuations about his spendthrift ways, an accurate reference to his unfavorable opinion of marriage, and a tiresome account of his parents' miserable lives. Following it, however, was an unvarnished denunciation of him by his aunt, due to his "wild recent behavior and unrestrained manner of living," and a declaration from her that until he married, settled down, and became a responsible fellow and a credit to his family name, he would not be receiving another penny from her. In addition, she refused to be responsible for any of his debts, past, present, or future.

Oh, Auntie Pet, he thought in dismay, *what have you done?*

Even as he asked himself that question, he remembered his aunt's visit this morning and his butler's words about it.

She has expressed the wish to discuss with you the matter of your recent conduct.

Why, he wondered with a grimace, was hindsight always so damnably clear? He ought to have seen Auntie this morning instead of putting her off. His decision not to receive her had obviously miffed her enough to warrant this declaration to the evening papers. He ought to have endured the inevitable lecture, made his abject apologies, declared that honor prevented him from offering explanations, and assumed full responsibility for the entire disgraceful evening. That might have mollified her and prevented her from taking such drastic and public action.

Although, he reflected, his gaze scanning the article again, any expression of penitence and desire to atone on his part might not have changed a thing. The report here made it plain that Auntie was not above using his conduct at the ball as an excuse to bring him to heel about matrimony, and anything he might have said this morning might well have fallen on deaf ears anyway.

Whether he could have averted this disaster by seeing his aunt earlier today might be open to question, but when Rex looked up from the newspaper in his hand to the girl sitting opposite, he knew one thing.

He did not have Clara Deverill backed into any sort of corner.

Rex drew a deep breath and put the paper on her desk. She may have called his bluff, but he'd be damned before he'd show his cards. "Thank you for your offer, Miss Deverill, but despite what appears in the newspapers, I have neither the desire nor the need to accept employment."

Her expression did not change, but he wasn't fooled, for he saw the dismay in those expressive eyes.

"Then there's nothing more to be said." She swallowed hard and lowered her gaze to her desk. "I shall expect the news of Lady Truelove's identity to begin appearing in the gossip columns of our competitors within a day or two." She stood up, and as he followed suit, she looked at him, squaring her shoulders. "The reports will be gleeful, I'm sure."

Rex noted the proud lift of her chin and felt the sudden, inconvenient prick of guilt. She'd precipitated all this, he reminded himself, trying to ignore the bleakness in her eyes and the whispers of his conscience. Because of her, he was in a fine mess, damn it all, and he'd have the devil of a time getting out of it. Served her right to dance in the wind for a bit, to spend the next few days poring anxiously over the newspapers before she realized the truth.

"Good day, Miss Deverill," he said, bowed, and turned to leave.

He got as far as the door. His hand on the knob, he stopped, gave an aggravated sigh, and looked at her over one shoulder. "Despite what you think of me, I am not the sort of man who would blackmail a woman—with knowledge of her secrets, or anything else. I have no intention of telling anyone about Lady Truelove, and never did have."

She stared, her pale pink lips parting in astonishment. "You were bluffing?"

"Yes. To no avail, it seems." He turned away and yanked open the door. "What the hell I'll tell my aunt and my friend," he added under his breath as he walked out, "I have absolutely no idea."

UPON LEAVING CLARA Deverill's offices, Rex instructed his driver take him to Petunia's house in Park Lane, and as his carriage carried him back across town, he considered how he might be restored to Auntie's good graces. He'd have to offer an apology for his conduct, of course, something he'd intended to do anyway. He'd also have to promise future good behavior, and that, he knew could be problematic. And though he didn't think she would seriously hold an income over his head to force him to marry, he knew he'd be required to at least put himself fully at her disposal for the remainder of the season, accepting whatever social engagements she deemed suitable as she shoved marriageable girls in his face.

By the time his carriage reached his aunt's residence, Rex had reconciled himself to three months of balls and dinner parties and countless conversations with young debutantes, but he was given no opportunity to make that sacrifice, for upon inquiry of Auntie's butler, he was informed that she was not receiving.

Rex feared he knew what that meant. "Not receiving any callers, Bledsoe?" he asked with a wink, smiling on the outside, bracing himself on the inside. "Or just misbehaving great-nephews?"

Auntie's butler was the stuffy, old-fashioned sort who gave nothing away. His countenance remained coldly impassive. Fortunately for Rex, Bledsoe's unwillingness to part with information didn't matter too much, for he knew where Auntie would be this evening. Adding abject groveling to the list of what would be required of him, Rex handed over his card to the butler and departed for home to change into evening clothes.

He'd barely stepped across his own threshold, however, before he was presented by his footman with a new and far more serious problem than anything he'd faced yet today.

"The Countess of Leyland has called, my lord."

Rex froze in the act of handing over his hat, staring at the servant in horror. "My mother called here?"

"Yes, my lord. She's in the drawing room."

"Good God!" He shoved his hat into the footman's arms. "Mama, in my drawing room?"

"Yes, my lord. She said it was most urgent she speak with you at once, and Mr. Whistler showed her into the drawing room to await your return."

"Damn Whistler for a fool," he muttered as he smoothed his tie and gave his waistcoat a tug. "That man has always had a soft spot for Mama. But then," he added as he passed the footman and started for the stairs, "most men do."

Making a mental note to reiterate to all his servants who was and who was not allowed to cross his threshold and that his dear mama was most decidedly in the latter category, Rex ascended the stairs to the first floor. With a quick raking of his hands through his hair, he entered the drawing room.

As he watched his mother turn from the window, it struck him anew that no one who ever saw them together could ever doubt that they were mother and son. Their coloring and features were strikingly similar, a fact which explained, he had no doubt, his father's resentful temper whenever he was in the old man's vicinity.

"Mama, what the devil are you doing here?"

She came toward him, hands outstretched. "Rex, my dear," she began, then stopped, her hands falling to her sides, staring at him in horror. "Good heavens, your eye!"

"It's nothing."

"A black eye?" She came closer and gave a cry of dismay as she saw the violent red gash on his temple. "My darling boy, what has happened to you?"

"It looks worse than it is." He waved aside this show

of motherly concern with an impatient motion of his hand. "Why have you come here, Mama? The last time you were here, if you recall, I told you quite clearly that you could never come again."

"I know, I know. But I really didn't see any alternative, since you refuse to answer my letters."

"I cannot correspond with you. You know that."

"Just so." She made a self-evident gesture. "Which means that if I wish to see my son, I really have no choice but to come in person."

He gave a laugh, a harsh and jaded one that made her wince. "Why do I have the feeling that fondness for me is not what has inspired this visit? Perhaps the fact that the last time you called upon me, Papa cut off my income!"

"I am so very sorry about that. I knew he'd be angry if he found out I'd been to see you, but I never dreamt he'd cut you off. Although, upon reflection, I suppose I should have known he'd be capable of it. It's just the bitter, vindictive sort of thing he would do. He's—"

"Don't!" he said fiercely. "Don't. And spare me any pretense that maternal affection has brought you here. If you had any consideration of that sort, you'd have stayed well away."

"As I said, I really didn't have a choice—" She broke off at his warning look and gave a sigh. "Oh, Rex, I do love you, whether you believe me or not."

The nauseating thing was that he did believe her. Worse, despite that she sponged off him at every possible opportunity, he loved her, too. And that made him all kinds of a fool. "However pressing your need to contact me, I don't suppose you could have sent a servant in your place?"

"No." She looked down, pretending a sudden vast interest in the state of her gloves. "I'm afraid not. I didn't bring any servants with me."

He frowned. "Not even a maid?"

"I'm only staying two days, so it hardly seemed necessary." She left off studying her gloves and looked up. "I'm at a hotel."

That bit of news did not surprise him. After the separation, she had taken to spending most of her time in Paris, and there, she had plenty of friends whose hospitality she could take advantage of. Here in London, however, it was a different matter. The French adored having scandalous friends, the English not so much.

Her lack of a maid, on the other hand, was rather a surprise, but he wasn't curious enough to inquire further on the subject. "What do you want, Mama?"

She smiled, causing Rex to suck in a sharp breath, for his mother's smile was strikingly similar to his own, and the sight of it never failed to inspire in him a rather sick feeling of dismay. No one he knew was more charming, more beguiling, or more willing to exploit her good looks than his mother, and he sometimes feared that a similarity of appearance was not the only trait he had inherited from her. "The usual thing, I'm afraid," she said.

"Already?" Given his mother's knack for heedless spending, he should not have been surprised, and yet, he was. "God, Mama, I gave you seven hundred pounds less than a month ago. That's not gone already, surely? What have you spent it on?"

She waved a hand vaguely in the air. "Well, darling, everything is just so expensive nowadays. Clothes, you know, and cosmetics, and entertainments . . ." Her voice trailed off, her blue eyes widening with kitten-like innocence. "I don't know where it goes, honestly. But it does vanish at an unaccountable rate."

"Doesn't it, though?" he said, pasting on an air of careless amiability he did not feel in the least. "It does that to me, too, especially when you come calling. Unfortunately, the last time you were here, you not only took all my golden eggs, you managed to kill the proverbial goose. As a result, I haven't a shilling to give you."

"I thought . . . that is, I heard . . ." There was a delicate pause. "I heard you were in funds again, despite your father."

"Ah, so word of Auntie's generosity reached you in Paris, did it? And you've come, hoping for a bit more of the swag? Yes," he went on before she could reply, "Auntie was kind enough to give me an allowance until I can manage to restore myself to Papa's good graces, but I'm rather on the out with her at present."

Her skin paled at this bit of news, making the rouge on her cheeks seem more obvious. "You can't raise a . . . a loan?"

Rex frowned at the faintness of her voice. She sounded more than dismayed. She sounded . . . afraid. It was an act, of course, and yet, even as he told himself that, he felt a hint of alarm. Showing it, though, would only encourage her to continue playing on his sympathy. "No, Mama, I can't. You'll have to look elsewhere."

She swayed on her feet.

Despite his certainty that he was being manipulated, Rex moved at once, closing the distance between them and catching her arm to keep her from falling. "Steady on, Mama," he said and led her to the nearest settee. "Sit down."

She complied, and he sank down beside her. "What is it?" he asked sharply. "What are you not telling me?"

"It doesn't matter, unless you have money."

"It does matter if you ever wish me to give you any money in future. You must be honest with me about why you've such a pressing need."

"Very well." She sighed and looked at him unhappily. "I haven't been spending what you've been giving me for living expenses or clothes or anything like that."

"Then where's it going?"

She stirred on the settee. "You know I had a . . . umm . . . a spot of bother a few years ago?"

He wasn't about to let her get by with euphemisms. "Gambling debts, you mean."

A frown marred her perfect forehead. "Really, Rex, must you be so tactless as to remind me of my past mistakes?"

Unimpressed, he folded his arms, propped his back against the arm of the settee, and prepared himself for what he was certain was coming. "So, you're gambling again. That's where the money's going?"

"No, no!" she cried. "That's not it at all."

He raised a skeptical eyebrow.

"It isn't! Rex, I swear to you, I have not gambled since then. Not once. It's understandable if you don't believe me," she added as he made a scoffing sound, "but it's the truth."

With Mama, the truth was a malleable thing, but

there was no point in arguing about it. "What are you spending your money on, if it's not gambling?"

"You remember how I paid those gambling debts?"

"Yes. You sold your jewels."

"That's just it. I didn't."

He stiffened. "So that was another lie? Why am I not surprised?"

"I couldn't sell them. When I took them to sell, the jeweler told me they were paste."

"What? How?"

"Your father, of course! Well, who else could have done it?" she asked when he made a sound of exasperation at this mention of his other parent. "He must have taken the jewels out at some point before we officially separated and had them replaced with replicas."

Or she had done so and was lying straight to his face. Either scenario was possible. "So how did you pay the gambling salon?"

She sighed. "I borrowed from moneylenders. The seven hundred pounds you gave me was to pay interest on the debt."

"Interest? Not all of it, surely?"

"Yes, all of it. The rate is quite high, you see."

"High? It's exorbitant! Your gambling debt was only . . . what . . . five hundred pounds?"

"I didn't have much of a choice, Rex. Given my circumstances, the only moneylender who would grant me a loan was . . . somewhat unsavory."

He thought of her a few moments ago, pale and faint, and he straightened in alarm, unfolding his arms. "How unsavory?"

"Enough to send one of his toughs to pass some very explicit threats to me via my maid. She was terrified enough to depart my employ."

"Good God, Mama!"

"I know, I know. But what else could I do? Anyway, I thought the money you gave me would pay the principal amount owed as well as the interest, but then, I was told no, that because I hadn't paid in a timely manner, more interest had accrued and a punitive fee added, so I still owe more money."

The greedy bastard. Rex pressed his tongue against his teeth, working to contain the anger rising inside him. "How much more?"

"The total is now one thousand pounds. If I don't pay it by Saturday, it rises again to fourteen hundred."

"But a thousand in this man's hands by Saturday clears your debt in full?"

"I have been told so, yes. But what does it matter? If you don't have it to give me—"

The door opened, interrupting her, and his butler came in. "My lord, your father is here."

Rex groaned. Could his day get any worse?

"He insists upon seeing you at once," Whistler went on.

"I'll bet he does," Rex muttered, thinking of the newspaper article Clara Deverill had shown him. "He's heard Auntie Pet has cut me off, and he sees a vulnerability to exploit."

"That sounds like something he'd do," his mother put in, causing Rex to round on her at once.

"Pipe down, Countess," he ordered. "You've no moral high ground with me."

His mother had the grace to look abashed, and he returned his attention to his butler. "Did he happen to have a newspaper with him?"

"He was carrying one, yes, my lord."

Rex sighed. "I was afraid of that."

"Do you wish to receive him, sir?"

"Here?" Rex jumped to his feet, appalled by the prospect. "My father and my mother in the same room? Are you mad?"

His butler stiffened as if affronted by that question. "I had thought," he said with dignity, "to put Lord Leyland in the study."

"No, that won't do. If you don't bring him to the drawing room, he'll immediately start speculating why, and I'll never get my quarterly allowance back if he goes down that road. Tell him I'm not receiving. Got in a fight, head trauma, all that rot."

"No," his mother interjected before the butler could move to depart. "See him. He's your only hope for an income, especially if Petunia is being chary. Best not to antagonize either of them." She stood up. "I'll go, and slip down the servant stairs so he won't see me."

"That's not necessary, Mama, for I have no intention of seeing him." He paused to wave Whistler out of the room to carry out his instructions. "Not after the day I've had."

"But you might be able to return to his good graces, and if so, he'd resume your allowance, and you could then pay off the moneylender—" She broke off, and had the grace to blush at her own self-absorption.

"I'm so happy to know how concerned you are about my well-being, Mama," he said dryly. "But never fear, I'm sure Auntie and I will work things out and all will be well. In the meantime, if Papa wants to reinstate me, that would be lovely, but I'm still in no mood to eat the crow he wants to dish out, nor do I want to hear a vituperative tirade about you for the second time in a week."

Even his mother didn't dare to press the topic any further. "What about the moneylender?" she asked in a whisper. "If I don't pay him . . ." She paused, pressing a hand to her throat as if unable to continue.

"I'll take care of it," he said harshly, well aware he was making a promise he was in no position to keep.

"You'll raise a loan, then?"

After what had appeared in the paper, he doubted he could raise a loan for omnibus fare, much less one for a thousand pounds, but he didn't say so.

"I already told you I would take care of it," he said, leading her to the writing desk by the window and thrusting a pen into her hand. "Write down this moneylender's name and exactly where in Paris one might find him."

"But where are you going?" she asked as he turned and started for the door.

"To make certain Papa has really left and isn't still lurking somewhere about the house. God knows, if he saw you here, I doubt he or Auntie would ever speak to me again, much less reinstate my allowance, and I'm not about to let that happen."

Upon verifying that Whistler had seen Papa get into his carriage and that said carriage had definitely departed Half Moon Street and turned onto Piccadilly, Rex returned to the drawing room, where his mother presented him with a folded sheet of paper.

"The man lives in a little cul-de-sac near Montmartre," she explained. "You should be able to find the place easily enough."

"Me, go to Paris?" He shook his head. "No, I can't. I need to make amends with Auntie Pet, and if she were to hear I've gone to Paris, she'll think it's to visit you. Papa will hear of it, too, and the fat will really be in the fire. I will send my valet. He's a trustworthy, responsible chap. And he's discreet. The debt will be paid by Saturday, you may be sure."

"Thank you, Rex. I am truly grateful."

"Are you?" He took a deep breath, looked into his mother's eyes, and worked to add another layer of armor to the ones already encasing his heart. "If so, then I trust you will show your gratitude by staying the hell away from me."

Despite his efforts, the hurt in her eyes pierced his chest like a knife, making it clear that a few more layers of that armor would be required. "Go," he ordered, "before I realize just how great a fool I truly am."

He turned away and walked to the writing desk without a backward glance. He sat down and made a great show of retrieving paper, envelopes, and stamps from the desk as if to demonstrate that he'd already dismissed her from his mind, but it was a pose, for he found himself holding his breath until he heard the door behind him open and close.

He waited a moment longer, then glanced over his shoulder to find that she was indeed gone. Only then, did he allow himself a sigh of relief.

That relief, however, was short-lived, for as he'd told his mother a few moments ago, he had to mend his quarrel with Auntie. He also had to obtain a thousand pounds and get it to Paris by Saturday.

Suddenly, it occurred to him that both these problems might be solved at the same time, and by one action. He considered a moment how best to proceed, then he drew a sheet of paper closer, pulled the pen out of its holder, and flipped open the inkwell. After taking a moment to compose in his head just what he wanted to say, he inked his pen and began to write.

Chapter 8

Though Clara had lived in London her entire life, she had been inside the Royal Opera House at Covent Garden only once, and the view she'd had then from her inexpensive seat in the stalls could not compare to the view she had now.

The theater's domed gold-and-white ceiling, its crimson velvet seats and draperies, and the dazzling light from its hundreds of gas jets made an even more breathtaking display when one was seated in a box three floors above the stalls.

"Let me say again how glad I was that you were able to accept my invitation this evening, Miss Deverill."

Clara turned her gaze from the dazzling vista below to the elderly woman standing beside her. "I was happy to receive it, Lady Petunia."

"Surprised, too, I daresay." The older woman smiled, a gesture that deepened the good-humored creases at the edges of her pale green eyes. "It was such a last-minute business."

Clara had been surprised, but the spontaneity of the invitation had not been the reason. She hardly knew Lady Petunia Pierpont. To be singled out by someone of her rank not once but twice was a circumstance for which she could find no explanation, especially since the duke's family, having so recently been rocked by scandal, were receiving a decidedly cool reception from most of society this season.

If all that wasn't enough to make Lady Petunia's invitation to the opera surprising, there was also what had happened this afternoon. No doubt Lady Petunia's great-nephew would prefer Clara at the bottom of the sea right now than anywhere near the members of his family. Granted, Galbraith and his aunt were not on the best of terms at present, but still, one's own family was always more important than any outsider, particularly among the *ton*. And the viscount would surely have called upon his aunt after leaving Clara's offices with the intent of mending their quarrel and restoring his income. But given the fact that she was here tonight, Clara could only conclude that either he didn't know Lady Petunia had included her in their party, or he had not yet succeeded in regaining any influence with his elderly relation.

"I had no plans this evening but to have dinner at home with my sisters-in-law and retire to bed early," she replied. "Your invitation may have been spur-of-the-moment, but as I said, I was happy to accept, and I thank you for thinking of me."

"You are quite welcome, my dear, although as much as I should like to have the credit for inviting you this evening, I don't deserve it. No, the idea came from my great-nephew, Lord Galbraith."

Clara stared at Lady Petunia, astonished. "Lord Galbraith suggested that you invite me?"

"He did, and I was delighted to oblige him."

Galbraith's anger this afternoon had been plain, his refusal of her proposition quite clear. When he had departed from her office a few hours ago, they had seemed—to her mind, at least—at a stalemate. "I can't imagine what would inspire him to do such a thing," she said truthfully.

"Can you not, my dear?"

The implication in that softly uttered question was not only erroneous, it was also absurd, and the idea that Lady Petunia might be harboring the notion that Galbraith had any attraction to her filled Clara with dismay. Still, there was no way to explain the reality, nor was there any point, so Clara looked away, pretending vast interest in the boxes on the opposite side of the theater.

"I don't mean to embarrass you," Lady Petunia said, breaking the silence. "But whatever it was that Galbraith said to offend you so grievously the other night, I do hope you can forgive him."

She had no idea which of that outrageous man's words the other woman was alluding to, or how she even knew Clara had been offended by anything, but before she could inquire further on the subject, they were interrupted by the very topic of their conversation.

"I can mend my own fences, Auntie Pet. No need for you to do it for me."

Clara turned to find Galbraith standing behind her

chair. Despite his evening clothes and the flutes of champagne he was carrying, he looked every inch the golden, windblown Adonis of ancient Greece to whom she'd first likened him, so much so that Clara's pulses quickened in response, a reaction that filled her with chagrin.

"And in that spirit of fence-mending," he went on, lifting the filled glasses in his hands, "I've brought Miss Deverill a peace offering."

This certainly was proving to be an evening of surprises, and champagne was quite a delightful one, for she'd never tasted the stuff in her life before. But she held back from taking it, unwilling to seem too impressed and show how easily she could be disarmed, especially after the set-to they'd had earlier. "Champagne is a rather unorthodox peace offering, isn't it?"

He grinned. "They didn't have olive branches on the refreshments menu."

The laugh was out of her mouth before she could even think to check it, and she appreciated that though Galbraith might be an utter scapegrace, he also had charm. When considered in combination with his breathtaking good looks, it seemed terribly unfair, a cruel trick of Fate played on unsuspecting females, and Clara was heartily glad of the conversation she'd overheard in the tea shop that prevented her from being one of those females.

"I suppose not," she said, accepting the flute from his hand. She lifted it to her mouth, and took a tentative sip.

It was glorious, utterly glorious, and she smiled, feeling as if she'd just swallowed a mouthful of liquid joy. But when she lifted the glass again for a second, more eager taste, she caught him watching her, his head to one side and a slight smile on his lips, and somehow, the idea of him seeing just how unsophisticated she truly was seemed unbearable. She lowered the glass again, working to school her features to a neutral expression. "As peace offerings go, champagne is probably more successful than a fusty old olive branch. Thank you."

"I'm glad you're here at last, Galbraith," his aunt put in before he could reply. "I was just telling Miss Deverill how inviting her was your suggestion, and then I wondered if I ought to have admitted the fact, given the time. Being late isn't the way to make a favorable impression on new acquaintances, my dear."

"I'm not late though, am I?" he countered, leaning down to press a kiss to his aunt's cheek.

She sniffed. "Arriving only thirty minutes before the performance isn't what I'd call punctual, either, especially when we have guests in our box. My greatnephew," she added, turning to Clara, "is always the last member of the family to arrive for any event. I can never decide if it's because he possesses an inferior pocket watch, or if he just likes making an entrance."

Despite this rebuke and their recent quarrel, her affection for him was obvious, and Clara wasn't the least bit fooled by her disapproving tone. Neither, she noticed, was Galbraith.

"I'm usually the last only because the rest of my family believes arriving half an hour early is the height of punctuality. But," he added before Lady Petunia could offer a retort, "in this case, Auntie, you'll be happy to know I was not the last one here. I was, in fact, the first."

"But where have you been, then? We arrived ages ago."

"When I got here, you and the rest of our party were nowhere to be found, so I occupied my time by going back down and ordering refreshments." He held out the second glass to her. "Champagne?"

She waved aside the offered glass. "No, no, thank you. I had two glasses of wine with dinner. Champagne so soon afterward will make me tipsy."

"I believe I'd like to see that," he murmured, earning himself a look of reproof.

"Now that you are here, Galbraith, I shall leave Miss Deverill in your hands and mingle with some of our other guests. Try not to offend her again, if you please. And Miss Deverill?" She turned to Clara. "If he dares to be impertinent, you have my leave to turn your back on him and walk away, just as you did at my ball."

With that, she departed for the other end of the room, and Galbraith moved between chairs to join Clara at the rail.

Clara turned toward him. "Lady Petunia doesn't know about that, does she?" she asked in alarm, glancing back to be sure the other woman was out of earshot.

"About what?"

She faced him again, her gaze rising as far as his tie, but she knew from the heat in her cheeks that her face was about the same rose-pink shade as her evening gown. "What you said," she whispered, oddly more embarrassed now about his suggestion of kissing her than she'd been at the time.

But he only laughed. "God, no. If she knew I'd made such a naughty proposition to a young lady, she'd not only have stopped giving me an income, she'd have flayed me alive. No, that secret stays between us, if you don't mind."

Relieved, she lifted her gaze to his, and at the sight of those brilliant eyes, she suddenly wanted to know why he'd made that wicked proposition in the first place. But she'd have died rather than ask.

"I'm glad you came," he said in the wake of her silence. "I wasn't sure you would."

"Was my presence here really at your instigation?"

"You seem skeptical."

"Should I not be? When you left my offices this afternoon, you seemed angry enough with me to spit nails."

"That's true enough," he conceded, leaning one hip against the railing. "But if you knew me better, you'd know I don't hold grudges. I . . ." He paused and looked down, frowning into the glass in his hand. "Holding onto anger, Miss Deverill, is an ugly thing, something I've watched people do through most of my life, and it never answers. Therefore, I strive never to do it." He paused and looked at her again, lifting his glass. "Truce?"

"Truce," she agreed, clinking her glass to his. "I'm not the sort to hold grudges, either."

His eyes creased at the corners as he smiled. "Good, because I'm afraid my effort to mend fences with you has an ulterior motive. I'm wondering if your offer of employment is still open?"

Clara froze, her champagne glass halfway to her lips, feeling a jolt of hope, for her attempts to compose an answer for the Devastated Debutante after his departure this afternoon had been dismally unsuccessful. "Why do you ask? Have you changed your mind about accepting it?"

"That depends," he said, an ambiguous reply that reminded Clara getting one's hopes up about a man like this was a foolish thing to do, even as she mentally crossed her fingers.

"Yes," she answered, "my offer is still open."

"Before you say that, I must warn you, I have a few conditions of my employment. For one thing, my fee would need to be one hundred and twenty-five pounds per column."

"Done," she said, too relieved to quibble about an additional two hundred pounds, especially since the paper could easily afford to pay it.

"And," he went on, "I would require all the money in advance."

"All of it?"

"Yes, all. That is a nonnegotiable point," he added before she could reply.

"Wages are usually paid only after the work has been done," she felt compelled to point out.

"True, but anything less than one thousand pounds paid immediately negates my sudden need for funds." He did not explain further. Instead, in the wake of her silence, he raised an eyebrow, looking amused. "What's wrong? Are you afraid I won't come up to snuff and you shall have to give me the sack before I've earned my pay?"

"Let's just say I'm not sure I can trust you to take the responsibilities of the job seriously. Laughing," she admonished as his smile widened, "only underscores my concern. Writing the Lady Truelove column is not a lark, Lord Galbraith. It is a task that requires serious thought and deliberation."

"Inventing problems for fictitious correspondents

and scribbling advice to solve those problems seems rather a lark to me, but I won't debate the point."

She could have told him that the people Lady True-love advised were not fictitious, but she decided to save any explanations of what would be required of him for later. If he truly was serious about taking this on, she didn't want to scare him off. "I will pay the funds in advance. Are we agreed?"

He didn't answer at once. Instead, he turned toward the rail, staring out at the boxes across the way. "I have one other condition."

Clara frowned, hating the feeling of being on ten-terhooks. "You really do believe in pushing your luck, don't you?"

He gave a little laugh at that. "You have no idea how true that is," he muttered without looking at her.

"So," she prompted when he did not elaborate, "what is this third condition?"

"It's not so much a condition as it is a request. Or a warning, depending on how you choose to see it."

"Warning?"

"Yes." He turned again to face her. "I intend to begin paying you my addresses, Miss Deverill."

"Paying . . ." Her voice failed, and Clara stared at him, too stunned to continue any sort of reply. His aunt had hinted something like this might be in the wind, but she'd dismissed that as a ridiculous notion. It seemed every bit as ridiculous now. "I don't think I quite understand," she said at last.

"I wish to court you. I should like you to allow me the privilege."

"What?" She burst out laughing, her usual reaction

when anyone caught her utterly by surprise. "But we don't even like each other."

A hint of a smile curved his mouth. "You mean, you don't like me."

Clara made a face, not the least bit fooled by the qualification. "If you have any liking for me, it's only because you like women."

"So I do."

"And I happen to be a woman."

His gaze lowered, skimming over her body in that slow way of his, a look that in this small room full of people seemed as intimate as a caress. "So you are."

At that softly uttered acknowledgement, Clara's heart leapt in her chest with such force, it almost hurt. Her toes curled in her satin slippers, and heat flooded not only her cheeks, but her entire body, a reaction she found aggravating beyond belief.

She took a fortifying swallow of champagne, working to contain these traitorous and most unwelcome responses of her physical body and think with clarity. "If you have any liking for me, you didn't display it this afternoon."

"No, but I was very angry with you. As we already discussed, I've gotten over it."

"And what a relief it is, too. Now I can sleep at night."

He laughed. "You see? That is one of the things I like about you: your unflinching ability to put me in my place. Most women don't."

That, she feared, was nothing less than the truth. "Either way," she said, "the idea that you are inspired by any romantic notions about me is ludicrous. What is this really about?"

"Believe it or not, even I am capable of being romantic on occasion. But since you insist upon believing the worst about me anyway, I will lay my cards on the table and tell you the unvarnished truth. You will no doubt be relieved to know that in this case I am not being romantic."

Having never had much in the way of romance, Clara wasn't quite as relieved as she probably ought to have been, especially when she looked into his devastatingly handsome face. "I see."

"As the Earl of Leyland's only son and heir, I am entitled to an allowance from the estate, but that allowance is bestowed at my father's sole discretion. Recently, in an attempt to control my behavior, he cut me off."

"Yes, I had heard gossip to that effect. Something about too much high living," she couldn't help adding.

He gave a short laugh, though he didn't really seem amused. "That is the gossip, certainly. And now, as you already know," he added before she could ask if there was more to the story, "my aunt has withdrawn the income she was so kindly providing me."

"But why should that prompt you to . . . to p . . . pay addresses to . . ." She paused, feeling as if a thousand butterflies were suddenly fluttering around in her stomach. Taking a breath, she tried to ask her question in a different way. "What does any of that have to do with me?"

He met her inquiring gaze with an unwavering one of his own. "If I begin courting a woman, my income will be reinstated."

Despite her knowledge of his character, Clara felt a stab of disappointment. It was an emotion with which she was quite familiar—the disappointment of the wallflower when the handsome man walked right by her to ask her prettier friend to dance or when the man seated beside her at dinner kept talking to the girl on his other side. In this case, however, Clara knew feeling let down was not only irrational, it was stupid. But it hurt, damn it, salt in the wounds of all her insecurities.

Still, she couldn't afford to show any of that, not with the future of Lady Truelove at stake. And it wasn't as if she wanted him. She was far too clear-eyed about him to do so. Nonetheless, she couldn't prevent an acerbic bite in her voice as she replied. "I'm flattered, Lord Galbraith. How could I not be, in the face of such overwhelming attentions?"

"Would you prefer it if my reason were the usual one?" His lashes lowered a fraction. "If my request were borne of a deep and passionate regard?"

"God, no!" she cried, alarmed by the prospect, though she wasn't sure what, precisely, she found so unsettling.

He shrugged. "There we are then."

His nonchalance was another prick to her pride, but Clara ignored it. "What makes you think courting a woman will soften your aunt's position?"

"It's not my aunt I'm concerned about, but to answer your question, no man can be expected to conduct a courtship if he hasn't the income to support a wife. If I begin paying you my attentions, my great-aunt will inform my father, and if Leyland thinks I am at last intending to find a wife, he will resume my allowance from the estate."

"Or he'll suspect it's all a hum."

"He can't afford to take the chance. Leyland needs

me to marry to secure the succession of the earldom to his own son. His pride, you see, can't bear the idea that the title and estates could pass to a distant cousin who earns a living making boots. On the other hand, he can hardly expect his ambition to be fulfilled if I have no income, for no woman would take a man's courtship seriously if he has no money to support her. By courting you, I force my father's hand."

Clara took a deep breath and shoved down any silly notions of disappointment. "Why choose me? There are many women, I'm sure, who would welcome your suit. Why direct your attentions to me?"

"Despite what you may think of me, I have no wish to encourage an unknowing woman's expectations."

"And I wouldn't have such expectations?"

"Of me?" His expression turned rueful. "Be honest, Miss Deverill. We both know you wouldn't marry me if I were the last man on earth."

Last man on earth, a little voice inside her head piped up to say, *might be a bit of an exaggeration.* Clara tore her gaze from his stunning face and told the little voice in her head to shut up.

She gazed out at the crowd and tried to consider with objective detachment the ramifications of what he was suggesting. From his point of view, she supposed it made a sort of sense. For her, however, it was untenable.

"You're quite right that I wouldn't ever dream of marrying you," she said at last, returning her gaze to his. "But that fact brings up another fact, one that— even if I conceded all the things you are telling me as true—makes what you are asking impossible."

"What's that?"

"Unlike you, I want to marry. That is one of the main reasons I am participating in the events of the season, to meet eligible young men."

"Ah." That reply seemed to indicate that he appreciated her point, but his reply, when it came, demonstrated otherwise. "All the better, then, for both of us. What's the problem?"

She frowned, bewildered by the question. "I beg your pardon?"

He shrugged. "If finding a man to marry is your goal, I can't think of a better way to accomplish it than by agreeing to my plan."

Clara began to wonder if he was touched in the head. "But if you are paying me your attentions openly, other men will see that."

"Yes." He nodded. "Exactly."

"They will assume that I am . . . that we . . . that I have regard f . . . for . . ."

She stopped and took another deep breath. "Other men will see us together," she said after a moment, speaking with deliberate care so that she didn't stammer. "They will conclude that my feelings are already engaged, that I have formed an attachment to you. They will steer clear of me altogether."

"No, my sweet lamb, that's exactly what they won't do."

"I don't see how you make that out."

"Men thrive on competition, and yet, we are also deathly afraid of rejection. If you are not dancing, for example, most men assume it's because you don't want to do so, and so they don't ask you. But if you agree to my plan, other men will see you dancing with me, be encouraged, and start approaching you."

"Will they?" She made a face. "They didn't after we

danced the other night. I spent the rest of the evening in my usual place, with the other wallflowers. Your attentions didn't change a thing."

"Only because you snubbed me by walking away after our dance was over, preventing me from doing the proper thing and escorting you back to your place. My aunt assumed your action was the result of something I said that must have offended you, but most men wouldn't draw such a conclusion. Any men observing us no doubt concluded that you were the one who snubbed me."

"And therefore, I would also be likely to snub them?"

"Just so. The opposite is also true. If you draw my attentions, you will draw theirs. Trust me on this."

"Asking me to trust you," she said, "is asking a lot."

He grinned. "I'm sure. But look at it this way. You want me to take on the role of Lady Truelove, which is to give people advice. Why would you do that if you can't even accept the advice I give you?"

"Somehow, it seems easier to unleash you on the rest of the world than upon myself," she confessed. "If you're wrong, you know, I spend the next two months with no male company but yours."

"A fate worse than death," he said gravely.

"You have no idea," she muttered. "But even if you're right, what you're asking me to do is to deliberately mislead the members of your family."

"No, I'm simply asking you to not spurn me outright if I pay you my attentions. Dance with me at balls, accept invitations to dinner where I will also be invited, play an occasional duet with me at the piano, talk with me for more than two minutes at a party and seem pleased to see me—" He broke off, flashing her a smile. "Really, Clara, you needn't look as if I've just suggested you eat raw lemons."

"Well," she began, but he forestalled her before she could applaud the aptness of that comparison.

"You've already made your opinion of me clear as glass. No need to hammer my masculine pride into the ground, is there?"

"You could do with a bit more hammering of that sort, in my opinion. Just how long," she hastened on before he could reply, "would you require this charade to go on?" Even as she asked the question, she couldn't believe she was even considering his mad idea.

Mad ideas, her pesky little voice reminded, *have become your special gift.*

"The two months I am in your employ should suffice. By then, my father will undoubtedly have reinstated my allowance."

"And then?"

"I propose marriage, you refuse me. Devastated, unable to even think about courting anyone else—at least until next year—I depart London for a cottage in the country, where I shall spend my time working to mend my broken heart. You, meanwhile, will enjoy the rest of your season surrounded by men who adore you madly and are heartily glad I'm now out of the running."

"You seem to have given this plan a great deal of thought. What if during this supposed courtship your aunt asks me about my feelings for you? What then? Am I supposed to lie?"

"I've seen firsthand your ability to dissemble when the occasion calls for it," he countered dryly. "But, no, you needn't worry, for Auntie would never dream of inquiring into your feelings for me. That would be an unspeakable invasion of your privacy. She will merely observe my interest in you and cross her fingers in the hope that her matchmaking efforts on my behalf might be paying off at long last."

"You can twist this any way you like, but you are still attempting to deceive her, and your father, too."

"During the next two months, I shall fervently deny any romantic interest in you at every possible opportunity."

"An action which will only serve to reinforce the opposite notion in their minds!"

He shrugged. "I can't help it if people don't believe what I say."

She laughed, shaking her head, amazed anew at how skillfully he could paint a picture for people that was completely different from reality without actually lying. "You really are a scoundrel."

"I know it seems that way."

"I don't see how any other interpretation is possible."

He studied her thoughtfully for a moment before he replied. "It must be lovely to have the luxury of such strong, unshakable ideals," he murmured. "To be able to distinguish so clearly what is right and what is wrong."

She stirred, those words making her feel oddly defensive. "Some rights and wrongs are plain enough."

"Are they? Honesty, most would say, is a virtue. Yet honesty has done little to help me, for I have always been scrupulously honest about my determination never to wed, yet certain members of my family refuse to accept it. Absolute honesty, Miss Deverill, has gotten me nowhere."

"They don't believe your resolve sincere?"

"They don't want to believe it. My father's motivation stems from the need to preserve the earldom with a secure succession. My aunt's reasons stem from her deep love and affection for me, and she has conveniently convinced herself that marriage would be a good thing for me, that it would settle me down and make me a responsible chap."

"And it wouldn't?"

His lips twisted in a crooked, sideways smile. "You seem to understand me enough to judge. What do you think?"

Clara thought of Elsie Clark tripping over herself to please him, and she appreciated that only a woman with a heart of stone or one with no sense of self-preservation would ever agree to marry him. "Let's just say that I long ago stopped confusing wishes with realities."

He laughed. "As I said, you have a very clear-cut view of the world. My relations, alas, are not inclined to share such a view, at least not when it comes to me."

"You could simply tell them all to go hang. Your reluctance to do so tells me that you want the money your family provides you, and you also want the freedom to do just as you please."

"Well, I do like having my cake, I confess," he said, the very blandness of his voice making her certain he was teasing her.

"Why is money so important?" she asked, refusing to be diverted.

"For one thing, it's deuced hard to pay rent and buy food without it."

"It's also hard to enjoy life's more frivolous pursuits, such as—how did you put it in the tea shop?—'wine, women, and song.'"

Her reply bothered him, she could tell, though whether that was due to her reminder of his lifestyle or the consequences of his conversation with his friend, she couldn't be certain. When he spoke, however, his voice was light and careless.

"It's the women that take the lion's share, I'm afraid." He smiled, but it was one that didn't reach his eyes. Defiance seethed in their blue depths like the turbulence of a stormy sea, telling her any disapproval she might feel could go straight to perdition. "Women, experience has taught me, are deuced expensive."

Those words seemed to confirm everything she knew of him, and everything she'd heard, and yet, they rang strangely hollow. As she studied his face, Clara felt a sudden, inexplicable pang of doubt about her own judgement. Was he really as great a rake as she thought him to be?

The moment the question crossed her mind, she wondered how many other women before her had asked themselves the very same thing. How many had longed, however much they knew it was futile, to believe he was a better man than his reputation and his actions painted him? How many had confused wishes with reality? Dozens, she'd wager.

Clara decided it was best to return to the topic at hand. "Do you really expect me to agree to help you manipulate your family?"

He shrugged. "Certain members of my family wish to manipulate me into something I have already made clear I do not want. Is it so wrong of me to exercise a little manipulation of my own? Besides," he added before she could think of how to answer, "if any manipulation is required, I shall be the one doing it. You, my lamb, are only required to do one thing."

"Which is?"

"Be nice to me." He stirred, leaning a fraction closer to her. His gaze lowered to her mouth, and his smile faded away. "Would that be so hard, Clara?"

At the soft murmur of her name, her throat went dry. Her lips parted, but no words came out of her mouth. Under his heated gaze, the alarm she felt whenever shyness tied her tongue seemed ten times worse than usual, pressing against her chest like a weight.

"No harder than having teeth drawn," she managed at last, but the tartness of her words was utterly spoiled by the breathlessness of her voice.

He laughed softly. "Fair enough," he said, his eyes meeting hers. "I'll settle for having your polite tolerance. Will you allow me that?"

"I s . . . s . . . suppose I can manage that much," she said. "I sh . . . shouldn't like to b . . . be rude to anyone, not even you."

"Do we have a bargain?"

She glanced away, her gaze skimming over the people gathered around the table of refreshments nearby. She did not like the idea of helping him encourage an impression for his family that wasn't authentic, and she wasn't at all sure that other men would find his attentions to her a spur of encouragement rather than a deterrent. But what other choice did she have? Irene was counting on her, and as Lady Truelove, she was a painfully inadequate substitute for her sister. She could not bear the idea of failing in her assignment and letting Irene down. And though this afternoon Galbraith had told her his threat to reveal Lady True-love's identity had been a bluff, she wasn't altogether sure she could trust him on that score.

"Very well," she said before she could talk herself out of this. "We have a bargain. I'll have a footman deliver the latest batch of Lady Truelove's letters to you first thing in the morning, along with a bank draft of one thousand pounds."

"Letters?" He gave a laugh, staring at her in disbelief. "You mean real letters from real people?"

"Of course. What?" she added, savoring his surprise. "Did you think we invent them?"

"Something like that, yes," he confessed, sobering, and she could tell he was appreciating the reality of what he'd just taken on.

"Sorry if you were hoping to spend the next two months writing fiction," she said, rather relishing his chagrin. "But being Lady Truelove requires you to help actual people resolve genuine problems. As I said, I'll have the latest correspondence delivered to you in the morning. From those letters, you must choose one, write a response suitable for publication, and deliver it to me by two o'clock tomorrow afternoon."

"Two o'clock? That's cutting it a bit fine, isn't it?"

"I regret the short deadline, but it can't be helped. You'll have more time for your future efforts, but the upcoming edition goes to press Saturday night."

"Today is only Thursday."

"I require time to contact your chosen correspondent and acquire formal permission to publish their letter. I will also need to make sure your answer is appropriate."

"I daresay even I can manage to be appropriate when the occasion calls for it," he said, his voice suspiciously grave.

She frowned. "Don't be glib about this. The people who write to Lady Truelove will be counting upon you for genuine guidance. I intend to make sure you don't disappoint them or guide them in a morally improper direction. And I expect you to take this job seriously."

"I shall do my best to come up to snuff. Just remember, this sort of thing works both ways."

"Meaning?"

"You've told me what you expect of me, but I haven't yet told you what I expect of you."

Clara's heart gave a hard thump against her ribs, and it was several seconds before she could respond.

"But you did tell me, remember?" she said at last, managing to inject a deceptive sweetness into her voice. "You intend to court me." She gave him a wide, bright smile. "I merely have to tolerate you."

He laughed, but before he could reply, the bells sounded, indicating that the performance was about to begin. Clara turned away and took her seat, but when Galbraith moved behind her chair and bent down close to her ear, she discovered their conversation was not quite over.

"I realize I'll be doing all the work," he murmured, his voice low so the others moving to take their seats would not overhear. "Nonetheless . . ." He paused, his warm breath against her ear making her shiver. "I think I got the better bargain, Clara."

Suddenly, every cell in her body was tingling with awareness. She could smell the sandalwood fragrance of his shaving lotion. She could feel the tickle of one unruly lock of his hair against her temple. She could almost hear the hard thud of her own heartbeat.

Thankfully, the lights dimmed. He straightened to take his own seat somewhere behind her, but though he was unable to see the evidence of how his closeness and his words affected her, she feared he was fully aware of the feelings he had evoked. He was, she acknowledged in chagrin, that sort of man.

The orchestra began to play the overture to Verdi's *Aida*, but even over the music, she could still hear his words from that afternoon echoing in her mind.

I know women.

He certainly did. And though he might be right that he was the one required to do all the work, their bargain wasn't going to be a stroll in the park for her, either. Quite the contrary, for only a few suggestive words on his part, and she could barely draw breath.

Clara pressed a hand to her tightly corseted ribs and grimaced. This mock courtship hadn't even begun, but she feared she might already be in over her head.

Chapter 9

Rex had no illusions about his own character. He liked women, he'd discovered just what delights they could offer about the time he turned fifteen, and he had never suffered any pangs of conscience about the fact that most of the delights he preferred were carnal in nature.

And though he did have certain strict rules when it came to his conduct with women, he'd never been one for suppressing naughty thoughts about them, particularly nowadays when thoughts were all he could afford. By the time he sat down behind Clara, the image of her laughing face and the orange-blossom scent of her hair had already lit the erotic fires of his imagination.

Unfortunately, the view he had of her now afforded that fire little in the way of fuel. Her back, sheathed completely in deep pink silk, her hair, swept up in its usual severe braided crown, the back of her long, slender neck—he stopped there, his gaze caught at her nape just above the edge of her evening gown.

In the dimness of the theater, her pale skin seemed to gleam like alabaster, but he'd wager it was as soft as velvet. If he leaned forward and kissed her there, he could find out for sure.

He closed his eyes, savoring the imagined texture of her skin against his mouth, and the desire in his body deepened and spread. His breathing quickened at the imagined scent of orange blossoms. A picture of her formed in his mind, an image of all that brown hair unbraided and falling loose around her small, round breasts and pale pink nipples.

Fully aroused, he shifted in his seat and grimaced, appreciating that this sort of thinking did have its drawbacks. Unrelieved, it would soon make him deuced uncomfortable. And since with her it could never be relieved, going down this road was probably unwise.

Clara Deverill was not a dancer at the Gaiety, or a woman on the town. She was innocent, pure, and definitely marriage-minded. Her opinion of his character put him just a little above—or perhaps even below— the slimy muck that lined the bottom of ponds. She might look as soft as a lamb, but she had a surprisingly steely core and a staunch sense of morality. And though she had a bit of a stammer when she was nervous, her tongue could sting him quite well when the need arose.

If he hoped any of that would put paid to his erotic imaginings, however, he was mistaken, for he immediately began contemplating various ways Clara could employ her tongue for purposes more pleasurable than stinging him, and he shifted in his seat again.

"For heaven's sake, Rex," his cousin Henrietta whispered beside him, "what is wrong with you? You're wriggling like a boy at Sunday service."

Rex gave a caustic chuckle. "You have no idea how inappropriate that analogy is right now, Hetty," he muttered and opened his eyes.

"Indeed?" purred his cousin. "Dare I wonder who is the subject of these irreverent thoughts? Do tell."

Rex cast a sideways glance at her, noting her amused expression. "Nothing to tell," he said and looked away, pretending a sudden interest in the performance going on below. "And even if there were," he added, striving to sound carelessly blasé, "it wouldn't matter. As a gentleman, I am obligated to keep mum."

"Such discretion does you credit, of course, though I shouldn't think it necessary. But then . . ." She paused, her gaze glancing sideways to the seat directly in front of his. "Perhaps we're not talking about a Gaiety Girl."

There was a question in those words, giving him the perfect opportunity to begin playing the part he'd created for himself, but before he could affirm the direction of her speculations, Clara's words of a short time ago came back to him.

What you're asking me to do is deliberately mislead the members of your family.

He stirred in his chair again, frustrated by something beyond mere physical discomfort. Guilt was an emotion he did not care for and could certainly not afford to indulge.

He did not respond to Hetty's inquiry, however. He simply smiled, and his cousin, thankfully, returned her attention to the stage.

Rex tried to do the same, but it wasn't long before

his gaze strayed again to the woman in front of him, and his imagination once again set to work. As he contemplated undoing the silk-covered buttons down her back and kissing the soft skin of her neck, he succeeded in banishing from his mind any notions of guilt about his chosen course, but these delightful contemplations also caused his lust to flare up even more hotly than before, and he appreciated he had another problem, one far more inconvenient than the whispers of his conscience, one with implications he hadn't really considered until this moment.

Clara was a woman he could not bed, and though a few lusty thoughts about her made for a damned fine diversion, if he allowed them to become a habit, his life would become damnably frustrating. Unrequited lust was a devilish thing.

The first act came to an end, and Rex knew he had about three quarters of an hour before the intermission to bring his body and mind back under stern regulation. In most cases, that would be more than enough time to distract his thoughts from a particular woman, but as he studied Clara's slim, straight back and the long, delicate line of her neck, he suspected he would need every one of those forty-five minutes.

ATTENDING THE OPERA provided few opportunities to converse with others, and Clara could only be grateful for the fact, for Galbraith's extraordinary proposition had left her rather at sixes and sevens. Looking back on it the following morning, the entire episode felt like something out of a dream.

Reminding herself that its dreamlike quality stemmed

from the fact that it was a sham courtship, Clara strove to remember her priorities. As promised, she sent him Lady Truelove's correspondence first thing in the morning, and on impulse, she enclosed a personal note as well, suggesting he consider the Devastated Debutante's letter for his first column. She strove to give her recommendation an appearance of professional interest by stressing the wide appeal of the Debutante's problem, and she hoped he wouldn't realize her action was motivated by a deeper purpose.

After dispatching the bundle of letters to his residence in Half Moon Street, she turned her attention to the articles Mr. Beale had selected for that week's edition and the layouts he had designed for them, but she couldn't seem to concentrate longer than five minutes at a time. Despite her best efforts, Galbraith and his outrageous proposal insisted on invading her mind.

I wish to court you. I should like you to allow me the privilege.

Some girls, of course, had men lined up around the block who were eager to express such sentiments, but for Clara, that sort of thing was rare indeed. Even now, eighteen hours later, his words still evoked the same undeniable thrill they had the night before. Her lips still tingled at the memory of his heated gaze.

He'd been thinking about kissing her last night. Clara had no experience with kissing at all, but she'd recognized the look in his eyes as he'd stared at her mouth. It was the same look he'd given her on the dance floor at his aunt's ball.

A kiss would break quite a few rules, wouldn't it?

The thrill within her grew stronger, and Clara scowled down at the layouts on her desk, aggravated with herself. For a man like him, a kiss was probably nothing—as easy as winking and just as easily forgotten. As for this courtship, it was a charade for the morally-questionable purpose of misleading his family, and when she thought of them—Lady Petunia, Sir Albert, and the various cousins she'd met last night, Clara couldn't help doubting herself for agreeing to such an outrageous proposition.

Still, the deed was done, the agreement made, so she tried to look on the bright side. Perhaps he was right that his notice of her would draw her to the attention of other possible suitors, suitors who might also wish to pay her romantic attentions, who might want to kiss her.

Somehow, that didn't seem quite as thrilling a prospect, and Clara tossed down her pencil with a sigh of exasperation. Damn the man, what was it about him—

A knock on her door interrupted, and Clara hastily seized her pencil. "Come in," she called, bending over the layouts and striving to seem hard at work as the door opened.

"Miss Deverill."

She looked up and felt again the inclination to sigh, but for a completely different reason. "Mr. Beale," she greeted the editor without enthusiasm. "What can I do for you? If you've come for the layouts, I've not quite finished with them, but I'll bring them to you the minute I've finished—"

"Lady Truelove's column has not yet arrived," he cut in with his usual impatience. "At least, that is what Miss Huish told me just now before she departed for lunch. Is that true?"

"Miss Huish is only going to lunch now?" Clara glanced down at the brooch watch pinned to her lapel. "But it's nearly two o'clock."

"I instructed her to wait until after she'd sorted the afternoon post, and it was late in arriving today."

Clara frowned. "It is not right to keep someone this long without a break for lunch."

"I haven't had my lunch, either, Miss Deverill," he answered sourly, "not that I expect you to care about that."

Deciding she must prove him wrong on that score, Clara wiped any hint of disapproval off her face and assumed a manner of concern, hoping to get the wretched man out of her hair as expeditiously as possible. "Oh, but I *do* care, Mr. Beale. It's abominable that you should have to go this long without your lunch! Why, you might faint away from malnourishment," she added, trying to sound appalled rather than delighted by that notion, "and then where would we be? You must go for your lunch at once."

She waved him toward the door, but to her dismay, he didn't move. "Lady Truelove's column," he reminded. "Where is it?"

"The deadline isn't until five o'clock, and since it is now only just two, I hardly think we need feel any anxiety—"

"Her column has always arrived in the Thursday afternoon post, but for the second week in a row, it has not come as expected. So, where is the blasted thing? Don't tell me the woman is late again this week?"

"I'm told the column is being delivered by hand," she replied, crossing her fingers beneath the edge of her desk where he couldn't see them, and hoping to heaven Galbraith wasn't going to let her down. "A . . . ahem . . . friend is bringing it. Any moment now—"

"A friend of hers, or yours? Either way," he added before she could answer, "I am hardly reassured, Miss Deverill."

Clara was tempted to reply that reassuring him was not one of her highest priorities, but she refrained, knowing she had to preserve at least a semblance of harmony with the man until Irene returned. At that point, Mr. Beale would become the thorn in her sister's side, thank heaven, and cease to be hers.

"That is a shame," she murmured politely and sat back down. "But for my own part, I am confident the column will be here well before the deadline, so—"

"See that it is," he interrupted again, glaring at her. "You oversee the woman, and if her column is late, I shall know who to blame."

"No need for blame," a male voice intervened, and recognizing it, Clara gave a sigh of relief. She looked past Mr. Beale to the doorway where Galbraith was standing, an envelope in his upraised fingertips and a smile curving his lips. "Lady Truelove's words of wisdom have arrived, ready to be shared with all her avid readers."

Despite this welcome news and the breezy tone of his voice, there was a curious tenseness in his wide shoulders and a strangely brittle quality to his smile, and Clara watched him in puzzlement as Mr. Beale turned and started toward the door.

"About damned time," the editor said, pausing beside Galbraith and holding out his hand.

The viscount, however, ignored him. Instead, he removed his hat and offered Clara a bow, then moved to one side of the door so that the editor might pass through.

With a sound of impatience, Mr. Beale reached out as if to take the envelope, but Galbraith evaded the move, lowering his arm and tucking the missive behind his back, still smiling, his semblance of careless ease still in place.

"You may give Lady Truelove's column to me," the editor said, his hand outstretched as if still expecting the viscount to hand it over.

Clara opened her mouth to belay that order and ask that the column be brought to her, but as she looked at Galbraith, she saw Galbraith's smile vanish, and she knew her intervention would not even be needed.

He glanced over the other man, but he didn't speak. Instead, he merely raised an eyebrow, a tiny gesture that somehow managed to convey polite disinterest and utter contempt at the same time.

From her position, Clara could only see a fraction of the editor's face, but it was enough to reveal the red flush that flooded his cheeks, and she found the picture of a discomfited Mr. Beale so delightful that she almost laughed out loud.

Despite his obvious awareness of the snub he'd just received, Mr. Beale did not take the hint and depart with good grace. "I am the editor of the *Weekly Gazette*," he said, his hand still outstretched.

"How edifying." With that, Galbraith stepped around him and started toward Clara's desk. It was a clear dismissal, and though Mr. Beale turned to scowl at the viscount's back, he did not attempt any further discussion of the subject. Instead, he stalked out of the office without another word, but he made his displeasure quite clear by slamming the door behind him.

"I believe I've given offense," Galbraith said, grinning a little as he paused in front of her, not seeming the least bit bothered by Mr. Beale's offended sensibilities.

"With that man, it's not a difficult thing to do," she assured him. "Would you mind opening the door again? The last thing I need is for any members of the staff to start gossiping about me because I'm alone with you behind closed doors."

"I don't know why you're worried about that," he said as he set aside his hat, retraced his steps, and opened the door. "It would further our purpose, wouldn't it?"

"It would not," she replied primly as he returned to her desk. "The only reason," she added, lowering her voice as she glanced past him to the open doorway, "an unmarried couple should be in such an intimate situation is if the man intends to propose. And we are hardly at that stage. You have quite a few more columns to write first."

"Quite right," he agreed. Leaning closer, he added *sotto voce*, "And we've no need to talk in whispers about Lady Truelove, Clara. There's not a soul out there."

"Everyone must be at lunch, then, even Mr. Beale. Thank heaven he's gone. We don't get on very well, I'm afraid."

"Why don't you sack him?"

Clara sighed, giving him a rueful look across the desk as she waved a hand to the chair opposite her own seat. "It's not that simple."

"I don't see why not." He settled into the offered chair. "You're in charge, aren't you?"

"Only temporarily. The paper belongs to my sister, and I am managing it only while she is away on her honeymoon. She hired Mr. Beale. Firing him is not my decision to make."

"You shouldn't have to tolerate working with horrid people."

Clara couldn't help a laugh. "Says the man who's never held a job."

He grimaced. "Sorry. That did sound terribly privileged, didn't it? Still, he was abominably rude to you."

"I'm used to it." Clara made a dismissive gesture that banished Mr. Beale. "It doesn't matter."

She stretched out her hand for the envelope, but Galbraith didn't give it to her. Instead, he frowned, tilting his head to one side and giving her a thoughtful look across the desk. "You don't really believe that, surely?"

She stared back at him, uncertain what he was referring to. "Believe what?"

"That the way you are treated by others doesn't matter."

She watched his frown deepen as he spoke until it was almost a scowl. "You're angry," she murmured, taken aback.

"Should I not be? To see you undeservedly berated and then to hear you confess you are accustomed to such treatment and that it doesn't matter . . . should I not be angry?"

She stared at him, noting the glint in his brilliant eyes and the rigid set of his perfect jaw. She'd seen him angry before, but this time, she realized, it was different. This time, his anger was on her behalf.

Tightness squeezed her chest, making it hard to

breathe, or even think. Her lips parted, but any sort of reply proved beyond her, and before she knew it, her lips were curving into a smile instead.

That smile seemed to make him self-conscious, for he stirred in his chair and looked away. "Any man would be angry, I daresay," he muttered. "I could hardly restrain myself from seizing him by the collar and hurling him into the street."

The pleasure she felt widened, opening inside her like a flower in the sun, because despite what he seemed to believe, men willing to toss other men into the street on her behalf had until now been a nonexistent species.

He looked at her again, and Clara pressed the smile from her lips, for he seemed embarrassed, and she didn't want to exacerbate it. "As much as I appreciate your offer to dispatch Mr. Beale into the street, I'd rather you didn't. It would be momentarily satisfying, I admit, but it would also make my life more difficult. As for the rest," she added as he opened his mouth to argue the point, "when I said I'm used to it and it doesn't matter, all I meant was that he makes it plain what he thinks of me at every opportunity, but I don't set enough store by his opinion to care."

"And what is his opinion?"

"That I am just a silly girl, too immature and foolish to be involved in business matters."

"Then he's the foolish one."

"Perhaps, but to be wholly fair, it's true that I have no experience being in charge. I was Irene's secretary for a time, but that's all. And Mr. Beale's understanding was that he'd be working under my brother Jonathan's supervision. Upon my sister's marriage, my brother was supposed to come home from America, go into partnership with her, and take over managing things. Mr. Beale took the position as editor under those terms. But Jonathan kept putting off his return, and now, he has decided to stay in America for the foreseeable future, so Mr. Beale and I are stuck with each other until Irene returns."

"None of that is your fault. The man ought to accept the situation as it stands with good grace."

Clara made a face. "He doesn't yet know about my brother's decision to stay in America. I keep putting off telling him about Jonathan, because when I do tell him, I'm sure he'll resign. Still, I suppose it's unfair of me to keep the knowledge from him—"

Galbraith's sound of derision interrupted her. "I shouldn't worry about that, not with a man like him. What's unfair is that your brother and sister have left you here to deal with their problem."

"About my brother, you may have a point, but as for my sister, it's not like that at all. Irene has always looked after me and our father. When we had no money and we were about to lose our home, she was the one who saved us. She started this paper and earned enough of an income from it to provide for us, and I am glad of the chance to do something for her. That said, when she returns, I shall happily hand the paper back over to her, and Mr. Beale along with it."

"At which point, he'll learn he'll still be working for a woman, and he'll probably quit anyway."

"Possibly, but Irene can hire someone else at that point. As for Mr. Beale, I don't know that his resentment stems from working for a woman per se, or if it's that he just doesn't like working for me. I'm afraid my sister does a far better job of being a publisher than I do."

"Stuff. I've no doubt you're doing an excellent job in your sister's stead. You've enough sense to hire excellent staff," he added with a grin, pointing at himself, "and that's probably the greatest talent one needs when one's in charge of a business enterprise."

She gave him a wry smile in return. "Thank you for the vote of confidence, but I can't imagine I'm a better judge of who to hire than my sister. Irene is usually an excellent judge of character. She's also a suffragist, and if Beale held any resentment against women with careers, I can't imagine that she wouldn't have sensed it when she interviewed him."

He shrugged. "Not everyone proves to be as worthy at their job as they might seem in interviews. Any butler or housekeeper could tell you that. And your sister was about to be married, wasn't she? She might have been too preoccupied with wedding plans to notice his defects."

"Perhaps." Clara was doubtful. "Distracted or not, it's not like Irene to make a mistake."

"Everyone makes mistakes."

"Not my sister." Clara laughed at his frown of skepticism. "It's obvious you've never met her."

"I shall look forward to the privilege of doing so," he murmured, a frown etching between his brows. "I've never met a paragon."

"Not a paragon, but close to it," Clara assured him, happy to boast of Irene's many talents. "She succeeds at everything she does. She's brilliant, confident, accomplished, clever, and if all that's not enough, she's beautiful, too. And she has excellent business instincts."

"Does she?" His frown deepened, and a muscle moved at the corner of his jaw. "Does she, indeed?"

His voice was tense, the question terse, and Clara looked at him in bewilderment. "What's wrong? You seem quite vexed."

"Do I?" His frown vanished at once. "I daresay it's watching you pull your punches with Mr. Beale that's put me out of sorts."

Clara blinked in surprise. "But why should you care? It's not as if—"

She broke off as that hot tightness squeezed her chest again. It felt like one of her bouts of shyness, only more acute, and yet . . . sweeter, too. He spoke as if he were genuinely concerned about her well-being, and yet, they barely knew each other.

She swallowed hard, reminding herself that making any woman, even one he didn't know, feel singled out and extraordinary was as natural to him as breathing. It didn't mean anything to him, not really. She cleared her throat, and when she spoke, she worked to put an indifferent note into her voice that she was far from feeling. "I don't see why it matters to you."

"Well, for one thing, you never pull your punches with me," he grumbled. "How is it that man gets more polite accommodation out of you than I do? It hurts, Clara, really."

She smiled, recognizing that he was teasing now. "The reason's plain enough, isn't it? Beale might quit on me. You can't."

"Thank you for the reminder. I feel so much better about it all now."

"In all seriousness, despite his antipathy for me, Mr. Beale is an excellent editor." Even as she spoke, she felt a sudden whisper of doubt. "He must be," she added at once, squelching that traitorous feeling before it could take hold.

"Of course," Galbraith agreed, his voice so agreeably bland that she felt compelled to justify.

"It's not really my place to judge the editor's qualifications. Besides, editor is the most crucial person on the staff, and if Beale quit, I'd be lost. I feel obliged to muddle through with him as best I can, don't you see?"

"I do see. And that's why it's aggravating as hell." Despite his words, his voice was gentle. "What you really mean is that you have doubts about his abilities, but because he was your sister's choice and your sister seemingly never makes mistakes, you tell yourself over and over that the man must be worthy of the post and that your own instincts, not your sister's, must be at fault. In other words, Clara, you lack confidence in yourself, and because of that, you trust your sister's judgement more than you trust your own."

She inhaled sharply, surprised by the accuracy of his conclusions, though she knew she shouldn't be. His understanding of people was what caused them to seek his advice and the entire reason she'd thought him qualified to write Lady Truelove in the first place. "You're very perceptive. But you're not here to talk about me," she added at once. "You're supposed to be solving someone else's problem, not mine, remember?"

"In this case," he said gently, "it's rather the same thing, isn't it?"

At once, she knew what he meant, and she looked

away, her face growing hot. In recommending the Devastated Debutante's letter, she ought to have known he'd perceive her true motives. How could he not? She looked at him again, forcing a laugh. "And I thought I was being so subtle."

He held up the envelope, smiling a little. "Would you like to know what advice I gave the Devastated Debutante?"

She was dying to know, but she shrugged, pride impelling her to assume a diffident air. "I shall know at some point, since I have to approve what you wrote."

He chuckled. "Quite right," he agreed, but when she held out her hand for the envelope, he didn't give it to her. Instead, still smiling, he propped his elbows on her desk, broke the seal, and pulled out the folded sheets within.

"'Dear Debutante,'" he began, casting aside the envelope, "'navigating the social season can seem a daunting task, particularly for the shy, but take heart. There is a secret to attracting others, even those of the opposite sex, and if you can successfully implement it, I promise that a more enjoyable season and life await you. That secret, my dear, is simply to *relax*.'"

"Relax?" Bemused, Clara made a face. "That's your advice?"

"Yes," he answered firmly. "And if you'll allow me, I am happy to elucidate further."

She sat back, lifting her hands in a gesture of capitulation. "Carry on, then."

"'To accomplish this, to achieve the ease of manner that will draw others to you, I advise beginning with the simplest changes first: those regarding your appearance—'"

"I don't see what one's appearance has to do with anything," she interrupted again, a bit nettled.

He looked up again with a sigh, giving her a look of mock sternness over the top of the pages. "And you never will see if you keep interrupting."

"Sorry," she mumbled. "Go on."

"'Gentlemen, it must be said, are visual creatures, but this does not mean they care about fashion. Leave tight corseting and high-heeled slippers behind, for they do little to help any young lady feel comfortable and relaxed. If you have fine eyes, avoid wide-brimmed hats unless you are in the sun, for though such hats may be fashionable, they prevent young men from looking into your eyes, and eyes are the windows to the soul. If you have a nice smile, bestow it as often as you can comfortably do, for it will draw others to you and help you feel more at ease, attractive, and confident. Find a modiste whose gowns will enhance the favorable aspects of your figure, and trust me when I say that if a young lady has marital ambitions, displaying a bit of décolleté in her ball gown is not a bad thing.'"

Clara made a sound of derision, causing him to pause again, though not, she soon discovered, to chide her for interrupting.

"I take it you don't agree?" he asked.

"I doubt a girl's odds of fulfilling her marital ambitions would be all that enhanced by lowering her neckline. Seems terribly superficial, if you ask me."

"Indeed?" His gaze swept down, making her blush all over and giving her cause to wish she'd kept her mouth shut. After a moment, he looked up again. "As a man, Clara, I have to say that you underestimate the power of a well-cut ball gown."

She wriggled in her chair, acutely self-conscious. "Isn't it at least as important to suggest ways the poor girl can make conversation?"

He laughed. "In a word, no."

Unamused, she folded her arms, giving him a pointed look across the desk.

"Oh, very well," he said with a sigh. "Since you're so insistent . . ." With that, he lifted the pages and resumed reading.

"'But what, you are surely asking, do you say once you've succeeded in attracting some splendid young man and he is standing in front of you? If you can think of nothing to say about yourself, seek a topic that enables the other person to talk. Being a good listener is always appreciated and far more charming to others than being a skilled conversationalist. Whatever you say, strive to put the other person at ease, and you will soon find that skillful repartee is not necessary. If all else fails, there is nothing wrong with acknowledging your shy nature. The response you receive will often be relief and a similar confession, thus giving you and your new acquaintance something in common to talk about. And remember, if you say something silly or make a mistake, acknowledge it at once and laugh about it.'"

"That's easy to advise," she objected, causing him to look up. "But it's not so easy to do."

"It's not easy at all," he said. "But it's useful."

"Is that why you do it?"

He smiled and returned his attention to the pages in his hand. "'Self-deprecation,'" he read, "'is not only a disarming quality, dear Debutante, but if you learn to employ it, you will soon discover benefits to yourself.

For the ability to laugh at ourselves and our mistakes is incredibly liberating. It frees us from any burden of worry over saying or doing the wrong thing. And that brings me back to my first point, one I cannot stress strongly enough to you. Shy people worry too much.'"

Clara grimaced, for that was a contention she could not refute, at least not about herself.

"'Convinced every eye in the room is upon them and that everything they do is being judged unfavorably,'" he went on, "'shy people find it impossible to relax. Their worries are usually unfounded, for other people are far too preoccupied with their own concerns to worry much about anyone else, but shy people, alas, never seem to believe this. Dire predictions of social failure fill their heads, preventing them from attaining the relaxed air so necessary to attract and hold the attention of others, and as a result, shy people spend most of their time at social functions wishing they were anywhere else. This demeanor, though not the true reasons for it, is painfully obvious to others, who react by seeking more ebullient companions. Thus, the shy person's exaggerated fears become self-fulfilling prophecy, and the shy find little enjoyment in the pleasures and pastimes of society.'"

Clara bit her lip, appreciating that he had just given voice to the pattern of her entire social experience.

"'Do not shortchange yourself this way, dear Debutante. The quality of your season does not depend on one dance, or one conversation, and the quality of your life does not depend on one season. Strive to set your fears aside. Cast away your expectations, forget the ambitions of your parents, and set aside the goal of seeking someone to marry. In all your engagements, strive only to enjoy yourself. Smile and laugh and savor every moment of your life, and one day, you may find someone at your side who longs to share that life with you.'"

He looked up, lowering the pages, and Clara suddenly felt it was of vital importance to tidy her desk. She straightened her blotter and moved her inkstand a bit more to the left, donning an air of businesslike nonchalance.

"Well?" he prompted when she didn't speak. "Don't keep me in suspense. Is my first attempt to be Lady Truelove satisfactory?"

Satisfactory? Her hand tightened around a sheaf of papers. What a tame word to describe the sort of insight she'd been looking to find ever since she turned thirteen, put up her hair, and went to a party where there were boys. She'd always been aware of her inhibited nature, yet she'd never appreciated just how much it could inhibit others. "It's—" She broke off, set the papers aside with a cough, and looked at him. "It's very good. Excellent, in fact."

"Thank you, but . . ." He paused, giving her a grin. "You could at least smile when you say that."

She laughed, and for no reason she could define, his grin vanished.

"Now, that's a bit of all right," he murmured. "Smile like that at the next ball, Clara, and you'll have every man in the room eating out of your hand."

She sobered, swallowing hard. He was exaggerating, of course, but she didn't say so. Instead, she held out her hand for the pages.

"I'll have Miss Huish type this," she said forcing herself to sound briskly efficient as he gave her the column, "and deliver it to Mr. Beale with the instruction that he isn't to edit a single word. Although . . ." She paused, tapping her index finger against one line of his handwriting as a thought struck her. "This bit about how a good listener has more charm than a good talker . . ."

"Yes? What about it?"

She looked up. "That's what you do, isn't it?" As she asked the question, she thought of Elsie Clark, and she knew the answer. "You're not a shy person, but you do that with people, don't you? Listen, rather than talk. Is it to get people to like you or is it a natural talent for you?"

"Both, I suppose." He made a face. "I fear you've uncovered my deepest secret, Clara. I have a compulsive desire to be liked. It's something I've had all my life, but it stems—I have no doubt—from the fact that I have a pair of self-absorbed and completely impossible parents. They spent most of my youth so occupied with destroying each other that they often forgot I existed. It hurt, you see. It hurt like hell." He paused and drew a breath. "Still does, if you want the truth."

She studied his face, suddenly seeing past the flawless symmetry of his features, past the perfect aquiline nose and splendid square jaw and azure blue eyes, seeing the boy he'd once been and the parents he'd just described. Somehow, imagining it hurt her, too, and she couldn't help wondering again if her first impression of him as a heartless cad might have been utterly wrong.

Before either of them could speak, a cough interrupted, and Clara looked past him to find Annie standing in the doorway.

"Begging your pardon, Miss Clara, but . . ." Annie paused, giving her a look of warning that put her instantly on guard. "Your father sent me down."

"What a timely interruption," Galbraith murmured, his voice light. "Another moment, Clara, and God only knows what further confessions you'd have gotten out of me."

He turned toward the doorway, and Clara saw Annie's eyes widen in pleasurable surprise. It was the sort of reaction he probably got from every housemaid who ever laid eyes on him, and one that brought Clara squarely back to reality.

"Yes, Annie?" she asked. "What does Papa want?"

The maid tore her gaze from the viscount with what seemed to be a great deal of effort. "He wants to know about tea, Miss Clara."

"Tea?" She stared back at the maid in dismay.

"Yes, miss." Annie's pale gray eyes took on a hint of apology. "He wants to invite his lordship up to the drawing room for tea."

At that unthinkable prospect, Clara's dismay deepened into horror. She loved her father, but tea with him was always a difficult business, and with a stranger present, it would be unbearable. "For heaven's sake," she mumbled, rubbing her fingers over her forehead, "how does Papa even know Lord Galbraith is here?"

"I believe I can explain that," the viscount put in. "I came to your front door, not perceiving there was an entrance to the newspaper office beside it. The woman who opened the door to me offered to bring me through the house and around, but I told her not to bother and I would use the street entrance. But I did leave my card with her, of course."

"Mrs. Brandt, that would be, my lord," the maid volunteered. "She's the housekeeper. If you do decide to come up, she'll be wanting to know if you prefer India or China tea?"

"It's only half past two," Clara put in before the viscount could answer, and the sharpness of her own voice made her wince. But she couldn't help it, for she was desperate to prevent this calamity. "It's far too early for—"

"Tea would be lovely," Galbraith said cutting the ground right from beneath her feet, and Clara nearly groaned aloud. "Tell Mr. Deverill I would be delighted to accept his invitation, Annie, thank you. And please inform Mrs. Brandt that I would prefer whichever tea is Miss Clara's particular favorite."

The maid giggled at that, but then she caught sight of Clara's face and sobered at once, giving a cough. "That be India tea, my lord," she murmured. "Darjeeling."

"Excellent." With a nod to the girl, he turned back around, returning his attention to Clara, and Annie departed, giving Clara a glance of sympathetic understanding just before she vanished from view.

The maid's sympathy only deepened her dismay, and Clara frowned at Galbraith. "That was rather high-handed."

"Was it?" he asked in surprise. "The invitation was directed to me, and I accepted it. Speaking of invitations, I have one to give you." He started to reach into his breast pocket, but stopped as he caught sight of her expression. "My apologies," he said quietly, his hand falling to his side. "I didn't realize you would mind if I came to tea."

"It's not that," she cried. "I don't mind . . . exactly. It's just—"

She broke off, for the truth was too humiliating to utter, and her mind couldn't seem to fashion a believable reason for her reluctance.

"I'm supposed to be courting you, remember?" he said, a gentle reminder that only seemed to make everything worse. "Meeting your father is something I would be required to do at some point, Clara."

He was right, of course. "Very well," she muttered and stood up, chin high, trying to ignore the shame that was already flooding through her. "Let's have tea. Just don't expect a party."

Chapter 10

Rex had never considered himself a dense sort of chap. In fact, he rather took pride in his ability to appreciate the undercurrents of a social situation and the reasons for them. In this case, however, he had to admit himself utterly baffled.

Clara didn't want him to meet her father—that much was clear. Her shoulders were set, her chin high, her expression wooden, and as they crossed the foyer, her profile reminded him of nothing so much as the nautical figurehead of a ship as it sailed into the teeth of a storm. The rapidity of her stride told him she wanted that storm over as quickly as possible.

She led him up the stairs and along a corridor, offering no explanations along the way, but once in the drawing room, the introduction to her father had barely been made before Rex realized no explanations would be needed.

The man was sodding drunk.

Quite accustomed to men in their cups, Rex schooled his features in the polite civility required of a gentleman and bowed, but as he straightened, he cast a sideways glance at Clara, and his polite veneer almost cracked.

Her face bore its usual placid coolness, but her eyes gave her away. They stared into his chin, dark and bleak and filled with shame. Looking into them was like looking into an abyss.

"Forgive me for not standing up to receive you, Lord Galbraith," Deverill said, a distinct slur in his voice and a strong waft of brandy in the air as he spoke. "Blasted gout."

Rex returned his attention to her parent, noting the wheeled chair in which he sat, and the foot propped on a heavily padded stool in front of it, and he wondered if the drinking had caused the gout, or vice-versa. "There is no need for apology, sir. Gout, I understand, hurts like the devil."

"It does, it does." Deverill picked up his teacup from the table beside him, and his hand trembled as he raised it to his lips, causing the amber liquid to spill over and another wave of brandy scent to hit Rex's nostrils.

Clara must have detected the scent as well, for she moved away from her parent, making for the settee across the room. "Will you sit down, Lord Galbraith?" she said, issuing the invitation with a painfully obvious lack of enthusiasm, and as she sank down on one end of the settee and gestured for him to sit at the other end, he wondered if he ought to make some excuse and leave instead. On the other hand, a hasty departure was probably the usual reaction of guests when faced with this situation, and if he ran for the door, it might serve only to deepen her shame. Besides, he still had Auntie Pet's invitation in his pocket.

"Thank you, yes," he said, then set his hat on a nearby table and moved to take the offered place on the settee, striving to act as if nothing at all was amiss.

"Delighted you could join us, my lord, and that Clara has a suitor at last."

"Papa," she protested, giving Rex an agonized glance, which he ignored. Since being a suitor was just the image he was attempting to convey, he had no intention of contradicting the description by word or deed.

"Now, Clara," Deverill said, heedless of his daughter's protest, "it's nothing to be embarrassed about. You've only been out for a short while. Clara's sister, Lord Galbraith, married the Duke of Torquil not long ago." It was a boast, dragged into the conversation by a man who wished to impress another with his connections. Clara knew it, too, for when Rex cast a sideways glance at her, he saw her wince and turn away to reach for the teapot.

"Would you like tea, Lord Galbraith?" she asked, her voice sounding an octave higher than usual as she began to pour.

"Thank you, yes. Plain," he added as she reached for the sugar tongs. "No sugar or milk."

She turned in his direction to hand him his cup and saucer, but she didn't quite look at him.

"Notice she doesn't offer her father any tea," Deverill said, lifting his own cup, tilting it back and forth a little, grinning as he gave Rex the knowing look of one man of the world to another. "She knows it's not necessary. I've got my tea already."

Rex felt a wave of pity. "Yes," he agreed mildly. "So it would seem."

His reply must surely have conveyed something of what he felt, but Deverill didn't seem to notice. His daughter, however, was a different matter.

"Sandwich?" she asked, her voice still unnaturally bright. "Or would you prefer a scone with cream and jam?"

When he looked into her face, he banished any hint of pity from his own, for that emotion was one he sensed she would not welcome. "A scone would be lovely, thank you."

"Do you know His Grace?" Deverill asked.

"Not well, I'm afraid." Rex took the plate Clara handed him, placed it on his lap, and once again turned his attention to the other man. "Though we have met, of course."

"He and Irene are in Italy on honeymoon. Taking their time about it, too," he added with a chuckle. "Marriage seems to agree with her. Would you ever have guessed that, Clara?"

"Not in a hundred years, Papa. My sister," she added for Rex's benefit, "had often declared quite adamantly that she'd never marry."

Deverill gave a bark of laughter. "Funny that. The daughter who vowed she'd never marry has made a brilliant match and is off on her honeymoon, and the one who's always wanted a husband and children more than anything is still waiting her turn. You've

got the connections now, Clara, so best get on with it."
He gave Rex a meaningful glance as he spoke. "Don't
want to be forever outshone by your sister, do you?"

Rex slid his gaze to the girl beside him, watching
as the color in her cheeks deepened, and he decided it
was time to offer her Auntie's invitation and take his
leave. He finished his scone, but before he could down
the last of his tea and depart, the door opened and a
man entered the room.

"Begging your pardon, sir," he said to Mr. Deverill,
"but Dr. Munro is here for your weekly appointment."

"Bah, doctors," Deverill said, an indignant sound
that made his opinion of the medical profession quite
clear. "Send him away."

"Really, Papa, you do need to see the doctor occasionally," Clara said before the manservant could turn
to leave again. "And you never know. He might have
some new treatment to offer."

"I doubt it. Munro's a dour Scotsman. His idea of
how to prolong one's life is to take away all the things
that make life worth living."

"See him for my sake, then," she said, beckoning
the servant into the room. "If not for your own."

"Oh, very well," he grumbled as the servant crossed
the room toward him. "But it's so unnecessary. All
Munro will do is look at me with all that disapproval
of his, and tell me not to drink."

"Then your meeting with him should be blissfully
short," she pointed out, the cheery determination in
her voice reminiscent of a nursery governess dealing
with a recalcitrant child.

"I doubt it," he shot back as the manservant moved
behind his wheeled chair and released the brake

mechanism. "The list of things I'm not supposed to have grows longer by the day. No strong cheese, no animal fats, no drink of any kind, no sugar, no milk— not even in tea . . . I ask you, Clara, what's left on a man's plate after all that's taken away?"

She didn't offer a reply to his question, but as the valet rolled her father's chair past her seat, she stood up, signaling the manservant to pause.

Rex rose as well, watching her as she leaned down to kiss her father's cheek, a tender regard for her parent that—in his opinion at least—the other man did not deserve.

"I will see you tomorrow, Papa," she said as she resumed her seat. "In the meantime, do try to obey the doctor, hmm?"

Still grumbling, he was wheeled out of the drawing room, but as they departed, he gestured for his valet to close the door behind them, giving his daughter a conspiratorial wink over his shoulder just before it swung shut.

Clara's cheeks were now absolute scarlet. She made a sound, half sigh and half groan. "I am so sorry about that," she mumbled, lowering her head into her hand as if to hide her hot face. "One's parents," she added with a smothered laugh, "can be so embarrassing."

Despite the laughter, it was obvious that she was not amused. "I am the one who should apologize," he answered at once. "Forgive me. If I had known—"

"It's quite all right," she interrupted, sparing them both his self-recriminations on the subject. Lowering her hand, she straightened in her seat and looked at him. "As you pointed out, you'd have been expected to meet him sometime."

"Yes, but we could have arranged it for a time when he would be . . . himself."

"I doubt it. He hasn't been himself since I was eleven." The moment the words were out of her mouth, she grimaced, pressing her palm to her forehead. "Heavens, I don't know what made me say that. Most of the time, other people have to pry words out of me." She stirred a little on her end of the settee. "But you already knew that," she added in a low voice.

"Yes, although . . ." He paused, giving her a frown of mock aggravation. "I've not seen much of this reticence, myself, Clara. You don't ever seem to hold your tongue with me."

"Goodness, I don't, really, do I?" she said with a laugh. Then her smile faded a bit as she considered. "That's because of you, I expect, not me. You're very good at . . . drawing people out."

"That can be said to work both ways, for I rarely talk about my parents, particularly about what life with them was like before they separated. I certainly never discuss it with anyone outside the family. Well, now," he added, trying to inject a lightness into his voice, "today has been quite the day for sharing confidences, hasn't it? Given how we started, who'd have thought you and I would ever be doing that?"

"Neither of us, that's certain. Are we . . ." She paused, her expression taking on a hint of surprise as she turned toward him on the settee. "Are we becoming friends, do you think?"

Through the window beyond her shoulder, sunlight suddenly flooded the room, making him blink. Leaning sideways a little to keep the light out of his eyes, he studied her where she sat at the other end of the settee.

The ray of sunshine that fell over her formed a nimbus of light behind her coronet of soft brown hair and gave her an angelic appearance. But when he looked down, he noted that the sun also made the silhouette of her body plainly visible through her white shirtwaist.

At once, desire stirred within him, making it clear that his body, at least, did not want to be her friend.

Still, with a girl like her and a man like him, there was no other course possible, and with profound regret, he tore his gaze away from the shadowy outline of her shape. "Perhaps we are," he said and took a swallow of tea, rather wishing his own cup had brandy in it, for he could really do with a drink. Absent that, conversation seemed his only distraction from the dangerous direction of his thoughts.

"What happened when you were eleven?" he asked, handing over his empty plate and settling back against the arm of the settee with his tea as the sun moved behind clouds again. "Sorry if I'm prying," he added at once, hoping she'd tell him anyway.

"My mother died. My father was quite a hellion in his youth, but when he married my mother, he promised her he'd reform. Unfortunately, he kept that promise only until she died. After that, he took to drink again. I suppose after her death he saw no reason to refrain."

"No reason? What about you and your sister?"

"Until this year, he's been manageable enough. But now, with Irene married, and me staying with the duke's family for the season, he's gotten much worse. There's no one here to check him, you see. It seems any time I come up to visit him, he's always—" She paused, lifting one hand toward the door. "Well, you've seen for yourself how he is."

"And your brother? Could he do nothing about it?"

"Papa would never listen to Jonathan. They quarreled years ago, Papa tossed him out of the house, and he went to America to make his own way. They haven't spoken since, for my father refuses to answer Jonathan's letters or heal the breach. So, even if Jonathan were here, he'd hardly be able to exert any influence. In fact, if my brother crossed our threshold, I doubt he'd have the chance to give Papa a lecture on his drinking. The house would combust before he could get in a word."

Rex smiled in commiseration. "I know what you mean. I shudder to think what might happen if my mother and father were ever in the same room together again. One of them would end up dead, I've no doubt. Your father and your brother sound very much the same. Did your father's drinking cause the breach?"

"Partly. Papa became erratic and foolhardy, making foolish business decisions and spending money like water, and the drinking contributed to his poor judgement, I'm sure. When Jonathan pointed that out, that's when Papa tossed him out." She paused and took a sip of tea. "You know, when I see my father like this, I wonder if I should forgo the remainder of the season. Perhaps I should return home before he gets any worse."

"I doubt it would matter if you did."

"I daresay you're right. Irene and I used to search the house, tossing out his brandy bottles whenever we found any, but he always managed to get more somehow. His valet, I suppose. Anyway, I would ask that you disregard the things he said. Particularly," she added, wincing, "his blatant matchmaking efforts."

"My great-aunt is rather the same. Another thing you and I seem to have in common." Rex smiled, hoping to ease her embarrassment. "It's awful when they're so obvious about it, isn't it? Still, however clumsy his efforts, you can't really blame him for trying to help you gain what you want from life."

"I don't blame him," she answered at once. "I realize he is motivated by a genuine concern on my behalf. I think he knows—" She broke off and a hint of pain crossed her face. "I think he knows," she resumed after a moment, "that he'll kill himself with drink one day, and I think he wants to see me settled properly before that day comes."

"He knows, and yet, he won't stop the drink?"

Clara's sweet face took on a hard glimmer of cynicism that hurt him, somehow. "Should he?" she asked. "Can a rake ever genuinely reform?"

He inhaled sharply, sensing they were not talking only about her parent any longer, but what could he say in his own defense? He'd indulged his rakish tendencies at every opportunity when he'd been able to afford it, and though he lived more like a monk than a rake nowadays, no one knew that. And besides, he'd probably go back to his previous wild ways at the first opportunity, because . . . why not?

"No," he said, the admission a bit bitter on his tongue. "I suppose true rakes don't reform. But let's talk about a more pleasant subject. You, for instance."

"Me?"

"It's a more interesting topic than your father's fondness for brandy."

"Well, a less embarrassing one, at any rate," she said with a hint of humor. "What would you like to know?"

He considered a moment. "Why do you want so much to be married?"

"Nearly every girl wants that, I suppose."

"An answer which neatly sidesteps the question. I'm curious as to why you want it."

She seemed a bit surprised, as if the answer was obvious. "Until a woman marries, she has no real purpose in the world. Oh, she can work for charity and help the vicar with parish activities and perfect her needlework. If she's fortunate, she can go into society, but unless she wants to be like my sister and defy all the conventions, she's stuck in a life that is quite dull, until she marries."

He couldn't help a laugh at that. "I know many married women, and I can assure you that most of them are bored silly."

"Perhaps, but God willing, a married woman has at least one preoccupation that is denied to single women. She has children to care for."

"Not all women would regard that as a blessing. How do you know you would do so?"

She laughed. "I've known since I was thirteen. Our cousin Susan became ill that summer, and I went to Surrey to help care for her. She and her husband have eight children and a big house in the country, and because my father had taken to drink again, Irene thought it would be good for me to go away for a bit. In Surrey, I discovered not only how much I love children, but also that I have a talent for managing them." She paused, and though she didn't smile, her face lit up suddenly, as if the sun had just come back out, as if she was looking through him, past him, into her future. "If I had children, I'd never be bored."

His cynical side was impelled to remind her of reality. "Yes, you would."

"Well, perhaps I would sometimes," she said. Unexpectedly, she grinned. "But not often, I can promise you, because like my cousin Susan, I intend to have at least eight. Maybe ten. How often can one be bored with a family of ten? What?" she added, her grin changing to a puzzled frown as he laughed.

"Ten children, my sweet, is not a family. It's a village."

"Oh, I want that, too," she assured him. "A village, I mean."

"Greedy girl."

"I am, I confess it. I want that big house in the country, and I want a village nearby, and thatched-roof cottages, and a parish church. And horses and dogs and apple orchards and a husband who loves me like mad."

"And you'll all live happily ever after," he said solemnly.

She made a face at him. "Make fun of me if you like, but that's the life I want."

"Is it?" he asked before he could stop himself. "Or is it merely that you want escape from the life you've had?"

Her smile vanished, her face went stiff, and he wanted to bite his tongue off. Still, damn it all, with that rosy picture in her head, she was just begging for life to disappoint her. Worse, he was reasonably sure she had no idea how easy it would be for a man to take advantage of her idealistic view. He could just imagine some wastrel with a glib tongue and an eye on her newly-acquired connections giving her a line of patter about life in the country and plenty of children, and she'd fall right into his lap like a ripe plum. Her father would certainly not be able to protect her from such a man.

Still, it wasn't any of his business what she chose for her life. "My apologies," he muttered. "That was a boorish thing to say."

"Yes," she agreed, giving him no quarter. "It was."

"You mustn't mind the things I say, Clara. Anyone who knows me well knows I'm a terribly cynical fellow."

Strangely, the stiffness eased out of her face, and she smiled a little. "I don't know you well at all, and I'm already aware of that fact."

He chuckled. "Fair enough. I just hope I haven't ruined this friendship of ours before it's even begun? Because if I have," he added before she could answer, reaching into his pocket and pulling out the invitation, "you won't accept this, and my great-aunt will shred me into spills, a painful experience I'd prefer to avoid."

"And what is this?" she asked as she took the envelope from him.

"Petunia and several of her friends have arranged a picnic party in Hyde Park for Wednesday next. I called upon my aunt earlier today, and when I mentioned my next order of business was a call upon you, she asked me to deliver it. The duke's family is included in the invitation, by the way."

"Thank you. It was very kind of your aunt to invite me, and to include them. I can't say if we are free that day until I ascertain their schedules."

"Of course. The doings will be just across from Galbraith House, so come through the Stanhope Gate.

They're setting up a big marquee, I understand, so you're sure to find us."

She nodded and set the envelope on the tea tray beside her, then returned her attention to him. "About what you said a moment ago . . ."

"Yes?" he prompted when she paused.

"I don't deny that I am hoping to trade the life I have known for one that I believe would make me happier. You think that is my attempt to run from my father's drinking?"

"Isn't it?"

She thought about it for a moment, then she shook her head. "No, I don't think so. Because no matter how much I might wish to escape—as you put it—I would never make a marriage for any reason other than deep and mutual love."

"Love?" He sighed. "My dear girl, why would you ever marry for love? Don't you want to be happy?"

"Says the man who tells me not to pay attention to anything he says."

"In this case, you should, because I'm in dead earnest, Clara. If you are looking for happiness in marriage, love is hardly a reliable indicator."

"Oh?" she countered, quirking a brow at him as she lifted her teacup. "And I suppose your experience as a single man has given you such extensive experience with matrimony?"

He stirred, suddenly on the defensive. "I've never been married, that is true. Nor even in love, actually, but—"

"What?" she interrupted, staring at him as if she couldn't believe what she was hearing. "You've never been in love before?"

"No."

"Never?" She straightened on the settee, glanced away, set aside her tea, and looked at him again, still seeming quite confounded by this news. "Not even once?"

"No."

She shook her head, laughing a little. "And of the two of us, I thought I was the one with the lack of experience in matters of romance," she murmured. "Heavens, even I have been in love before."

He stared at her, too surprised to point out that one could have a great deal of romance without falling in love. "You have?"

"Of course. His name was Samuel Harlow, and he was the best-looking man I'd ever met—well, except for you, of course. He—"

"Wait," he begged, holding up one hand to stop her, for he needed a moment to absorb what he'd just heard. "You think I'm good-looking?" He paused and laughed in disbelief. "*You* do?"

"Oh, stop fishing for compliments. You know you're a handsome man, and you hardly need me to tell you so."

Well, yes, he supposed he did know it, and yet, from her, it seemed something of a revelation. "On the contrary," he murmured. "In this case, I think I am in need of a compliment or two. Besides, we've become friends now, and one ought to compliment one's friends. But I can see you've no intention of buttering me up any more today," he added with a sigh of mock regret when she made no reply, "so carry on. Who was this Harlow chap?"

"Mr. Harlow arrived in our parish the summer I

turned seventeen, and I fell in love with him the moment I laid eyes on him. We saw each other quite often, for he lived just two blocks from here. I also saw him at church, of course, and sometimes we would invite him to luncheon or tea with us afterward—Papa wasn't as bad then as he is now. In those days, he didn't usually start drinking until well after tea time. Anyway, whenever Mr. Harlow came, I was always the one to whom he paid his attentions. Me," she added as if in surprise, pressing a hand to her chest. "Not Irene."

Rex felt a surge of frustration at this self-deprecating comparison to her sister. He thought of how she'd looked a few moments ago, with the sun revealing her lithe, slim silhouette to his gaze, and he was sorely tempted to haul her over to his end of the settee and show her a few of the reasons a man might pay her his attentions. With great effort, however, he managed to refrain. "And you found such attentions surprising, did you?"

"Well, it had never happened to me before. Men are usually too occupied with staring at my sister to notice I'm even in the room." She paused and laughed. "But then, of course, Irene would say something about her goal to achieve the vote for women, and we'd never see the chap again." Her laughter faded to a thoughtful frown. "I sometimes think she said things like that on purpose, to drive them away because they admired her instead of me, as if afraid my feelings would be hurt."

He didn't want to talk about her practically perfect sister. "So, you fell in love with this man," he said. "What happened next?"

"One day, we were in the vestry alone together. It was after some parish meeting for a charity bazaar."

He lifted a brow. "Why, Clara, you naughty girl."

Her tiny nose wrinkled up ruefully. "It wasn't my intent to be naughty, but even if it had been, it wouldn't have done me any good. There we were, alone together. A perfect opportunity, and he didn't even kiss me."

At once, Rex's gaze moved to her pale pink lips. "He was probably just trying to behave himself," he said, striving to think of all the reasons he needed to do the same. "Anything else would be conduct unworthy of a gentleman."

Even as he spoke, arousal stirred inside him, making it clear his body didn't care a jot about gentlemanly conduct.

"That's what I thought, too, at first," she said. "After all, we were inside the church."

Rex studied her, thinking of all the shadowy corners in his own parish church back home that would be perfect for cornering Clara and stealing a kiss or two. "I'm not sure being in church would be much of a deterrent," he said, his control slipping a notch. "To a determined man."

"I rather think it is, at least if you're the vicar."

Those words were sufficiently astonishing to divert him from his rather irreverent fantasy. "You fell in love with a vicar?"

"I wasn't the only one. Most of the girls in our parish were in love with him at one time or another. As I said, he was very good-looking. Church was never as full before he came. And you wouldn't believe the number of knitted gloves and embroidered tea cloths he received at Christmas."

Rex grinned, imagining the picture. She was a good storyteller. "No doubt."

"Anyway, that afternoon in the vestry was rather a disappointment to me, but afterward, he continued to pay me a great deal of attention. He never showed any interest in the other young ladies in the parish, even the bolder ones who flung themselves at him. So, I thought . . . I hoped—" She stopped, and shrugged. "It was foolish."

"What happened?" he asked when she didn't go on. "He proposed to someone else, I suppose?"

"Oh, no," she replied at once. "He proposed to me. But I refused him."

"What?" Rex straightened on the settee, staring at her as she turned matter-of-factly to reach for her tea. "But you were in love with him, you said."

"I was. Madly. But when he proposed, I realized I couldn't marry him. It was the way he put it. He said he had a warm regard for me." She paused over her tea, making a face. "A warm regard. I ask you," she added, sounding suddenly indignant, "is that the sort of feeling that's going to set a girl's pulses racing?"

"Probably not, but how do you know he wasn't just being respectful and considerate of your maidenly sensibilities?"

"Oh, I'm sure he was. Too considerate. He told me that because I was so sweet and so pure, I would be the perfect wife for a vicar. We would have, he said, a truly celestial marriage."

Rex frowned, utterly at a loss. "What sort of marriage is that?"

She stirred, setting her cup and saucer aside again

with a clatter. "That's what I wanted to know! I was forced to ask him straight out if he was saying he didn't want children. What?" she added, her cheeks going pink as he gave an astonished laugh. "I know the stork doesn't bring them! Heavens, I'm not that innocent."

She was every bit that innocent, even if she was aware of basic human biology. But there was no point in launching a discussion on the topic of lovemaking, for he'd just be tormenting himself. "The things you know and don't know sometimes confound me, Clara," he murmured instead. "But what was his answer?"

"He said children would not be a consideration for us. Our union, he said, would be above such base carnality."

Rex's gaze slid down, and he wondered how any man, even a repressed vicar, could think that living with her and not bedding her would be anything but a living hell.

"The man's clearly touched," he muttered. "And wound tighter than his own church clock. But there are some women who would see a marriage like that as quite appealing."

"Well, I didn't. I'm not a celestial being, and I don't want a celestial marriage. I want children, and I told him so."

"And what did he say to that?"

The color in her cheeks deepened. "He said that if I was insistent upon it, he would agree, but the . . . the act w . . . would be distasteful to him." She paused, swallowing hard. "That's what he said. *Distasteful.* What man thinks that?"

Rex stirred in his seat. "Not this one," he muttered, acutely aware of the fact at this moment.

"We're not Shakers, for heaven's sake," she went on in bewilderment, not seeming to have heard his muttered words. "Why would he want such a marriage?"

Rex could see only two possible reasons—sexual repression or homosexuality, or possibly both. "Until he became better acquainted with you, he never paid much attention to any of the young women in the parish, you said?"

"No attention at all. He seemed to prefer the company of the young men."

That, in Rex's mind, rather settled the matter. "It's only a guess, but I'd say he suggested this arrangement because he was about to be arrested."

She frowned, looking surprised. "He did leave the parish afterward, but I thought it was because I refused him. Why would a vicar be in fear of arrest?"

Rex was in no frame of mind to explain some men's desire for other men or that such desires were illegal or that becoming a vicar and getting married were possible ways for such a man to divert suspicion from his preferences and avoid prison. "Never mind," he said before she could delve into what he meant. "Did you ask him what his reasons might be?"

"No. I was too busy asking myself why he thought I would accept such a marriage." Her round face twisted suddenly, went a bit awry. "Did he think me so desperate to be married that I would be willing to forgo physical love? Or did he think me so undesirable that I could not realistically expect to ever receive it?"

Her questions, and the rawness in her voice as she

asked them, threatened to send Rex straight off the rails and over the cliff. He curled his hands into fists, took a deep breath, and reminded himself sternly to stay on his side of the settee.

"Well, he was wrong," she choked. "I may be plain, and I may not have men tripping over themselves to propose to me, but even so, I would prefer never to marry than to settle for a marriage like that. I would rather have no husband at all than one who thinks me so undesirable that a true union with me would be distasteful."

Like a dam breaking, his control crumbled, desire overcame him like a flood, and he found himself beside her before he'd even realized he was moving.

"You're not undesirable," he said, his voice savage even to his own ears. "For God's sake, if you pay no attention to anything else I ever say, Clara, pay attention to that. You, my sweet, are eminently desirable, and any man who can't see that making love to you would be like heaven on earth is an idiot, or a fool, or doesn't desire women at all. I am none of those things, which is why during the entire time we've been sitting here sipping tea like civilized people, I've been having thoughts about you that would burn your wretched vicar's notions of your purity to a crisp."

She stared at him in astonishment, her face pink as a peony. "You have?"

"I have, so put that in your pipe and smoke it. And while we're on the subject," he added, appreciating too late that telling her about his erotic thoughts was only fanning the flames inside him, "you're not the least bit plain, so rid yourself of that notion, too, if you please."

She frowned, a hint of wary skepticism coming into her face. "You don't need to soothe my feminine pride, you know," she said. "I'm no great beauty, and I accepted the fact long ago."

"Beauty, my luscious lamb, is in the eye of the beholder." He leaned closer, irresistibly drawn. "When I look at you, would you like to know what I see?"

"I—" She folded her arms, as if propping up a shield between them—very wise of her given his confession of a moment ago. Her frown deepened. "I'm not sh . . . sure."

"I shall tell you anyway, because you are clearly in need of additional opinions on the subject. The first time I ever saw you in that ballroom, I likened you in my mind to a morsel of shortbread on a tray of French pastries."

She made a face, clearly not thinking much of the comparison. "So, plain and ordinary, in other words."

"I happen to adore shortbread, I'll have you know, and so do a lot of other people."

"Shortbread, indeed." She made a scoffing sound. "What's next? A mention of my sweet disposition?"

Despite what his body was enduring, he couldn't help a grin. "Hardly, since I've yet to see it. With me, you're usually prickly as a chestnut, Clara."

She sniffed, her round chin jerking a little. "I've had some provocation on that score."

He had no intention of being sidetracked now. "I'm going to tell you exactly what I think of your looks, all right?" He took a profound, shaky breath, knowing what he was about to say was deuced important, and he had to keep his arousal in check or he'd never be able to say it without hauling her onto his lap and kissing her senseless. "I'm going to start with your eyes, because if memory serves, I told you once that you've got expressive eyes, and it's quite true. Unless you're embarrassed, your face rarely gives you away, so if I want to gauge what you are really thinking, I look in your eyes."

She ducked her chin, clearly uncomfortable with the idea of him being able to discern what she was thinking, but he wasn't about to let her get by with that. Touching her right now, however, would be akin to lighting a match in a room full of powder kegs, so he bent down, tilting his head so that she had nowhere else to look but at him. "Eyes like yours are dangerous, Clara. They can slay a man with a look like an arrow through the heart. I should know," he added, smiling a little, "because I've had to dig several arrows out of my chest since we met."

"Don't," she ordered in a fierce whisper, lifting her face to scowl at him. "Don't tease."

He wasn't teasing, not a bit, but he decided not to hammer the point. Safer for him if she didn't appreciate the power she had to wound him. "You've got lovely skin," he said instead, and because it was suddenly impossible not to touch her, he lifted his hand and allowed himself the torture of sliding his fingertips slowly across her cheek. It was like touching warm silk. "And some pretty freckles, too, I've noticed."

"F . . . freckles aren't p . . . pretty. That's absurd."

"Haven't we already established that your opinion on this topic isn't to be trusted? Now, where were we? Ah, yes," he added, pressing the tip of his index finger to the patch of skin between her brows, smoothing out the frown that had appeared at his mention of freckles. "I think we were coming to your nose."

"What about my nose?" she cried, telling him he was touching on a vulnerable point, and he decided a frank acknowledgement was his best bet.

"Well, it's tiny, Clara." He slid his fingertip slowly down the bridge. "It's the tiniest button nose I've ever seen."

She sighed, her breath a soft huff of acknowledgement against his palm. "It's a ridiculous nose, I know," she whispered. "I used to pinch it all the time when I was a girl, hoping it would turn Grecian, but it never did."

"Good thing, too, because it's adorable just as it is." He pulled his hand back a fraction to plant a kiss on the turned-up tip.

She gave a startled gasp at the contact and unfolded her arms, pressing her palms against his chest as if to push him away, impelling him again into speech. "And lastly," he said, "there's your mouth."

Her palms stilled against his chest.

"It's my favorite part of your face." He opened his palm to cup her cheek and touched his thumb to her lips, giving in to the inevitable. "It's because of your smile. When I was giving the Devastated Debutante examples of how she might draw men's attention, and I put in the part about smiling, I was thinking of you."

"Me?" The word was a squeak of surprise.

"Yes, you." He moved his thumb, sliding it back and forth across her mouth. "Surely you know why?"

"Not really," she confessed in a strangled whisper. As his thumb grazed her lips, he could feel her breathing quicken, and he knew he ought to stop, for what he was doing was well beyond the pale and no doubt beyond her experience as well. In fact, this might even be the first time in her life she'd been intimately touched by a man.

If he possessed any hope, however vague, that reminders of her virginal innocence would give him the will to call a halt, he discovered at once that the very opposite was true. Her innocence seemed to inflame the wickedest desires within him and make him want her even more. He wasn't certain how much longer he could keep lust at bay. And yet, he could not pull back.

"You might think I put in that bit to help you overcome your shyness and further your goal of finding a husband," he went on, "but that wasn't my reason at all."

"It wasn't?"

"No. My reason was purely selfish. You see, you have this stunning, absolutely ripping smile, and I'd really like the pleasure of seeing it more often. Most of the time, you're so damnably serious. But when you smile . . ." He paused, his thumb stilling against her parted lips. "Ah, Clara, when you smile, you light up the room. Surely you know that?"

She squeezed her eyes shut, shaking her head a little, as if she wanted to deny it or she didn't believe him. "This is not a real courtship," she said, her lips brushing against his thumb as she spoke, her hands curling into fists against his gray morning coat. "There is no need for you to pay me compliments."

There was every need, since it was clear she'd received precious few of them in the past, but he didn't debate the point. "Which doesn't make what I've said any less true."

"I'm not sure I can trust you to tell the truth about anything," she mumbled against his thumb.

"What if I stop using words altogether, then, hmm?" He slid his thumb under her chin and pushed gently against her jaw, lifting her face. "Words aren't necessary anyway."

"They aren't?" she whispered.

"Not for what I want to say." With that, he bent his head and kissed her.

Chapter 11

The moment his mouth touched hers, Clara experienced a pleasure so keen it was almost like pain, so intense it was almost unbearable. The press of his lips was light, and yet, she felt it in every part of her body. From fingertip to fingertip, from the bottoms of her feet to the crown of her hair, it seemed as if every cell and every nerve ending she possessed was awakening to this new experience.

Her first kiss, she thought and closed her eyes, a move that ignited other senses. She became aware of his scent—a mixture of sandalwood and castile soap and something else, something deeper and earthier. She heard the tick of the clock on the mantel and the thud of her own heartbeat. She felt his warm palm cupping her cheek, his fingertips caressing the nape of her neck, his forearm brushing against her breast. In some vague corner of her mind, she knew it was all terribly improper and she ought to stop it, but she could not move. She could only feel, as the sweetness of it all washed over her and through her, becoming more potent with each tick of the clock. When his lips moved against hers and his tongue touched the seam of her closed lips, she stirred in agitation, giving a soft moan against his mouth.

He pulled back a fraction, his lips brushing hers in a teasing caress. He lifted his free hand to slide his arm around her shoulders, and as his fingertips ran lightly down her spine, any notions of stopping this wondrous experience went out of Clara's head and vanished into space. When he pulled her closer, she came willingly, gladly, her arms wrapping around his neck, her sound of assent stifled by his mouth capturing hers again.

This kiss was more ardent, more demanding, his lips urging hers to part. When they did, his tongue entered her mouth—a shocking thing, and yet, as he tasted deeply of her, the pleasure within her deepened as well, bringing heat, and the sweetness of the first kiss gave way to a new sensation in the second, something hungry and wild, something almost desperate.

His tongue pulled back, and driven by instinct, she pursued. As her tongue entered his mouth, the strange hunger in her rose even higher, grew even hotter. This was the most intimate thing that had ever happened to her, and yet, strangely, it wasn't intimate enough. She pressed her body closer to his, her arms tightening around his neck, and suddenly, she was falling forward and he was falling back. As their bodies sank together onto the settee, Clara felt an exultation unlike anything she'd ever felt before.

He moved beneath her, making a rough sound against

her mouth as if he were surprised, and who could blame him? Women weren't supposed to be so brazen. And yet, he didn't seem to mind, for he broke the kiss only long enough for both of them to take in air, and then, he was kissing her again, his tongue in her mouth and his arms tight around her. It was glorious.

His arms were like steel bands, holding her. The strands of his hair felt crisp and silky as she raked her fingers through them. She could taste tea and strawberry jam on his mouth. Held in his embrace, captured by his kiss, her senses filled with him, everything else in the world faded to insignificance.

Beneath her, his heat seemed to sear her through all the layers of her clothes. His body was lean and hard—particularly where his hips were pressed to hers with such shocking intimacy. She stirred against that hardness, and the pleasure brought by the tiny move was so sharp, so exquisite, that she tore her lips from his with an astonished gasp.

For an instant, they stared at each other, and then, his embrace suddenly slackened and his arms slid under hers, his hands lifting to cup her face.

"This has to stop," he said, his voice a rasp in the quiet room. "It has to stop now, or God help us both."

Pressing a quick, hard kiss to her mouth, he gripped her shoulders, then he shoved her backward and sat up. Planting her firmly in her own seat, he let her go and slid at once to the other end of the settee.

Clara turned to stare at the clock on the mantel ahead of her as she worked to regain a sense of equilibrium. It wasn't easy. She felt as if she'd been running, and because of her corset, she couldn't take deep breaths, and in consequence, she felt a bit dizzy.

Her body seemed afire, burning in all the places he'd touched her and even in some of the places he hadn't. She'd often tried to imagine what kissing a man might be like, but heavens above, her imagination had never conjured anything even close to the reality.

Was it the same for men? she wondered, and cast a sideways glance at him.

He was not looking at her, but at the floor, his forearms resting on his parted knees. His breathing was hard, deep, and labored. Watching him, her question was answered, and the knowledge that she had evoked in him the same feelings she had experienced made Clara want to laugh with joy, because for the first time in her life, she knew what it was to feel beautiful.

Somewhere in the distance, a door banged. Though the sound was muffled by the closed confines of the drawing room, he heard it, too. He stirred, lifting his head, and she looked away, her happiness at what had just happened fading a little as it dawned on her how lucky they'd been. If anyone had come in and caught them—

"Forgive me," he said, interrupting that alarming line of speculation. "I have to go."

His voice was a welcome diversion from the sobering turn her thoughts had taken, and Clara jerked to her feet.

"Of course," she said, turning toward him as he stood up, and she worked to don a demeanor of polite civility and speak naturally, as if the most extraordinary experience of her life had not just happened. "Please express my thanks to your aunt for her kind invitation, and tell her I will respond as soon as I have spoken with my sisters-in-law."

He gave a nod and bowed, then walked toward the door, taking up his hat from the table where he'd left it earlier as he went. But then, he stopped, hat in hand, and turned to look at her over his shoulder, his perfect countenance graver than she'd ever seen it, his eyes so brilliantly blue that it almost hurt to look into them.

"You've never been kissed before," he said. "Have you?"

His voice was so matter-of-fact, it wasn't really a question, and she colored up at once, wondering how he could possibly be so certain.

"No," she admitted. "You were . . . you were the first."

He didn't seem gratified to hear it. He pressed his lips tight together, gave a brief nod of acknowledgement, and turned away to open the door, leaving her with no idea what had given her away. Perhaps she'd done it wrong somehow, made some terribly gauche mistake.

That was a mortifying possibility, and yet, Clara's joy refused to be dimmed. It lingered inside her—like sunshine caught in a box—even after he was gone.

DAMN, DAMN, DAMN.

The oath reverberated through his head like a series of gunshots, condemning him with every step he took down the stairs, across the foyer, and out of Clara Deverill's house.

He walked straight past his driver, who had hopped down from the box and was waiting by the carriage door, opened umbrella in hand. "Go on, Hart," he ordered over his shoulder without breaking his stride. "I'll walk for a bit, then take a taxi home."

"But, sir, it's raining."

"Is it?" He strode rapidly on, his body in the hot, agonizing turmoil of unrequited lust, his mind glad of the cool drizzle already dampening his hat and coat. "Good."

"But, sir," Hart called again. "You'll catch cold."

He made short shrift of the inclement spring weather and its possible consequences with a wave of his hand, and kept walking. A cold, he could not help but feel, would be no more than he deserved for breaking his cardinal rule about women.

Stay away from the innocent ones.

Innocent young women invariably expected matrimony, and who could blame them? For a girl of good family, marriage was the only socially acceptable path through life, the only means of fulfilling physical desires, ensuring a stable future, and having children. His conversation with Clara over tea had only served to underscore why he'd established his cardinal rule in the first place.

But for a man, even a peer, marriage was not a necessity, a fact for which Rex daily thanked heaven. He'd spent his entire youth watching his parents destroy not only each other, but also the passionate love that had brought them into matrimony in the first place. To love and then come to hate what you had loved—he could imagine no greater hell. And though he couldn't remember the exact moment he'd decided never to wed, not once since then had he had cause to regret his choice, or even to doubt it.

He still didn't. And that made what he had just done all the more reprehensible.

For Clara, marriage was not a mere necessity of exis-

tence. Romance, marriage, children, love everlasting—
these things comprised the dream of her life. They
were things she wanted and deserved, things he would
never willingly offer any girl.

A cold gust of wind came up, taking his hat. He
watched, indifferent, as his gray felt derby tumbled
through the air ahead of him and landed in a curbside
puddle with an unceremonious plop.

Rex stepped over it and kept walking.

He passed Mrs. Mott's Tea Emporium, and he
couldn't help giving it a resentful glance as he walked
by, wishing he'd never agreed to meet Lionel there for
tea. Why there, of all the bloody tea shops in London?
Why her, of all the women in the world? It was laughable, ridiculous, and aggravating as hell that he should
be lusting after a girl he could not have, a girl who
wanted everything out of life that he avoided like the
plague.

The rain was falling harder now. Ahead of him, people caught out in the deluge were huddling under their
umbrellas—an inadequate protection, given the wind.
Those without umbrellas were darting into doorways
and ducking under awnings, seeking shelter. Not Rex.

Rex kept walking.

He welcomed the rain that pelted his bare head and
soaked his gray morning coat and dark blue trousers.
He savored the cold wind that had taken his hat and
was now whipping his coattails. These were just what
he needed, for the sweet taste of Clara's mouth still
lingered in his own, the scent of her hair still filled
his nostrils, and the imprint of her body on his still
burned him like a brand.

Worse, her innocence itself inflamed him. The hunger in her inexperienced kiss, the passion that had led her to abandon maidenly restraint and push him down on the settee, the awareness that he was in territory no man had ever explored—all these had acted on him like paraffin tossed onto flames, flaring the darkest, most erotic parts of his imagination more strongly than the naughty wink of a Gaiety Girl or the knowing smile of a courtesan ever could.

And he'd known, damn it all, known instinctively when he'd sat behind her at Covent Garden, that he might be getting into something he would find hard to master. He'd barely made his arrangements with her before his oh-so-clever scheme had come back to taunt him. Even while indulging in erotic notions about her, he'd sensed just how strong was the fire that he was playing with. His body had tried to warn him, and he had not taken warning. Today, that fire had nearly flared out of control. Had he not stopped when he had, he might very well have taken her virtue, right there on a settee in her father's drawing room.

He felt like a dog. He watched people peeking curiously at him from beneath the brims of their umbrellas as he passed them, and he wondered if their curious stares were because he was walking, coatless and hatless through a pouring rain, or because he was emanating lust for all to see. Either way, getting drenched was just what he needed and what he deserved.

He was soaking by the time he picked up a taxi at the Holborn Hotel, but thankfully, by then his ardor had cooled, and his body was once again under his strict regulation. Innocent young women with big dark eyes, romantic ideals, repressed passion, and marital ambitions were once again relegated to the same place in his mind that he put oysters, Afternoon-At-Homes, Evensong, and aspic: things that were not for him.

"And all's right with the world," he muttered, but as the taxi carried him back to the West End, he felt anything but right. Clara Deverill had shown him how erotic innocence could be, and if he couldn't keep that newfound knowledge at bay, her virtue, her dreams for her future, and her blissfully sweet notion to marry for love would all be in jeopardy.

He didn't want any of that to happen to her. He didn't want to kill her dreams, or taint her ideals about love and romance. Hell, he must have had some romantic ideals himself at one time, even if he couldn't remember them anymore.

A CARRIAGE CONTAINING four women was not usually a place one would expect silence, particularly when it was conveying them to a picnic on a fine, sunny afternoon, but as the Duke of Torquil's open landau made the journey down Park Lane from the duke's home in Upper Brook Street to the Stanhope Gate of Hyde Park, all four ladies in the duke's carriage were silent.

Carlotta, usually the first to point out the negative aspects of any situation, seemed in a happy frame of mind today, content with enjoying the beautiful afternoon and anticipating the event ahead. Married to the duke's brother, Carlotta was Clara's chaperone while Irene was away, but that duty had been quite a dull one until Lady Ellesmere and Lady Petunia had conspired to bring Clara out. That decision had benefitted the duke's entire family, and Carlotta was too relieved by the re-elevation of their social status to complain about anything.

Nor was the silence from Sarah all that surprising. The youngest of Clara's three sisters-in-law, Sarah was a quiet girl by nature. Sarah's sister, Angela, however, was usually a lively and outspoken sort, but as the carriage rolled down Park Lane, even Angela was uncharacteristically silent.

For her own part, Clara sensed a certain tension among her sisters-in-law, but at the moment, she was in no frame of mind to wonder at its cause, for she was gripped by tensions of her own, and those dominated her thoughts to the exclusion of all else.

In only a few minutes, she would see him again. A week had passed since that extraordinary kiss, but though she had seen his great-aunt at several social events during the past seven days, she had not seen him.

The prospect of seeing him today, however, did not bring the happy anticipation that a girl ought to feel about seeing the man who had so recently kissed her. No, Clara's anticipation at the notion of seeing Galbraith again felt more like dread.

The joy she'd experienced during those extraordinary moments in her father's drawing room had, alas, faded over the past seven days, supplanted by her innate common sense. Her dazed wonder had slowly, inexorably, given way to a sobering appreciation of harsh realities.

For one thing, her actions had been foolish. Galbraith was not a man any girl could rely upon—not for marriage anyway, and for her own life, she wanted no path but marriage. Despite that, she had allowed him the liberty of kissing her, knowing he had no honorable intent of courtship or view to matrimony. What did that say about her self-respect?

She had been very wrong to allow it, and even now, she didn't understand what had possessed her. How could she have ignored her scruples, abandoned her customary caution, and gone against her very nature? She was not, she reminded herself, an intemperate person. She was calm and steady. She was plain. She was shy.

The image of her pushing Galbraith down onto the settee flashed through her mind again, bringing all its glory and agony. There hadn't been any temperance or shy modesty about her that afternoon. On the contrary. She'd been indiscreet, forward, downright wanton.

If all that wasn't enough to force her into sober reflection, she had also put her reputation at grave risk. If they had been caught, if her father and the doctor had come in, or if—God forbid—one of her father's acquaintances paying a call had been ushered up to the drawing room, the sight that met that person's eyes would have been a shocking one indeed.

She imagined it as a witness might have done—with her prone body shamelessly on top of Galbraith's, her hands raking through his hair, her mouth taking his with hungry abandon.

It was a painful picture.

Had anyone walked in on them, the result for her would have been abject shame, disgrace, and possibly ruin. It had been a mistake of epic proportions, and she needed to make that fact plain to Galbraith at the first opportunity, lest he assume her brazen behavior had been permission for him to take further liberties in future.

Even as she took that stance of firm resolve, the memory of his body beneath hers and his strong arms around her made her pulse quicken and spread aching heat through her limbs. Even as she reprimanded herself for a fool, her soul yearned to experience it all again, to know, if only for a few more shining moments, how it felt to be a beautiful and enticing woman.

Heavens, she was in such a muddle, how could she ever face him? How could she sit across from him on a picnic blanket this afternoon and not think about the two of them on that settee locked in a passionate embrace? How could she be in the presence of his family and act as if he had not given her the most singular experience of her life? She'd been tempted to refuse the invitation, but she hadn't had the heart to do that to her sisters-in-law, who were receiving precious few invitations this year. It would have been selfish, and cowardly, too. And ultimately futile, for she'd have had to face him sometime. They'd made a bargain. She couldn't back out.

And as the carriage made its way down Park Lane, she knew she had only a few precious minutes to piece her wits together. Because unless she found a way to spend the afternoon in his company without showing the world what he'd made her feel, she'd spend her season pursued by him alone—a man who could only offer a sham courtship. Unless she wanted to become known as a flirt and a jilt when she refused his suit in two months' time, she had to regain the cool façade of polite tolerance she'd originally decided upon. How easy polite tolerance had seemed ten days ago, and how impossible it seemed now.

"All right, that tears it," Angela suddenly burst out,

breaking the silence in the carriage. "I don't know about the rest of you, but I can't tolerate the suspense a moment longer."

She turned toward Clara, lively curiosity and expectation in her gray eyes. "What is going on?"

Alarm seized Clara's insides, clutching like a fist. There was no way her sisters-in-law could know what had happened between her and Galbraith, but it was clear they sensed something was afoot, and she knew it was time to put on the mask of indifference she was supposed to be wearing. "I'm sure I don't know what you mean, Angie," she said and looked away, pretending a vast interest in the tall elms around them.

This pretense seemed to exasperate Angela. "Really, Clara!" she cried. "You are like a sphinx when you choose. Days and days have passed, and still, you haven't explained a thing. When are you going to tell us about it?"

She resisted the temptation to look down and see if she had a big scarlet A emblazoned on the front of her blue-and-white striped outing gown. *They can't possibly have guessed*, she told herself, hoping she wasn't engaging in mere wishful thinking as she turned again to the woman beside her. "But what am I expected to tell?"

"Everything about *him*, of course! Is he as charming as they say?"

At once, Clara's cheeks grew hot, a reaction that did not go unnoticed.

"Ooh-la-la," Sarah piped up, laughing. "See how she blushes, Angie, and you haven't even uttered his name."

"Shall I say it, and watch her blush deepen? Lord

Galbraith is the man I'm talking about, Clara, you oyster! Viscount Galbraith, the handsomest devil in the entire *ton*. So," she added, nudging Clara's knee playfully with her own, "do you intend to keep us on tenterhooks, or shall you tell us what's between the two of you?"

"And don't say there's nothing," Sarah interjected as Clara opened her mouth to say just that. "Because it's plain as a pikestaff you've caught his eye."

"Have I?" Had she put the proper amount of innocent surprise in her voice? she wondered.

Angela made a scoffing sound. "Oh, you know you have. First, he singles you out to open Lady Petunia's ball, and then she invites you to sit in Leyland's box at Covent Garden. And now, we're off to spend the day with them."

"It's just a picnic," she began, but Angela cut off her attempt to downplay it.

"One with a family we are barely acquainted with. The point is, all these things are because of you. As Sarah said, Galbraith's interest is clear, and yet, for all you talk of him, he might as well not exist."

"That will be enough, girls," Carlotta put in, the rebuke severe enough to demonstrate how seriously the duke's sister-in-law took her role as matron and chaperone of her unmarried companions. "Despite Lord Leyland's scandal-ridden wife, his aunt is quite well-regarded in society, and if she is willing to help bolster our social position after your own mother's unfortunate elopement, I shall not take issue with it. And, more importantly, if Clara doesn't wish to confide in us or seek advice," she added with an injured sniff, making it clear who she thought ought to be dispensing said advice, "then you've no right to press her."

"It isn't that!" Clara cried, her mask slipping a notch. She wished she could confide in them, for the feelings that had been plaguing her ever since that extraordinary afternoon were heady and overwhelming and wholly alien to her, and she'd spent most of the week torn between wanting to laugh with joy and wanting to die of mortification. She would have dearly liked to hear other feminine opinions on the subject, but she could not allow herself that luxury.

If she told her sisters-in-law that Galbraith had kissed her, they would surely assume an engagement had been made, and upon finding out that no such honorable proposal had been offered, they would be outraged on her behalf. Knowing Clara's own father was hopeless at parental duties, Carlotta might even go to her husband, the duke's brother, and honor would require Lord David to see Galbraith and demand he do right by her, a ghastly and humiliating prospect that Clara could not bear to contemplate.

She would then be obligated to take responsibility for her part in what had occurred, own up to the fact that she had been as much to blame as he, and how could she tell anyone that? How could she make the humiliating admission that she had allowed a man to whom she was not affianced an unpardonable liberty? More than allowed it—she had enjoyed it, reveled in it, pushed him down on the settee and shamelessly demanded more of it. Clara could no more have confessed such things than she could have turned herself into a frog and croaked out a mating song.

She swallowed hard and made herself to say something. "It's just that there's nothing to tell," she said. "I hardly know the man. Yes, I danced with him at his aunt's ball, as you saw for yourselves. And as I told you at the time, I didn't think much of him."

"A feeling that is obviously *not* mutual," murmured Sarah, giving her sister a wink across the carriage, and Angela's responding giggle only increased Clara's dismay.

"His great-aunt is a friend of my grandmother," she reminded them. "As I told you before the ball, Lady Ellesmere prevailed upon Lady Petunia to help bring me out. That is the reason for all these invitations, I'm sure."

"That explains Lady Petunia's attentions," Carlotta put in dryly. "But hardly Galbraith's."

Clara stirred on the seat, her lips tingling, some of Galbraith's more improper attentions becoming even more vivid in her mind. "I don't see that he's been so very attentive," she said, hoping to heaven lightning didn't strike her dead for such a bold-faced lie.

"Don't you, my dear?"

Desperate for a distraction from this topic, Clara looked past the other woman to the carriage behind them. "Lord James shall have his hands full today, I think, for his boys seem in even higher spirits than usual. Colin is climbing out onto the boot of the carriage, and Owen is sitting on the back of his seat. Your husband does not look happy, Carlotta, riding with them. I told Lord David I would take his place, so that he could sit up here with you, but he declined."

"My husband can hold his own with his nephews, I assure you," she answered without turning her head to look. "And if Jamie's sons are hellions, it's his own fault. As for you riding in the other carriage, that would not have been appropriate. Jamie is a widower, and you are unmarried. Speaking of single men," she added, making Clara groan, "as you are in my charge for the season, my dear, I am obligated to point out that Galbraith's attentions to you were made plain at Covent Garden. A single man who was not interested in you would never have allowed himself to be seen tête-à-tête with you at the rail of his father's box, in full view of all society."

"It was hardly tête-à-tête," she objected. "Lady Petunia was less than a dozen feet away."

"But the conversation was *intime*, so I've been told."

This confirmation that gossip was already circulating about Galbraith's interest in her made it even more crucial that she don the veneer of polite tolerance she and the viscount had discussed. She pasted on a dismissive smile and braced herself to tell more lies. "It doesn't have the significance you impart to it. Nothing intimate was said. And anyway, it's common knowledge that Galbraith would never seriously consider courting any girl."

"All the more reason he would take pains to avoid speculations on the subject, then," Carlotta said and leaned back, still smiling.

"And perhaps his views about courtship have undergone a transformation," Sarah put in. "At least since he danced with a certain girl we all know," she added with a wink.

"This is absurd," Clara cried, even as she reminded herself that this sort of thinking was just what her arrangement with Galbraith was supposed to bring about. "Even if what you say is true, Sarah, my opinion of the man hasn't changed."

But as she spoke, her body proved her a liar not

only to herself, but to all the ladies riding with her, for she blushed as she spoke. The other three women giggled—including Carlotta—and Clara jerked her chin, turning her head to the side and her attention to the view of Hyde Park as she struggled to regain her composure. "Any young lady," she said through clenched teeth, "would be a fool to want Galbraith's attentions."

Her own words made her grimace, for she was well aware of how shamelessly she'd responded to some of those attentions. And now, as she thought of that kiss, all the heat, shame, and exultation she'd felt that afternoon came roaring back and underscored the galling truth that Galbraith was not nearly as low in her estimation as she'd previously believed. Either that, she thought dismally, or he had awakened her to her true nature as a strumpet.

Clara wasn't quite sure which possibility was worse, but as the carriage turned to enter the park, she knew one thing for certain. It was going to be a long and awkward afternoon.

Chapter 12

$\mathcal{D}$espite his driver's prediction, Rex did not catch a cold after his walk in the rain, and even if he had, it would have been worth the sacrifice. His drenching in that storm did the trick, and by the time of his aunt's picnic, he had managed to shove any erotic thoughts about Clara down into the darkest corners of his imagination. And he knew it was best if they remained there.

Now that he had managed to wrestle the dragons of lust into submission, however, Rex still had to deal with the scorched earth left behind. There was no acceptable excuse for what he'd done, and he owed Clara an apology for his conduct. In addition, it was quite likely his actions had led her to expect more of him than what he could offer. Most young ladies would, understandably, expect a marriage proposal after a man had taken the liberties he'd taken the other day, and if Clara was no different, if the mutual passion of their kiss had led her to develop expectations of that sort about him, it would be best if he extinguished them straightaway.

By the time of her arrival, he'd managed to compose a speech that detailed everything he needed to say, but as he watched the Duke of Torquil's carriages turn at the Stanhope Gate, he was tempted to abandon speeches and apologies and plans to atone and just hurl himself into the path of an oncoming train instead. The latter course seemed far easier than the former.

Nonetheless, as the duke's carriages rolled toward their party, Rex excused himself from the guests he'd been speaking with, and he crossed the turf toward them as the duke's drivers assisted the passengers to alight. Lord James St. Clair's twin sons needed no assistance, for they both vaulted over the side of the open landau before the doors were opened and, kites in hand, they raced past Rex hell-for-leather across the lawn. Their father followed them, giving Rex a wave of greeting as he ran by. Lord David Cavanaugh came toward him at a more leisurely pace than his brother-in-law and nephews had done, escorting the ladies.

"Cavanaugh," Rex greeted the duke's younger brother with a nod as they came abreast.

"Galbraith." The other man gestured to the redhead in green beside him. "You know my wife, of course?"

"I do, indeed." He removed his hat with a bow. "Lady David, it's a pleasure to see you again."

"And you as well," she replied. "Though seeing you moving in society is rather a surprise, I confess. How has your great-aunt managed to drag you out? I don't recall her having much success there in the past."

"Even I have been known to enjoy the pleasures afforded by good society, ma'am."

"Yes," she murmured, giving him a knowing little smile in return. "But more so this season than usual, it seems."

That remark evoked stifled giggles from the dark-haired girls beside her, and Rex decided that until he could ascertain just what Clara's expectations were, his best course was to downplay his attentions toward her and keep mum.

When he slid his gaze to Clara, however, she gave him no clue as to what she might be thinking or feeling. Her head was tilted down as she occupied herself with refastening the pearl button of one white glove, and the brim of her hat—an enormous concoction of straw, white feathers, and blue ribbons—prevented him from seeing her eyes. What he could see of her face, however, appeared as smooth as polished marble, with nothing to give her away, and he wondered if perhaps she had chosen to overlook the events of a week ago.

Even if she had, it would not relieve him of his obligations as a gentleman, however, and he knew he had to find a way to speak with her alone.

"Sarah, Angela," Lady David said, gesturing to the pair of giggling girls, "may I present Viscount Galbraith to you? Lord Galbraith, the duke's sisters, Lady Angela Cavanaugh and Lady Sarah Cavanaugh. And you know Miss Deverill, of course?" she added as he bowed to the girls.

"I do, indeed." He turned to Clara. "It is a pleasure to see you again, Miss Deverill."

Faced with his direct attention, she was forced to

leave off buttoning her glove. She lifted her head, and when he looked into her face, all his efforts to bury that kiss were obliterated in an instant. Her dark eyes were like a mirror, reflecting all the desire he felt and was working so hard to suppress. The sight threw him strangely off-balance, as if the world had just tilted a bit sideways. Any apologies for his conduct suddenly seemed like lies because he wasn't sorry, and any reassurances that she would be safe from further improper advances on his part seemed laughable and absurd.

"Lord Galbraith."

Despite what he saw in her eyes, her voice was cool, polite, and distant, reminding him forcibly of their original agreement and what civility demanded of him now. Like the spring rain a week ago, her voice acted on him like a bracing splash of cold water, and thankfully, the world shifted back into its proper perspective.

He turned, gesturing with his hat to the large tent behind them. "My great-aunt and my uncle Albert are by the marquee," he said to Lady David, offering her his arm. "Shall I take your party to them?"

Lady David acquiesced to this plan, placing her hand on his arm and walking beside him, while her husband fell back to escort the other ladies.

His great-aunt and his uncle were standing just inside the marquee, and as they came forward to greet the new arrivals, Rex gave way.

"Lady David, how lovely to see you again," Petunia said as Rex moved to stand beside Clara at the back of the group. "And your sisters-in-law as well. Do please come into the shade here, for the sun is quite warm."

As the rest of the party complied, Rex took that opportunity to lean closer to Clara. "Might I beg your indulgence for a private word?" he murmured by her ear.

The moment the request was out of his mouth, he felt the need to clarify it, lest she think his private word meant something it did not. "By 'private,' I only meant that I don't wish our conversation to be overheard. We'll be within sight of everyone the entire time." He gestured to a pair of empty lawn chairs on the grass about a dozen yards away. "If you were to stroll over in that direction, might I join you there?"

She nodded. "I should greet Lady Petunia and Sir Albert first."

"Of course. I shall see you in a few minutes, then." With that, he bowed and left her.

Feeling restless, knowing what he had to say and dreading the prospect of saying it, he occupied himself with a stroll about the lawn. He paused to listen to the string quartet for a bit and chatted with several acquaintances, but as the minutes went by and Clara made no move to depart the marquee, his restlessness and his apprehension grew.

Never before had he put himself in the risky and vulnerable position of having to apologize to a young lady for untoward advances, and by the time she excused herself from his relations and started toward their appointed meeting place, Rex felt like a cat on hot bricks.

She was standing by the lawn chairs when he reached them, and the fact that she had chosen not to sit down only made him more nervous, but he halted in front of her, took a deep breath, and plunged into speech. "Clara, about the other day, you mustn't think . . . that is, I never intended any impropriety, or meant anything by it—that is, anything untoward. I mean, what I did was untoward, of course it was, but . . ."

He paused, aware that what he was saying wasn't anything like the speech he'd prepared. This was an incoherent, rambling jumble of words, not at all germane to the point. He took a deep breath and tried again. "What I mean to say is that I wasn't thinking about propriety, or the ramifications, or any of that when I kissed you. You seemed to be expressing the fear that you weren't a desirable woman, and it was frustrating as hell listening to it, because you're not undesirable at all—quite the contrary, in fact, and my only intent was to let you know that, and—"

He stopped again, for talking of her desirability was sending him onto very dangerous ground. Besides, he wanted to be as honest with her as he could be, and his intentions when he'd kissed her were far less noble than he was making them sound. Aware that this second effort was just as inept as his first, he gave up any attempts to be eloquent, took another deep breath, and cut to the chase. "What happened a week ago was a mistake."

The moment those words were out of his mouth, he grimaced at how blunt, even cruel, they sounded. Her lips parted, and though he didn't know what he expected her to say in reply, when she swallowed hard and pressed a hand to her chest, staring up at him with those big brown eyes of hers, he felt every bit the cad she'd initially thought him, and he braced himself for either a blistering and well-deserved tongue-lashing or a storm of feminine tears.

"Oh, thank heaven," she breathed, laughing, displaying nothing of what he'd feared. Instead, she looked . . . relieved. "I'm so glad you said it first!"

He blinked, utterly taken aback. "I beg your pardon?"

"I've been in a state all week, dreading this encounter, thinking I'd be obligated to chide you for what happened, and I really didn't want to do that."

"No? I'd deserve it."

"It would be a bit hypocritical of me, wouldn't it?" she whispered, lowering her gaze to his mouth. "After I . . ."

Her voice trailed off, but he knew she was thinking of her own actions—of her own ardent response to his kiss. The effect of that knowledge on his mind and his body were immediate, but his imagination had barely started down that delightful, agonizing road, before her next words hauled him firmly back.

"I'm not saying what we did wasn't wrong." She glanced around to verify no one had strolled within earshot. "If anyone had come in—"

She broke off, as if unable to voice that unthinkable possibility, and he stepped into the breach. "We'd have been in dire straits, no question, and it would have been utterly my fault. My actions were appalling."

Her cheeks went pink, and she stirred. "I wouldn't quite say that," she murmured, touching her gloved fingers to the side of her neck.

That gesture of feminine arousal impelled him to qualify his statement. "Don't misunderstand me, I beg you. I'm not saying that kiss wasn't wonderful. It was."

"Yes." The acknowledgement was soft, breathed on a sigh. "It was, rather."

"More than wonderful," he went on. "Earth-shattering,

as kisses go, if you want the truth." Even as he spoke, he was baffled as to why he was being so frank. Telling her just how ripping that kiss had been hardly served to bolster the regretful apology he was attempting to make. "But," he said with all the firm conviction he could manage, "it was still a mistake."

"I agree." Her hand fell to her side, and her manner became brisk. "We should not have done it."

"You mean I should not have done it," he corrected. "Please, Clara, do not keeping saying 'we'. You are not in any way to blame for what happened. All the blame is mine, and you have my deepest apologies. And if . . ." He paused and took a breath, but he knew he had to say the rest. "If my actions have led you to any expectations, I could not blame you for them. Please believe me when I say that if I led you on, it was inadvertent."

"Led me on?" She frowned, staring at him in bewilderment. And then, as she realized what he meant, her eyes widened. "You thought I'd expect a marriage proposal? From *you*?" Her emphasis on the last word made him grimace, and then, she laughed, laughed so merrily that he felt like a complete idiot.

"I need not have worried on that score, it seems," he muttered, watching her.

"Goodness, no!" Sensing that he was not as amused as she, Clara sobered and gave a little cough. "You may rest assured, Lord Galbraith, that the expectation you fear never entered my head. And if it had, I'd have booted it out again straightaway. We both know you're not a marrying man."

"Quite so." Despite everything, he felt off-balance again, and truth be told, a bit nettled as well. She really was the most unaccountable girl.

"While I," she went on, "am definitely a marrying sort of woman."

"Yes," he hastened to agree, nodding to emphasize that important point. "Most definitely."

There was a pause. They seemed in complete agreement on the matter, and yet, he felt dissatisfied, as if there was something still unsaid, leaving him no clue at all what to say next.

"Our truce remains intact, I hope?" he said at last.

"Of course." She gave a deep sigh as she looked up at him. "Oh, I'm so glad we've had this conversation," she said, laughing again. "I feel so much better now. Although . . ." She paused, her smile fading, a little frown etching between her brows that gave Rex renewed cause for concern. "In a way, you're right that you've given me certain expectations, though not quite the ones you feared."

Rex readied himself—for what, he wasn't quite sure. "Indeed?"

"The last time you attempted to broker a peace with me, you brought champagne." She spread her gloved hands wide, demonstrating his failure in that regard, and gave him a look of mock regret. "You set a very high standard for yourself, Lord Galbraith, and now, I'm afraid you must live with the consequences. I'm not sure that I can accept any apologies from you if champagne is not offered in accompaniment."

He laughed, and the tension and guilt he'd been flaying himself with all week broke apart and floated away on the warm spring breeze. "Now that," he said as he ushered her to a nearby lawn chair, "is an expectation easily fulfilled. But only if you stop referring to me by my title and start calling me by my name.

It's Rex, by the way," he added over his shoulder as he walked away, making for one of the footmen milling about with champagne, sherry, and lemonade. He plucked two flutes of champagne from the tray and returned to her side.

"Here we are," he said, offering her one of the glasses before settling himself in the chair opposite hers. "It's Laurent-Pierre, '91," he added as she lifted her glass. "A vintage as excellent as that ought to put me firmly back in your good graces, I should think."

"Mmm," she said, an appreciative murmur as she swallowed a sip of sparkling wine. "It's lovely, but I'm not sure what that opinion's worth, since I wouldn't know one vintage from another. In fact, until the other night at Covent Garden, I'd never had champagne in my life."

"Yes," he said, smiling as he remembered her happy surprise upon discovering the magic of champagne. "I suspected as much. But I can't imagine what took you so long."

"Irene felt, and I agreed, that to imbibe spirits of any sort around Papa would only encourage his drinking, so we both chose to abstain while at home. So, thank you," she added, raising her glass to him. "For introducing me to my first champagne."

Among other things.

Thankfully, he managed not to voice that rather naughty thought out loud. "It's understandable you and your sister would choose to abstain at home, though I don't know why you haven't had any champagne in the duke's household, for they are not teetotalers. In fact, I see Lady David sipping champagne as we speak."

"Lady David is married. She is also a very strict

and watchful chaperone. I drink only what Sarah and Angela are allowed, which is a little taste of each wine served at dinner, and no champagne has been served at home. Unfortunately."

"Best pace yourself, then," he advised, grinning as she took another appreciative sip, "since you're not accustomed to spirits. As for Lady David," he went on, turning his head to glance again at the woman talking with Auntie Pet, "she seems to be in a more liberal frame of mind today. She's looking right at us, and she doesn't seem at all put out that you're drinking a full glass of champagne in the middle of the day."

"Yes, well, Carlotta is feeling amiable today."

That took him back a bit, for Lord David Cavanaugh's wife wasn't known to be the friendliest of creatures, particularly not to his somewhat tarnished family. "Indeed?"

"You don't have to sound so surprised," Clara said, laughing. "Carlotta is capable of amiability . . . sometimes."

Rex laughed, too, enjoying the wicked pause she'd put into her remark. "And what accounts for her friendly manner this particular afternoon?"

"That we're here. The duke's family hasn't received many invitations this season."

"Ah, yes," he said, remembering what Auntie had told him about her family. "The Dowager Duchess's scandalous marriage. It hurt the family's social position badly, did it?"

"It did, indeed. Your great-aunt's invitations—the ball, and now this picnic—have been welcomed with great delight by all of them, including Carlotta."

"Well, if anyone knows what the duke's family is

going through, my family does. My parents made my family a favorite target for gossip and a juicy topic of London's scandal sheets for years." The hint of bitterness in his voice was unmistakable, even to his own ears. "Sorry," he added. "I don't mean to denigrate your family's livelihood, Clara."

"No need to be sorry. You have every right to feel as you do. If it's any comfort, my family didn't publish scandal sheets at all until my sister invented one. For a time, the *Weekly Gazette* was a scandal sheet called *Society Snippets*, and the only reason Irene did that was because a scandal sheet can be very profitable, and we were in desperate need of money at the time."

"Another thing I completely understand," he assured her. "And I imagine your father's drinking made him a very poor businessman?"

She nodded. "His father was the one who turned Deverill Publishing into an empire, but my father managed to destroy it all in less than a decade. Irene got us out of queer-street with *Society Snippets*, but when she fell in love with Torquil, she changed it back into an ordinary newspaper because she didn't want to print gossip about his family. And given your history, I don't wonder that you hate newspapers."

"I grew weary of seeing my mother's latest love affair or speculations about my paternity splashed across the pages."

She grimaced. "I used to enjoy reading the gossip columns, I admit, but then, after I saw what gossip did to people—the duke's family in particular—I acquired a distaste for it. But I don't think we ever printed anything about your family in *Society Snippets*, and . . ." She paused, smiling at him. "I'm glad of it."

"So am I," he said, "if it makes you smile like that."

The smile faded at once, much to his regret. "And," he went on, feeling the need to keep talking, "I can't really resent newspapers so much now, can I? I work for one. Speaking of Lady Truelove, did you receive my column yesterday? I sent a footman with it."

"I did receive it, yes. And it's every bit as good as last week's. You have a true talent for giving advice, even if I sometimes question the morality of it."

That dry qualification compelled him to respond with his best innocent stare. "My advice to 'Speechless in South Kensington' was immoral?"

"You know I'm talking about your advice to your friend, Lionel. Although while we're on the subject, I'm not sure advising a young man to arrange a supposedly accidental encounter with the object of his affections while walking the most adorable puppy he can find is quite aboveboard."

"I don't see why not. The poor fellow's desperately in love, but the girl takes no notice of him. He wants to gain her attention and begin a conversation, and a puppy is an effective way to do both. A baby would have been even better, of course, but I couldn't imagine any young man would be willing to walk down the street in front of his ladylove's house pushing a pram. So, I settled for a puppy."

She laughed. "A wise decision. Though you do realize that within a week, young men all over town who are in love will be acquiring adorable puppies and walking the streets with them?"

"Well, if they keep the puppies, London will have fewer stray dogs, and more young couples will fall in love. I'm not sure I see a negative aspect, except that they'll all be expected to get married, poor devils. Speaking of marriage-minded people," he added, glancing past her, "I see Lady Geraldine Throckmorton is here today. Dina," he clarified as he noted Clara's bewildered look, "to her friends. Dark hair," he added as Clara turned her head. "Green walking suit, walking a white poodle on a lead."

"She's quite elegant, isn't she?" Clara commented, sounding a little surprised.

"Very," he agreed as she returned her attention to him. "Also, fashionable and sophisticated. That's what drew her to Lionel, I expect. The attraction of opposites." He paused, looking at Clara, appreciating that truth about human nature more than he ever had before. "People tend to be rather perverse that way."

"I wasn't." Her absurd little nose wrinkled up as she grinned. "I fell madly in love with a vicar."

"True," he agreed, and laughed a little. "Your tastes seem to have changed since then."

He regretted that careless comment at once. He'd meant it to be self-deprecatingly witty, but that wasn't how it had come out, and he rushed to qualify it. "I didn't mean to imply that I think you're falling for me. I'm not the sort to suit your preference. God knows, that's been clearly established, and—" He broke off, feeling deuced awkward, something he wasn't accustomed to and didn't like in the least. "What the devil is it about you, Clara Deverill?" he muttered in chagrin. "You're the only woman I've ever met in my life who can make me stammer like a schoolboy."

"I certainly seem to be making you stammer today. I rather like it, actually."

"Like it?"

"Yes." She smiled that wide, pretty smile of hers. "I'm usually the one doing the stammering."

That smile not only left him tongue-tied, it also caused the world to tilt a bit sideways again. He looked away, wondering in desperation if this topsy-turvy state was going to continue indefinitely, a question that impelled him to down his remaining champagne.

Fortified, he set his empty glass on the table beside his chair and returned to their previous, much-safer topic. "Unlike Dina, Lionel isn't the least bit elegant, I'm afraid. He's more like Fitz—that's his dog," he added, as she gave him a bewildered look. "Fitz is a sheepdog, and Lionel's a great deal like him— friendly, ambling, loyal. Dina, on the other hand, is very much like her poodle, elegant, sharp, perfectly groomed. People are rather like the dogs they choose, aren't they?"

"Are they?" She tilted her head, studying him. "Which breed are you?"

"Wolf," he said at once, not knowing if he was reminding her of that fact, or himself.

She made a face. "I meant, what breed of dog do you own?"

"Hounds, though strictly speaking, they aren't mine. They're my father's, and used only for foxhunting. At Braebourne, you see, we don't breed ratting terriers, or retrievers, or anything remotely practical."

She laughed, then sobered. "How does your friend, Lionel? Is he all right? Or is he still in the throes of heartbreak?"

"I don't know, actually," Rex confessed, keeping his voice light. "I've called twice, but his servants have told me both times that he's not receiving. And I've not seen him at White's when I've been there. Unless I want to chase him through the corridors of Parliament, I'm not sure what else I can do but wait for him to soften."

"He still thinks you betrayed his confidences, then?"

"Seems so. In fact, I'm sure that suspicion is becoming more cemented in his mind with each passing day."

"Why now?"

He met her gaze. "Word is starting to get 'round that you've caught my eye. That, I'm sure, is reinforcing his belief that I was indiscreet."

She bit her lip. "I'm sorry you're on the outs with your friend over my actions, and perhaps it was wrong of me to interfere, but his courtship—if one can call it that—was not aboveboard, so I can't find it in my heart to regret that Lady Throckmorton ended their amour because of what I wrote. And I still think it was very wrong of you to advise him as you did."

"I did it in the hope of giving them both more time together so they could decide how they truly felt about one another."

"You did it to help him avoid the dreaded state of matrimony."

"Not true. Be fair, Clara, if you please, and recall precisely what I said. I first told him he ought to break it off, since he wasn't sure he wanted to marry her, but when he expressed reluctance to do that, I gave him another option."

"A morally questionable one."

"But a better one than having to part irrevocably, in my opinion. And far, far better than to marry in haste and repent at leisure."

"I don't know." She paused, considering. "There could have been serious consequences, you know, to what they were doing. For her, particularly."

"You mean a child, I assume?"

"That, yes, but if they were caught, there would have been disgrace, ruin, and shame for her, child or no."

"Lionel would stand up, do the right thing, if any of that were to happen."

"You seem sure of that."

"I am sure. I've known Lionel since school days. He's an honorable man. Despite," he added as she raised a skeptical eyebrow, "what you might think."

"Then I don't see why he can't court Lady Throckmorton in an honorable fashion, especially now that he knows marriage is her expectation."

"Once two people take the step Lionel and Dina have, they've rather crossed the Rubicon." As he spoke, he wondered if his words were in defense of his friend or a reminder to himself. "Chaperoned walks and a stolen kiss or two behind the hedgerows might seem a bit tame to them now."

"Or it might have the opposite effect. It might serve to increase their anticipation by suspense."

"It might." Irresistibly drawn, he looked at her mouth, then wondered why he was torturing himself. "At least until the poor chap hurls himself off a bridge," he muttered, leaning back again in his chair.

Desperate for a new distraction, he looked away, and was heartily glad to see Lord James St. Clair walking toward them. "St. Clair," he greeted. "God, man, you look like the devil."

"No doubt," the other man agreed as he sank down, breathless and disheveled, beside their chairs, then fell back into the grass. Rolling his head, he looked at the girl beside him. "Why didn't I bring Nanny, Clara? Remind me."

"Because it's her day out." She looked him over, then she laughed. "Galbraith's right. The boys seem to have worn you to a nub already."

"They have, and I'm not ashamed to admit it. William's with them now, but if that continues too long, the poor fellow's likely to resign. If Torquil comes back to find we've lost our first footman, he'll be fit to be tied."

Rex moved to rise. "I can send a footman to fetch your nanny, if she's at Torquil House."

"That's all right," Clara said, standing up, bringing Rex fully to his feet and impelling St. Clair to rise as well. "Let Nanny have her day out. She's earned it. I'm happy to take the boys for a bit." She glanced at Rex, then back again. "If you will both excuse me?"

Rex bowed. "Of course."

"You're a brick, Clara," St. Clair called after her as she crossed the turf toward the twins and the poor footman who was trying valiantly to assist them in launching their kites.

"Your footman deserves a tip," Rex said, turning to the other man. "Helping you look after those boys of yours today."

"He'll have a large one, I assure you. But if you'll pardon me, Galbraith, I must take advantage of this heaven-sent opportunity and help myself to some of the sandwiches while I have the chance. Join me?"

Rex shook his head. "Thank you, no. I'll eat later."

With a nod, St. Clair moved off, headed for the marquee where refreshments had been laid out. He'd barely departed, however, before Rex was joined again, this time by Hetty, who was carrying two flutes of champagne.

"Here," she said, offering him one. "I noticed your glass was empty."

"You're an angel, Cousin."

"Angel?" Hetty laughed, sinking into the chair vacated by Clara. "I do believe that's the first time anyone's called me that."

"For good reason." He resumed his seat and took an appreciative swallow of champagne. "And given this most uncharacteristic show of solicitude on your part," he added, leaning back in his chair, "I can only conclude you have a deeper purpose."

She grinned at him from beneath her yellow straw hat as she tucked a loose tendril of her chestnut hair beneath the crown. "Curiosity. Miss Deverill," she clarified when Rex gave her an inquiring look.

"Ah," he said, pretending to be suddenly enlightened. "But why ask me about her? You met her yourself at the opera."

"A quick introduction before you cut her from the herd. And then the performance started." There was a wicked, knowing gleam in Hetty's green eyes that recalled his acute discomfort on the night in question.

"I can't be of much help in satisfying your curiosity, Cousin, for I met Miss Deverill myself only a few days before you did. Best ask Auntie Pet, if you want to know more about her."

"Auntie Pet is the one who sent me over here." She paused and took a sip of champagne. "She seems to think you have a romantic interest in the girl."

"Hope springs eternal."

"Auntie's terrible, I know. She's the same way with me and my sisters and brothers—shoving potential spouses at us every chance she has, if that makes you feel any better."

"It doesn't. As for Miss Deverill, I can assure Auntie—and you as well, for I know perfectly well that Auntie is not the only one in my family crossing her fingers and hoping for miracles—that the girl is not the least bit attracted to me." Even as he spoke, the damnable memory of sinking beneath Clara on that settee flashed through his mind.

"A woman who can resist you? Heavens."

Clara's lack of resistance seven days ago was, he feared, going to be a fundamental source of torment to him for the foreseeable future. "God, Hetty, you talk as if all the pretty girls of London are falling at my feet."

His cousin stared at him, her eyes going ingenuously wide. "Is this one pretty? I hadn't formed an opinion, myself, but it seems you have."

He gave her a warning look, but of course, being Hetty, she ignored it. Sitting up a bit straighter, she turned in her chair and studied the girl who was standing on an open stretch of turf, holding a reel of kite wool and talking with the twins. "She has a lovely figure," Hetty said after a moment and sighed. "So dainty. I'd kill for that tiny waist and those long legs."

Rex set his jaw, valiantly resisting delicious contemplations about Clara's figure as he watched her attempt to launch the kite. Her effort failed however, crashing the toy almost immediately into the turf and sending her and the two boys into peals of laughter.

If I had children, I'd never be bored.

"She seems quite sweet."

He stiffened, looking at his cousin. "Are you being catty?"

His voice was quiet, but a hint of what he thought of that comment must have shown in his expression, for looking at him, even his intrepid cousin shrank back a little.

"No, Rex," she said. "I'm not, actually. That was my impression when I met her, and it's still my impression."

Something in him relaxed.

"I only remark on it because . . ." She paused. "Sweet girls aren't your usual cup of tea, that's all."

The attraction of opposites.

He hastened into speech. "Miss Deverill and I are just friends."

One of Hetty's dark brows lifted a fraction. "Friends? You and any girl alive . . . friends?"

Her skepticism about that notion made him feel oddly defensive. "Is it so hard to imagine?"

She laughed. "Frankly, yes! Granted, you seem on very friendly terms with women of a certain type, much to Aunt Petunia's dismay. But I doubt any demirep could be described as your friend. And you're amiable as can be to women you consider out of bounds—married women, women in love with other men, etcetera. But when it comes to young, unmarried ladies, we know you pay no attention to them at all, as a rule, which is quite right of you, you rake. So, tell me how this particular girl could possibly have become your friend."

Because God has a wicked sense of humor.

Rex shrugged. "These things happen," he said lightly.

"Not to you." She sobered. "Be careful, Rex. Don't . . . hurt her."

He stirred, already quite aware of the damage a man like him could inflict upon a girl like Clara if the desire he felt for her was allowed free rein. "I told you, Miss Deverill has no romantic aspirations about me whatsoever. She knows me for just what I am."

"That's rather what I'm afraid of." With that enigmatic comment, Hetty rose and walked away, leaving Rex to watch Clara and battle the dragons of his lust.

Chapter 13

During the remainder of the picnic and the fortnight that followed it, Clara played the role she'd agreed upon. At every social function to which she and Rex were both invited, she greeted his attentions with the polite tolerance she'd promised, but nothing more.

As for Rex, he became the quintessential gentlemanly suitor, interested but not too interested. He sent his next two columns to her office through the post, for as he explained on one of the rare occasions when they could manage a private word, if he came to her office every Thursday on Lady Truelove's behalf, the members of her staff were sure to suspect the truth. And though he occasionally called on her at the duke's house, with Carlotta hovering as a proper chaperone should, slipping her a letter of any sort would have been impossible.

His interest in her was duly noted by society, as was her indifference to him, and not only did it give the gossip columnists a great deal of amusement at his expense, it also succeeded in drawing the notice of other men, just as he'd predicted it would.

Clara, who hadn't really believed him on that score, was rather taken aback when several young men, as well as the members of their families, began calling on her. Unprepared, she found it hard to manage the newfound attention, but she resisted the urge to withdraw back into her shy shell.

She did her best to apply the advice Rex had given the Devastated Debutante to her own situation, and she was amazed to discover that though she might not be as beautiful as her sister, she did have certain powers of attraction. And though she stammered her way awkwardly through quite a few conversations, she soon learned the art of making fun of her own stammering tongue. In every conversation, she strove to set aside her self-consciousness, and she worked hard to make every person she spoke with feel at ease in her company. Slowly, gradually, she grew more comfortable with attention, began to relax, and gained a measure of confidence that she'd never possessed before. For the first time since she entered society, she began to truly enjoy herself.

But it was in early June, at her second ball of the season, when Clara realized just how much society's view of her had changed. She'd barely greeted her hosts and entered the ballroom before one of the many young men she'd met during the past two weeks approached her and asked for his name to be placed on her dance card. He'd barely departed before there was another, and then another, and within fifteen minutes her dance card was nearly full.

"Heavens, Clara," Sarah said, laughing. "You are the belle of the ball this evening."

Astonished, pleased, and more than a little bemused, Clara glanced over the names on the card attached to her wrist. "It must be the dress," she said, making her friends laugh even though she'd only been half joking.

"If it is the dress," Angela put in, "then I definitely deserve some credit."

"You?" Sarah made a sound of derision. "I'm the one who advised her to pick the rose-pink silk at *Vivienne* because pink's her best color."

"Yes," Angela responded at once, "but I'm the one who advised her to lower the neckline."

"Only because we read it in Lady Truelove."

As her sisters-in-law debated the issue, Clara glanced down, dubious. Low neckline or no, she doubted her less-than-impressive bust was the reason for her recent social success, and when she looked up again, she knew it for a fact, because standing only a few feet away was the real reason.

He was watching her, his face grave, hands in the trouser pockets of his evening suit and one shoulder propped against a marble column. Windblown, rakish, a modern Adonis come to earth, and her breath caught in her throat.

Perceiving her gaze on him, Rex straightened away from the column and came toward her. "Good evening, ladies," he greeted with a bow. "I'd have stepped forward sooner, but I was waiting for the crowd to clear. I thought I might be trampled."

Stifled giggles from her companions greeted this declaration, and then, somehow, Angela and Sarah were gone, and she and Galbraith were alone.

"I hope I didn't wait too long to ask to be added to your dance card?" he said. "You've been surrounded ever since you arrived, penciling in name after name."

"I have, haven't I?" She laughed. "Heavens. How astonishing."

"Very," he agreed, his mouth curving at one corner. "Who'd ever have predicted such a thing?"

She made a face at him. "You were right," she conceded. "Is that why you came over here? To gloat?"

"Not at all. I told you why I came." He nodded to the card dangling from her wrist. "Unless I'm too late?"

"I have a few places left." She caught up her dance card and glanced over it. "I still have the Roger de Coverley, two quadrilles, a mazurka—"

"Not a mazurka," he cut in. "Those are dangerous."

The memory of their conversation the first time they'd danced together made her smile, and when she looked up, she found that he was smiling, too. "And do you have nefarious intentions?" she asked, putting on a frown of mock disapproval.

"Always." It was a rake's answer, careless and glib, and for some reason, it hurt.

She returned her attention to her dance card. "I have one waltz left, too, if . . ." She paused, her voice suddenly failing as she thought of being in his arms again. It was only a dance, in full view of everyone, not an intimate embrace on a settee, but that distinction didn't seem to matter, for at the thought of it, heat flooded her body and all her newfound poise started dissolving. Her gloved fingers tightened around the card as that old familiar shyness pressed her chest, but she made herself finish what she'd intended to say. "I have one w . . . waltz left . . . if . . . if you w . . . want it."

He didn't answer, and when she looked up, his faint smile was gone, but his eyes were as blue as the sea. "I want it, Clara."

She inhaled sharply as her heart slammed against her ribs with painful force, and she looked away again. She reached for the little pencil tied to her wrist, but when she glanced over her card to find the place to put his name, she couldn't help being amazed anew at how few lines were blank.

"It is astonishing, you know," she confessed softly, staring down at the list of penciled names. "At least to me. I've never had a dance card before." She looked up with a laugh. "Never needed one before."

He didn't laugh with her.

"It's because of you," she blurted out, nodding to the card in her fingers. "All this."

His mouth tightened. "No, it isn't," he said, shaking his head. "Every rose blooms at some point, Clara. I just happened to be here when it happened to you."

He spoke again before she could reply. "Best put my name down," he advised. "Otherwise, you might forget, and if some other chap steals my waltz, I shall demand pistols at dawn."

He bowed and walked away, and as she watched his broad-shouldered frame meld into the crowd, she knew he was wrong. She was only blooming now because of him, because of what she saw in his eyes when he looked at her, and what she heard in his voice when he said her name, and what she'd felt that glorious afternoon when he kissed her. He had awakened things in her that she'd never felt in her life, things she'd never known existed. If she was the rose, he was the sun and spring rain that had lifted her out of a lifetime of winter.

Maybe that, she thought, was what rakes were for.

IN CLARA'S CASE, a rake's kiss might have inspired her to bloom like a rose, but only an hour later, she discovered that not every rose was the same.

Having just made use of the lavatory, she was still in the water closet, adjusting her skirts, when she heard the outer door open and two women came into the ladies' withdrawing room, one of them clearly in great distress.

"I can't believe he's here," she sobbed. "Oh, Nan, it was awful."

"Now, now, everything will be all right. Just sit down here and catch your breath." There was a pause as the door was closed. "Seeing him must have been a terrible shock."

"It was! I haven't seen him, you know, since I broke things off, and I felt as if I'd been struck by an omnibus."

Clara bit her lip, acutely aware that this was the second time in a month she'd been privy to a confidential conversation. Deciding it was best if she exited and made her presence known to the other two women as quickly as possible, she finished settling her skirts, but when she turned to open the door of the water closet, the woman called Nan spoke again, stopping Clara in her tracks.

"But what is Lionel even doing here?"

Clara froze, hand on the doorknob.

"I don't know," the first woman sobbed. "And given that he's made no effort to speak to me, I shouldn't even care why. But I do care," she added on another sob.

The woman called Nan gave a cry of sympathy. "Oh, Dina, my dear."

At the sound of that name, Clara's hand fell away from the doorknob, and she stayed right where she was, listening for all she was worth.

"This is a charity ball," Dina said with tearful indignation. "Lionel never attends public balls. How dare he come here?"

"He's such a cad. Handkerchief?"

"Thank you." Dina sniffed. "I suppose it's just one of those cruel twists of fate."

"Or perhaps he knew you'd be here. As you said, he never comes to these charity affairs, and you are on the committee."

"Do you think he may have come to make up our quarrel?" There was so much hope in Dina's voice that Clara's heart twisted with renewed compassion.

"It's possible. But of course, it may also be that it's sheer coincidence. Not everyone bothers to read the list of sponsors before purchasing vouchers. And anyway . . ." She hesitated, then said, "Don't be offended, darling, if I ask this question, but do you really want him back? I mean, you were the one to break things off."

"Oh, he deserved it! When he gave me that ridiculous speech, it was so much like Lady Truelove's column, it was uncanny."

Not really, Clara thought with a grimace.

"Why, I felt as if Lady Truelove was almost talking to me," Dina continued, "instead of to that other poor girl. I knew just what Lionel was trying to do, the scoundrel."

"Well, I think you were quite right to call his bluff."

"Was I?" She gave a sob. "Now that I've seen him again, I'm not so sure."

"Oh, my dear!"

There was a momentary pause, probably for a comforting hug, and then Dina said, "I knew I was getting into deep waters when I told him I loved him. I never should have said it first!"

"A woman should never say it first. Have another handkerchief."

"It just came spilling out. And when he said he loved me, too, of course I thought that settled it, and we'd marry. That's what people are supposed to do when they love each other, isn't it?"

Dina's starting to feel guilty.

Rex's words from that afternoon in her office came echoing back, and Clara wondered just how large a part guilt had played in the other woman's decisions and actions. Perhaps more, she was forced to concede, than she had first thought.

They've known each other a month. Do you really think they are in any position to commit to each other for the rest of their lives?

"Well, yes," Nan said, her voice intruding on Clara's memories of her debate with Rex a few weeks earlier. "Getting married is the customary choice. But it's not as if it's required, not for the two of you. You're a widow, so if you're discreet, and take the proper precautions, of course, there's no reason you can't just pick up where you left off, is there? There are risks, of course, but you know that already—"

"But that's just it," Dina cut in, "I don't want to go back to that. Oh, it was all right at first, terribly exciting, and such wicked fun. But it's all different now. I love him."

"Do you truly want to marry him, then?"

"I don't know! When he said he loved me, I was sure he meant it, but after that ridiculous speech, how can I ever believe he was telling the truth? After he tried to pull the wool over my eyes, how could I ever trust him? If I hadn't read Lady Truelove that very afternoon, I might have fallen for it, too! But Lady Truelove was right to say, 'When a man declares his love, he should be prepared to demonstrate it by an honorable courtship.' Oh, Nan, that's not too much to ask, is it?"

Of course not, Clara answered silently, her sympathy for the other woman deepening, along with her sense of responsibility. Surely something could be done to make Lionel step up and behave honorably.

"Still," Dina said, sniffing, "I doubt it matters, since it's clear he's not willing to do the right thing."

"Do you want to leave?" her friend asked. "Shall I have them fetch the carriage?"

"Run away like a rabbit? Never. I'm all right now, and I have no intention of leaving just because he's here. Let's go back—no, wait. Do I look a fright?"

"Not too bad, but . . . here. Put on a bit of my face powder. It's wonderful stuff. A few dabs of that, and no one will know you've been crying."

The face powder must have done the trick, for a few

seconds later, Dina gave a deep sigh and said, "Oh, that's better. I feel myself again."

"If Lionel does approach you, what will you say?"

"If he's not willing to court me in an honorable fashion, there's nothing to say."

That sound observation was punctuated by a decisive slam of the door. Clara waited a few moments, but when she heard nothing further, she emerged from the water closet to find herself alone in the withdrawing room, except for the maid in attendance.

Clara paused before one of the pink marble washstands, considering the situation as she washed her hands. The conversation of the other two women made it clear Dina was still in love with Lionel, and that what she wanted was demonstrable proof he could be trusted with her heart and her future before she decided to marry him. Rex had acknowledged that Lionel loved Dina, but he just wasn't sure they knew each other well enough to wed. If that was still the case, perhaps something could be done to bring these two people back together. She and Rex would have to be the ones to make it come about, since the other two were far too proud and hurt to do it themselves. And, besides, she and Rex had been the ones responsible for tearing the two lovers apart in the first place.

A short while later, however, when Rex claimed his waltz with her, he didn't seem to share her point of view.

"Is eavesdropping on conversations something you do with everyone?" he asked as they swirled across the ballroom floor. "Or just my friends?"

"Do be serious. She's devastated, Rex."

"Possibly. Or she sees that he's out about town again, having fun, and she regrets tossing him aside."

"Dog in the manger? I don't think that's it at all. I think she really is heartbroken, and bewildered that he's not willing to do right by her."

"Perhaps. Either way, what's it to do with us?"

"We caused it. Yes, we," she emphasized when one of his brows lifted in a sardonic curve. "Isn't there something we can do?"

"I think we've both done enough already, don't you?"

"We broke them apart. Can't we reunite them?"

He shrugged. "To what end?"

"Honorable courtship, of course. And," she added firmly as he groaned, "a view to matrimony."

"A view aspired to by no sane man, ever. And Lionel, I assure you, is quite sane. He asked for my advice to avoid matrimony, remember?"

"You could persuade him."

"Send a man to hell before he's even dead?" Rex quipped. "Why would I do that?"

"You said you're not against marriage for everyone," she reminded.

"I support it for my friends only if they are sure it's what they want, and a month isn't long enough for anyone to be sure."

"It's nearly two months now."

"During which time, they've not seen each other, as your account of Dina's conversation with her friend makes clear. And," he added before she could reply, "even if I were willing to try bringing them back where they were, I'd have little opportunity, since—as you may have noticed—Lionel is still not speaking to me."

"All the more reason for us to do something, then. What better way to regain his goodwill than to reunite him with the woman he loves?"

He muttered an oath, then sighed. "I assume you have a plan in mind to achieve this miracle?"

"You had a plan already, remember? Is your friend a man of discretion? If I did what you first asked me to do, if I explained to him what really happened, could he be persuaded to keep my secret?"

"Since his entire reason for being so angry with me is my supposed lack of discretion, he's hardly the sort to tell tales himself. If you told him about Lady Truelove and asked him to keep it to himself, he wouldn't breathe a word. But at this point, he'd never believe you. It's known now that I'm paying you my addresses, and I'm sure he's more convinced than ever that I gossiped to you, and that you used that gossip as fodder for the column. How could he ever be made to think otherwise?"

"By the fact that you'd never court me if I had used you so despicably?"

"There's something in that, I suppose. But you'll have to sound very convincing when you explain to him what really happened."

"It's not hard to sound convincing if one's telling the truth."

"It won't all be true. For I assume you're not going to tell him I'm writing the thing now."

"Heavens, no. That would confirm all his worst suspicions even more strongly. I shall let it be assumed I'm still Lady Truelove. Well?" she prompted when he didn't reply. "Will you help?"

"I'd be very glad for him to know what really happened, and even more glad if it succeeds in mending our quarrel. But as for the rest, I'm not sure it's right to interfere."

"Well, that's the thing about giving advice. You are required to bear some responsibility for the consequences."

"Coming from you," he said dryly, "that's rich."

Her answering look was wry. "Why do you think I didn't want the job of being Lady Truelove in the first place? But working to bring them together for an honorable courtship is the right thing to do."

"Only from your point of view, and only if it stays that way. As I told you at the picnic, they've crossed the Rubicon. An honorable courtship, with all its constraints, would be something they'd probably find unbearable. Neither of them will be able to tolerate it now, at least not for very long. If we bring them back together, I give them a fortnight before they either capitulate to society's rules and rush into marriage—the very thing I wanted them to avoid—or passion will out, and they'll resume their secret assignations at discreet London hotels—a situation you have deemed dishonorable and immoral."

"She's heartbroken, Rex. She thought he loved her, that he'd come after her when she ended things, and that he'd do the right thing. She's entitled to expect honorable courtship of a man who professes to love her, isn't she?"

"Oh, good Lord." He sighed, tilting his head back to glance at the ceiling. "Women," he said as if talking to God, "are the very devil."

He looked at her again. "If I agree to this, I want it understood that whatever decision they make is theirs, and the affair ceases to be any of our business. If they resume their illicit liaisons, I don't want to hear one word from you about how he's being dishonorable."

She nodded, lifting her hand from his shoulder to make a crossing gesture over her heart. "Not one word, I swear. But," she couldn't help adding, "if they decide to get married, you'll have to put on your best morning coat, go to the wedding, and give that speech about true love and happy marriage. You said you would, if it came to it."

"Don't remind me."

She ignored that. "So, the question is, how can we maneuver Lionel into listening to me long enough for me to explain what I did?"

"That is the first bridge to cross, I agree." He paused, and for several turns around the ballroom, they were both silent.

"There might be a way," he said at last. "I know you're quite the social butterfly this evening, but have you any dances left on your card?"

"One, I think." She pulled her hand from his and flipped over the card that dangled from her left wrist. "The one directly after this. Why?"

"Because Lionel is going to ask you to dance."

With his surprising prediction still hanging in the air, their waltz came to an end. They pulled apart and made their bows, but as Rex escorted her back to her place, she was impelled to point out the obvious flaw in his idea. "Your friend doesn't know me. He and I have never even been introduced."

"Believe me, that is the least of our problems."

"He'll never ask me to dance," she said as they paused beside Sarah and Angela. "Why would he?"

"Says the girl with the full dance card."

"You know what I mean. I'm sure he blames me as much as he does you for what happened. Why would he ever ask me to dance?"

"To make me jealous, of course." Rex bowed over her hand, and as he straightened, there was a look in his eyes she recognized, one that made her already-rapid heartbeat quicken even more. "And if he makes you smile, Clara, he'll succeed."

"WELL, I'VE DONE what you asked." Hetty shook her head in obvious bafflement as she joined Rex at the edge of the dance floor. "Though your reason for asking me to introduce Clara to Lionel Strange escapes me. Look what happened." She waved a hand toward the ballroom floor. "He immediately asked her to dance."

"Did he?"

"An event which doesn't seem to surprise you," Hetty murmured, staring at him. "You wanted him to dance with her? But why?" she asked when he nodded. "Why would you want that?"

"I know what I'm doing," he assured, but Fate seemed inclined to test his declaration, for at that moment, Clara smiled at Lionel, and Rex experienced an almost primal urge to snarl, an echo of what he'd felt earlier as he'd watched London's young turks gathering round her asking for dances. Not wanting to be a glutton for punishment, he'd escaped to the card room after securing his own dance with her, but in this case, he was obliged to watch her dancing with another man, and though he could not deny his own jealousy, he tried not to explore it too deeply, for there was nothing he could do about it. Still, he couldn't help being glad Lionel's heart was already taken.

"Do you, Rex?" Hetty asked, bringing his attention back to her. "Do you know what you're doing? Lionel Strange is one of London's most eligible bachelors. Not much money, of course, but being an MP, he has an income. And he is rising in the Labor Party, I understand. He could be Home Secretary one day. He's very good-looking, too. And, like Miss Deverill's father, he comes from the middle class. Many would consider Lionel and Miss Deverill rather well-suited, in fact."

Rex didn't reply.

"Oh, I don't understand you at all!" she cried. "I thought you liked this girl."

"I do like her." Deep inside, lusty dragons rumbled, reminding him how much. "But she and I are just—"

"Just friends," she finished for him. "Yes, so you've said. But since you talk with her at every party, you accept invitations to events you know she will attend, and you dance with her at balls, you are giving everyone in society the impression you're quite keen." She looked at the dance floor, then back at him. "And yet, I have observed that she does not seem all that taken with you."

He thought of that afternoon on the settee, of Clara's passionate response to his kiss. Guilt rose in him, and was at once snuffed out as desire took over. He stirred, looking away.

"Ooh-la-la," Hetty murmured, watching him. "Perhaps the shoe's on the other foot, at last."

He set his jaw, working to muster his dignity, but dignity was a difficult thing to find when memories of Clara's kiss were making his body burn. "That," he said, "is absurd."

"Is it? Perhaps Lionel is out on the dance floor with her to plead your suit?"

Despite what he was feeling, that suggestion was almost enough to make him laugh. "Didn't you hear what happened at Auntie's ball? Lionel knocked me unconscious."

"Oh, you two have been friends forever. Whatever your quarrel was about, it's obvious you've made up by now. Because I can think of no other reason why you would willingly push Miss Deverill, a woman you clearly have a passion for, into the arms of a man so perfectly suited to her."

He did not reply, and after a moment, Hetty gave a vexed sigh.

"Oh, very well, since it's clear you're in no mind to part with further details, I shall take myself off and go in to supper."

Hetty walked away, and Rex returned his attention to the ballroom floor, shoving memories of that afternoon on the settee with Clara out of his mind even as he searched for her among the dancers. When he found her, he observed that Lionel was listening quite closely to what she was saying, a very good sign, indeed. And when the dance was over and he escorted her off the floor, he nodded to Rex as he passed by.

That, Rex knew, was an even more encouraging sign, but it was only as Lionel escorted Clara in to supper and she gave Rex a nod over her shoulder that he allowed himself to believe Lionel was willing to forgive and the plan had succeeded.

Not that he shared Clara's romantic view of what success entailed, but that, he decided, was another battle for another day.

Chapter 14

With Lord and Lady Montcrieffe's charity ball, Clara's season took an even more frantic turn. The next day, invitations began to pour in, and within two weeks, she found that every moment, from breakfast to the wee small hours, was being conscripted for some activity. Luncheons, picnics, charity meetings, Afternoon-At-Homes, and water parties filled her days, while dinner parties, theater, opera, suppers at the Savoy, cotillions, and balls filled her evenings. The pace became so rigorous, that had she only had herself to consider, she might have begun refusing invitations to give herself a rest.

But the duke's family benefited greatly from her elevation in status, for almost all the invitations included them as well, and she didn't have the heart to turn away any opportunity to help them.

As for Rex, she continued to treat him with the same

offhand disinterest she had before, and he continued to play the role of interested suitor in pursuit. For Clara, however, the charade seemed harder to maintain after the ball than it had before. The image of him, one shoulder against a marble column and his face so grave, often came into her mind, and whenever it did, a tiny throb of sweet pain always hit her square in the chest.

Sometimes, she would catch him looking at her as he had that night—across someone's drawing room, or down the table at a dinner party—and his voice— low, vibrant with intensity—would echo in her ears.

I want it, Clara.

Sometimes, he would invade her dreams at night, his mouth on hers and his arms around her and his body hard beneath her, and she'd wake up with her lips tingling and her body aching as if she had a fever. She ought to have found it easier as time went on to put that forbidden afternoon out of her mind, but as the days passed, the memory only seemed to grow stronger, ever harder to suppress.

As for their efforts to reunite Dina and Lionel, Rex reported that he and his friend had forged a truce, but beyond that, he knew nothing of how the other man's romance with Dina was progressing, or if it was progressing at all. He continued to send the Lady True-love column to her through the post, and she never found cause to change a single word he wrote. His advice to London's lovelorn was always spot-on, and morally acceptable, though whether the latter fact was due to her influence, Clara could not have said.

She tried to carve out at least an hour or two each day to spend at the paper, but she couldn't always manage it. One morning about a fortnight after the Mont-crieffe ball, a glance through her calendar at breakfast revealed that a full four days had gone by since her last visit to Belford Row. Worse, it was Friday, which meant she had not yet read Rex's column, nor had she reviewed that week's layout of the paper. Constructed by Mr. Beale the previous day, the layout was probably sitting on her desk, still waiting for her approval. Either that, she thought wryly, or Mr. Beale had used her absence as an excuse to increase his own authority and had taken it upon himself to approve the layout. He may even have opened and read this week's Lady Truelove column, perhaps even editing it himself. With that thought, Clara knew a visit to Belford Row was in order.

Truth be told, she was rather relieved to take a bit of time away from luncheons and parties and have a bit of peace and quiet in her little office. Cancelling all her appointments for the afternoon, she took a taxi to Belford Row.

But the moment she arrived at the newspaper office, she realized peace and quiet were the last things she was to have. She'd barely opened the door a fraction when Mr. Beale's enraged voice poured to her through the doorway.

"This is the most idiotic piece of writing I've read in my life, Miss Trent. You call this journalism? It's shallow, facile rubbish."

"Shallow and facile?" a female voice countered. "That's a bit redundant, isn't it, sir?"

That pert reply earned stifled giggles from the other women on the staff, but when Clara pushed the door fully open, she found Mr. Beale wasn't laughing with them. Instead, he was glowering at the petite Elsa Trent, his usual sour expression replaced by one of unmistakable outrage.

"Mr. Beale, what is going on here?" Clara demanded as she stepped inside the office.

The other women glanced at her, but by Mr. Beale, she was ignored. He didn't even glance in her direction.

"I'll have none of your cheek, miss," he said to Elsa, waving a sheaf of papers in the girl's face. "To read this was difficult, to edit it is impossible. Throw it out and start again."

"But, sir, I'm not sure what's wrong with it. If you could just tell me—"

"Start again," he interrupted her, "and if I hear one more word of argument, you'll be looking for other employment." And with that, he tossed the pages in Elsa's face.

Fury erupted inside Clara, and before she knew it, the door had slammed behind her, and she was across the room, coming between Elsa and Mr. Beale as the pages of the other woman's composition fluttered to the floor around them.

"That will be enough!" she said. "Mr. Beale, cease this unthinkable abuse of Miss Trent at once."

"Abuse?" He left off berating Elsa and turned to scowl at Clara. "The abuse is upon me, Miss Deverill, that I am expected to edit fluffy stories about nothing by silly women who can't write, and that I should suffer cheek from them when I order changes to be made. But the most galling part," he added, as she opened her mouth to reply, "is that I should be reporting to a chit of a girl who's half my age, and hasn't a fraction of my experience. And," he went on giving her a disdainful glance up and down, "to be upbraided by someone unworthy of my respect when I am attempting to exert my rightful authority is unbearable. It's—"

"You're right," Clara interrupted, and she knew all the fury she felt was in her voice, because her two clipped words cut through his tirade at once. "It *is* unbearable, so much so, in fact, that I can't think of any reason I should tolerate it from you a single moment longer."

Her choice of pronouns was not lost on the editor. His jaw slackened and his eyes bulged, and Clara might have found his shock rather comical, if anger wasn't freezing in her veins like ice water.

"For three months, Mr. Beale, I have overlooked your bellicose manner, your arrogance, and your lack of consideration for the others who work here," she said, relishing every word as she spoke. "For too long, I have striven to see your point of view, and I have worked to ignore your denigrating remarks. But in berating a member of the staff," she went on as he attempted to object, "in this vicious manner, you have gone utterly beyond the pale." She took a deep breath, exhilaration making her almost dizzy. "Mr. Beale, you are fired."

"You don't have the authority to terminate my employment."

"No?" She laughed, savoring this moment far more than she probably ought, given the problems it would cause. But she knew she'd never have any regrets, no matter what happened next. "Who's to stop me?" She looked him up and down with scorn. "You?"

"As we have discussed many times, I do not work

for you, Miss Deverill. I was hired on the understanding that I would be working for your brother—"

"But my brother is not here," she cut in, spreading her arms wide in an encompassing gesture. "I am. And as the only Deverill on the premises with the authority to act, I am terminating your employment immediately. This decision," she added as he attempted to speak, "is not open for discussion."

"I refuse to stand for this. I shall go to your father."

"Oh, do." Clara laughed again, a little wildly this time, for her exhilaration was deepening into absolute glee, and she wondered why she had ever tried to pacify this man or work with him or even tolerate him. She waved a hand toward the stairs behind her. "Please, do. He's upstairs in the drawing room. I'm sure he'll give you sympathy over how unfair I'm being and commiserate with you about how difficult and disobliging women can be. He'll probably even offer you a drink. But what he won't do is countermand my decision. He hasn't the legal authority to do so, nor—let us be frank—does he have the will."

"He owns this building—"

"But he does not control, nor even own, the newspaper, and he certainly does not control or own me. Now, remove yourself from these premises at once. The personal items in your desk, as well as all wages owed you until this moment, will be forwarded to your residence by the end of the day. Don't expect a letter of character, for there won't be one. And don't," she added as he stepped closer to her, his fists clenched, "make me call a constable."

He stood there a moment, staring at her, his jaw working furiously. Clara stared back, unblinking, and after a moment, he turned away with an oath and stalked toward the door. He paused only long enough to pull his mackintosh from the coat tree before walking out and slamming the door behind him.

The sound reverberated through the silent room like a gunshot, but no one moved. The three other women in the office stared at Clara in wide-eyed shock, but none of them, it seemed, knew quite what to say.

Clara drew a deep breath, feeling a bit shaky now that the deed was done. She glanced around. "Has he been as abusive as this every time I've been away from the premises?"

The women exchanged glances, but none said a word, and Clara had her answer. "I see. Ladies, you have my deepest apologies, for I have unforgivably neglected my duty to you and to the newspaper. None of you should ever have to put up with such appalling behavior from anyone, man or woman. If it ever happens again, you must report it to me immediately. You will never be in trouble for doing so, I promise you. As for my part, I will do my level best not to neglect you again. Now, Evie?"

She turned to the secretary. "Ring up Merrick's Employment Agency, and inform Miss Merrick we require a newspaper editor. Someone experienced in the position, and—preferably—pleasant to work with. Make it clear the person must be not only knowledgeable and experienced, but also comfortable operating under a woman's authority and, when needed, supervising a female staff. As owner of her own agency, I'm sure Miss Merrick, of all people, will appreciate our reason for such requirements."

The other three women laughed, and the tension broke.

"Hazel," she went on, turning to the blonde young woman beside Miss Huish, "since you've donned your coat, I take it you were on your way to lunch? Are the advertisements ready for typesetting?"

"Yes, Miss Deverill."

"Then, I hope when you return, you'll be willing to compose an advertisement stating our need for a new editor?"

"Yes, ma'am. I'll even work through lunch."

Clara smiled. "I appreciate the sacrifice, but I think we can spare you for half an hour. After you've composed the advertisement, bring it to me for review. Once I have approved it, Evie will arrange to have it inserted in the appropriate newspapers."

"Will they accept it, do you think?" Evie asked. "Being competitors?"

"Some may not, but some will—particularly the larger papers up north. Try the *Manchester Daily Mail* and the *Leeds Gazette*, for a start. And all of Lord Marlowe's papers. Even his London papers will likely accept an ad of that sort. Marlowe's never had to be afraid of losing staff to his competition. And," she added, returning her attention to Hazel, "we shall put a quarter page announcement in this week's edition of the *Gazette*, inviting qualified candidates to apply, so I'd like you to design that as well."

"What about the layout?" Hazel asked. "Mr. Beale's already done it. There's nowhere to add another advertisement, not one of that size."

"I will reconstruct the layout. You design the advertisement, Hazel, and I'll make it fit. A full quarter-page."

"Yes, ma'am. I'll just get a sandwich and apple from the costermonger and come straight back." Hazel departed, and Clara turned to the woman whose latest article had been the catalyst of this showdown, but she had no chance to give Elsa any instructions.

"I am so sorry, Miss Deverill," the other woman burst out. "I didn't mean to give Mr. Beale any cheek. Truly, I didn't. And now, we've no editor. I know I've put us all in the devil of a mess—"

"Please, Elsa, do not apologize. What happened was not your fault in any way. The man is impossible, and I thought you remarkably restrained, given the circumstances. I put up with him for far too long, I know, but I can assure you, I don't consider his departure any great loss. However, if you believe any of the comments in his tirade to be valid—and try to be as honest with yourself as you can about that—then I want you to incorporate them into your piece. Put anything else that awful man may have said to you out of your mind, all right? Once you've finished reviewing your work," she added as the other woman nodded, "type a final draft and put it on my desk for editing."

"Does that mean you'll be our editor until you hire a replacement?"

"I shall have to be."

Elsa smiled, clearly relieved by that news, but Clara could not really share the feeling, for the position of editor was arduous and difficult, even for someone experienced at the job, and Clara wasn't at all confident she could do it properly. And as she'd told Rex, good editors were a rare commodity, so it would probably take some time to find the right person, which meant her first season in society might well be over.

On the other hand, when she thought of Mr. Beale's shocked face, she knew that forfeiting the rest of her season was a small price to pay. And, more importantly, she also knew that no matter how many mistakes she made in her new role, she would never again make the worst one of all. She would never trust anyone else's judgement, including her beloved sister's, more than she trusted her own.

REX HAD NEVER been the sort for self-torture, but after the Montcrieffe ball, it soon became clear he'd somehow become addicted to it, at least as far as Clara was concerned.

In the two weeks since the ball, he'd spent most of his time searching for her amid the crowds at whatever event they both happened to be attending. Whenever he had happened to catch sight of her, she always seemed to be talking to some other man. At dinner parties, silly rules of precedent always prevented him from sitting beside her at the table, and though she'd saved him a dance at every ball, it hadn't always been a waltz, worse luck. As a result, he'd spent most of his time since the Montcrieffe ball tamping down either lust or jealousy, perfectly aware he had no right to either, and by the time two weeks had passed, he was in a state of such acute frustration, he felt ready to chuck the entire business and go find some form of employment that was more relaxing to his mind and easier on his body—prizefighter, perhaps, or lion tamer.

But after a fortnight of this frustration, he found him-

self relieved of it, and his mood took a decided turn
for the worse. She vanished from society altogether,
and after a full week passed with no sign of her at any
party or ball, he decided to find out what was going on.
Catching Lady David at the opera during intermission,
he asked after Clara and was assured that though she
was quite well, she had been obligated by unforeseen
circumstances to return home for an indefinite period.
A press for more details yielded no additional information, and Rex, not knowing whether to be worried or
exasperated, decided it was time to find Clara and hear
from her what these unforeseen circumstances were.
On the off-chance he might be responsible in some
way for her absence, he acquired a bottle of champagne from the refreshments steward, then he left Covent Garden and took a taxi to Belford Row.

When he arrived at Clara's home, the windows of
the newspaper showed the front office to be dark and
empty, but there was light spilling from Clara's office into the corridor at the back, and he concluded
she must be working late. He tried the door, and finding it unlocked, he went inside, but when he called
her name, there was no answer. Despite that, he went
inside, thinking it best to extinguish her lamp before
presenting himself at her front door, for an unattended
lamp was a fire hazard. As he crossed the outer office,
he made a note to give Clara a sound lecture about
leaving lamps lit and doors unlocked, but when he entered her office, he found her still there, and at the
sight of her slumped over her desk, sound asleep, her
cheek pillowed on the back of her hand, the fingers
of her other hand still clenched around a pencil, any
lectures about anything died on his lips.

He removed his top hat and took a step closer, then stopped, realizing he probably ought not to wake her, and yet, he could hardly think leaving her to sleep this way, hunched over her desk, was a better idea. Before he could decide, however, some instinct woke her. She jerked upright, an abrupt move that rolled her chair back a few inches and sent a lock of her hair tumbling down over her face.

"Rex?" She brushed the loose lock of her hair back from her forehead, blinking sleepily at him. "What are you doing here?"

"A courtship, even a sham one, takes two people, I'm afraid."

She sighed and pulled her chair close to her desk again. "Sorry, but I've been terribly busy with the paper."

"Ah." He glanced at his surroundings, noting the untidiness of her office, a characteristic he did not remember from his previous visits here. Stacks of newspapers, files, and other documents seemed to be everywhere—on chairs, on filing cabinets, on the floor, and on her desk. Also on her desk were sheets of drawing paper, charcoal pencils, and various other stationery supplies. "Yes, so I see."

He looked at her again, noticing that her hair wasn't fashioned in its usual austere crown. Instead, the locks were piled in a careless, haphazard sort of chignon at the back of her head that was soft and pretty and looked ready to tumble down at the slightest provocation.

That was dangerous thinking, but even as he gave himself the reminder, he said, "You've changed your hair."

She flushed. "I don't have a maid here, and I've been too occupied to bother much with it," she mumbled, lifting her hands to the messy chignon as if to tidy it.

"Leave it," he ordered. "It's deuced attractive that way."

The moment the words were out of his mouth, he wanted to kick himself in the head.

"It is?" She touched the chignon self-consciously, giving him a dubious look. "But it's so untidy."

He had no intention of explaining why that might have a certain appeal, and fortunately, she spoke again, preventing him from having to invent some absurd explanation.

"You brought champagne?"

"I did." Pushing aside the images of her with her hair tumbling down around bare white shoulders, he came in and set the bottle in front of her. "You've been missing from every social gathering this week. Lady David assured me you weren't ill, but she was so evasive on the subject that I thought your absence might be my fault. So, I decided to find out what was going on. I hope I haven't blotted my copybook in some way?"

"Oh, no, it's nothing to do with you. As for Carlotta, she hates having to explain to anyone that I have an occupation, especially one as middle-class as running a newspaper. That's probably why she refused to enlighten you. It embarrasses her that I'm engaging in a profession, however temporary it might be."

"I see. But what is all this?" he asked, gesturing to the disarray all around her with his hat. "What's happened?"

"I fired Mr. Beale."

"You did?" He grinned, setting his top hat aside as

he sank into the swivel chair opposite her. "What delightful news."

She made a face at him as she shoved her pencil behind her ear. "Yes, well, I've been paying for that delight ever since. First, the typesetter quit. Being the only remaining male employee in a company of women made him uncomfortable, he said. So, Hazel and I had to typeset last week's issue ourselves. Then, the printing press gave out—after, I'm thankful to say, we'd printed all the copies. I had to scramble like mad to find a qualified firm to contract the typesetting and printing for this week's issue, and I'd barely done that before Hazel's aunt came down with flu and she had to go home to Surrey. I meant to let you know what was happening, but, honestly, Rex, I just . . . forgot."

She gave a little laugh, shaking her head and sending the looser lock of hair tumbling down again. "Terribly rude of me, wasn't it?"

"Not at all. Perfectly understandable." He leaned forward, frowning as he noted the tired lines and shadows of her face. "You look quite done in, my lamb."

"I am a bit tired," she admitted and attempted to shove the loose tendril of her hair back again, but when it immediately fell back over her brow, she left it there, as if too weary to bother trying to tuck it into place.

He did it for her, reaching out to curl it behind her ear. Fighting the temptation to linger and touch the soft skin of her cheek, he let his hand fall. "More than a bit," he said gently, leaning back in his chair.

"It's not only work here that's worn me out. The season had become this mad dash from party to party."

"It tends to get that way."

"It's been rather nice to have a change, even if the pace of my days hasn't slowed." She gave a laugh. "The odd thing is that I'm actually enjoying myself here. That's something I never thought would happen."

"Still, I daresay you're due for a rest. Perhaps you should go upstairs and go to bed."

"I can't." She gestured to the pages spread across her desk and the credenza behind her. "I have to finish this first."

"And what is so important that it can't wait until morning?"

"With Hazel gone, I'm not only the publisher and the editor, but also the advertising artist. I have a meeting with Ebenezer Shaw first thing in the morning in which I'm supposed to show him ideas for advertisements to launch his company's newest product. Hazel left me with some conceptual ideas, but she did not have time to do any sketches before she left, so I must do them. I've been trying, but . . ." Clara's shoulders slumped as she stared down at her efforts. "Sketching is something for which I have little talent, I'm afraid."

He glanced at her pathetic attempts and was forced to agree.

"They're awful, I know," she said as if reading his mind. "But I can't cancel the meeting. He's such a curmudgeon, he's likely to withdraw the entire campaign if I'm not prepared, and if he does that, we could lose over a thousand pounds in advertising revenue. More, if he's in a sour mood."

"Never fear." Rex stood up and began unbuttoning his black evening jacket. "You shall not lose a single penny."

"What are you doing?" she asked as he slid his jacket off his shoulders, slung it over the back of his chair, and began unfastening his cuff links.

"What do you think I'm doing?" He dropped the heavy silver cuff links into her pen tray and began rolling up his shirt sleeves. "I'm going to help you."

Chapter 15

*I*f Rex had any hope his announcement would cause Clara to deem him her knight in shining armor, rush into his arms, and shower him with grateful kisses, he was immediately disappointed.

She frowned, her skepticism obvious. "Have you any talent for drawing?"

"More than you, my sweet," he countered, plucking her charcoal pencil from behind her ear. He spread out her sketches, and a quick glance over her stick men, skewed bottles, and scribbled notes told him what she was attempting to do. "Shaw's Liver Pills has a new patent medicine, I see."

"A cure for colds."

He made a scoffing sound that earned him a disapproving look.

"Disparaging our advertiser's product," she said dryly, "is not inspiring my confidence in your ability."

"Perhaps this will." Rex pulled a fresh sheet of drawing paper in front of him, bent over the desk, and began to sketch. It only took a few quick strokes to capture the essence of a happy baby and relieved mother, and by the time she had circled around to his side of the desk, he'd added a replica of a medicine bottle to one side and scrawled the Shaw's insignia at the top. "There," he said, straightening. "How's that?"

Staring down at the page, she made a choked sound of relief, something halfway between a sigh and a sob, and he began to think her initial dim opinion of him was getting a polish at last. He wasn't sure if he deserved it, but he savored it just the same.

"It's good. Truly good." She turned toward him, pressing a hand to her chest. "Oh, thank you, Rex. Thank you."

Her brown eyes were filled with enough gratitude and relief that he thought of pushing his luck and demanding some sweet, sweet compensation, but he refrained. "I just wish I'd known you were in this sort of difficulty earlier," he said instead. "I'd have come straight here this evening and spared myself the pain of listening to two hours of Wagnerian opera."

"Is that where you were? Covent Garden?"

He nodded. "That's where I spoke with Lady David. I saw her across the way, in the duke's box, noted you weren't with her party, and decided it was time to run you to earth."

"I'm so glad you did. Can you . . . would you mind doing a few more of these?"

"That depends. Have you anything to eat?"

"You want food?"

"Well, there are other compensations I could ask

for," he couldn't resist saying, "but I'll settle for a plate of sandwiches."

"I think I can manage that." She gestured to some handwritten pages piled on one side of her desk. "Those are the notes of my meeting with Hazel before she left for Surrey. Read those and you'll have an idea of what we had in mind. We want to propose six advertisements."

"So, six sketches?" When she nodded, he resumed his seat and reached for her pile of notes. "Consider it done."

Clara went off in search of sandwiches, and after reading through her notes, he set to work. By the time she returned, he had completed two sketches and was halfway through a third, but when he caught sight of the tray she put on the desk beside him, he stopped.

"What's wrong?" she asked as he stared askance at the four miniscule triangles on the plate.

"If you expect work out of a man, you'll have to feed him better than that, Clara."

"It doesn't seem like much food, I suppose, not to you. But—" She stopped, and as he turned in his chair to look at her, he noted in some surprise the hot color flooding her cheeks. "It's j . . . just that our cook is still in the kitchen. Sh . . . she's always the last to . . . umm . . . to go to bed. If I had asked her for more food than I usually eat . . ."

"She'd get the wind up?" he finished for her when she stopped again.

Clara nodded, looking at her feet. "It's not really proper, you know," she whispered. "You being here. Alone. With me."

It wasn't proper at all. More than that, it was risky as

hell, especially given what had already passed between them, but he had no intention of pointing that out.

"I understand. Though I can't imagine how even a dainty creature like you can subsist on a meal like that," he added, waving a hand at the sandwiches. "It isn't even a meal, now that I think on it. It's a snack."

"I can bring you more in a few hours, after Mrs. Gibson's gone to bed. That is, if you're still here by then."

"I'll stay as long as you need me to."

She smiled, and as always when she smiled at him like that, Rex felt the world slipping dangerously sideways.

He looked away, gesturing with his pencil to the sketches he'd completed. "You might look over those and tell me I'm on the right track," he said. "Then I suggest you fetch a glass, if you can sneak it out from under your cook's prying eyes. If not, we'll both be swigging that champagne from the bottle."

She complied, giving him the reassurance he needed to continue, then she went in search of a glass. Unexpectedly, she brought back two, because as she explained, champagne flutes were part of the crystal, and weren't kept in the kitchen but in the china cupboard in the dining room. Mrs. Gibson wouldn't miss them.

"Just be sure to wash them and put them back before morning," he advised, "or heaven knows what your cook will think. Can you open it?" he added, gesturing to the champagne.

"I can try."

She did, but once she'd removed the wire cage and begun working to free the cork, he decided he'd better intervene. "The last thing we need is to have the cork go flying, break something, and make such a racket it brings your cook swooping in to see what's going on. Here, let me show you how it's done."

He moved to stand behind her, his arms coming around her to grasp the bottle, demonstrating how to open it and stealing for himself a few tantalizing moments of having her in his embrace. Once the champagne cork had popped, however, even his lame excuse for standing behind her with his arms around her was gone.

He didn't move.

Neither did she, and he took advantage of it, turning his head to inhale the delicate orange-blossom scent of her hair. He closed his eyes, thinking how easy it would be to pull her back against him, to bend his head and kiss her neck . . .

Christ, he was making himself insane.

He lowered his arms and stepped back, stepping to her side to pour champagne, and he decided it might be best to start a conversation on a safe topic.

"So, you fired Mr. Beale. How did this momentous event occur?"

"I lost my temper, and before I knew it, the words, 'you're fired' were out of my mouth. Words, I must say, that gave me great delight."

He grinned as he handed her a glass of champagne and began to pour one for himself. "What happened to all that rot you tried to tell me about having no authority to give him the sack, doing one's best to get along, and respecting your sister's judgement?"

"I didn't really think about any of that. He was abusing a member of the staff, and I just . . . let fly." She gave a sigh. "I'm living with the consequences now, though, I'm afraid."

He set aside the bottle and glanced at her, noting again the weariness in her face. "Which have been arduous, I see."

"Well, as I told you once, editor is the most important position on the staff. I'm not accustomed to making these decisions. I knew how hard my sister worked, of course, but I never realized until now the burden of being in charge. I've never really overseen anything, you see. Most of my life, Irene has protected and looked after me. I've been quite sheltered."

Rex couldn't summon any regret that her paragon of a sister wasn't hovering over her like a hen with one chick. Although as he shot a considering sideways glance over her, he appreciated that her current lack of a chaperone made the temptations tormenting him even harder to resist.

"And with Mr. Beale gone," she went on, bringing his thoughts back to the matter at hand, "I'm in charge of everything. It's rather daunting."

"You're doing all right so far," he said and picked up a sandwich.

"Am I?" She rubbed her nose, looking doubtful. "I hope so."

"Buck up. Paper's getting printed, all's right with the world."

"I suppose that's the only way to look at it at this point." She paused and took a sip of champagne. "Has your father relented yet and reinstated your allowance?"

He shook his head. "Not yet, I'm afraid."

"I only ask because our bargain might be in jeopardy. I may not be able to finish the season. If I don't find an editor, I shall have to carry on here until Irene comes back. I doubt I'll have time to do both, especially if this past week is any indication."

"No applicants for the post?"

"We've had a few. They all seem qualified, but none seem right." She paused, considering. "I don't know if that's true, actually, or if I'm just terrified of choosing wrong and I'm procrastinating over the decision out of fear."

"You can't let fear stop you from making decisions like that."

She laughed. "Says the man who'll never marry."

"Really, Clara." He made a scoffing sound, set aside his champagne, and reached for his drawing pencil. "It's not the same thing at all."

"Yes, it is. It's exactly the same." She laughed again as he shook his head in denial. "All right, then," she added, settling herself on the edge of the desk beside him as he took his chair. "How is it different?"

"An editor can be sacked," he pointed out as he resumed sketching. "A spouse, alas, cannot."

"I agree the risk is higher, but surely the rewards are, too."

"What rewards?"

"Love, for one."

He made another derisive sound to show how unimpressed he was by that argument. "My parents were in love, passionately so, if their friends' accounts can be trusted."

"It wasn't a marriage of alliance? I thought it might have been."

"Why? Because they didn't live happily ever after?"

She gave his leg a kick with her shoe, demonstrating how little she appreciated that acerbic rejoinder. "So, if they were in love, what do you think happened?"

"My mother was unfaithful. She had affairs. I thought everyone knew that."

"So, it was all her fault?"

"It was if you ask anyone in our family. Both sides condemn Mama and blame her for the whole messy business. Even her own relations won't have anything to do with her."

"What about you? Do you condemn her?"

"I wish I could," he said with a sigh. He put a last flourish on the sketch before him, set it with the others, and pulled out a fresh sheet of paper to start the last one. "My life would be so much less complicated."

Before she could ask what he meant by that, he went on, "Don't think I deem her blameless, because that's not the case, either. My mother is beautiful and weak and terribly, terribly insecure. She needs constant reassurance and support. My father, being an impatient man, and blunt to a fault, was never capable of filling that sort of need, or even understanding it."

"What you're saying is that they were never suited."

"About as suited as oil and water. From what I understand, I had barely learned to walk before they drifted apart, and by the time I went off to school, they could only tolerate each other's company if it presented an opportunity to blame each other and tear each other to bits. After I left for Eton, my mother launched her first affair, and . . . well, the rest, as they say, is history. I'm surprised you don't know all about it. It was reported in the papers in lurid enough detail."

"I was only a little girl when they separated, far too young to be interested in reading newspapers. I don't know any of the lurid details you speak of."

"You've missed nothing by not knowing. When love goes awry and turns to contempt, it's always a sordid tale." He paused for another sandwich and a swallow of champagne. "Given the sort of people they are, I can't fathom how my parents ever thought it could be otherwise."

"For some, love is blind."

He nodded. "In my parents' case, very much so. Especially my father. My mother was already a scandal before they ever met, from what I understand. How he ever thought she'd transform into a faithful partner and loving helpmate, I have no idea. Anyone with sense could have told him that she could never be what he wanted her to be."

"There was no way they could reconcile their differences?"

"My parents?" The idea was so absurd, he laughed, and it must have been a harsh sound, because she winced.

"Sorry," he said at once, "but it's clear you've never met them. In most cases when a marriage falls apart, it's true that the two people attempt to put things back together. If that fails, they still soldier on, being discreet and presenting a united front to the world, even if they privately go their separate ways."

"What did your parents do?"

He gave a laugh. "They threw discretion to the winds. My mother stopped making any attempt to hide her affairs—she wanted Papa to divorce her, you see, so she gave him ample grounds, again and again, but he refused to free her. He dug in his heels, and the next few years provided the press with plenty of mutual mudslinging to report, damaging my entire family's social position. The one bright spot was that the scandals spurred the family to work on my father, and though he still refused to divorce her, he did agree to legally separate from her. The separation has failed to rid either of their souls of the acrimony they feel toward each other, but it has at least made it less likely that one of them will kill the other, something that was always a distinct possibility when they lived under the same roof."

"Not all marriages are like your parents'. My parents were happy together. Until—"

She stopped, but he knew what she'd been about to say. "Until your mother died."

"Well, yes, and then Papa rather went to seed. But love's hardly to blame for the fact that he chooses to drink."

"It's unfair for me to blame love, I suppose, but there it is. My father chooses to remain bitter and wounded and unforgiving. He won't let go of a woman whose love for him vanished over twenty-five years ago. My mother, on the other hand, being both more affection- ate and more shallow than my father, loves love so much she does it every year, rather like debutantes do the season. Every time, she's sure this time the love is true and everlasting, only to find herself crushed and disappointed when it all falls apart. My parents, your father . . ." He shrugged and took a swallow of cham- pagne. "What good did love ever do any of them?"

"I've known from the start you were a cynical man," she said. "I suppose I just didn't realize how cynical. But Rex, some people who marry are happy."

"Yes, so the matchmaking members of my family remind me daily. Even my father, who to this day refuses to quit the hell he made for himself, wants me to marry. But what's the point of it? Why should I?"

"What about children?"

"I have an heir, and though he may be a distant cousin, at least the estates won't revert to the Crown when I die." He shrugged. "Marriage is a difficult business. To my mind, frankly, there's not enough reward in it for the risk."

"Perhaps if you ever truly fell in love you'd change your mind."

"I doubt it." That reply was so uncompromising, Clara's face so solemn, watching him, he felt he had to lighten the moment. "I think if I ever had an inclination to love, I'd just want it over as quickly as possible. Love is painful, they say," he added, forcing a laugh. "Why prolong the agony?"

She didn't smile in return. Instead, she gazed back at him, her eyes dark and steady, and in their depths, he saw—God help him—a hint of pity.

He sobered at once, looking away, reaching for the bottle to refill their glasses. "And how does one know it's true love anyway? That's the trouble with it. Infatuation and desire blind you, so there's no way to know if you've got something that will last through a lifetime. When you fell in love with your vicar, you were sure you wanted to marry him, but you must agree that if you had done so, he could never have made you happy."

She considered. "I don't think I thought about it from that standpoint. It all seemed very simple and straightforward to me. I loved him. If he loved me, then of course we would marry. What else is there?"

His hand tightened around the glass in his hand as he slanted a glance at her, the devil inside him appreciating all the delicious possibilities. "What, indeed?" he countered, holding her filled glass up for her.

She took it, making a face at him. "Free love, I suppose," she said, and took a swallow of champagne. "Hardly the culmination devoutly to be wished."

"Depends on one's point of view," he countered, setting the bottle aside and settling back with his glass. "I could say the same about marriage."

That bit of wit did earn him a smile, rather a rueful one. "God help any woman who falls in love with you," she said, shaking her head. "As to my vicar, I was only seventeen when I fell in love with him, so I'm sure infatuation was a large part of what I felt. But that wasn't all of it. I cared very deeply for him, and though I couldn't give him the sort of marriage he wanted, I still believe he cared for me."

Rex considered that, and gave a nod. "Yes, I think he did. Otherwise, he would not have been so honest with you. It's lucky he was. Had he not told you just what sort of marriage he was hoping for, you'd have wed him in ignorance, only to be shocked and disappointed when the truth was revealed. And you'd also have been stuck for life with a man who could never have made you happy."

"Thank you, but . . ." She paused, giving him a rather tipsy smile over her glass as she swirled her champagne. "Had we ever married, I'd like to think I would have eventually persuaded him to abandon his notions of a celestial marriage."

A picture formed in his mind at once, of Clara standing in a bedroom somewhere in corset and drawers with that smile on her face, and his throat went dry, leaving him in need of several swallows of champagne before he could reply.

"In the case of most men," he said at last, "no persuasion would be needed, Clara, I assure you. But for your vicar, it's my guess all the persuasion in the world wouldn't have availed. I saw enough of that sort of thing at Eton to know."

Her smile vanished, and she gave him a puzzled frown. "What sort of thing?"

"There are some men who just don't desire women. Any women. Ever. Poor devils," he added, shaking his head. "It's illegal for men to desire other men, you see."

She stared at him, aghast and shocked, heaven bless her sweet, innocent mind. "That's what you meant about being arrested?"

"Yes."

"Good heavens." She shook her head, still trying to assimilate this theory of the events surrounding her marriage proposal. "It wasn't me, then," she said after a moment, and began to laugh. "It wasn't me at all. It had nothing to do with me."

He took a deep breath, unable to look away from her laughing face even as he tried to shove images of her in a corset out of his mind, appreciating more than ever his newfound pleasure in self-torture. "Really, Clara, I don't know why that's such a revelation now," he muttered. "I told you weeks ago it wasn't you. I even demonstrated the fact, quite strongly, as I recall."

She stopped laughing, her smile faded away, and suddenly, in her face, he saw all the same desire he felt. Or at least, he saw what he wanted to see. "And really," he added, taking refuge in teasing, "I don't know why you needed a demonstration anyway. Why can't you just trust me when I tell you things?"

"Maybe because . . ." She paused and licked her lips as if they were dry, drawing his gaze like a moth to a flame. "Maybe because you're a rake and not to be trusted?"

"I'm not though," he blurted out. "Not a rake, I mean. Not anymore."

She laughed, clearly skeptical of that contention. And who could blame her?

"Oh, I used to be," he went on. "Don't misunderstand me. I was once one of the most notorious men about town, and my reputation was well-earned. Drink, cards, low company, women . . . especially women. God," he added, laughing in disbelief at how much his life had changed, "so many women. I chased skirts from the West End to the East and back again. Actresses, Gaiety Girls, mistresses, courtesans—any woman who didn't expect marriage and wasn't already taken was fair game to me."

"You speak as if all that's in the past."

He gave a nostalgic sigh. "Well, let's just say my wild ways have been temporarily suspended."

"Oh, I see." Her brow cleared and she gave a nod. "Women, you said once, are deuced expensive. And now that your father and your aunt have both cut you off, you can no longer afford such things."

"Well, that's true, yes, but I'm afraid this sad state of affairs came to pass two years ago, long before my father stopped my allowance."

"Years? The gossip columns say otherwise. They . . .

h . . . have you with some new . . ." She paused and looked away. "You seem to . . . have a new m . . . mistress every other month."

"I know, but that's all a hum, Clara. The women, the cards, the drink . . ." He paused, waving a hand vaguely in the air. "All that's just a charade nowadays. A charade I created over two years ago, and one I maintained up until the night we made our arrangement at Covent Garden."

"But why would you do such a thing? For what purpose?"

He shrugged. "I had to find some way to explain why I'm always short of funds."

"And why are you?"

He took a deep breath. "I give my mother money. Everyone believes I still spend whatever I get on rakish pursuits, but as I said, that's tosh. Whatever I don't spend on my own household has been going to my mother for quite some time. I'd ask you to keep this knowledge to yourself, for if my father found out, I'd never get my allowance back."

"Of course, I won't tell anyone, but why should your father care?"

"In the separation agreement, he stipulated an allowance for my mother. It's enough to live on, but only just. Mama can't afford a household, so she's drifted all over the Continent, from friend to hotel to friend to hotel, but after a decade of this, she has pretty much used up all her friends' goodwill, and hotels have stopped allowing her accommodation, for though she's a countess, she's a disgraced one, and she always ducks her bills. She tried to bolster her income with gambling, but of course, that didn't work. She only got into more debt. Debt that my father, understandably, refused to pay."

"So, she began applying to you for money, and you give it to her?"

"Yes. That's the reason my father cut me off. I don't know quite how, but he discovered what I was really doing with my income. Detectives, I'd guess. He's employed enough of them to trail my mother in the past, God knows. He probably has a firm of those good gentlemen on permanent retainer."

"But keeping you continually short of funds only hurts him. If he wants you to marry—"

"Even the ambition to see the estates secured to his own bloodline is not stronger than his need to try to control my mother. He can't accept that he never could do that and he never will. And he can't bear to think my allowance from the estate might be circumventing his control over her."

"He hates her that much?"

"He hates her as much as he loves her." Rex laughed, and even to his own ears, it had a bitter tinge. "I think if she ever expressed the desire to come back to him, he'd let her. But, of course, he'd also make her pay for it. Love, Clara, can be a terrible thing. Which is why I've so little use for it."

"I do see your point of view a little better now, I suppose. But, still, as terrible as it can be, love can also be beautiful, surely? If it's true?"

"Perhaps—that is, if true love exists at all, which my cynical heart is inclined to doubt. I think romantic love is a bit like a pot of gold at the end of a rainbow."

"A mirage, you mean?"

"Yes. Sorry if that disappoints you." He tilted his

head, giving her a curious look. "Aren't you going to ask me why I do it?"

"Why you give your mother money? It's obvious, isn't it?"

"Is it? The family—both sides, mind you—think I ought to have told her to go to the devil. And that I was a fool for risking my father's wrath for her."

"I don't think you're a fool. You obviously love your mother."

He smiled, raising his glass. "That's what makes me a fool."

She shook her head. "No, Rex, it doesn't. You are trying to help her as best you can. It's . . ." She paused, looking at him thoughtfully. "It's quite noble of you."

He choked on his champagne. "Noble?"

"Yes." She frowned as he laughed. "Why are you laughing?"

"Clara, in over three decades of life, no one who knows me has ever deemed me noble."

Her frown cleared, and her smile came back. "Now who's hiding their lights under a bushel?" she asked and swallowed the last of her champagne.

His amusement vanished, for in her face, he saw something he'd never seen there before, something that shouldn't be there. He saw a hint of admiration. "If you knew what I've been thinking about you ever since I walked through that door, my sweet lamb, you'd never call me noble."

She set aside her glass and slid off the edge of the desk. "And if you knew what I was thinking about you right now," she said as she turned his chair toward her and leaned over him, "you'd never call me sweet."

She kissed him, and the moment her mouth touched

his, Rex decided to rid her of any ridiculous notions of his nobility in the best way a rake could do. He broke the kiss long enough to stand up, and then, he wrapped his arms around her and took her mouth again, not with any tenderness or gentle regard for her inexperience, but with all the passion he'd been keeping under such tight, agonizing control.

From the moment he'd first kissed her on that settee, he'd been able to think of little else but doing it again, of tasting her mouth and unleashing the sweet passion he'd so unexpectedly uncovered that afternoon. Yet now, as her arms came around his neck, he reached up to grasp her wrists, the vague notion in his head that he ought to stop this, that he ought to exercise at least a shred of the nobility she'd attributed to his character.

But then, her lips parted, he tasted champagne on her mouth, and any thought of stopping crumbled into dust. He deepened the kiss instead, sliding his tongue into her mouth.

Her response was immediate, her fingers raking through his hair as her mouth opened wider, her tongue meeting his with all the same sweet eagerness she'd displayed during their first kiss. She wasn't thinking of boundaries or consequences, he knew. She was only drinking in all these sensations still so new to her, and he wanted, more than he'd ever wanted anything in his life, to give her more.

Keeping one arm tight around her waist, he slid his free hand up along her ribs. Through her shirtwaist, he could feel the rigid whalebone stays of her corset, a barrier and a reminder, but he moved his hand higher, embracing her breast through her clothes.

She gasped, turning her head away to break the kiss

even as the rest of her body pressed closer. "It's all right," he murmured, his palm cupping her through the rigid corset, his other arm tight around her waist as he trailed kisses from her cheek to her ear. "It's all right."

Her skin was like velvet, her hair held the sweet scent of orange blossoms, and her breathing was shallow and quick against his neck. When he pressed his lips to the side of her throat, he could feel tendons there quiver beneath the caress of his mouth. When he moved higher, pulling the lobe of her ear into his mouth, she moaned. Her hips stirred against him, sending fissures of pleasure through his body, pleasure so intense, it almost knocked him off his feet.

He pulled back, sliding both hands to her waist. She was so slim, so delicate, that his hands encircled her waist completely as he lifted her on to the desk.

He reached up to the thin bow of ribbon at her throat, yanking it free, then he began unbuttoning her shirtwaist.

"Rex?" Her hand encircled his wrist, and he stopped. Hands at her collar, he made himself to look into her face. He couldn't see into her eyes, worse luck, for her gaze was lowered, her lashes tilted down.

Not yet, he thought, desperate. *God, Clara, not yet.*

"Not yet, then," she whispered, and only then did he realize he'd uttered his agonized plea out loud. But he wasn't going to let a trivial thing like his pride get in the way now, and when her hand slid away, he worked his way down, unfastening buttons as fast as he could.

When he reached the waistband of her skirt, he paused to take a deep breath and remind himself there would come a point soon when he would have to stop. Praying that when that moment came, it wouldn't annihilate him completely, he pulled the edges of her shirt-waist apart. As it opened, revealing the muslin and lace of her sweet, white undergarments and the delicate pink flush of arousal on her pale skin, his own arousal deepened and spread.

He leaned closer, and the soft, pristine scent of talc mingled with the orange-blossom scent of her hair, flaring arousal into lust, making him dizzy. He pressed a kiss to her collarbone, and she stiffened, sucking in a sharp breath at the sensation.

Her hands came up to cradle his head, pulling him closer as he trailed kisses along her collarbone to her shoulder, then he buried his face against the warm skin of her throat, and lifted his hand to once again embrace her small, round breast.

He wished he could unlace her, but removing that barrier, he feared, would break his already shaky will-power utterly apart, so he was forced to be content with shaping her through the corset. He pressed a kiss to the soft white crest of her breast above the edge of her undergarments, and she moaned in response, her body stirring in agitation.

Gently, still kissing the talc-scented skin above her breasts, he grasped folds of her skirt in his free hand and began pulling the soft, thin wool upward, work-ing to get his hand beneath the layers of skirt and pet-ticoats.

She made a faint, maidenly sound of what might have been protest, her hands coming to rest on his shoulders. Rex went still, waiting, expecting her to push him back, but when she didn't, he resumed, shaping her thigh through her drawers as he slid his hand upward.

He was rock-hard now, aching with weeks of pent-up lust, but oddly enough, he didn't mind that, for he was driven by a far greater need: the need to pleasure her. He wanted her to know just what the culmination of passion felt like, the release and the exquisite bliss that followed it.

Kissing her all along the curve of her neck and shoulder, he shoved folds of her skirt upward, then slowly eased her backward onto the desk, moving to lay beside her as he slid his hand up a few more inches and eased it between her thighs.

She stirred again, but he wanted to deprive her of any ability to call a halt, and he turned his hand, cupping her mound through her drawers. Her hips jerked sharply, and she gave a soft cry of surprise.

He kissed her, hard, catching her cry in his mouth. His hand moved between her legs, using the friction of his caress against the damp fabric to arouse her further, but it wasn't enough. He wanted more, and he eased his fingers inside the slit of her drawers.

She was wet, ready, and as he caressed the crease of her sex, he relished the soft, desperate panting sounds of need she made. She was nearing climax, he knew, and he used his voice to inflame her further.

"That's it, sweetheart," he said softly. "You're close, so close. Let it happen."

As he spoke, her hips began pumping faster, moving against his hand in awkward, frantic jerks as she strove toward the peak, and when she came, he felt the sweetest pleasure he'd ever felt in his life.

She collapsed back against the desk, panting. He waited until the last waves of her orgasm had subsided before he pulled away, easing his hand from under her skirts. He was aware of the painful, aching need in his own body, and when she opened her eyes and smiled at him, he knew he couldn't stay here one more minute without crossing the Rubicon.

He moved at once, rolling away and sliding off the desk. "I've got to go."

Even as he said it, he was aware of all the times he'd said those exact same words to women before, of all the times he'd rushed to dress and raced for the door. This time, his reasons for dashing off were totally different—rather the opposite, in fact. The irony of that was not lost on him.

"It's terribly late," he felt it necessary to point out as he reached for his jacket and slipped it on. "And you need sleep. Try to get some, all right?"

"You, too."

He laughed, a caustic sound in the quiet room.

"You always laugh at things I say when I'm not trying to be funny," she accused, sitting up.

"Sorry," he said and bent to retrieve his hat from where it had been pushed off the desk, a move that exacerbated the pain of his unrequited lust. "But somehow, I doubt I'll sleep much tonight."

He retrieved his cufflinks and turned away without looking at her. "Good night, Clara."

He could feel her gaze on his back as he departed, but he kept walking, vanishing from view into the corridor. As he traversed the short distance from her office to the outer one of the newspaper, he realized he hadn't even kissed her good-night.

He stopped. Any woman deserved at least that much, Clara especially.

He couldn't do it. He couldn't go back, not even to offer her such a simple consideration. Anarchy was inside him, and if he went back, her virtue would be utterly lost before any good-night kiss.

"Lock the door after I'm gone," he called back over his shoulder, "and from now on, if you're going to work late, then keep it locked. If you don't, any scoundrel could walk in. God knows, I'm living proof."

With that, he left the newspaper office, but even then, he did not depart. Instead, he crossed Belford Row, where he paused in the doorway of a darkened building and waited in the shadows, watching the windows across the street. With his body in agony, it seemed an eternity before she came into view, a lamp in her hand, but it was only after he had seen her lock the door and draw the blinds that Rex turned away and started up the street to find a taxi.

Chapter 16

*I*t must have been the champagne.

Clara didn't know how else to account for what had just happened. The passionate kiss she and Rex had shared in the drawing room upstairs had been sweet and exciting and so, so lovely, but that kiss was not anything like what he had had done to her tonight. His searing touch, her own rising tension and hungry, aching need, and then . . . waves of pleasure, shattering her again and again, like nothing she had ever felt before, or could ever have even imagined. It had all been wickedly shameful, and yet, she'd felt no shame. Even her usual shyness had been burned away by his hot caresses, and long after he was gone, she couldn't summon so much as a speck of maidenly modesty.

No, the only thing she felt was a euphoric happiness that didn't disperse even after she'd disposed of the empty champagne bottle in the rubbish bin out back and washed the glasses and returned them to the china cupboard. As she went upstairs, undressed, and got into bed, she felt gloriously wide-awake, and she was sure she wouldn't sleep a wink.

In that, however, she was wrong, for she fell asleep almost at once, and when she woke the next morning, her theory about the champagne seemed the most logical explanation for her wanton behavior the night before. And whenever she thought of Rex's scorching caress, euphoric joy rose inside her like champagne bubbles, a fact that made her meeting with Mr. Shaw even more difficult. Every time she presented one of Rex's drawings, she was reminded of what had occurred, and though she did her best to present a brisk and businesslike demeanor, an occasional euphoric giggle did slip into her presentation.

Still, old Mr. Shaw was favorably impressed by what she had to say, and by Hazel's plan and Rex's sketches, so much so that the old devil not only approved the entire advertising plan, but also commissioned an additional series of advertisements for the new cold remedy that would run throughout the winter. This happy conclusion filled Clara with a sense of triumph and satisfaction she'd never experienced before, and for the first time, she truly appreciated just why Irene had been so passionately involved with the newspaper.

Clara had no opportunity to tell Rex about today's success, however, or thank him for the enormous part his drawing talents had played in achieving it, for that afternoon, she learned that he had left town, a piece of news that turned her bubbly euphoria as flat as day-old champagne.

The bearers of this information were Hetty and

Lady Petunia, who came to call on her at the newspaper office, and though Clara tried not to show any feelings about his departure one way or the other, she knew at once she hadn't quite succeeded.

"There, Auntie Pet," Hetty said only seconds after imparting the news, "I told you she'd be as disappointed about this as we are."

"You are mistaken," Clara rushed to reply, working to wipe any trace of emotion off her face, even as she wondered if last night's episode had driven him away. "I'm not disappointed."

That was not only a flagrant lie, it was also a rude thing to say. "Forgive me," she added at once, grimacing. "I didn't mean that the way it sounded. It's only that I've been so hard at work, you see. We lost our editor, and then our advertising artist had to go to nurse a sick relative, and of course, with my sister away on honeymoon—" She stopped, appreciating that she was rambling. "It's just that I shan't have much time to see anyone for the time being, and it does no good to be disappointed about it."

"But Rex going away is a disappointment?" Hetty asked. "Oh, Clara, do say it is! You must like him, at least a little."

Thankfully, Lady Petunia intervened before Clara could reply. "Henrietta, that will be enough. You mustn't press Clara and invade her privacy this way."

"Sorry," Hetty said at once. "Forgive me."

"Not at all," Clara replied, striving for something innocuous to say. "And yes, I do like your cousin. We have become friends, you see." Even as she spoke, she thought of last night, of how she'd leaned down and kissed him, and of the sensations his caress had evoked in her, and she feared she was beginning to like Rex in a way that had nothing to do with friendship.

"Friends, hmm?"

Hetty's amused, teasing voice lurched her out of her contemplations, and Clara realized something in her face must have given her away.

"Henrietta, stop this at once," Lady Petunia said, her voice a sharp rebuke. "Clara is not required to confide anything to us, and why should she, given your relentless teasing? If you keep on this way, she'll never agree to come to our house party."

"House party?" The other woman frowned a little, turning to look at her great-aunt.

"My dear girl, don't tell me you've forgotten our Friday-to-Monday six days hence?"

There was a moment of silence, then Hetty gave an exclamation. "Right, of course! You mean the weekend party."

"It's a Friday-to-Monday," Petunia said with a sniff, "and that's a house party, regardless of what you young people call such things nowadays."

"I hadn't forgotten," Hetty said. "I just hadn't realized it was so close. My, how time flies in the season."

"That's just why a Friday-to-Monday is so perfect for July." Petunia turned to Clara. "I am chaperone to Henrietta, as you know, as well as to her younger sister, May, and because May is just out this year, it's been an especially busy time. But I'm getting on in years, you know, and the season is becoming so frantic, I will soon need a rest, or I fear I won't be able to continue. So, after May has been presented at court, we shall be having a little Friday-to-Monday at Lisle. That's the home of my nephew, Sir Albert—Henrietta's father, you know. We should dearly love to have you join us, my dear. And the duke's family, of course."

"Lisle's a lovely place," Hetty put in, "even if I do say it myself. Do say you'll come, for I should very much like to show it to you."

"I'd like to come," Clara assured her. "But as I said, things are very busy here. I'm not sure I can afford to be away."

"It's in Kent, down toward Dover," Hetty said. "And that's a very short journey, with trains running multiple times a day. If anything untoward were to arise, you could be home within a few hours. And if you've been working as hard as you say, you'll surely need a good rest by then. Not that we'll rest much if the weather's fine, for there will be croquet and tennis and perhaps some punting on the stream. We may even go to Dover and picnic on the cliffs overlooking the sea."

"That would be lovely, for I've never been to Dover. But—"

"There, then, it's decided," Hetty cried. "I don't want to hear any buts, Clara. It'll be great fun, I promise, and though there will be plenty of new people for you to meet, you needn't fear you won't know anyone. Rex is there already, along with my brother, Paul, who you met at the picnic."

As she remembered, Hetty's brother Paul was very nice, and the idea of meeting new people didn't intimidate her nearly as much now as it would have done just a couple of months ago, but it was the mention of Rex that caused Clara to capitulate. "Very well, then," she said, and the moment those words were out of her mouth, all her earlier euphoria came rushing back. "If the duke's sisters are free to accompany me, I should be delighted to come to Lisle."

THERE WAS NOTHING like the country if a man wanted to regain his sanity. A long, hard ride across the downs on horseback every morning, followed by a hike through the woods or along the cliffs after luncheon, and a few vigorous sets of tennis with his cousin Paul in the late afternoon all helped Rex put himself to rights. The tennis, he found, was especially effective, for not only was his cousin as fiercely competitive as he and almost as skilled a player, Paul was also a full decade younger, which meant that although sometimes Rex won and sometimes he lost, he never failed to be thoroughly done in afterward. And if thoughts of Clara still prevented him from sleeping, a few dozen laps in the pond were sufficient to cool his blood.

After half a dozen days of vigorous exercise, and nights of tumbling into bed exhausted, Clara Deverill at last stopped bedeviling his mind and body. The feel of her, so warm and sweet, became a memory rather than a torture. The sound of her soft cries of release stopped invading his dreams, meaning that he no longer woke up hard and aching in the middle of the night. By the afternoon of the house party, he felt he was at last himself again.

He and Paul were on the court when Hetty, May, and Auntie Pet, the only members of the family not already at Lisle, arrived from the station. Tea had been laid out on the south lawn near the tennis court, and some of the guests were already partaking as Uncle Albert's carriage pulled into the drive, but it wasn't until the vehicle stopped nearby and Hetty called a greeting to them that Rex noticed another vehicle coming around the south lawn. More guests, he supposed.

"Everyone seems to be here at last," Paul called to him, returning Rex's attention to the game. "Do you want to stop for tea?"

"Tea?" Rex shook his head, laughing. "Now, when I'm a hairsbreadth from winning this match? Not a chance."

"Hairsbreadth?" Paul echoed, making a sound of derision as he prepared to serve. "That's rich."

The ball rose high in the air, then Paul's serve sent it flying across the court to a tricky corner. Rex's backhand, as deadly a weapon as his cousin's wicked serve, sent the ball flying back across the net, but then, Rex thought he heard Hetty call Clara's name.

Startled, he glanced sideways and found all his worst fears confirmed by the sight of Clara's slim figure crossing to Hetty's side, and his concentration shattered to bits. He heard the thwack of Paul's racquet against the tennis ball, but still looking at Clara, it took him a millisecond too long to respond, and by the time he dove for the ball, he was already too late. He missed it entirely, his body went stumbling forward, carried by sheer momentum.

He landed hard, his shoulder and hip slamming down on the turf of the tennis court less than ten feet from the very woman he'd been trying for nearly a week to forget, his gaze riveted to a view of Clara's dainty, leather-clad toes and lace petticoats peeking out from beneath the pleated hem of a blue traveling skirt.

Christ, almighty.

He turned away from that delectable vision at once,

grimacing in pain and aggravation as he rolled onto his back, Paul's merry laughter ringing in his ears.

What the hell, he wondered, staring up at the sky, had he done to deserve this?

"Are you all right?" Paul asked, still laughing.

"Shipshape and Bristol fashion," he called back. "Why do you ask?"

He stood up before Paul or anyone else could question that lie. Giving his shoulder an experimental shrug, he was glad to find he'd suffered no serious injury, and he glanced around for his racquet. It had landed nearly on the chalk line, a fact that forced him even closer to where Clara stood at the side of the court with Hetty.

"Rough game?" his cousin asked as he bent to pick up his racquet.

"Apparently so, Hetty. Miss Deverill," he greeted with a bow, but he didn't look at her, and before she could reply, he turned away, returning to the court. He wiped the sweat off his brow with his wrist, and readied himself for Paul's next serve, but suddenly the idea of playing any more tennis, knowing Clara was here, that she'd be watching, was just too much to bear, and he waved Paul to stop before the other man could serve.

"What's wrong?"

He shrugged his shoulder again, and gave an exaggerated grimace of pain. "Let's stop," he said. "I'm done in. I concede," he added before Paul could reply. "I'm going to bathe and change for dinner."

"Concede?" his cousin echoed as he walked off the court. "But you never concede."

"I just did," he called back, fearing it wasn't just the tennis match he'd given up on.

HE DIDN'T SEE her again until dinner. Fortunately, he was not seated anywhere near her at the table, but that wasn't as much of a blessing as it might have been, for he could still see her plainly from where he sat. Paul, seated beside her, must have been in quite a mind to be witty and charming company, because every time Rex took a glance her way, she seemed to be laughing at something his cousin had said. Lisle had no gas jets in the dining room, and the candlelight gave her pale skin a luminous glow. Her hair was done up in that pretty chignon he'd complimented that night in her office, which only led him to remembering what had happened there, and he was heartily glad when dinner was over and the ladies had gone through to the drawing room.

After the port, when he and the other gentlemen joined the ladies, Rex kept his conversation with her to the politest possible minimum, but there were times when he couldn't resist edging close enough to hear her voice. It was an exercise in self-torture, and one that soon paid him out in spades, when he heard her describing the beauty of her yellow bedroom to her sister-in-law, Lady Angela. There was one, and only one, bedroom at Lisle done up in yellow.

The moment he discovered the location of her room, he tried to put the knowledge out of his mind, but he feared it was rather like putting Pandora's gifts back in the box, because lying in bed five hours later, the location of her room seemed to be the only thing he could think about.

Images of her there danced tantalizingly across his mind, of her hair tumbled down around her, of small, round breasts, pale, luminous skin, and long, slim legs.

He breathed deep, imagining the scent of orange blossoms and past the roar in his ears, he remembered her soft cries of climax as his own lust rolled in him like thunder, rising, thickening, until it was pain.

He slid his hand along his hip, thinking to relieve the agony with simple expediency, something he'd been doing quite often during the past two months, but then he sighed and let his hand fall to his side. What good would it do? Any relief would be temporary, for just one sight of her smile and he'd be reduced to this state again.

Shoving back the sheets, he got out of bed. Time for another midnight swim, he decided. After sliding on black trousers and his heavy indigo satin smoking jacket, he left his room. Barefoot, he went downstairs and slipped out into the moonlit summer night.

He walked across the cool turf, circling the house toward the north side, making for the millpond, though he feared that was nowhere near far enough to get clear of her now. Maybe he could go rent a cottage in Ireland, he thought in desperation, or go to his father's hunting lodge in Scotland, but neither of those seemed far enough away. Hell, with how he felt right now, even Shanghai might not be far enough to keep her safe from him.

After stripping naked, he dove into the pond, and he counted thirty full laps before the ache in his loins eased, the driving need for her slid back into mere discomfort, and he began to think Shanghai might not be necessary. But on his way back, he saw a light in one of the windows, the only light still lit on this side of the house. He counted the windows twice just to be sure, but even as he did so, he knew quite well it wasn't necessary.

This was fate. One of those things a man just couldn't fight. His attempt to do so had been a worthy, perhaps even noble battle, but now he knew it had also been a pointless one because when he saw the light in the Yellow Room, he knew he'd just lost the war.

He began walking toward the house, his steps quickening as he crossed the grass, slowing to a soft and quiet tread once he reentered the house. He went up the south staircase because it didn't creak, traversed a maze of corridors, tiptoed past the quietly snoring hall boy, and turned toward the suites of guest quarters. He paused at the start of that corridor, noting the light that shone from beneath the door of the Yellow Room, and he didn't know whether to be glad or not.

He counted doors as he walked toward her room, verifying his earlier calculations. Outside her door, he paused. Taking a deep breath, he considered with great care what he was about to do, what it would mean, and the inevitable consequences it would bring. Then he put his hand on the doorknob. Turning it, he opened the door, stepped inside, and crossed the Rubicon.

Chapter 17

The click of the latch caused Clara to look up from her book, and as the door swung open, she gave a startled gasp and bolted out of bed, only to freeze, riveted, at the sight of Rex coming into her room.

Her bedroom.

He put a finger to his lips and stepped farther into her room, closing the door behind him. When he faced her again, she realized his hair was damp and he was only partially dressed, as if he'd just come from his bath, and she stared in shock at the vee of his bare chest, visible between the edges of his smoking jacket. She'd never seen a man's bare chest before.

Heat unfurled in her belly.

He started toward her, and she took an involuntary step back, her legs hitting the bed behind her.

He stopped.

"Rex?" she whispered. "What are you doing here?"

He didn't answer. Instead, he looked down, and as his gaze slid over her body, Clara's question was answered.

The heat inside her deepened and spread.

His roaming gaze stopped at her feet, and she curled her toes, tucking them under the hem of her nightgown. "Rex, you shouldn't be here."

"I know."

At that soft admission, the heat inside her flared into a sudden, violent surge of anger. She strode across the room toward him. "You were barely civil to me when I arrived," she reminded in a fierce whisper as she stopped in front of him.

He stirred. "It caught me off guard, seeing you here. I didn't expect it. No one told me you were coming."

"So, shock was the reason you looked at me as if you wanted me banished to perdition? And why you've been avoiding me ever since I arrived, and why you've treated me as if I have plague?"

"I've been trying to keep you safe."

"Safe from what?"

He looked up, his eyes like blue flame. "From me."

She sucked in her breath, that simple answer and the desire in his eyes robbing her of anger, leaving only heat.

"If you want me to go," he said, his voice a low, harsh rasp, "say so."

She should. Of course she should.

She opened her mouth, but the words wouldn't come. Of all the times for her tongue to fail her, this shouldn't be one of them, but after what had happened between them that extraordinary night in her office, after his scorching kisses and caresses, notions of propriety seemed absurd. Worse, far worse, she didn't want him to go. She wanted all those scorching kisses again. She didn't speak.

Slowly, he moved, easing closer, and with every fraction of an inch he bent his head, her heartbeat quickened. By the time his lips brushed hers, her heart was racing.

"You know what it means, Clara, if I stay?"

She knew. He would lie with her. It was a risk. It could be ruin. And yet, with the light brush of his lips, she ceased to care. She nodded. "Yes."

With a suddenness that took her breath away, his arms were around her and his mouth was taking hers in a lush, openmouthed kiss.

And she relished it—relished all the scorching intimacy of it, tasting him as deeply as he tasted her. His arms around her, so strong. His body, so much larger than hers and so, so different. His mouth and his taste, familiar to her now. She melded against him, and moved to wrap her arms around his neck, but to her astonishment, he stopped her, his hands encircled her wrists.

She made a sound of protest against his mouth, but he ignored it, pulling her wrists down as he broke the kiss. "I've got to slow things down," he told her, but even as he spoke, he was reaching for the ties of her robe. "I don't want to ruin it for you by going too fast."

"Whatever you do will be wonderful."

He gave a laugh low in his throat. "I wish I shared your confidence," he muttered. "Just remember, we'll have to be very quiet. The rooms on both sides of you are occupied."

He pulled at the edges of her robe and slid the garment from her shoulders. Then, to her astonishment, he took up the end of her braid, and with a tug, he untied the ribbon and began unraveling the plait.

"There now," he murmured after a moment, spreading the long locks of her hair around her shoulders. "I've been wanting to do that almost from the moment we met."

"What?" Clara blinked, staring up at him. "On the dance floor, you were thinking of unbraiding my hair?"

"I was. I wanted to take it down, see it fall, run my fingers through it."

"Goodness." It was a faint sound to her ears, barely audible.

His palm glided along her cheek, and then, he raked his hand through her hair, and with a fistful of it in his grasp, he tilted her head back and kissed her again, a long, lush kiss, more tender this time, but still hot enough to burn her everywhere. "And that," he said, pulling back a little. "I was thinking about doing that, too."

"I knew about that part," she gasped, trying to catch her breath. "You told me as much."

He chuckled, disentangling his fingers from her hair. "So I did. I'm such a scapegrace."

He lifted his hands to her collar, and Clara felt a thrill of anticipation and a throb of fear as he unfastened the top button of her nightgown. He worked his way down, and the tension within her grew with each one that came undone. By the time he reached her navel, she was shaking inside, and when he pulled the garment off her shoulders, down her arms, and over her hips, then shoved it down to her ankles, she gasped at the sensation of cool air on her skin, for her body ached and burned with heat.

Abruptly, he stopped. He leaned back, his lashes lowered as he slanted a glance down over her, and she appreciated, too late, that she was completely naked. All the thrills died at once, and she wanted desperately to hide.

He wouldn't let her. "No, no," he murmured, catching her hands before she could think to cover herself. "I've been imagining this for a long time, Clara," he whispered, spreading her arms wide even as she resisted. "Don't deny me this."

"I can't," she whispered, arms outstretched, his hands clasping hers, her body fully exposed. "Since you've already done it."

He chuckled. Then his laughter faded away, and she knew he was looking at her body. Even with a corset, she didn't have much in the way of curves, and without one, she knew her shape was more reminiscent of a stick than an hourglass. She endured his gaze, but she couldn't look at him. Instead, she stared into his chin as he looked his fill, her tension growing. He was silent so long she could only fear the worst.

"You're lovely," he said, and then, to her utter amazement, he sank down to his knees in front of her. "Even more lovely than I'd imagined." He laughed softly, his hand gliding up her hip and over her ribs. "Given how vivid my imaginings of you have been, that's saying a lot."

She did look at him then. She couldn't resist, and when she saw his face, saw the hunger in his expression as he stared at her naked body, her relief was so profound, she almost sank to her knees, too.

He lifted his hand and cupped her breast in his palm, and her relief dissolved into a jolt of pleasure so strong, she gasped. The feel of his palm against the bare skin of her breast was exquisite, and when he took her nipple between his thumb and forefinger to gently toy with it, she couldn't help a soft moan.

"Ssh," he admonished, then he kissed her there, a sensation so sharp, so exquisite that she had to bite her lip to keep from crying out. And when his mouth opened over her nipple, her knees gave way beneath her. He caught her before she fell, his arm wrapping tight around her hips, as his mouth suckled her breast.

She stirred against him, for what he was doing made her want desperately to move, but he wouldn't let her. His arm tightened around her hips, pinning her to his body, bondage that only seemed to enhance the pleasure he was evoking with his mouth.

As last, she could take no more. "Rex," she gasped, raking her hand through his hair, pulling his head back.

He relented, easing away, reaching for her hands, pulling her down to join him, and as she sank to her knees in front of him, he shrugged out of his smoking jacket.

He moved to kiss her, but Clara stopped him.

"What's wrong?" he asked, his breathing uneven.

"Nothing. I just—" She stopped, her gaze lowering to his chest. "I think it's my turn to look."

He laughed low in his throat. "Fair enough. Look your fill."

She did, her gaze roaming over his wide chest and powerful arms, and as he watched her, he realized that looking at him pleased and aroused her, and for the first time in his life, Rex was grateful for the good looks he'd inherited from his mother.

When she lifted her hands to his chest and touched him, he bore the sweet agony of it. But when her gaze slid to his trousers and her hands followed, he shook his head and pushed her hands gently away. "A man can only take so much torture," he told her. "If you start undressing me, I'll go to bits and our evening will be over far too soon."

"But you got to undress me," she protested.

"That's different." He kissed her to stifle any further discussion on the subject, then he eased her down onto the carpet.

That didn't seem to please her, for at once, she wriggled, making a face. "It's itchy. Can't we lay on the bed?" she whispered.

He shook his head. "Iron beds make too much noise."

"Oh." She blushed as she realized why, and it made him laugh. Never in his life would he have thought sweetness like hers would be addicting, but he craved it now, as if it were a drug.

"Really, Rex, I don't understand the things you think are funny."

"I know." He kissed her. "I know."

Straightening, he reached for his smoking jacket. "Here," he said, spreading it out. "Lay on this."

She complied, and the sight of her stretched out naked on top of his jacket was the most erotic thing he'd ever seen. He ran his gaze over her sweet, round breasts, her slim waist and hips and her long, long legs, coming at last to the soft brown curls at the apex of her thighs. He wanted her so badly, it was making him dizzy, but he had to bank his own need just a little bit longer, for her first time was going to be the most beautiful, romantic experience he could make it.

Not that he quite knew what he was doing there, he realized, a thought that almost made him laugh. All the women he'd had, and yet, that sort of experience did him no good with Clara. He'd never made love to a virgin before, and he hadn't been this intimidated by the act of love since he was an adolescent.

He took a profound, shaky breath, then eased down beside her. His weight on his forearm, he spread his hand over her stomach.

She responded to his touch at once, a low moan in her throat as her hips arched. He smiled at that. She was so delicate, and yet, the passion inside her was titanic. Nonetheless, when he eased closer and his erection pressed against her thigh, she shied away a little, opening her eyes.

"Rex?"

"It's all right," he promised. "Trust me."

He kissed her, slow, deep kisses, as her body slowly relaxed. Still kissing her, he slid his hand to her breast, shaping it, toying with her for a bit, then he bent to take her nipple into his mouth. She moaned again, and earned herself another admonition to be quiet, and when she lifted her arm, pressing her wrist over her mouth, he smiled.

Still suckling her, he slid his palm down her ribs, across her stomach, and between her thighs to touch

the soft triangle of her curls. She gasped, her legs
squeezed convulsively around his hand, her hips working as he caressed her.

She was wet, ready, and yet he waited, stroking her
as he had that night on her desk, gliding his finger
back and forth along the crease of her sex, watching
her face as her eyes closed. Her arm fell to her side, her
breathing quick, her hips working against his hand.

"Remember this?" he whispered. "Remember the last
time I did this?"

"That's not—" She paused, panting, hips working.
"That's not something a girl's likely to forget."

He laughed, a chortle that he quickly snuffed. She
said the most unexpected things.

Clara heard his laugh, but as usual, she didn't understand it, and right now, she was too overwhelmed
to care about figuring it out. Each stroke of his finger
was sending a throb of pleasure through her body, until she couldn't bear it. She shattered apart, just like
before, a sob of ecstasy tearing from her.

He caught the sound in his mouth, kissing her, his
fingers continuing to pleasure her, even as she collapsed, panting, against the carpet.

"Clara, it's time." His voice was harsher than she'd
ever heard it before, vibrating with need she instinctively understood. "I can't wait any more."

She nodded, letting him know she felt the same, that
she was ready for what she only vaguely knew was
about to happen, but then he withdrew his hand and
rolled away from her. Surprised, she opened her eyes
and turned her head, watching him as he unbuttoned
his trousers, and pulled them off.

She slid her gaze down his body for her first glimpse

of what she'd wanted to see earlier, but the sight was sufficiently shocking that she stared, aghast, sudden trepidation vanquishing any curiosity she might have felt.

"Rex?"

He came over her at once, and beneath him, she squeezed her eyes shut. With his body, solid and heavy on top of her, and the hard, swollen part of him pressed between her legs, she wasn't at all sure she wanted to continue.

He sensed what she felt. He must have, for he stilled, and she felt his hand cup her face. "Clara, look at me."

She forced herself to open her eyes.

His seemed vividly blue even in the lamplight, and his voice when he spoke was strained with need. "This part is probably going to hurt you. There's no way to avoid that, I'm sorry to say." He paused and kissed her. "I'll be as gentle as I can. All right?"

She nodded, and sucked in a breath. "Yes. All right."

She felt his hand ease between their bodies, moving to push her thighs apart. "Open for me, sweetheart."

She did, spreading her legs apart, and at once she felt him against her, hard and scorching hot. When he moved, the friction was luscious, and her earlier excitement came flooding back as the tip of his hardness pressed against her and into her.

"My God, my God," he groaned against her neck. And then, his hips surged, and his hardness was fully within her.

The pain was even more acute than she'd expected, a deep, hard, bruising pinch that blotted out any pleasure she'd been feeling. She cried out, but he smothered it, kissing her as his body stilled on top of her.

He kissed her, a long, deep, tender kiss. Then he lifted his head. "Are you all right?"

His voice was so strangled, the words were barely understandable, telling her the strain he was under. She stirred, wriggling her hips, but the pain, thankfully, was easing. "Yes." She nodded. "I think so, yes."

He kissed her again, and then, he began to move within her. It hurt still, a little, but there was pleasure, too—pleasure in the hard, thick fullness of him inside her and the way he moved, and she tried to move with him.

Her efforts quickened his pace, and each time he thrust into her, it was a little harder, a little deeper, but that was all right, for her pleasure was deepening, too.

Then, without warning, the explosive sensation she'd only felt from his touch before roared up inside her, a violent, beautiful jolt that sent spasms of pleasure through her whole body. She wrapped her legs around him, her body clenching him tight.

He made a rough sound against her mouth. His arms slid beneath her back, as if he wanted to be even closer to her. Locked in this embrace, she relished it as he thrust into her again, then again, and yet again, and then, shudders rocked his body, and she knew he was feeling the same exquisite pleasure in this coupling that she'd just experienced. Three more times, he thrust into her, and then, at last, he stilled, the weight of his body settling over her. His arms still tight around her, his breathing hard and labored, he turned his head, burying his face against her neck.

Dazed, Clara stared up at the ceiling, her hands caressing the smooth, hard muscles of his back. The pain was gone now, and with his strong body heavy and solid on top of hers, part of him still joined with her, and his arms around her so strong and tight, all she felt was a sweet, singing joy and an overwhelming tenderness.

He stirred on top of her. "Does it still hurt?" he asked, pressing a kiss to her throat. "Tell me."

She shook her head. "No. Oh, no."

"Good." He kissed her mouth, then he stirred again, as if to roll away, but she tightened her legs around him, reluctant to let him go.

Smiling, he lifted himself far enough to look into her face. "I'd love to stay," he murmured, "but I can't. I have to be back in my own room before the maids wake up."

She nodded, knowing he was right. Her legs relaxed, opened, and he lifted his hips, slipping free of her. She grimaced, appreciating that she was still sore, more so than she'd realized. She was also sweaty and sticky, especially in her most intimate place. Lovemaking wasn't quite as romantic afterward.

He stood up, and held out his hand to pull her to her feet as well, then he paused, smiling, his gaze drifting down over her naked body, a look that made her feel terribly shy and flustered, but pretty, too, and she revised her opinion. Even afterward, there was romance in the act of love.

"Why are you smiling?" she asked, but she knew. She touched a hand to her hair, her blush deepening.

"You look delicious," he said.

"Do I?" She gave him a wry, sideways smile. "Like shortbread, I suppose?"

"Yes, thank God." He kissed her. "Because I adore shortbread."

He turned away to find his clothes, and she tilted her head, studying his body, appreciating the view. He had such splendid shoulders. And also, she realized as he bent to reach for his discarded trousers, a very splendid bum.

He turned back around and caught her watching him. She tried to paste on an innocent, lamblike stare, but he grinned, not the least bit fooled.

"Enjoying the view?" he asked and pulled on his trousers.

She made a face at him. "I was, until you put on those trousers and ruined it."

He laughed softly as he reached down to retrieve his smoking jacket from the floor. He started to put it on, but then, he stopped, and for no reason she could think of, he bundled it into his hand instead. He went still, staring at it for a moment, then he pressed his lips together and lifted his head to look at her. His face was so grave, it startled her.

"Rex? What's wrong?"

"Nothing." He smiled a little. "Try to get some sleep tonight, all right?"

Sleep? She stared at him in disbelief as he turned away to open the door. She couldn't possibly fall asleep now. She'd never felt more awake, more alive in her entire life. She felt as if she could conquer the world. Did people truly fall asleep after such an extraordinary experience?

But before she could ask him that question, he was already gone.

Chapter 18

Perhaps it was the amazing and strenuous adventures of the night, or perhaps the fact that she'd been working so many late hours at the paper, but whatever the reason and despite her predictions on the subject, Clara succumbed to sleep the moment her head hit the pillow, and the only reason she woke was the fact that someone was moving around in her room.

Eyes closed, her senses still groggy, she wondered what Rex was still doing here. Hadn't he gone? A vague memory of him slipping out her door came into her sleep-dazed mind, but the moment it did, any speculations about what he was doing back again vanished as she remembered the amazing things he'd done earlier.

Never, until last night, had she ever felt truly pretty. But when he'd knelt in front of her and called her lovely, when she'd heard the hushed, awestruck quality of his voice, it had made her heart sing with a joy and a confidence in her own feminine power that she'd never possessed before. When he had kissed and caressed her, she'd felt every bit as lovely as he'd deemed her, and a lifetime of gawky awkwardness, of feeling overlooked and plain had melted away under the scorching heat of his eyes and his hands and his mouth. Even now, it was still with her, that feeling, and she smiled in her sleep.

A drawer opened and closed, intruding on blissful, dreamlike memories, and she decided Rex could not possibly still be in her room, for why would he be opening drawers? With an effort, she dragged her eyes open to find the gas jets lit, a bright crack of light coming through between the closed draperies, and her maid putting undergarments away in the chiffonier.

"Forrester?" she mumbled, blinking against the light. "What are you doing?"

"I'm sorry, Miss Clara." The maid turned, offering her an apologetic look. "You were sleeping ever so sound, I didn't think putting away a few things would wake you."

"It's all right." She rubbed the heels of her hands over her eyes, trying to come awake. "What time is it?"

"Quarter past eleven."

"Eleven? What?" Astonished, Clara bolted upright, fully awake. "So late?"

The plump, middle-aged maid nodded. "Yes, miss. I'd have woken you, but you were sleeping ever so, and I thought it best to let you be. You've been working so hard and been so tired lately. I hope I haven't done wrong?"

"No, no, of course not," she hastened to assure. "And

I suppose you're right that I must have needed the rest. Quarter past eleven? Goodness, I never sleep so late."

Even as she spoke, she thought of what she'd spent her night doing, and she hastily turned away before Forrester could see any hint of her thoughts in her expression. Shoving aside sheets and counterpane, she got out of bed on the opposite side from where her maid was standing and walked to the window. Pulling back the drapery a fraction, she blinked a little at the bright sunlight. "What a lovely day. What are the carriages for?" she asked, noting several broughams and landaus in the drive.

"Miss Chapman has arranged a picnic luncheon to the White Cliffs for anyone who wants to go," Forrester said. "There will be luncheon here, too, of course, for anyone who chooses to stay behind, and after the picnicking party returns, there's to be croquet and tennis."

"Tennis?" Clara thought of Rex, how splendid he had looked on the court in tennis whites. And how much more splendid he'd looked without them. She closed her eyes, picturing his naked body, his wide shoulders, the powerful muscles of his back and arms, the lean and luscious lines of his bum. She'd sensed the first time she'd ever seen him how athletic he was— more suited, she remembered, to some ancient Olympiad than to a sedate little London tea shop. Seeing his magnificent body had proved her instincts right.

What about her other instincts? she wondered suddenly. Which had been right, the ones that had deemed him a rake and a cad, or the ones that had allowed him to stay with her and lie with her? Maybe both, she realized, and she felt a sudden jolt of misgiving.

I've been trying to keep you safe . . . from me.

She shivered, and the question whispered through her mind of what would happen to her now.

"Do you want to go, Miss Clara?"

She jerked, startled, and opened her eyes, the curtain falling from her fingertips as she turned to her maid. "Sorry? What?"

"The picnic. If you want to go, we'd best get you dressed. The carriages are supposed to be off at twelve sharp, so Miss Chapman said."

Clara gathered her scattered wits, pushing delectable thoughts of Rex's magnificent body and forebodings about the future out of her mind. "I do want to go, yes," she answered and turned from the window. "Hetty promised me an outing to the White Cliffs, for I've never seen them, and I don't want to miss the chance."

It was a mad dash to get her ready in time, but Clara soon learned that the White Cliffs might have to wait for another day. The big grandfather clock on the landing had already chimed the hour by the time she raced past it down the stairs, and when she arrived at the bottom, she found Carlotta waiting for her.

"Sorry," she said, skidding to a halt, out of breath as she tucked her parasol under one arm and worked to button her gloves. "Am I terribly late? Is everyone waiting on me, or have they already left?"

"No, no, they haven't gone yet, but I don't think you'll be wanting to join them, in any case."

Clara frowned, puzzled, especially because Carlotta was smiling like the Cheshire Cat, and that almost never happened. "What do you mean?"

Carlotta slid her arm through Clara's. "Let's take a walk, my dear."

Her bewilderment deepening, Clara allowed her

sister-in-law to lead her across the foyer and out of the house. "Where are we going?" she asked as they turned in the opposite direction from the carriages in the drive.

"The rose garden is lovely, with everything in bloom," her sister-in-law said. "I thought we might go there."

"What about the picnic?" Clara asked as they rounded the corner of the house and started across the south lawn. The question was barely out of her mouth, however, before she saw Rex standing by the entrance to the rose garden, hat in hand, and any thoughts of the picnic or seeing the White Cliffs of Dover went straight out of her head.

Lord, he was handsome.

All the memories of last night came flooding back in a burst of pure joy, and she smiled.

He didn't smile back.

Clara's steps faltered, but Carlotta's arm was still entwined with hers, impelling her forward. As she approached, his face was so grave, she immediately wondered if something terrible had happened.

She glanced at Carlotta, and her anxiety eased, for the other woman was still smiling.

She turned to Rex again. "What is this about?"

Instead of answering, he gestured to the path. "Take a turn with me?"

Carlotta's arm slid away, and to Clara's astonishment, her sister-in-law gave Rex a nod, turned around, and departed, leaving them. "Carlotta?" she called, but the other woman kept walking away. "Where is she going?"

"Out of earshot." He slid his arm through hers. "Walk with me, please."

He pulled, urging her gently into the rose garden, but even as she walked with him, she was looking back over her shoulder. "What on earth is she thinking? She can't leave us alone out here. She's my chaperone."

"We're a bit past the point of chaperones, don't you think? Clara," he went on before she could reply, "I asked Lady David to arrange a private meeting between us, and when I explained my reasons, she consented."

Reasons? There was only one reason a man would make such a request of a chaperone.

With that thought, a torrent of emotions surged through her all at once. Disbelief, dismay, jubilation, trepidation, joy, hope—in a flood, they came, simultaneous yet distinct, each one powerful enough to overwhelm her. She stopped walking, unable to take another step, and yanked her arm out of his hold.

He stopped as well, turning to face her. "Surely you can guess what my reason is?"

One emotion nudged upward past all the others, rising above the tide, threatening to carry her utterly away. It was hope.

And yet, hope of what? Not happy matrimony, because he wasn't the marrying sort, and she'd always known that. Just as important, she wasn't at all sure she wanted to marry him, for she'd never contemplated it, not once until this very moment. So, why was hope rising inside her, wrapping around her heart, squeezing her chest with such dizzying excitement? What was she hoping for? She honestly didn't know.

She looked down, staring at the gravel path under

their feet, trying to set aside any romantic notions and remind herself of realities. This was Rex, which meant the idea of marriage was absurd anyway, so—

He reached for her hands, interrupting this chaotic stream of thought, and she watched as he clasped them in his, his bare fingers entwining with her gloved ones, turning her toward him. "Clara, we have to get married."

Not so absurd after all.

And yet, oddly enough, it wasn't quite a proposal.

"Have to?" she echoed, trying to make light of it, striving to think. "Heavens, that's quite a definitive statement from a man who doesn't believe in marriage and openly advocates free love."

"Don't tease, Clara. This is hard enough."

It shouldn't be hard at all, should it?

"You can't possibly want to marry me," she said.

"Yes, I do."

"Don't!" she ordered fiercely, lifting her head, yanking her hands free of his, every instinct she possessed telling her he didn't mean that. "Don't lie, Rex, for God's sake."

He inhaled sharply and looked away, confirming that at least in this case her instincts about him were sound.

"Very well," he said after a moment. "Since you are demanding precise language of me, let me give it. What I want, Clara, is you. I have wanted you ever since you gave me cheek on that ballroom floor. I still want you."

Now that, she thought with a delicious thrill and hint of relief, was more like what she'd been hoping for.

"And if we were anywhere private," he went on, "I'd ravish you quick as lightning, whatever the risk, right here, right now, if you let me."

Laughter bubbled up and came spilling out. "I fear if we were somewhere private, you wouldn't be the only one doing the ravishing."

He didn't seem pleased to hear it. "That's why we have to marry. You're not the sort of woman a man can ravish and leave."

She stiffened, any tendency to laugh vanishing as quickly as it had come. "Are there such women?"

"I think you know there are," he said, "so please don't go all prickly on me, Clara. There are mistresses, courtesans—"

"Widows," she cut in. "Lady Dina Throckmorton, for example. Your friend Lionel seems to think she's that sort of woman. Is she?"

"Let's not get into the weeds by talking about Dina and Lionel, all right? Let's leave them to sort out their own affairs while we sort out ours."

"But you seem to think that she and I are different, that we deserve different consideration from our lovers," Clara persisted. "I want to know why you think so."

"Do you really need to ask? Dina was not an innocent woman and Lionel did not ruin her. I, however, did ruin you, despite all my efforts not to. I tried to stay away from you. God knows, I tried." Unexpectedly, he gave a laugh, and the harshness of it made her wince. "I failed, as the events of last night so aptly demonstrated."

She felt cold, suddenly, all her joy in their night together fading. "So, what you are saying is that you wanted me against your will, fought it as long as you could, but having failed and succumbed to your passion for me, you now feel honor bound to offer me marriage, even though you don't really want to make a life with me, or any woman. Do I have it right?"

She didn't wait for an answer, but turned away. She'd heard enough.

He wouldn't let her go. "Not quite," he said, stepping in front of her. "When I came to you last night, I knew just what I was doing, and what the consequence would be. It was a choice, Clara, one I did not make against my will. It was a free, conscious choice. I wanted you, and I accepted that marrying you was the price I would have to pay to have you."

"Price?" she echoed in disbelief. "There is no price, Rex. A life with me is not something that can be bought."

"I didn't mean—"

"You made a choice for yourself."

He stirred, looking away. "You could have told me to go. You didn't. You let me stay. You made a choice as well."

"I am not disputing that, but you assume that our choice was the same one. It was not. Do you remember," she went on before he could reply, "what I said that afternoon in the drawing room of my father's house? When I told you what I wanted for my life?"

"I do, yes. Believe me when I say I have not failed to take that into consideration."

"Indeed?"

"You want honorable marriage, which I am offering, though a bit late in the day, I grant you. You also want children." His gaze lowered, then lifted. "A de-

sire that might already be in the process of being fulfilled. Have you thought of that?"

She hadn't, heaven help her, not until this moment.
And Irene had explained the facts of life to her so
painstakingly when the vicar had come courting. A
lot of good it had done her.

"Oh, God," she whispered, seized by a sudden jolt
of panic.

Rex grasped her arms as if perceiving her suddenly wobbly knees. "It's all right," he said, his voice
savage. "There'll be no shame for you. No ruin. I
swear it. We'll be married straightaway, and no one
will know. We'll live at Braebourne, of course. Don't
worry," he added, his voice gentling. "It's a big house,
enormous, wings sticking out every which way, plenty
of room for a dozen children. It has dogs, horses, apple
orchards. It's in the Cotswolds—Gloucestershire, to
be exact. Our village is Stow-on-the-Wold. Very pic-
turesque. Lots of thatched cottages, rambling roses,
and bilberries everywhere in summer."

She felt the appeal of what he described. How could
she not? "It sounds like everything I've ever wanted,"
she whispered and felt an absurd desire to burst into
tears. "But it doesn't have the one thing that matters,
does it, Rex? You want me, you are willing to marry
me, but—" She took a breath, looked into his stunning
blue eyes, and made herself to say it. "But you are not
in love with me. Are you?"

His lips pressed together. He stared back at her, his
face showing regret for what he did not feel and probably never would. The silence seemed endless. "No,"
he said at last, a simple reply, brutal in its honesty.

Again, she tried to turn away, but he would not release her. "Clara, I realize this is not the most romantic situation, and I'm sorry for that. You talk about love, but I honestly do not know what you mean by the word. Infatuation? Passion? Companionable friendship and affection? What sort of love is true and lasting, and what love is not? How does one know the difference? As I've said, I desire you. I think very highly of you—"

"Very highly," she echoed dismally. "Goodness. That's almost as romantic as celestial marriage."

"Well, I'm not offering that, just so you know."

How absurd, she thought. For the second time in her life a man was proposing marriage to her, the first because he didn't desire her at all, and the second because he desired her too much. But neither had offered marriage out of love for her. She had a penchant, it seemed, for men incapable of loving her.

"Well, there we are, then," she said. "You do not love me. And—" She stopped, unable to say she did not love him. She couldn't say it, for it would be, she realized, a lie. She did love him. She'd been falling in love with him all along, bit by bit, starting that very first moment she'd seen him in the tea shop.

How mortifying to know she was such a fool.

Pride came to her rescue, enabling her to say something. "And that means you will marry me, not out of love, but out of obligation." Pain pierced her chest at the word, her heart cracking wide open, breaking right there in front of him. "An obligation inevitably becomes a burden. I will be no man's burden."

"And the child, Clara? What will the child be if you refuse me?"

She flinched, drawing back as far as his hold would

allow, desperate for space and time to think. "We don't even know if there will be a baby."

His gaze was steady, calm, as cool as ocean waters. "And if there is, it will be my bastard, if you do not let me do right by you."

"I'll decide what to do about that when it happens, if it happens, which it probably won't."

He shook his head in adamant disagreement. "The longer we wait, the more risk of scandal. I have no intention of compounding the wrong I've done you by risking your reputation."

"And I have no intention of making an irrevocable decision because you insist upon it. My answer is no. I will not marry you."

"And if there is a child? Will no still be your answer then?"

She didn't reply, and she could feel panic setting in again, not the panic of an illegitimate child, of giving it up or raising it alone, or of her own possible ruin. If she stood here much longer, she would waver in her decision. She might even relent, and then, she would be trapped. She could see her future with him, a future that was secure and safe and bleak. She could see herself years from now, still in love with a man who did not love her, a man who'd had more women than he could count and had never loved any of them, who could very well not be capable of love at all and who might not even manage to be faithful. She would want him to love her and only her, she would hope for it, yearn for it, and if he could not give his heart and be a true husband to her, it would destroy her.

She looked at him, knowing he was still waiting for an answer to his question. "I refuse to worry about things that haven't happened," she said, and jerked hard, wrenching free of his hold. She ducked around him, fighting back tears as she walked away.

"This isn't over, Clara," he called to her.

Yes, it is.

She did not say it out loud, and she did not look back, and as her heart broke into pieces, her only consolation was her absolute certainty that refusing him was the right thing to do. Whatever it cost her, giving him her heart was not worth the price of her soul.

Chapter 19

Clara sat in a train carriage compartment, staring out the window at the fields and hedgerows of Kent, watching as they gave way to the coal-dusted streets and sidewalks of London. Her companions all had books, but she feared they were only pretending to read, for whenever she chanced to glance at them, their gazes were on her. When caught watching, they always returned their attention to their reading, but not before Clara saw the bewilderment in their eyes.

Carlotta, not usually the most understanding of women, had displayed a surprisingly tender regard for her well-being upon learning she had rejected Galbraith's proposal. She had offered no lectures and asked no questions. Leaving Clara with her maid to pack, she had gone at once to inform their hosts and her sisters-in-law that a matter of urgency had arisen for Clara that required them to return to London immediately, and she had made all the arrangements for their departure from Lisle.

Carlotta must also have instructed Sarah and Angela to ask Clara no questions, for as the late afternoon train carried them back to London, no one spoke. Even the usually lively Angela was silent. None of them pressed for details, and Clara was relieved, for what could she say?

Lord Galbraith proposed, but only out of a sense of obligation. I lay with him last night, you see, so he feels he must do the gentlemanly thing and offer me marriage. I love him, but he doesn't love me, so I refused him. My virtue is lost, I may be pregnant, and now that I have rejected him, what will become of me?

All of that sat like dead weight inside her, pressing on her heart and laying like a stone in her belly. Fear whispered in her ear, reminding her of what happened to unmarried women who did what she'd done, of what the children of such liaisons were called.

It will be my bastard.

Even now, Rex's words made her flinch. Even now, she did not know what she would do if and when the worst happened. Now, in the cold light of day, she wondered what had possessed her last evening and how she could have forgotten all of Irene's explanations and warnings. And she wondered, after everything she knew about him, after everything he had told her and everything she had told herself, how she could ever have let herself fall in love with him.

But love, she was beginning to see, was a choice of the heart. Common sense and reason played little part, or if they did, hers had both taken quite a holiday.

Looking back on everything that had happened these

past two months, she realized that falling in love with him was something she'd feared all along.

From the beginning, she'd sensed he had the power to steal her heart, and that if he ever succeeded, her heart would be returned to her in pieces. Her reasoning mind had tried to protect her with disapproval of his profligate living, questions about his morality, and reminders of all his flaws, but from that first moment in the tea shop, her soul had not cared about any of that. Her soul had only known this man could make her feel beautiful and desirable, and unmoved by the cautions of her reasoning mind, her soul had insisted on turning toward him again and again, the way a plant in a window turned continually toward the sun.

That unknowing, unreasoning instinct, she appreciated now, was why she'd asked him to be Lady Truelove—she'd known somehow that he would teach her things about herself no one else could. It was why she'd agreed to his sham courtship—because she'd sensed it might be the only true romance she ever had, and her heart had not wanted it to pass her by. It was why she'd managed to ignore all her own high-minded principles about virtue and marriage and had lain with him, sacrificing all the dreams she'd ever had for her future. And it was why, though she might be ruined forever, she felt no shame and no regret. Deep down in the dark, secret recesses of her soul, she'd wanted this, every beautiful, shining, heartbreaking moment of it.

You're lovely. Even more lovely than I'd imagined.

Shame and regret, she supposed with a newfound cynicism, might come later, when his awestruck voice and tender words and scorching caresses had receded from her memory. And if the worst did happen, an illegitimate baby would probably be quite effective at snuffing out any yearning for romance that might still be lingering within her.

The train slowed, coming into Victoria Station, and Clara shoved aside grim speculations about the future. If there was a baby, she'd cross that bridge when she came to it.

A smile touched her lips. In the midst of the worst crisis of her life, and yet, she was still such a procrastinator.

CARLOTTA MUST HAVE telegraphed ahead to Upper Brook Street, because the duke's carriage and a dog-cart were waiting for them at Victoria. At Carlotta's direction, porters separated Clara's trunks from the others, strapped hers to the carriage boot, and piled all the remaining luggage on the dogcart. Twenty minutes later, the duke's dogcart and its driver were halfway to the West End, and his other driver and footman were carrying Clara's trunks into the house at Belford Row and she was bidding farewell to her sisters-in-law.

"We shall see you for dinner soon, I trust?" Angela's arms wrapped her in a hug, then she pulled back and looked into Clara's face. "I shan't ask any questions, but I hope you feel you can confide in me—in any of us—if you need to."

"Of course." Clara smiled, gave her friend a reassuring pat on the back, and decided it was best to leave things like that for the present. A few minutes later, the duke's carriage was off again, and Clara was taking off her traveling cloak, hat, and gloves in the foyer and handing them over to her maid.

"Have everything taken to my room, Forrester," she instructed. "I'll see Papa, inform him I'm home, and then—"

"Clara!"

That familiar voice brought a burst of happy surprise, lightening her heavy heart, and she turned to find her sister running up the corridor from the newspaper office, arms outstretched.

"Irene?" She laughed, stretching out her own arms and running to meet her beloved sister halfway. "You're home again!"

"Just an hour ago." Irene's affectionate and comforting arms wrapped around her, and suddenly, the powerful emotions that Clara had been keeping at bay all day refused to remain wholly submerged. A sob surged up inside her, cracking her hard-won fortitude, and she had to bite her lip hard to keep it from escaping.

"Henry's on his way to Upper Brook Street," Irene said, still hugging her tight. "But I wanted to see you first, and Papa, so Henry dropped me here and took all our luggage on. But then I discovered you had gone to the country. I was about to leave you a note and depart."

Clara worked to regain her composure. "I wouldn't have gone anywhere, if I'd known you were arriving home today," she said and pulled back, pasting on an expression of mock censure. "You are terrible about writing, dear sister."

"Me? What about you? Only two letters from you forwarded to me through Cooks' these past two months."

"I'm not the one who has things to write about," she lied. "You're the one gallivanting across the world."

"Yes, and when I come home, I find you've gone gallivanting off to the country with people I've never even met. Speaking of which . . ." Irene paused, frowning. "Why are you here? Annie told me the house party you were attending was supposed to go on through the weekend, and today is only Saturday. Isn't it?"

Irene laughed, shaking her head, her frown clearing as she brushed back a lock of golden-blond hair that had tumbled over her forehead. "One tends to lose track of what day it is after four months of traveling, and—"

She broke off, all the laughter dying out of her expression, and Clara knew something in her own face must have given her away.

"Clara?" Irene put a hand on her arm and cupped her cheek, her hazel eyes filled at once with protective, sisterly concern. "What is it? What's happened?"

Heartbreak, fear, panic all welled up, blurring her sister's beloved face, but she blinked back tears and tried to smile. "I've fallen in love."

THE RULE THAT Irene and Clara had established not to partake of alcohol in their father's house was broken that night, and Clara was able to add the drinking of brandy to her ever-growing list of life experiences.

Across her desk in the privacy and quiet of the newspaper office, over a snifter of brandy, she told her sister everything about her transformation from wallflower to belle of the ball to fallen woman, and all things considered, Irene took the entire narrative rather well, at least after she calmed down and promised not to shoot Lord Galbraith with a pistol. There were no recriminations regarding Clara's lost virtue, no lectures on why she ought to have accepted his marriage proposal, several faithful pledges not to tell the duke anything about it, only one sobering mention of the possible consequences and choices Clara might have to face, and then, at last, Irene asked the vital question.

"What are you going to do now?"

Perhaps it was the steadying effects of a few sips of brandy, but Clara was able to give her sister a calm and reasoned response.

"Carry on, of course. What else is there to do?"

"Carry on with what, though?" Irene asked, her voice gentle. "If the worst happens . . ."

Clara nodded as Irene's voice trailed off. "I know. But if there is no baby, or if there is and I give it up, then I shall need an occupation, a distraction, a purpose, and even if I go back into society, I don't think that alone would be enough to satisfy me now. I think . . ." She paused, took a deep breath and waved a hand to their surroundings. "I think, perhaps . . . the paper."

"The *Weekly Gazette*?" Irene stared at her as if she'd grown a second head, and no wonder, for in the past, Clara had never expressed a fraction of her sister's passion for the family business. "You want to run the paper with me?"

"Well, Jonathan's not going to do it," she reminded. "Not now."

"As long as there's silver in that mine of his, I expect you're right. But when did you become so interested in running the newspaper?"

Clara began to laugh. "Well, I didn't have much choice after I sacked your Mr. Beale."

"What? You sacked him? Why? Was he awful?"

"You have no idea." Clara explained how firing the editor had come about, and she didn't mince words regarding her opinion of the man or how difficult it had been to work with him.

"Heavens," Irene said when she'd finished, shaking her head, looking even more confounded than before. "I had no idea when I interviewed him that he was anything like what you describe. He was so highly recommended, and seemed to radiate competence. And I certainly never would have hired him if I'd known his opinion about working for a woman! Although . . ." She broke off, frowning a little. "Now that I think about it, he did ask several times about Jonathan. He must have wanted to be absolutely sure he'd be reporting to our brother rather than to me, though I can't believe I didn't notice his reasons at the time."

"Well, you were a bit busy. Wedding plans and all that."

"I suppose so. But still . . ." She slapped a palm to her forehead. "How obtuse of me."

"Everyone makes mistakes, Irene, though until Mr. Beale, I never thought you did."

"Oh, darling, I make mistakes all the time! I've just tried not to let you see them. I've always wanted to protect you. Speaking of which," she added before Clara could reply, "why didn't you ever cable me and tell me of your difficulties? I'd have come home at once."

"I know, and that's just why I didn't do it. You deserved every minute of that trip, and I wasn't going to deprive you of it. And the funny thing is that even as hard as I've been working, and as scary as taking this on has been for me, it's been rather fun, too. I never thought I'd say this, but I'm really starting to enjoy it—being in charge, making the decisions, exercising my own judgement."

Irene grinned. "Fun, isn't it? Still, I'm astonished at all these changes in you. You're quite transformed, Clara, really. But . . ." Irene paused, her grin fading as she leaned forward across the desk to put a hand on Clara's forearm. "If there is a baby, we shall have to consider carefully what that will mean and what to do."

Clara nodded, appreciating that it was time to put aside procrastination, and prepare for the worst, just in case. "Because I shan't be able to do both, you mean?"

"Well, I wouldn't say that. If you gave the child up, of course you could work here at the paper. In fact, since no one knows what happened between you and Galbraith, your life could pretty much go on as before."

"My life will never be what it was before."

Her sister winced at that. "No, darling," she agreed tenderly. "I don't suppose it will. But baby or no, are you absolutely sure refusing Galbraith was the right thing to do? You've always wanted to be married. And you do love him."

"But he does not love me. He admitted the fact."

Catching sight of her sister's scowl, she rushed on before Irene could go on a hunt for Papa's pistol. "So, if there is no baby, I would like to carry on with the paper. If I am with child—" She paused, her voice failing, and it took her a moment before she could go on. "I would have to go abroad to have it, Irene. And if I kept it, I would have to stay abroad."

Her sister gave a cry of dismay. "No, you wouldn't.

You could put the child with a family in the country, pay them to care for it, make it your ward, see it during holidays . . ." Her voice trailed away as Clara shook her head.

"I think we both know that wouldn't be possible. People would eventually put two and two together and make four. I could not shame you by staying in England."

"Nonsense," Irene said stoutly. "You think I care about that?"

"You would have to care. You're married now, and your husband and his position would have to be considered. He is a duke. He could not have a wayward sister-in-law and her love child living nearby, and certainly not coming to visit. And what of his sisters? Their social position has already been damaged—"

"I would never turn my back on you!" Irene interrupted fiercely. "Not even for Henry would I ever do that."

"I know." She paused. "And we don't even know if there will be a child. But if there is and I decide to keep it, you will have to come abroad to visit us, without Henry."

Irene gave a sob and caught it back. "You would be giving up everything, Clara. Your life, your future, all your hopes—" Her voice broke, and she stopped.

Watching her, Clara smiled a little. "Dearest Irene," she murmured. "All this must be so hard for you, for you have always tried so hard to protect me. But I cannot marry a man who does not love me just to be safe and protected. And I can't always take the easy way through life, even if a life of ease is what you want for me."

Something in her voice, perhaps the resoluteness of it, caught her sister's attention, for Irene pressed her lips together, and a sweet, poignant sadness came into her lovely face.

"What are you thinking?" Clara asked, watching in astonishment as a tear rolled down her sister's cheek.

"I think . . ." Irene choked up again, then gave a little sniff and leaned forward to take her hands. "I think my little sister is all grown up."

SHE WOULDN'T SEE him.

At least twice a week, Rex called at Belford Row, only to be told by their grenadier of a housekeeper that Miss Deverill was not receiving. He tried calling at the newspaper office, but that strategy brought no greater success, for her secretary always informed him that she was busy. He tried using charm, but he must be losing his touch with the ladies, for Miss Evelyn Huish remained adamant and unimpressed, a stalwart sentry at Clara's gate. Resisting—for the present anyway—the temptation to invade Clara's office by force, he turned to other means of dealing with the situation.

He wrote letters. She did not reply. He sent flowers. She sent them back. He got drunk, often. It didn't help. One night, God help him, he even found himself standing on the pavement outside the newspaper office, champagne in hand, staring through the lit windows hoping to catch a glimpse of her. He even attempted to go in, but the door, when he tried it, was locked. A good thing, probably, for all the instincts that had made him such a rake in his salad days told him that invading her privacy would only hurt his cause. Left with no other options, he was forced to wait.

He had a slew of relations and friends, and once the news spread of his marriage proposal and Clara's rejection, all those friends and family attempted to distract him. During the seemingly endless days of summer, invitations poured in from every quarter, beckoning him to the country for hunting and house parties, but he refused them all. He had no intention of being away, should Clara write him with news of her condition or decide to take pity on him and agree to receive him.

When friends came to town, however, he was happy to spend an evening with them. Lionel he saw more often than most, but though the two of them managed an occasional game of tennis, and one rousing night of celebration in late August when he learned of Lionel's formal engagement to Dina, Rex preferred to spend the majority of his time alone. He walked the streets of London a lot, usually places with some connection to Clara—Upper Brook Street, the sidewalk in front of Montcrieffe House, Mrs. Mott's Tea Emporium, the newspaper office. He even returned to the spot in Hyde Park where she'd tried to launch that kite, and as he thought of her laughing with her nephews, he wondered when he would hear news of a baby. Oddly, he was sure there would be one, perhaps because he'd been prepared for that outcome from the moment he'd entered her bedroom that night at Lisle.

His father, probably in the mistaken belief that Rex's proposal had been rejected for financial considerations, not only reinstated his estate allowance, but doubled it.

Usually, when Rex was in funds, his mother managed to learn the fact and came calling for a touch, and sure enough, only days after his father's reinstatement of his income, his mother was at Half Moon Street asking to be received. To his surprise, however, he soon learned that money, for once, was not her reason for coming.

"Rex," she cried, beautiful as ever as she came across his drawing room, hands outstretched in greeting. "I've just heard. Oh, my darling boy, is it really true, or is it just a rumor?"

"Is what true?"

"That you proposed marriage to a young lady and she refused you? It must be gossip, for no girl would ever turn you down, but my source was quite adamant—"

She stopped, and he realized something in his countenance must have given him away, for she gave a cry of dismay and yanked her hand from his, cupping it to his cheek with what he thought might be genuine motherly concern. "It is true! Oh, Rex, my dear."

He pulled out of his mother's hold, forcing a laugh. "Only time in my life I shall ever propose to a girl, and she turns me down flat. One of life's little ironies, what? And just what I deserve."

"Nonsense. Any girl would be lucky to have you. And besides, you shall persuade her. You're not giving up after one refusal, surely?"

"More than one, I'm afraid." He pressed his lips together, smiling a little. "She refuses me every time she refuses to see me, Mama."

"But why? The only reason she could have for turning you down is money, and your father reinstated your allowance—by a substantial amount, I understand."

He sighed. "How you ferret these things out never ceases to amaze me."

She shifted her weight from one foot to the other, tugging at her ear. "I have my spies," she murmured.

"Yes, my butler, no doubt. Every time I pay him whatever back wages I owe him, I'm sure he fires off a letter. He's a fool for you."

"Yes, well . . ." His mother paused, smoothing her skirt and trying to look modest, but she succeeded only in looking like a contented house cat. "He is such a dear, sweet man. If he wasn't a butler, I'm sure I'd have fallen in love with him ages ago."

"Oh, I'm sure," he agreed. "So, now that you've heard my income's reinstated, is that why you've come?"

"No, no, I don't need a penny, but it's very sweet of you to offer."

He hadn't offered, but pesky little details like that always sailed right past his mother's beautiful head. "You not in need of money?" He laughed. "My, there's a first time for everything."

"No, I came because I have news of my own, darling, which I shall tell you presently. But first, you must assure me that you're not giving up on this girl you're after."

"Really, Mama, of all the people in the world, I'd have thought you the last one to encourage anyone to get married."

"Nonsense. How else will you be ensured a steady income?"

"How, indeed." He folded his arms, bracing himself. "What's your news? But I think I can guess," he added, noting the little smile that curved his mother's lips. "A new man, I assume?"

She heaved a dreamy sigh and pressed a hand to her bosom, confirming his theory. "And what a man he is, too. Handsome, charming, quite rich."

"Naturally. Am I entitled to know who he is?"

"Of course! Our affair is not a secret, and even if it were, I'd tell you, for you can always keep a secret."

He thought of the night he'd spilled secrets to Clara about his parents, himself, and how he spent his money. She was, he realized, the only person in his life who could loosen his tongue. "Not always, Mama. But carry on. Who is this new man of yours?"

"It's Lord Newcombe. We met at Cannes in January, then again at Zurich in July, and now . . ." She paused, one that was clearly supposed to be dramatic. "I'm in love!"

"What a surprise."

The ironic inflection of his voice seemed lost on his mother. "It was to me! Newcombe's ten years younger than I am."

"Newcombe?" He repeated the name, frowning a little as he began to appreciate who they were talking about. "You mean Baron Newcombe?"

"The very same."

"You realize he's married?"

She laughed. "So am I. What does that matter?"

"To you, it probably doesn't."

That dry comment earned him an unhappy sigh. "Really, Rex, I love you, but there are times when you remind me so much of your father."

He made a sound of derision. "I'm nothing like Papa."

"Not in looks, perhaps. And you're much more charming than he ever was. But you do have some of his qualities. Impatience, stubbornness, cynicism, and a rather tiresome way of putting a damper on the loveliest things."

"Things like true love?"

"Exactly! Do you know, Newcombe's taking me around the world on his yacht? He wanted to depart straight from Calais, but I insisted on coming up to London to see you before I go. Isn't it wonderful?" she added, clasping her hands together as if she'd just been blessed by heaven. "I shan't have any living expenses for months!"

He sighed, knowing that when those months had passed, Mama would be here again, and he'd be drying her tears and handing over whatever cash he could spare. He thought of his father, and he thanked God that his mother was mistaken in his character, for the last thing he ever wanted to be was a brokenhearted wreck of a man who, despite years of rejection, still loved one—and only one—woman.

"Just be careful, Mama," he said.

"Oh, don't be silly, darling." She smiled and rose on her toes to kiss his cheek. "I always land on my feet."

A cough sounded behind them, and both he and his mother turned around to find Whistler standing in the doorway, a silver salver resting atop his fingertips, an unmistakable admiration for the countess in his eyes. "Forgive me, your ladyship," he said, bowing, then turned to Rex. "The afternoon post, sir."

He caught a nuance of significance in the butler's last words, and when he shot Whistler a sharp, inquiring look, he was rewarded with a slight nod of confirmation.

At last. Relief flooded through him, and though he wanted to dash across the room and tear the letter open right then and there, he refrained, for he did not want his mother here when he read the news from Clara.

"Just put it there, would you, Whistler?" he said, working to keep his tone indifferent. Then, as the other man crossed the room to deposit his letters on the writing desk beneath the window, he turned to his mother. "I fear I must send you off, Mama, for I have an engagement and have to change."

"Of course. I need to be toddling along anyway, for as I said, Newcombe's awaiting me at Dover. *Au revoir*, my darling son." She cupped his cheeks. "If you want this girl, don't give up." With that bit of rather ironic advice, she kissed him and departed, following Whistler out the door.

Rex walked to his desk, took up the letter that reposed on the top of the pile, and turned it over. There was no name on the back, but there was a return direction. No. 12 Belford Row, Holborn.

Rex swallowed hard, bracing himself, and sat down at his desk. He moved to tear the letter open with his usual impatience, but then, he changed his mind and retrieved a letter opener from the desk instead, using it to slit the envelope neatly across. Drawing a deep, shaky breath, he pulled out the single sheet of notepaper, broke the seal, and unfolded it.

Lord Galbraith,
   It is now certain beyond any doubt that what you feared has not come to pass, and therefore, your obligation is discharged. I hope this letter brings you a measure of relief, and I wish noth-

ing for your future but good fortune and happiness.

    Sincerely,
    C.M.D.

He stared at the lines of Clara's prim copperplate script in disbelief. Throwing him off his trolley on a consistent basis seemed to be her special gift, but nonetheless, this was not the news he'd been expecting. He'd been sure beyond doubt there would be a baby, that his future with her was settled and inevitable, and this news left him feeling not only astonished and bewildered, but also strangely bereft.

He read the lines again. She hoped her news would bring him relief—well, that was a reasonable wish, he supposed. Most men, he thought cynically, would be dancing a jig after news like this.

He had never felt less like dancing.

He held the letter to his nose, and as he breathed in the scent of orange blossoms, he thought of that night in her office when she'd stood in his embrace and he'd shown her how to open champagne, and he suddenly realized that he might never have the chance to hold her in his arms again.

Suddenly, he saw a different future ahead of him than the one he'd lately been envisioning, a future like his past, a future without her. As his mind formed that picture, something deep inside Rex cracked and broke apart, and he realized in despair that it was his heart.

He set aside the letter and lowered his face into his hands.

Chapter 20

"I don't see why we have to go to Lionel Strange's wedding," Clara muttered for perhaps the fifth time since Torquil's carriage had left Upper Brook Street and started toward St. John's Church. "You don't even know him, Irene."

"But Henry knows him slightly, for he is an MP."

"A tenuous connection, hardly worthy of an invitation to the man's wedding."

"Not really. Dukes receive invitations to everything."

"Not your duke, not after his mother married the Italian."

"Yes, well, even slightly tarnished, Henry's still a duke. And since we received the invitation, I decided this wedding would be a good way for Henry and I to take our first step back into society after the Dowager's fall."

"But Henry isn't with us."

"He had another engagement, so he's meeting us at the church."

"It still seems quite odd that he agreed to come at all. I wouldn't have thought a Labor MP would impress Torquil enough to receive this sort of condescension. Your duke is difficult to impress."

"Henry's agreed to go for my sake. Lionel Strange favors the vote for women, and I intend to bend the man's ear at the wedding breakfast for ideas as to how we can gain more support in the Commons. Henry promised to put in a word of support as well."

"Lovely. So why were you so insistent I attend?"

"You were included in the invitation, so it's clear Mr. Strange and Lady Throckmorton want you to come. And why shouldn't they? From what you told me, you are directly responsible for bringing them back together. You and Galbraith."

"I'm surprised Rex hasn't convinced Lionel to call it off," Clara muttered. "I don't suppose there's any chance he'll stay away?"

"No chance at all, for I heard he's to be best man. He will be there, you may be sure."

Clara swallowed hard, dread like a knot in her stomach. "I was afraid of that."

"And even if he weren't attending his friend's wedding," Irene went on, "you're likely to see a great deal of him in future, just the same."

"Do you think so?" The knot of dread twisted tighter.

"You are the sister of a duchess, and he is the future Earl of Leyland. You are bound to see him quite often, especially in the season. Unless, of course, you intend to spend every free moment of the rest of your life working at the paper and brooding in your room."

"I have not been brooding. And it's laughable for you, of all people, to criticize me about working too hard on the paper. I remember all your late hours in that office before you married Torquil."

"My point, darling," Irene said gently, "is that you will have to face Galbraith sometime. The connection's made. One can't undo it now."

Clara grimaced, hating the fact, though she knew it was true.

"Will it be so hard to see him again?" Irene turned toward her on the carriage seat. "It has been over two months since you refused his proposal."

Ten weeks and six days, Clara corrected silently.

"That depends," she answered after a moment, forcing a laugh. "Are you talking about before or after he sees me and goes bolting hell-for-leather in the opposite direction?"

"Would he?"

"I can't imagine he wouldn't. He's safe now, isn't he?" She paused, staring down at the skirt of her deep green dress. "He was calling or writing to me every few days before, clearly because he felt obligated to do so. But since I informed him there's no baby . . ." Her throat closed up, but despite the pain she felt inside, she forced herself to say the brutal truth out loud. "It's been three weeks since then, and he hasn't tried once to see me. It's clear he wants nothing to do with me now that he knows he's free."

"Oh, darling," Irene cried, throwing an arm around her in a comforting hug. "I'm sure that's not true. If it were, he'd be the world's greatest fool. For you, my dear sister, are an angel."

Clara sniffed. "A fallen angel," she muttered.

Irene choked, stifling what had obviously been an involuntary giggle. "Oh, I am sorry," she said at once. "I didn't mean to laugh. That was awful of me." She paused, her arm slid away, and she pulled back. "I never told you just why Henry and I decided to marry, did I?"

Clara stared, astonished by this abrupt turn in the conversation. "Isn't it obvious? You love each other madly."

"Well, there's more to it than that. Henry and I— and you mustn't tell him I've told you about this, by the way—Henry and I married because his upright, honorable nature couldn't tolerate our love affair."

"What?"

Irene nodded, laughing. "Oh, yes, we were sneaking in and out of London hotels, signing in as Mr. and Mrs. Jones, having quite a torrid little fling. So, you see, you are not the only fallen angel in our family."

"I—" Clara stopped, and laughed, for she had no idea what to say. "Heavens."

"Are you very shocked?"

She considered. Six months ago, she'd have been shocked all out of countenance, for back then she'd possessed such a staunchly proper moral code that she doubted she'd have approved of free love for anyone, not even for her very modern, suffragist sister. But she'd become less of a prig since then, and Irene had always been rather a free spirit. "As to you, no, I don't think I'm shocked at all. Torquil, on the other hand . . ."

Irene laughed. "The affair only lasted a week before he couldn't stand it anymore, and he insisted upon making an honest woman of me."

"So that's why you never fired off any stern lectures at me about what happened at Lisle," Clara murmured, thinking it out as she spoke. "I wondered at the time."

"I couldn't do that, could I? It would have been terribly hypocritical. Oh, listen—I can hear the bells. We're nearly there."

The carriage pulled into Southwick Crescent and stopped as close to the doors of St. John's Church as the throng of vehicles would allow. Torquil's driver rolled out the steps, and Irene and Clara stepped down to find Henry waiting for them on the church steps.

They signed the book in the vestry and gave their names to the ushers. As acquaintances of the groom, they were led to a pew on the right side of the church, and rank having its privileges, that pew was very near the front, right behind the groom's family, which gave Clara an almost perfect view of Rex.

Lucky her.

He was standing by his friend, impeccably dressed in formal black morning coat, pale gray waistcoat and cravat, and darker gray striped trousers. Golden head bent, he was listening to Lionel as the shorter man murmured something in his ear. It must have been something amusing, for as he tilted back his head, the sight of his laughing face was as devastatingly handsome as she remembered.

The knot in her stomach pushed upward, pressing against her chest, so hard and painful that she could scarcely breathe.

And then he saw her, and as all the laughter went out of his face, Clara felt as if a fist was squeezing around her heart. It took every scrap of pride she possessed to keep her face expressionless, hold his gaze for two full seconds, and then look away.

The organ music, which had been soft and subdued, changed in tone, informing the guests that the ceremony was about to commence, and with the first notes of the wedding march, Clara moved into a blessed state of numbness.

She scarcely heard the vicar's gentle lectures from the Book of Common Prayer, and the marriage vows of the bride and groom. Perhaps it was because she'd now accepted that she would never give those vows herself, or perhaps it was because she was tougher than she'd ever thought possible, but Clara somehow managed to get through the entire ceremony without coming apart.

Afterward, she walked with Irene and Henry to the home of the bride and her parents a block away, and even with Rex's broad-shouldered form scarcely a dozen feet in front of her, Clara was able to remain tightly leashed and numb. Nonetheless, once they reached Hyde Park Square, she could only be grateful that a receiving line did not include a groom's best man.

For the wedding breakfast, long tables had been arranged in the ballroom, and as had been true for the ceremony, seating was based on rank. This placed Clara at the very first table in front of the bridal party, and since Dina and Lionel had chosen to sit at the head of their table rather than the center, Rex's seat was right in front of her. As she sat down, she could only be thankful that custom required a woman to keep her hat on during a wedding breakfast and that wide-brimmed leghorns were in fashion.

Avoid wide-brimmed hats unless you are in the sun, for though such hats may be fashionable, they prevent young men from looking into your eyes, and eyes are the windows to the soul.

Despite Rex's advice, Clara was happy to be a slave to fashion just now, for having him look into her soul was the last thing she wanted. She kept her head down and her gaze on her plate. From the soup to the wedding cake, she managed to choke down a few bites of each course, but when champagne was poured and toasts were offered to the bride and groom, she only made a pretense of drinking to their health as she stared into her glass and thought of the first night she'd ever had champagne.

They didn't have olive branches on the refreshments menu.

Had that really been almost five months ago? Clara bit her lip. It was all so clear in her mind, it could have been last week.

I wish to court you. I should like you to allow me the privilege.

She could still remember nearly every word of that extraordinary conversation, a conversation that had launched the most exciting, romantic time of her life. A time, she thought, her gaze stealing to him, that was now over and would never come again.

He was murmuring something in the ear of the head bridesmaid seated beside him, but then he seemed to feel Clara's gaze on him, for he turned his head, looked at her, and went suddenly still.

Their gazes locked, and this time, she could not look away. She could not run, she could not hide beneath her hat brim. And she could not, for anything, avoid the pain or conceal it from him. Inside, she began to shake.

He was the one who looked away, turning to signal the footman to refill his champagne glass. Once it had been filled, he took it up with one hand while reaching for a fork with the other. Then, he rose to his feet.

The tines of the fork tinged against the glass several times before there was silence. In the hushed room, with his glass in hand, Rex put down the fork and turned his attention to the crowd.

"Lords, ladies, and gentlemen," he began. "I have been asked by the groom to say a few words at his wedding breakfast, a request with which I was happy to comply. You see, some months ago, I had promised a friend . . ."

He paused and looked at her, and caught in his sights, Clara caught her breath, feeling as if his gaze had just pinned her to her chair. "I had promised a friend that if Lionel and Dina ever made a match of it, I'd put on my best morning coat, stick a carnation in my buttonhole, and give my best groomsman speech at their wedding breakfast, a speech extolling the wonders of true love and the virtues of matrimony." He paused. "Of course, I gave that promise never dreaming the day would come when I'd actually have to fulfill it."

Laughter ensued, indicating that many in the room were familiar with his long-held views.

"But here we are," he went on when the laughter had subsided. "And though everyone who knows me is aware I have been quite a cynical man about love and marriage for most of my life, here I stand. And though any speech I might have given on this topic a few short months ago might well have been poetic and romantic, it would not, sadly, have come from the heart. On this day, however, I'm happy to admit I'm not the same man now that I was then. I used to believe that true love and happiness in marriage were myths, but now, for the first time in my life, I know they're not. Now, for the first time, I'm able to see the joy that two people can find when they join their lives together."

He was still looking at her, and Clara's heart leapt with sudden, unreasoning hope. Did he mean—

He turned away, stopping the question in her mind before it was even complete as he looked at the couple sitting at the head of the table. Clara's flare of hope fizzled and died.

"We have the proof of true love before us," he said, still looking at his friends. "It shines like the sun in the faces of my two friends, and I defy anyone to look at them and not believe in it." He turned again to face the crowd, and when his gaze lit again on her, Clara strove hard not to wriggle in her seat.

Why, she wondered in desperation, did he keep looking at her? What she felt must be obvious now. Why was he tormenting her with it?

Look away, she told herself, but her mind could not will her body to obey her. She could only stare at him, helpless, as he went relentlessly on.

"Having attended many weddings, I've heard the words from the Book of Common Prayer many times. And yet today, those words resonated with me in a way they never have before. Perhaps that's due to the oratory skill of the vicar, or perhaps it's because I'm just not as cynical a chap as I used to be, but whatever the reason, when the vicar reminded us today of what marriage partners should be—counselors in perplexity, comforters in sorrow, companions in joy—I knew with the deepest conviction of my heart that Lionel and Dina will be all those things to each other."

He paused, smiling a little, a tender smile that took Clara's poor heart and shredded it anew, even as she strove to remember that he was referring to his friends, not to himself and her and the vows they might have made had she accepted him.

"And I can only pray," he said, his smile fading to a grave expression, his gaze steady as it looked into hers, "that one day very soon, a sweet and lovely girl will allow me the privilege of courtship, fall in love with me, and agree to make me as fortunate a man as my friend."

Clara pressed a hand to her mouth to hold back a sob as he looked past her to the crowd. "Lords, ladies, and gentlemen," he said, "please charge your glasses and let us drink a toast." Turning to his friends, he lifted his glass high. "To the happy couple, to the beautiful joy that marriage can bring, and to true love."

Clara could barely manage to choke down the customary swallow of champagne, for inside her, she could feel hopes rising up again, romantic hopes about him, hopes she'd tried to deny ever since she'd first set eyes on him. It was just a speech, she reminded herself, words he didn't mean, said for the benefit of his friends. She was reading things into it that weren't there, things that were impossible. He didn't love her. He'd said it straight out, no equivocations. And yet, what if . . .

"Clara?" Irene's voice intruded, and when she turned, she found her sister's hazel eyes filled with sympathetic understanding. "We can leave if you wish. Or," she added gently, "you could see him, if you want to. It can be arranged."

Agonized, she glanced at him again, wondering what to do. And then, as if it were an answer, he looked at her and his voice echoed through her mind.

Strive to set your fears aside. Savor every moment of your life, and one day, you may find someone at your side who longs to savor those moments with you.

"I want to see him." She turned, putting a hand on Irene's arm. "But will he see me? What if he won't?"

"He'll see you," Irene said firmly as she stood up, and she pulled Clara to her feet as well. "I know he will. Come with me."

"Where are we going?" she asked as Irene led her out of the ballroom and along the corridor.

"To the library."

"But I can't imagine you've ever been here. You can't possibly know where the library is in this house."

Irene stopped before a door about halfway along the passage and opened it. "I do know, as a matter of fact, but I'll explain that later. Go on," she added, urging Clara through the door. "I'll bring him to you."

"He'll never agree to come," she mumbled even as she walked into the library. She waited, heart in her throat, and though she didn't know how long Irene was gone, it seemed like an eternity before the door opened again and her sister ushered Rex into the room.

The pair of them paused by the door, and Clara did not miss the frown Irene gave him. "When you came to me a fortnight ago," she said, much to Clara's astonishment, "I agreed to help you arrange this meeting with my sister only on the condition that you behave impeccably. If I find that you have taken any liberties with her today, I will, quite literally, kill you."

Rex nodded. "I understand, Duchess. And thank you."

"Irene?" Clara cried, baffled. "You arranged this meeting a fortnight ago?"

But her sister did not answer. Instead, she turned away to open the library door. With one last stern glance at Rex, she walked out, closing the door behind her.

"We did arrange it, yes."

Rex's voice turned her attention to him. "Why?" she choked. "How?"

He started toward her. "As to how, I called on the Duchess at Upper Brook Street, presented an invitation to the wedding, and requested her assistance in persuading you to accept. She complied, and promised to allow a private meeting to take place between us, if you consented to it. As to why . . ." He paused, halting in front of her, and she watched as that tender smile curved his lips again. "I'd rather hoped my speech would answer that question."

"You couldn't have meant it," she burst out. "True love and happiness in marriage?" She shook her head. "You said it for them, for Lionel and Dina."

"No, sweet lamb. I said it for you."

Joy rose inside her, joining all her hopes and all her fears, and yet, she could not quite believe he meant what he was saying. "I already turned you down. There's no obligation for you to offer me marriage now."

"True," he agreed.

"There's no baby," she said. "Didn't you—" She paused, her voice failing, but she knew she had to ask the question. "Didn't you receive my letter?" she whispered.

"I did receive it, yes. It's right here." He patted the breast pocket of his morning coat. "Over my heart."

She made a choked sound, half sob, half unlady-like snort, but thankfully, he didn't seem to hear it. Instead, he reached for her hands, pulling her toward him. "I love you, Clara."

Such a declaration was impossible. It was absurd. "That day in the garden at Lisle, you said the opposite, quite unequivocally, as I recall."

"Yes. Because I'm an idiot."

"Well, that much I can believe," she muttered, glaring at him as he laughed.

"You always do manage to put me in my place, don't you?" he said tenderly. "When I said that, I believed it. I've never been in love in my life, you see, and though I desired you, I didn't understand that my feelings were actually far deeper than desire. The truth is, I've loved you for ages. In fact, when I look back on everything, I think I fell in love with you that afternoon on the settee."

She stared at him, confounded by yet another incredible piece of news. "When you kissed me?"

"No, earlier, when you asked me if we were becoming friends. I knew I wanted you like mad and that I didn't want to be your friend, but I didn't know at the time that was love. And I didn't know it that night in your office, either, or when I literally fell at your feet on the tennis court. I didn't even know it when I came to your room. That's why, when you asked me if I was in love with you, I said no. I didn't recognize it. I thought it was lust, and I didn't want to give you any false hopes that my feelings would deepen. I didn't think they would, and I didn't want to hurt you."

Her anger flared up, and she took a step back. "It was a little late by then," she choked, fighting tears.

His lips tightened, and he swallowed hard, watching her. "Yes," he agreed. "I'm just hoping it's not too late to win you back."

Inside, she was shaking. "When did you make the amazing discovery that you really do love me after all?"

"It was when I received your letter. Yes," he said as her gaze slid to his breast pocket. "That letter. You told me there was no baby and my obligation to you was now over, and that's when I knew—" He broke off, waiting until she looked up at him again to continue. "I knew I was in love with you because your words broke my heart."

His voice cracked on the last word, and Clara's protective shell cracked apart as well. "An organ," he added, laughing a little, "I didn't even know could be broken, until you."

A sob escaped her, a sob of joy that disintegrated all her anger, fear, and hurt. "Rex, I—"

"Let me finish, please. I must say these things now while I have the chance, for I know you may never give me another. Without a baby, you see, I knew I had nothing left to offer you, nothing to hold you. Your sister's returned, I'm not writing Lady Truelove for you anymore, and when I got your letter, I knew my only remaining link with you had been severed. I couldn't bear it, Clara. I still can't."

"Rex—"

"I'm not asking you to marry me, I'm asking you for the chance to court you honorably, as any woman deserves." He took a breath and grabbed her hands. "I want the chance to win you, to show you that my affections are unwavering and my love is true. I know you don't love me, and I know I can't make you do so, but I want to try anyway—"

"You're wrong," she cried, unable to bear it, unable to wait another moment to tell him what she felt. "I do love you."

"What?" He stared at her, understandably astonished. "You mean it?" When she nodded, he let go of her hands, cupped her cheeks, and kissed her mouth. "You're serious?"

"Yes. I love you. The truth is," she added, her voice going a bit teary and wobbly, "I've been falling in love with you a little bit every day, from the moment I first saw you."

"Well, why didn't you say so, woman, for God's sake?" he demanded and kissed her again. "You've been falling in love with me all along? And you never said. I lusted after you, ruined you, proposed to you, and fell in love with you, and you never said a word about loving me. Couldn't you at least have given me a hint?"

"No, because I didn't want to admit it, not even to myself. I fought it every step of the way, denying it because I was afraid, and I was trying to protect myself. I didn't ever want to fall in love with a man like you."

"Because you knew I was not a marrying sort?"

"Well, yes, that, and because of your reputation, and your looks and—"

"Wait," he cut her off. "You refused to let yourself fall in love with me because of the way I look?"

"Partly, yes. Well, look at you!" she burst out, pulling back, waving her hand in a gesture encompassing his perfect face and splendid body. "You could snap your fingers and have any girl you wanted."

"Not any girl," he said with a sigh, giving her a meaningful glance. "Or we'd have gotten married weeks ago."

"Nearly any girl," she said firmly. "I knew that from the moment I first saw you with Elsie Clark."

His brows drew together in puzzlement. "Who?"

"Elsie Clark, the waitress at Mrs. Mott's, the girl you practically charmed out of her skirts right there in the tea shop just to show your friend how it's done. And the fact that you don't even remember her," she added as he displayed no signs of recognition, "rather proves my point. I put any desire for you right out of my head, not only because it was always clear you're not a marrying man, but also because I knew it was a fairy tale. Why, I thought, would a man like you ever fall for a girl like me?"

"Wait." He stopped her, wrapping an arm around her waist and hauling her against him. "Stop right there. I'm not going to deny that looks matter, because yours do. They matter to me. From your adorable nose and ripping smile," he said, the fingertips of his free hand caressing her face, "to your mile-long legs and tiny, pretty feet, I love everything about the way you look. And," he added, "I believe I made my opinion on that score quite clear months ago, on that same settee we've been talking about."

She smiled, remembering that extraordinary afternoon and how he'd discussed her facial features one by one. "So you did. And what's so strange is that even as you made me afraid for my heart, you taught me how not to be afraid of anything else. All my life, I've been protected and sheltered by my sister, and I've allowed myself to be comfortable there. I wanted to be married partly so that I could continue to be comfortable and safe. The first time I ever had to be accountable for anything was when Irene went away on her honeymoon, and I had to start relying on my own judgement, but I didn't trust it. I was afraid of making mistakes, and to my mind, you would be any girl's biggest mistake. But I've changed, Rex, and you are the reason why."

He shook his head. "You don't give yourself enough credit, my lamb."

"No, it was you. It was all because of you. You saw me in a different light than anyone else ever has, you gave me my first real glimmer of self-confidence, bolstered my judgement when I made decisions—"

His chuckle of laughter interrupted her. "You mean Mr. Beale, I take it?"

"Him, for one. I hired you to write Lady Truelove, and though it was a move of desperation, I knew instinctively that you'd be good at it, and you proved me right. You're the one who told me I should trust myself—"

"Advice I've been questioning ever since you turned down my marriage proposal."

"Which I was quite right to have done," she countered at once. "But my point is that none of these changes in me would have happened if you hadn't come along. One week of doing Lady Truelove, and I'd have been begging Irene to come home. And I'd never have fired Mr. Beale, or learned not to worry about making mistakes, and I'd never have developed any confidence in myself or known what I was capable of. I've been running the paper, hiring staff, making editorial decisions, and it's been so much easier than I ever thought it could be, because I've learned to trust myself and my own judgement. If it weren't for you, none of that would ever have happened."

"Well, if that's true, could you exercise your judgement in a way that doesn't make me insane?"

Smiling, she slid her arms up around his neck. "Most important," she added softly, "I'd never have known that I was a desirable woman. You showed me that, when you kissed me. That was the turning point, really, for after that, I just started to . . . to bloom."

"Yes, so I noted at the time, and what an agony it was to watch it happen, let me tell you. All those other men dancing with you that night at the ball made me feel absolutely savage. And then, seeing you across the dinner table at Lisle, laughing with Paul—Paul, of all men, who is a bigger rake than I ever was—"

"Coming from you," she cut in, quoting his own words from the ball back to him, "that's rich."

"I'm not joking, Clara. The hearts of shopgirls all over Oxfordshire are broken now that's he done at university. And seeing you laughing with him that night at Lisle . . . well, that may have been what pushed me over the edge and brought me to your room that night. As for me," he added, his arms tightening around her waist, "I want to reiterate what I told you the night we had champagne in your office. I left my rakish ways behind quite some time ago."

"My sister would not agree with you there."

"Don't I know it? She was barely civil to me when I called on her a fortnight ago. I think if I hadn't declared right up front that my intent to marry you was undimmed, she might very well have shot me."

"Oh, I know she would have," Clara agreed, laughing.

"So," he murmured, his free hand sliding up her back to caress the nape of her neck and interrupting her laughter, "are you going to take pity on me at last, and allow me to court you in a true and honorable fashion?"

"That depends," she murmured, smiling. "Do you know any discreet hotels where we can retreat during this courtship and go back across the Rubicon?"

"Why, Clara Deverill, you naughty girl," he murmured and kissed her. "But no," he said, pulling back, "that won't be possible, because if your sister found out, she really would shoot me."

"No, she wouldn't. Not now that we're engaged. My sister has very modern views."

"Still, I don't think I'll risk it. But I would ask that we make the engagement somewhat short. When it comes to you, I'm not sure how long I can be honorable."

"Would three weeks be short enough?" she asked. "Just long enough for the banns to be read?"

"Three weeks, then," he agreed, then bent his head and kissed her, a kiss that was so deep and ardent, so passionate, that when he pulled back, Clara was breathless.

"Goodness," she gasped. "Perhaps we ought to get a special license and marry straightaway?"

"Banns, Clara." His voice was resolute. "This is true love," he added severely, overriding her protest. "And that's the trouble with true love. It has to be done the proper way."

"Oh, very well," she agreed. "But," she added, rising on her toes for another kiss, "I'm finding us a discreet hotel just the same."

His agonized groan just before their lips met told Clara a discreet hotel was definitely going to be needed.

*G*ive in to your Impulses!

These unforgettable stories only take a second to buy and give you hours of reading pleasure!

Go to ***www.AvonImpulse.com*** and see what we have to offer.

Available wherever e-books are sold.

AVONIMPULSE